KNIGHT'S DOMINION

KNIGHTS OF HELL, BOOK 4

SHERILEE GRAY

CHAPTER 1

ONE COOL THING about killing demons? When you cut off their heads, the fuckers turned to ash.

Made cleanup unnecessary.

Thank you, demon scum.

If things went the way Grace hoped tonight, she'd end her evening buried to the knees in that shit.

She quickly swiped another cotton pad over her face, the heavy mask she wore daily disappearing before her eyes. Music thumped through the floorboards. A song she recognized. Tina was on stage, doing her last dance of the night.

Adrenaline made her hands shake slightly as she brushed the tangles from her long blond hair and pulled it back into a sleek ponytail. Kicking off her six-inch heels and sliding off her pantyhose and garter, she wriggled into soft leather pants.

It took a few minutes, but she got the laces of her corset undone and tossed the final traces of her alter ego, Gigi Fury, on the bed.

After tugging on a long-sleeve, fitted T-shirt, she shoved

her feet in combat boots, did them up nice and tight, and bounced on the balls of her feet.

She caught a glimpse of herself in the mirror. *Could the real Grace Paten please stand up?* She didn't know who that was anymore, hadn't in some time.

Her hand automatically lifted to the gold rings hanging side by side from a delicate chain around her neck. They were warm from her skin, and she let the weight press against her palm, familiar, comforting—fuel for her rage.

What would her parents think of what she was, who she'd become? Would they know her if they passed her on the street? Would they want to?

Shutting those thoughts down quickly, she grabbed her crossbow and bolts, slinging them over one shoulder, snatched up her mask, and climbed out onto the fire escape.

The rusting steel groaned like it always did, like her own personal call to war.

The alley below was dark and still, but the streets beyond were alive with rowdy humans seeking a good time, laughing with friends, looking to escape their lives for one drunken night.

Whatever they were after, they made themselves easy targets.

The cityscape with its golden halo, caused by a multitude of streetlights and fluorescent signs, silhouetting skyscrapers and apartment buildings, was just like any other.

And if it wasn't for that pesky gateway to Hell right here in Roxburgh, it would be. The portal opened every solstice and equinox, spewing out demons faster than they could kill them.

And yep, the Knights of Hell were here, too—the half-demon, half-angel assholes created to control the invading monsters.

Unfortunately, they sucked at their job, and their "leader" Chaos was the absolute worst of them all.

The knights were supposed to protect her kind—demi-demons—demon–human hybrids who developed special abilities. Well, that was another thing they sucked at, and why Grace was heading out under the cover of night with weapons strapped to her body.

On light feet, she quickly climbed the ladder to the roof. She'd done it so many times, the darkness wasn't a problem anymore.

Three figures dressed in black stepped out of the shadows when she reached the top.

"We were starting to think you wouldn't show," Mark said, voice muffled under his mask.

She hadn't missed an equinox since she'd joined this fight, and she wasn't about to now. "I had to make sure the place was tip-top before I left. Vince heard through some goon of Oden's that he might stop by the club. Vince couldn't hide his boner, was all but frothing at the mouth waiting for him to arrive so he could fall to his knees and lick his leather Berlutis."

Mark made a gagging sound. "Nice mental image, thanks."

She loved Vince, he wasn't just her boss, he was family, but he was so desperate to find an "in" with some of the powerful demi-demons who occasionally popped by the club that he went a little nuts around them.

They'd ignored his overtures so far.

"Where's Tina?" Laney murmured from Mark's side.

Both worked at the club, Laney dancing and Mark behind the bar. Most of their crew worked at, or had once worked at Revelry, the burlesque club under her apartment. Grace pulled on her mask. "We'll give her a few minutes. She was still working when I left the floor. Has everyone else checked in?"

"Yep. We're all set to kick demon ass."

The wind picked up speed and tugged at Grace's ponytail. She fought the urge but couldn't stop herself from looking up to the night sky, almost expecting to see a pair of dove-gray wings.

A bolt to the junk might dissuade the arrogant knight from following her next time. The prick had tried again to get her to stand down a couple weeks ago. Nothing—not even an infuriatingly stubborn, immortal demon hunter—would get her to abandon the fight. She imagined the fury in his eyes, veins bulging in his neck as he clutched the family jewels in pain and had to fight back a grin.

"He'll be excited to see you, too," Mark muttered.

"Who?"

"Chaos."

Grace scowled.

"The terrible gleam in your eyes gave it away."

"He better not get in my way tonight." She wrapped her fingers around the handle of her crossbow, adrenaline racing through her veins at the prospect of the coming fight. That initial rush always made her hands shake, at least until she was in the thick of it—then she was in her element.

"What's with you two, anyway?" Mark asked.

"Nothing."

The guy snorted. "If all the eyeball daggers you shoot at the big bastard could draw blood, he'd be sliced to ribbons by now."

"And let's not forget the growing number of impressively creative insults and death threats," Laney added, a grin curving her lips. "I've got to say, I do enjoy those."

Grace clutched the cool steel of her bow tighter and felt the rise of cold determination and white-hot rage that was never far away around that male. "What can I say? I hate his guts."

The three settled into a comfortable silence while they waited for Tina. Minutes ticked by, but there was no familiar rattle of the fire escape.

Time was up; they needed to get going. "She'll have to meet us there."

They took off at a sprint, freerunning across the rooftop. Grace couldn't stop the smile that curled her lips as they leapt the meter-wide gap to the next building and kept going. The surge of adrenaline was addicting.

Dammit, they needed Tina and her skill with a crossbow. Their bolts immobilized the vermin scrambling out of the portal, giving her people enough time to move in and remove their heads, turning them to ash.

Of course, the knights would be fighting as well.

The arrogant bastards were failing miserably, failing the people they were created to protect, and that blame rested squarely on Chaos's shoulders. And if the guy hadn't already picked up that she despised him with a fierceness that bordered on psychotic, he was even more of a fool than she thought.

They leaped to the next building and kept on sprinting.

He had no idea what went on in this city, right under his damn nose. Someone had to stop the bloodshed, the slaughter and kidnapping of her people, and if the knights couldn't do it, she sure as hell would give it her best shot.

If Chaos didn't like it? Well, tough shit. She'd worked too hard, had sacrificed too much to back down now. She didn't answer to him, had been fighting for this cause since she was sixteen years old. And she'd continue to do so, with or without his approval. She sure as hell wasn't going to stop just because that growly bastard demanded it.

When they reached their destination, most of her people were already there, waiting, lining the walls above the alley. She joined them at the edge of the building and looked down.

It was dark, with oppressive shadows that seemed to creep in, covering everything in its path. The smell of evil, of death, clung to the brick walls and concrete floor, saturating the air around them.

And of course, *he* was there.

Chaos stood front and center like always, his massive body held rigid, looking surly as fuck. She was pretty sure that was the only expression he was capable of, with the exception of a few variations. There was grumpy: when both brows got in on the act. Pissed off: add in a wicked lip curl. And, of course, murderous: his whole face got involved with that one. Add in the short beard, buzzed hair, and the tattoo covering one side of his head, and he looked kind of like a Marvel super villain...or maybe a serial killer.

He was dressed in his usual uniform: worn jeans and a black T-shirt, black boots on his feet. She scrutinized him as he swung his short sword, limbering up. The muscles in his arm flexed, causing the tattoo-like markings each knight was born with to dance across his tanned skin.

Her belly tightened, doing a little flip, and she gritted her teeth.

Laney rubbed her arms. "I can already feel it. Gives me goose bumps every time."

Grace jumped up onto the taller lip edging the building. "Take your positions, everyone," she called to her people.

Yeah, she could feel it.

And she was ready.

CHAPTER 2

CHAOS STOOD in the center of the alley, his brothers with him. Rocco to his right, Kryos and Lazarus a few steps behind. Gunner had taken his left with Zenon close by but, as always, concealed in shadow.

For the first time in a long time, they were the tight, unbreakable unit they were meant to be.

Only the unit was missing one vital member. Tobias. And right now, the loss of their brother had never felt so raw. He should be there, standing with them.

A familiar energy shivered across his skin, lifting the hair on his arms. *Fuck.* He'd been expecting it, knew it was coming, and still the sensation unsettled him, made him restless, off balance.

She was here.

With her little posse of vigilantes.

He shook out his clenched fists, jerking his head from side to side, cracking his neck to release the tension flowing through his body at her arrival. He looked up, unable to stop himself.

Sure enough, his gaze instantly went to the slight figure

dressed in all-black. Her gentle curves were highlighted by the glowing neon signs behind her. Her fingers were curled around her crossbow, the thing hanging loose at her side—locked and loaded and ready to take someone's fucking eye out.

Roc snorted. "Persistent, aren't they."

"Suicidal is what they are," he ground out.

The female moved closer to the edge and had the damn nerve to wave down at him.

"She totally likes you, brother," Roc said.

Her hand was still raised, and he watched as she made a fist, then slowly lifted her middle finger.

Chaos clenched his teeth and bit back a growl.

"Aw, look at that, you're still her favorite," Lazarus said. "I mean, the death threats alone are a sure sign she wants you."

Rocco nodded. "Absolutely. I've seen those crazed eyes trained on you through that freaky black ski mask. How can you resist that whole Jason Voorhees, Friday The Thirteenth thing she's got going on? So hot, man."

Chaos pinned the guy with a cold stare. "Shut it."

Gunner chuckled, the scar through his upper lip making his mouth twist up on one side. The sound was rusty as hell but good to hear. Something was up with the male, had been for a while now, but so far, he hadn't been in the mood to share.

The wall in front of them shimmered to life, and all conversation died an abrupt death.

The metallic scrape of Chaos's sword being pulled free seemed loud in the silence. "No one's getting past us today."

His brothers grunted their agreement, aggression rolling off their powerful bodies as they shifted, preparing to fight.

"Never thought I'd say this, but Chaos is right. Kill anything that moves," the pain in his ass above the alley said, weighing in.

Chaos growled, not only at what she'd said but at the sound of his name coming from her smart mouth. That slightly husky voice echoing down at him caused fire to burn in his gut and lick over his tingling skin. He ignored it and aimed a hard stare at her. "Do *not* kill anything that moves. Some could be seeking refuge. Not all demons are created equal."

Her spine straightened. "You're so goddamned blind. As soon as you turn your back, they'll slit your throat..."

"You'll do as I say, or you'll leave."

She laughed, a bitter, raspy sound that skittered down his spine. "You gonna make me, princess?"

Rocco choked beside him.

"Yes."

"We don't answer to you. And I'd like to see you try; you have no power here," she called down, a whole lot of smug coming through every word.

She was right. This close to a portal minutes from opening, a knight's powers were rendered useless. Still, he had no idea why she thought that would stop him. "I don't need my powers to spank your stubborn ass."

She stiffened, and the sound of her sharp, indrawn breath traveled down to him, tugging somewhere low in his gut. *Why the hell did I say that?*

"I hate to interrupt foreplay, that's never cool, but y'know, demons," Rocco muttered.

Seconds later the wall ahead shimmered, golden light rippling across the brick surface like it was liquefying before their eyes.

Demons immediately scrambled through and charged them.

Chaos spun and with one swing removed the head of a demon coming at him full speed.

More quickly followed. Impaling one on the end of his

blade, he slammed his fist into the face of another. Rocco came up behind the demon and removed his head.

Chaos couldn't stop his gaze from lifting again to the most maddening female he'd ever encountered. She had her bow raised, body lithe and strong, movements graceful yet sure as she fired bolt after bolt with precision, picking off the demons one by one as they fought or ran to escape into the city. Her people rushed in, removing their heads.

The battle raged on, and although they fought to cut them back, the demons kept coming.

One ran out, rushing to the side, pressed up against the brick wall, arms in the air, calling for sanctuary.

It happened occasionally. Demons wanting out, wanting relief from the darkness. Before Lazarus's mate, Eve, had joined them, it had been near impossible to decide who should be allowed to remain. But now they took the demons to her. Her ability to read minds had grown and took out the guesswork.

Most of the demi-demons were now fighting side by side with the knights on the alley floor. Even though they were all dressed the same and wore masks, he knew exactly where *she* was and wasn't surprised when she made a beeline straight for the demon trying to stay out of the action.

Chaos ground his teeth. Killing indiscriminately was not something they could or should do, for several reasons. Something the little vigilante didn't have the first clue about.

Slinging her crossbow over her shoulder, she slid a blade from her boot and pulled back. Chaos grabbed her wrist before she could let it fly.

He squeezed, and she released the blade, the thing clattering to the pavement.

"Let me go, jackoff..." Her gaze snapped to something over his shoulder.

Chaos spun around.

Two orthon demons rounded the corner at the entrance of the alley and gunned it straight for the portal. Not the brightest bulbs in Hell but deadly, and once given an order they would not stop unless you put them down. A female screamed and fought between them. Her wild, dark hair obscuring her face as she struggled to get free.

Chaos sprinted toward them, but demons crawling from the portal crowded in, blocking his way, and by the time they'd cut them down, the orthon had made it to the gate.

An extremely tall male stepped from the portal, deathly thin, but the power he was radiating was worrying on many levels. He took the female from the orthon, wrapping his fingers around the back of her neck.

Chaos searched for an opening, a way to stop him without hurting the female, a way to get her back, and edged closer.

The powerful demon's gaze slid to Chaos, and he made a tutting sound. "Not another step."

Chaos froze, although it went against every instinct he possessed.

Maybe the demon wanted to make a deal? Negotiate his escape from Hell? He hoped like fuck that was it, because there was no way they could get to her. All the demon had to do was take a step back and they'd lose them.

The alley went silent, the fight ceasing all around them. No one drew a goddamned breath as they waited for what would happen next.

Zenon cursed beside him. "Taren. Diemos's right hand."
Fuck.

Taren smiled. "Run, children," he said to the demons still in the alley, and they immediately took off, disappearing into the city.

Taren's gaze shifted to Rocco, and the fucker's smile widened as he brushed the female's hair away from her face.

Rocco roared. The sound bounced off the brick walls, the pain of it hitting Chaos in the chest with force, and he instantly knew who that female was to his brother.

The female stared at Roc, confusion and terror twisting her gentle features. "Rocco? What...what's happening," she asked, terror making her voice brittle, small.

The sound that left Rocco was pure animal, so raw it grated like sandpaper across Chaos's skin.

And that's when he felt it, the reason Roc had kept this female under wraps.

Chaos's body went haywire. His spine torqued, followed by his demon rocketing to the surface, like the bastard was trying to jump though his skin. If they hadn't been at the portal, that's exactly what would have happened.

The female was a hellsgate, a demi-demon who could be used to open and close the gates of Hell at will, and powerful enough that even without going through her transition, without having developed her powers yet, he could feel it.

Taren wrapped his hand around the front of her, gripping her throat and leaned in, eyes still on Rocco, who shook with rage so fierce Chaos was surprised the ground didn't shake with him. "Say goodbye now. This will be the last time you see your female."

"Rocco!" she screamed, tears streaming down her face. "Please...oh, God, please, help me."

A bolt came out of nowhere and lodged in Taren's shoulder. Two more quickly followed, taking out both orthon at his side. Taren hissed in pain but held the female tighter, using her as a shield as he backed up.

"Kyler!" Rocco roared and exploded into action, running for them.

Chaos sprinted after him—

Taren yanked the female back, back through the portal.

It would remain open for another few minutes, but they

were fucked. Knights couldn't enter Hell. One step through that portal with the angel brands they'd each had burned into their skin, and they'd die almost instantly.

Rocco knew this as well, which was why he'd pressed the bloody knife in his hand against his own forearm and started sawing at the brand, cutting at his flesh.

They all moved as one. Zenon got there first, tackling him hard to the ground. Rocco fought and bucked, determined to go after her, the sounds of his anguish sending a shiver down Chaos's spine and tearing through him.

In the end, it took four of them to hold him down and wrestle the blade from his hand.

"*Get the fuck off me!*" Rocco's voice was almost unrecognizable, fear and rage strangling his vocal cords.

A flash of light lit up the alleyway, followed by a familiar pop, and the portal closed.

Rocco's tortured scream was like a wild animal being slaughtered in the most inhumane of ways, and they all felt his soul-deep agony. It shredded Chaos. It shredded all of them.

"What have you done?" Rocco rasped, the fight leaving him immediately. His haunted gaze locked on the wall where the portal had been moments ago. He moved up to it, pressing his hands to the cold brick.

"Brother," Zenon choked, stepping forward.

Rocco shoved him away. "If that was Mia?"

Zenon's jaw tightened, his face twisting in agony. "I couldn't let you kill yourself."

Now that the portal was gone, their powers returned, and Rocco shifted, immediately taking his Kishi demon form. His clothes, now nothing but tatters, lay scattered on the ground at his feet. His deep crimson skin, so dark it was almost black, gleamed under the dim light in the alley, making his enormous fangs and black horns almost sparkle. But there was barely anything left of Rocco in his dark blue gaze, and Chaos watched as obsidian crawled in from the edges of his irises, washing away the color completely.

Gunner reached for him. "Roc—"

Without a backward glance, their brother took flight.

Zenon began to strip, and Chaos shook his head. "Leave him. He needs time to cool off."

Laz's head jerked up and he turned to Chaos, disbelief in his bright green eyes. "Cool off?"

Chaos didn't know what the fuck to say.

"Our brother just lost his mate," Lazarus choked. "In the most horrific of ways. She won't even get the mercy of death. Rocco has to live with the knowledge that she is in Hell, suffering unimaginable torture at the hands of his enemy. Try to live, fucking breathe, while she is unprotected, afraid, in pain, and there's not one thing he can do to save her. And you think he needs time to *cool off?*" Lazarus's features twisted in rage. "I know you're made of fucking stone, brother, so let me spell it out for you. Rocco, as you know him, *is gone*. He will never be the same. Chances are, we'll lose him just like we lost Tobias. So, no, there will be no *cooling off*. No amount of time will make this better for him."

Chaos clenched his fingers into a tight fist, the hopelessness of their situation more than he knew how to deal with.

Watching Tobias's descent into darkness after the tragic death of his mate, as he'd willingly surrendered to his inner demon, choosing a life without the memory of her—as he'd turned against them, before they'd lost him forever—was something that none of them would ever recover from.

Gunner scrubbed his hands over his face. "We should have let him go."

"He would've died. We need him in this war," Chaos said.

Kryos planted his hands on his hips. "We've already lost him."

He understood their pain for Rocco, fuck, he felt it too, but no one was saying what this truly meant. "She was a hellsgate."

"Roc thought she was safe. She hadn't transitioned. He planned to mate with her before bringing her to the compound to be safe," Zenon said.

Lazarus's mate, Eve, also a hellsgate, had affected their inner demons in ways they couldn't fully understand, and being around her had almost tipped them all over the edge into darkness. "You knew about her?"

Zenon dipped his chin.

Rocco had kept this from him. He hadn't trusted Chaos enough to share he'd found his mate. Pain deep and raw burrowed into his chest.

"Why didn't he ask me for the amulet?" The piece of jewelry had been imbued with angelic power, and was strong enough to block a demi from demons. Eve had worn it when they found out what she was, before she and Lazarus had mated.

"He didn't think he'd need it. She didn't have her power yet and he planned to make her his mate as soon as she did."

Since mating would have rendered the hellsgate power inside Kyler useless.

"Let's hope like fuck Diemos doesn't have any of Golath's bones." With Kyler and a bone from Golath, the first demon Lucifer ever created, Diemos would have complete control over the portal.

Zenon pushed away from the wall, black leathery wings snapping out from his back, and without another word, he was gone, no doubt after Rocco.

Chaos worked to control his emotions. "I know this is hard, but we still have a job to do. Go scout the city."

Laz and Gunner aimed disgusted glares at him, and Kryos just shook his head—then they were gone as well.

Planting his hands on his hips, Chaos dropped his head and sucked back several deep breaths, trying to gather his control. When that didn't work, he smashed his fist into the brick wall with a roar.

"Fuck... *Fuck!*"

The scrape of a boot had him lifting his head. *She* stood there, and even without seeing her face, he knew she was pissed, could feel her anger washing over him. She was on her own, her people had gone, chasing the demons that had escaped tonight. Doing *his* fucking job.

"What in *the hell* just happened?" she hissed.

He reached out with his senses, to *feel* her. But she was locked up tight, like she always was. "We're fucked," he said.

"I'm gonna need a little more than that."

"As soon as that female"—he pointed to where the portal had been a short time ago—"comes into her powers, Diemos will have a key to open the gates of Hell at will. She was a hellsgate."

She flew at him without warning, taking him by surprise. Her spinning kick made contact with his shoulder. He managed to block the punch she threw with her left but wasn't quick enough to avoid her right hook. Her fist slammed into his jaw. Hard. He blocked her next few punches, not wanting to hurt her, but the female was good. She could fight.

She feigned right, then spun to the left and slammed the heel of her palm into his nose, breaking it. There was only one thing he could do to stop her without hitting her; he wrapped his arms around her in a bear hug, holding her immobile.

She hissed and smashed her head into his already busted nose.

"Fuck!"

"How could you let that happen?" She struggled like a wildcat in his arms.

"Calm down."

One of her hands broke free, and her fingernails dug into the side of his throat, scratching across his skin and taking a nice sample of his DNA with them.

"I have enough to deal with without some unstable demi getting in my face," he ground out.

She stilled and shoved at him. For some reason, a reason he couldn't explain, he didn't let her go.

"If it wasn't for this unstable demi, you'd be dead." She pushed at his chest again, clearly pissed. "I should have let that demon take your arrogant-fucking-head when he had the chance."

She'd saved his ass a while back and wasn't going to let him forget it. "You really do hate me."

"More with every breath I take."

He believed her, could feel her shake with rage beneath his hands. "That's a lot of hate."

"You have no idea, pencil dick."

Pencil dick was a new one. But he didn't give a shit about her name-calling, this wasn't the first time she'd said how much she hated him, and he wanted...no, needed to know why. "What did I do to you?"

"You were born."

"I didn't exactly have a say in that."

She released a shuddering breath. "Let me *the fuck* go."

"If you aim those claws at me again, I'll put you over my damned knee. I'll treat you like the immature, pain in the ass you're behaving like."

She jerked in his arms, and his dick got hard. What the fuck was wrong with him? He had to force himself to release her.

She stumbled back a step and reached behind her head,

yanking her full mask off, revealing herself. She was breathing heavily, fire flashing in her expressive, mahogany eyes. "Asshole."

He clenched his fists tighter. Her lips were full, and they thinned when her gaze locked on his, full of fury and hatred. She ran those long, graceful fingers over her hair, brushing back loose strands of the palest gold.

Finally seeing her face for the first time had a serious effect on him. So sudden, he had to lock his knees. The rich brown of her eyes, soft and sumptuous, like umber velvet, got darker. She took another step back, shaking her head. "Fix this. Do your goddamn job and fix this," she yelled, fury exploding from her.

Then before he could say another word, she spun and sprinted into the night.

Chaos stood there alone, boots all but buried in the ashy remains of the demons they'd slaughtered, but his mind wasn't on the coming war, or what he could do to stop what could only be described as the fucking apocalypse.

Worse, it wasn't even on Rocco and the pain he was going through.

No, all he could think was, he still didn't know her name.

CHAPTER 3

GRACE WIPED the sweat from her face and tossed the towel by her gym bag. Her advanced combat and defense class was coming along well, really well. In fact, there were three demi that showed real promise.

After what happened during the equinox, they desperately needed to increase their numbers. Recruitment was the main reason she'd started her advanced classes. The other classes she taught, the basic self-defense and assertive verbal skills classes, they were different. And to her, were just as important. No one, human or demi, deserved to feel defenseless, helpless. No one.

Most of her students had left, and she made her way over to the females gathering their stuff. "Mia?"

The lovely redhead turned to face her. "Hey, Grace. Class was awesome as always."

"You've been practicing while you've been gone."

Mia had been coming to her classes for a while, and Grace had immediately seen her potential, then she'd vanished for several months—thanks to one scary-as-fuck knight. She'd mated Zenon, which blew Grace's mind. The male was standoffish and terrifying, and Mia was all warmth and sweetness. But then, they say opposites attract. Though, attraction had nothing to do with it, did it? The bond between mates bypassed all of that—whether you wanted it or not.

Grace was also good friends with Mia's older sister, Chaya. Chaya had worked with her a few months back. Still worked with her when she could, getting intel through the sex club she owned with her husband, Brent.

Chaya had kept Grace's identity secret, and if Chaos hadn't seen her face, she wouldn't even consider revealing herself to the mate of a knight. But he had, and it was only a matter of time before Chaos found her, anyway. May as well go for it. And it wasn't like she was trying to recruit Mia, no way would Zenon let her fight.

But thankfully, she'd found her way back to Grace's classes here at Deluca Gym, and she'd brought two of her extremely skilled friends with her.

"Yep, I train most days." Mia motioned to her friends. "This is Eve and Meredith."

Grace shook their hands. "Where do you both train? You're amazing."

Eve smiled. "With my...husband."

Meredith nodded. "Me too. I mean, with mine. My ah...husband."

The three friends smiled, like they were having trouble controlling their amusement. Grace had never had that kind of friendship with anyone, too busy killing demons for close girlfriends and in-jokes. Whatever had them so entertained didn't have anything to do with her. These females could fight, and that's all she cared about.

"Would you mind sticking around for a bit? There's something I'd like to discuss with you."

Mia frowned. "Yeah, sure."

Grace led them to the small office at the back of the gym and shut the door behind her. She didn't waste time with chitchat. Eve and Meredith were either up for it or they weren't. "Did you tell your friends that I'm a demi?" Grace asked Mia.

Mia nodded, frowning a little.

Eve crossed her arms. "I'm usually pretty good at sensing it. But if Mia hadn't told me, I wouldn't have known." All three females' postures had changed, now defensive. And that just confirmed to Grace that she'd picked correctly. It was a damned shame Mia was mated to a knight. She could have been extremely useful.

Grace allowed her guard to drop. "I'm good at blocking. Excellent, in fact." Which was the truth. She'd had to be. These females didn't need to know that she didn't possess an actual power, that being proficient with a crossbow and being able to kick ass was all she brought to the war.

Grace leaned forward, resting her forearms on her knees. "Look, what I'm about to tell you is going to sound crazy. But will you hear me out before you run off or make an offhand decision?"

Mia did some more frowning. "Of course."

Eve and Meredith studied her for a few seconds, then both nodded.

Right. Here goes. "I'm part of a select group of demi from all over the city. We have different reasons for why we came together, but we all want the same thing, have the same goal. We hunt and kill the demons invading our city and I'd like Eve and Meredith to join us."

Mia's gaze sliced to her friends, and they all did that eye-widening thing again.

"You don't have to decide right now, of course. But this fight is going to get a lot worse before it gets better, and we need all the help we can get. You can both fight, and I can sense whatever your powers are, they're impressive. You're exactly the kind of demi we need in this war." She glanced at Mia. "Obviously, you're out. I can't imagine Zenon would want you fighting, but maybe Eve and Meredith are interested?"

Mia's lips tipped up on one side. "It's you. You're the one, huh?"

Grace said nothing. She didn't need to.

"Look, since you told us who you are. I think it's only fair we do the same," Eve said and glanced at Meredith.

Meredith nodded.

Eve winced. "We don't have husbands. We have mates."

Fuck.

"My mate's name is Lazarus."

"And I'm mated to Kryos," Meredith said. "I think you've met them?"

I'm dead.

Yep, Lazarus, Kryos, and probably Zenon as well, were going to make mincemeat out of her.

"Right." What the hell could she say? She'd just propositioned the females of two of the deadliest and frankly unstable males she'd ever come across. Several seconds ticked by, but she didn't miss the emotions that flashed across their faces.

"You're going to tell them I talked to you?" Grace said.

Eve looked up to the ceiling and let out a breath. "I think you're amazing. What you're doing is so brave, the guys think so, too…but we don't keep secrets from each other."

In other words, be ready for the fallout.

The knights thought she was brave? The female was obviously trying to be nice, because she knew of one knight who certainly didn't think she was brave. Immature? Yes. Reckless and stupid. Absolutely.

22

"If it wouldn't send Zenon over the deep end, I'd join you in a heartbeat," Mia said.

Grace was already toast, so she may as well dig her own grave. "Your mates don't need to know. We look out for each other, we have each other's backs. You could use a block so they don't know it's you. Plus, we conceal our identities." Well, she had until the other night. Why the hell had she taken off her mask and shown Chaos her face?

"You don't know how badly I want to say yes," Eve said.

Meredith tucked her dark blond hair behind her ear, her hazel eyes earnest. "Every time Kryos comes home bloody and exhausted, I feel so helpless."

"But our hands are tied, right now," Eve said. "And I won't lie to Lazarus."

Grace held her gaze. "I can respect that."

"But we think you're amazing. Don't stop fighting," Mia said.

"I'll never stop. And you know where to find me if you ever change your minds."

Grace watched the females leave.

Chaos would come for her after this.

By the time Grace got to Revelry, the place was filling up and the regulars had taken their usual spots for the night. She headed out back to the dressing rooms. A few other girls were there putting on makeup and getting their costumes on.

Vince had decided on a burlesque club because he said it made the place sound classier. Only the rich and influential residents of Roxburgh need apply for membership—if you told people something was exclusive enough times, they believed you and wanted in.

But really the only difference between Revelry and one of

the strip clubs on Emery Square was the fancier costumes. Vince made sure to deliver burlesque style down to their very shoes. Yeah, there was the occasional comedic act, and they did some group dances that involved them all performing a striptease, à la 1950s, with a lot of fake fur and faux diamonds.

But at the end of the day, they took their clothes off for an audience.

Grace would be just as happy dancing for Joe Schmo on Emery instead of Roxburgh's elite.

Emery Square was made up of four streets. It surrounded a park that the city had created in an attempt to drive out the local strip clubs, massage parlors, and adult shops in an effort to "claim back" the area. The venture that failed miserably because the good people of Roxburgh didn't want anything to do with that part of the city. Instead it had become a hive of nighttime activity. Mainly fucking and fighting, but also a favorite hangout for sex demons, and an excellent hunting ground for Grace and her crew.

"Has anyone seen or heard from Tina?" Grace asked.

"Nope." Laney finished applying glossy, pink lipstick. The color matched the bows at the top of her white stockings. "But Vince was bitching about being a girl down."

Laney was their resident Bo-Peep. Not very original, but the guys loved it. Then again, Laney could wear a sack and the men would throw money at her.

Like most of the dancers, Tina was a demi. She was also a bit of a loner, which seemed to be a common trait among their crew of fighters. Few had blood family or friends outside their own little dysfunctional family they'd created at Revelry. They may not live in each other's pockets, but they loved—and would die for—each other and their cause.

There could very well be a good reason why Tina had up and taken off. It wouldn't be the first time one of the girls had run away from this life, and she doubted it would be the last. But Tina was solid. The war was as important to her as it was to Grace.

The room cleared out, and she pulled her phone from her purse and texted Mark again. *Tina?*

His replay came a few seconds later. *No word.*

Dammit. She needed to go to Tina's apartment and make sure she wasn't there sick or hurt.

The door opened, and Vince strode in looking kind of wide-eyed and twitchy. "Hey, Gracie?"

"What do you need, Vince?" She gave him shit, and not strangling him on a regular basis was a test of her control, but the older demi had become a kind of father figure, not only to her, but to a lot of the demi working for him.

He slid his hands into his pockets, looking more anxious. "I have a special guest coming tonight. I thought you might entertain him for me?"

"Did you now." She inwardly groaned. This was obviously important to him, which meant some rich asshole that Vince was desperate to get close to.

"Oden's coming in tonight, and I thought you could make him feel special, show him some of that Gigi Fury magic," he said.

Oden. Just Oden. Like the fucker thought he was Prince or Madonna or Rihanna.

The powerful demi owned half of Roxburgh. He also had a reputation. Someone not to be crossed. Which meant, he could be useful. "Fine, but you owe me."

He grinned. "You're my favorite, you know that, right?"

"There was never any doubt."

He chuckled. "So you'll make Oden feel welcome?"

She most certainly would. Schmoozing the wealthy and influential was one of the reasons she continued to work here. There were demi in this war who couldn't physically fight, but still wanted to help. Despite Oden's reputation, he might be able to provide useful intel, resources, manpower, maybe even a donation to the cause, if she got him on her side. Males like him loved to talk about themselves, throw their money around.

To most she was just something nice to look at, and that worked in her favor. It was amazing how much you learned about a person—how loose tongues got—when you were grinding on top of them and shaking your tits in their face.

She would do whatever it took to get more demi on their side, and fighting against the demons in this city.

She smiled sweetly. "Of course."

Vince was the other reason she stayed here. He'd given her and many other demi a home, a job, when they'd had nothing and no one else. He'd believed in her ability to fight, had encouraged her when she'd sought out others like her— demi sick of sitting back doing nothing while the knights failed them. There was no one she trusted more. He'd seen her at her worst, knew all her secrets. Well, all except one. Her stomach twisted.

Vince's phone buzzed. "Oden's here early." His eyes lifted to hers, pleading. "I don't want anyone but you with him."

He also wouldn't be on board with her recruiting his customers to her cause. She kept that part to herself as well. She rolled her eyes. "Fine. I'll go now."

Relief washed over his face, and she followed him from the dressing room.

Laney was on the stage near the end of her performance, her Bo-Peep outfit gone except for her stockings, a pink garter, and tasseled pasties.

Nearly every set of eyes in the room were on her.

Grace scanned the crowd, spotting her friend for the evening.

Oden. His eyes weren't on the stage. They were on Grace.

He sat in a corner booth, sipping what had to be their top-shelf whisky. His gaze, the darkest of blue, almost black, glittered as she approached. Tingles, unpleasant ones, danced down her spine, an uneasy feeling making her want to turn around and walk the other way.

She had no idea why she was reacting that way, and honestly, it just made her more curious about him. She stopped in front of him, and knew she'd picked the right outfit by the hungry look on his face as he took her in from head to toe.

Her panties matched her beaded, dusky pink corset that cupped her modest breasts, pushing them up and making them look bigger than they were, and hugged her ribs, defining her waist and curving over her hips. The attached garter held up her natural-colored, silk stockings. They had small dusky pink frills that ringed the tops of her thighs and a seam at the back that led down to her spike-heeled, platform stilettos.

She smiled.

He said nothing, just stared at her.

Ice sliced through her belly. "I'm Gigi."

"Vince's told me all about you," he said, his oddly perfect features not moving, showing no emotion at all. "You're exquisite."

"Thank you, Mr. Oden."

He held out a hand and she took it. He gently tugged her closer, until she had no choice but to climb onto his lap.

His hands went to her hips and his nearly black eyes glittered. "Yes. So very beautiful."

"I'm glad you think so."

"Are you going to dance for me, Gigi?"

"If that's what you'd like," she said. The urge to run, to get the hell away from him, grew.

He dipped his chin.

She attempted to climb off him, but he gripped her hips tighter.

"Here," he said.

He wanted a lap dance. Not her first. She did them from time to time, especially if she thought she could extract information—a lot of the girls did. It wasn't a big deal, but something about Oden set off all her alarm bells.

Which told her this was exactly where she needed to be.

She forced a coy smile and straddled him, wrapping her arms around his neck. Then lifting up to her knees on either side of the padded bench seat, so the tops of her tits brushed his chin, she rolled her hips.

He tugged her back down so she had no choice but to sit on his obvious erection. He was hard, but the expression on his face was still carved in stone as he watched her. It was unnerving.

The music was slow, sensual, and she moved her hips to the lazy beat, grinding down as she leaned back, exposing her throat and pushing her tits out further. His hands skimmed up her sides and stopped just below her breasts.

She winked when his gaze darkened in a way that made her blood freeze and slid off his lap. Spreading his knees before he could protest, she spun around, then bent forward. Reaching back, she brought his hands to her hips, letting him draw her back in close where he wanted her, rubbing her ass against the poker in his trousers.

He spun her around, forcing her to straddle him again. His dick was so hard she knew he had to be hurting, but that terrifying expression was still carved in stone, the only change was a slight tinge of color on his cheeks.

His fingers dug in roughly. "Don't stop," he said, his voice deeper, darker.

One of his hands slid up her back and he fisted her hair. She looked over his shoulder and saw Vince watching. He looked on edge, chewing his nails to stubs. She'd seen that look on his face before. Something more was going on here. *Goddammit.* So instead of burying her blade in this fucker's eye socket, like she wanted to, she forced herself to stay where she was. "You like it rough, baby," she crooned.

His black eyes boring into hers. "Yes."

She'd thought Oden's reputation had been exaggerated. But every instinct she had told her that it had not. Getting involved with this male in any way would be a huge mistake.

She bit her lip and rolled her hips. "Are you and Vince going into business together?" If Vince was climbing into bed with Oden, they'd all need to be doused in Lysol at the end of it. And there would be an end. To men like Oden, Vince was disposable.

His grip tightened, telling her without words he was not in the mood to talk about business.

"You're pretty rich, huh? Is it something to do with the club?"

She knew she'd pushed it when he tugged her head back. "You ask a lot of questions."

She raked her fingernails down his chest. "What can I say, power turns me on."

"Let's go somewhere private."

She was a dancer, currently rubbing against the guy like a cat in heat. It wasn't a stretch to assume she'd be up for it. It wasn't the first time she'd been asked to cross that line, and it wouldn't be the last.

"Sorry, honey. That's not part of my job description."

"You're a tease. I don't like to be teased."

His fingers dug in painfully, but she didn't give him the satisfaction of seeing it on her face. Instead she moaned. "I think you're enjoying it just fine." She moved faster, ground harder, let the music thumping through the room take over.

She had to force herself not to gag when he wrapped an

arm around her waist and shoved her down on his dick, thrusting up against her.

Shit, was he going to...

His eyes rolled back in his head.

Yes, apparently, he was.

Grace wanted to shove the creep away, slam her fist in his face, but Vince was still watching them, still looking worried. It was obvious the idiot was up to his eyeballs in something that reeked, and it had everything to do with Oden. If he was in some kind of trouble, punching the fucker holding her painfully tight, while he dry humped against her could make things worse, so she forced herself to endure it as he upped his efforts, ramming his dick against her inner thigh repeatedly.

If he wanted to walk out of here with a wet patch on the front of his pants like a sicko perv? Fine with her.

He made a rough sound and shuddered against her.

So fucking gross.

"Like an audience, huh?" she said, still on his lap when she wanted to jump the hell off and take a shower to wash off the smell of his sweat and overpriced cologne.

"How much?" he said as he ran his thumb across her lower lip, stretching the skin painfully, and smearing her lipstick.

"I'm not for sale."

His jaw tightened. "Everyone has a price."

She smiled and began to ease off his lap. His fingers gripped tighter for a second before he let her go. "It's been fun, Mr. Oden," she said.

His gaze traveled over her curves. "Just Oden."

She nodded and backed up several steps, not wanting to turn her back on him. He was a predator, there was no doubt about it. Finally, gaining some distance, she spun and headed across the now full club.

When she found Vince again, because he was suddenly nowhere to be seen, she'd brake his goddamn arms, followed by both his legs. He was so far out of his league it wasn't funny, and if he thought he could whore her out to get in good with his new buddy, he was in for a major wake-up call.

But her plans to beat Vince's ass were waylaid when a wall stepped out in front of her. A hard, hot, growling, very pissed-off wall.

She'd been expecting him, but...

Fuck.

CHAPTER 4

CHAOS CLAMPED his hands down on warm, bare flesh. The skin beneath his fingers was smooth, supple. The muscle of her upper arms, firm and defined. Jesus, that corset barely covered her nipples, the mounds of her modest breasts forced up and together. And if she turned around, he had no doubt he'd be able to see the curve of her ass cheeks.

She looked up at him, defiance clear in her mahogany eyes.

The female was maddening...tempting.

And right then he wanted to throw her over his shoulder, walk out of this place, and spend hours punishing her—for attempting to recruit more demi into her little army and risking the lives of more ill-prepared civilians. But most of all, he wanted to punish her for what he'd just seen her do with fucking Oden.

Why the hell do you care?

He bit back a growl as she lifted her chin, looking up at him, and all that pale gold hair fell back, brushing her waist. She smirked. "How's the nose?"

His groin tightened. What the hell was it about this female? After what he'd just witnessed, he felt like a sleazy bastard, no better than all the other panting, desperate males in this room mentally fucking the hot blonde staring up at him.

"You never trained at the compound." He would have remembered if she had. All demi-demons trained with the knights when they came into their powers. Grace had not.

"Nope."

"Who trained you?"

"Not your business."

Jesus.

She eyed him from head to toe. "You found me quicker than I expected."

"What did you expect?"

"As it happens, not a hell of a lot when it comes to you."

He'd never met anyone more infuriating in his life. His gaze dropped to her mouth. And before he could stop himself, he'd reached out with his thumb and was wiping off the red lipstick smeared past the curve of her full, lower lip. A jolt shot up his arm at the contact.

Her nostrils flared, and she jerked back.

Shit, he'd lost his damn mind. He'd seen Oden do it, marking her, trying to make her feel small, and he hadn't liked it, any of it.

Again, why the fuck do you care?

"Enjoyed the show?" she said scowling, and not giving one shit what Chaos thought about what she'd just done with that asshole.

Despite the directness of her gaze and the fire in its depths, her voice was husky, different.

"Grace…"

"Gigi," she said. "When I'm here, you call me Gigi."

This was her work persona, the temptress, the dancer. A

33

female who would sell her time, a piece of herself to males like the conceited demi she'd been sitting on moments ago.

He didn't like that, either.

She saw it on his face, because just like that, the steel veil dropped into place, all softness washing from her expression. "Let's save us both some time, shall we? No, I won't stop what I'm doing. No, I won't stop recruiting. And yes, you are the biggest asshole I have ever had the misfortune to encounter. Does that about cover everything?"

This female pissed him off like no one else. Not even Rocco's smart mouth could piss him off like—

He slammed the door on that thought instantly. His helplessness and anger over what happened to his brother was more than he knew how to deal with. He gritted his teeth as anger forced its way forward. "Not quite. I have one more question."

Her hands went to the gentle curve of her hips. "Illuminate me."

"Do you enjoy the power you have over weak, spineless males like your friend Oden? Does it turn you on? Or do you feel shame after you've let them pant all over you?"

He didn't know where the words had come from, or why he'd lashed out, but it was too late to take them back now. Her entire body went rigid under his hands, and he realized he hadn't yet released her. What was he doing? It wasn't her he wanted to strangle...no, he realized it was Oden. And that loss of control pissed him off further—it also confused the hell out of him.

She moved quickly, flicking her arms out in an arch, forcing his hands from her upper arms, and shoved his chest.

A sneer twisted her features. "If anyone should feel shame, it's *you* for phenomenally sucking at your job, for failing those who rely on you most, those who are unable to protect themselves." Pain flashed across her eyes, but it was gone almost instantly. "And as for the power I hold over weak, spineless males"—her hand landed on his hard cock and she cupped him over his jeans with a firm grip and squeezed—"you tell me."

"Fuck." The word slipped out before he could stop it.

"My sentiments exactly. Only I don't fuck people I don't respect."

"Glad we're on the same page." Except he did respect Grace, he respected the hell out of her. He just didn't want her and her people fighting, not when it was his job.

She laughed, a mirthless sound that held so much behind it. "We're not even in the same damn book, Chaos."

His name on her lips again sent a shiver through him, and he scowled harder. She squeezed tighter and he didn't move, didn't shove her hand away, wouldn't give her the satisfaction. "Yeah, I'm hard. Big fuckin' deal. Any male would be when confronted with a blatant show of tits and ass. But the difference between Oden and me, is that I have a semblance of control, and most importantly, as far as you're concerned, I'm not the slightest bit tempted." *Yeah, right. Who are you trying to convince, her or your dick?*

Her hand dropped to his balls and he braced. But instead of squeezing the shit out of them, she gave him a light slap. Pleasure and pain shot up through his lower stomach. It took effort, but he managed to stop his eyes from rolling back in his head.

She laughed and leaned in. He had to fight not to do the same. "Like a little pain with your pleasure, do you, Chaos?"

He gritted his teeth. She had no idea what he liked, but fuck, he desperately wanted to show her.

"Have we finished here?" she said. "I have customers to see to, then I have demons to hunt and kill. Y'know, the job *you* should be doing instead of coming here to stare at my tits and lie about the real reason you tracked me down."

"And what reason would that be?" *Dammit.* He should keep his mouth shut and leave. This female annihilated his control.

The gentle muscles in her shoulders shifted in an attractive way when she shrugged. "You can deny it all you like, but you're curious. So I'll help you out." She tilted her head back, her gaze clashing with his. "I like it deep, and hard. *Rough.* All the fighting and dancing I do has given me stamina and flexibility... Oh, and I like to use my nails and my teeth."

All things he'd considered, and dammit, in his weakest moments, imagined.

She placed a hand on his chest, trailing it down to the waistband of his jeans. "But that's never going to happen, since I don't even tempt you. And of course, there's the fact that I'd rather fuck a cactus than you." She shrugged. "So you see, coming here was a waste of time."

The urge to prove her wrong pounded through him, to show her exactly how good he could make her feel, how he could make her scream his name in pleasure, hummed through his veins.

It took the last of his dwindling control to stop himself from hauling her closer and slamming his mouth down on her sexy defiant lips. *Fuck.* Unacceptable. "I'm here for one reason, and that's to tell you to stop this dangerous game you're playing. You get yourself killed, that's your own stupid fault. One of my brothers loses a mate because of you, and we will have a serious problem. There is nowhere on this earth you could hide that I won't find you. Do you understand? I will not lose another—" Shit, he stopped himself before he said too much, locking down the pain that shot through his chest again. Tight.

"How is Rocco?" she asked, reading him perfectly and picking at his wound.

Crossing his arms over his chest, he took a step back, like

the action had the ability to shield him from her questions. "My brother is no concern of yours. Just remember I warned you."

"Cool, I'll file that away with the rest of your orders and threats...under bullshit that doesn't concern me."

"Grace..." Her name slipped past his lips again, and he clamped them shut. He hadn't said her name out loud until tonight, since Mia had told him who she was. Saying it felt too personal, made him feel strange, unsettled. Angry.

"See you around, knight," she said and walked into the crowd without a backward glance, hips swinging, ass hanging out for anyone to see.

He had the sudden, unexplainable urge to go after her.

Which was why he turned and strode out, putting as much distance between them as he could.

CHAPTER 5

GRACE KNOCKED on Tina's apartment door. When no answer came, she checked for prying eyes, then quickly picked the lock and eased the door open.

She hadn't been able to get away the night before, not when Vince had pounced not long after her confrontation with Chaos, demanding every gory detail from her time with Oden. Thankfully, Vince's focus had been locked on the powerful demi walking around with a wet patch on his crotch and he'd missed her little conversation with the pissed knight.

Mark had swung by Tina's place, though, and he'd done a quick search, but Grace wanted to see it for herself.

She locked the door behind her and looked around the shadowed room. After speaking to Mark this morning, Grace was even more sure that something was seriously wrong. It wasn't like Tina to go off like this for more than a couple days, and she sure as hell wouldn't keep ignoring everyone's texts and calls.

Grace let out a relieved breath when the only lingering scent in the place was Tina's perfume with a chaser of sour milk. She flicked on the light, illuminating the tiny studio apartment. The place was neat, tidy. There was no sign of a struggle, everything in its place. Her bed was perfectly made and covered in overstuffed pink and purple cushions.

Two mugs, a bowl, and a spoon sat in the sink. They'd been there since she'd had breakfast the morning of the equinox, no doubt. A milk carton sat on the countertop, not quite empty, and the cause of the smell. Grace picked up the mugs, only one had lipstick on the rim. Tina had company that morning. She didn't have a boyfriend right now, at least Grace didn't think so. No one serious, anyway.

She put them back in the sink and began to methodically move through the room, checking for any indication that Tina had plans of leaving town or any clue as to who had shared a coffee with her that morning.

A small box sat beside the bed and she flipped open the lid. Lip balm, a pair of stud earrings. The box shifted slightly and something gold and black and shiny peeked out from underneath. She picked it up. A cuff link, weighty, solid. The bottom was gold, the top was black, and there was something carved into it, filled with gold, some kind of bird, or a dragon? She couldn't tell.

Tina's last boyfriend delivered pizza. Definitely not a cuff link kind of male.

It looked expensive. Maybe it was something, maybe it wasn't, but she snapped a photo, put it back, and left through the fifth-story window.

Scaling the fire escape, she climbed onto the roof and let the light breeze wash over her. Everything was a mess. Tina was missing. Something was up with Vince. And, of course, there was Chaos and the impending apocalypse. Helpless wasn't a feeling she liked, and right then that was the dominant emotion riding her.

After sending a quick text to Mark, in case he had any

updates, she worked at refocusing. She wasn't great with the whole communication thing, but her crew trusted her, believed in the cause, and most importantly, in her skill as a fighter. She chose to lead by example, and that meant killing demon scum.

She took off, sprinting across the roof toward the next building, and her gaze lifted to the sky, like it did far too often lately. No sign of gray wings glinting in the moonlight, not tonight anyway. Jesus, the sheer power she'd felt coming off Chaos when he came to the club was both impressive and intimidating. And she despised him for it. What a damn waste.

She still couldn't believe that she'd grabbed him. The weight of his erection, hot and hard, had branded her palm and affected her more than she thought it would.

But that was just plain old biology, right? She had no control over her body's reaction to him from what she understood. What would he do if he knew who she really was?

Her stomach tightened and her heart raced.

If she told him she was his mate?

If she dropped her rock-solid block, and she let him feel their connection. A whacked-out, soul-deep knowledge that she would have cut out of her body the moment she felt it if that were possible.

"Do you enjoy the power you have over weak, spineless males like your friend Oden? Does it turn you on? Or do you feel shame after you've let them pant all over you?"

She scowled. She'd die before revealing the truth to him.

The only one who should be ashamed was him. He'd failed her kind time and again.

Had failed her family.

She'd never see her parents, her brother, ever again because of him.

Pain washed through her, and she used it to drive her on, to run faster, harder, jump farther. That pain was her fuel.

Despite Chaos's power, he was failing in his task, and because of his arrogance, his ignorance, she'd lost everything. Her parents had suffered terribly before they'd been killed by rogue demons, demons that should have been tracked and killed as soon as they'd escaped Hell. Both her parents had held impressive abilities, especially her father, but he'd been no match for the creatures.

Both her parents had been demi, and Grace had assumed when she came of age, her powers would be stronger for it. Instead, she'd gotten the opposite: not a damn thing. She could lift an invisible shield, block herself—who she was, what she was—from other beings, knights…Chaos, but that was the extent of it.

Sometimes she thought she felt something deep inside swirling, restless to be set free, but nothing ever came of it. Phantom powers. She wanted them so badly, she imagined it.

Yeah, she could fight, but it was a demi-demon's unique powers that would win this war, she was positive of it. Which was why Chaos choosing not to utilize the demi willing to fight, when they were on the cusp of losing everything, infuriated her even more.

She picked up her pace, feeding off the rush of adrenaline as she launched off the ledge and leapt to the next building. Her boots hit the next roof, and she pushed her body to its limits, relishing the burn of her muscles, planting each foot against the rough surface beneath her feet to propel her faster, farther. She dipped her head, preparing to jump—

Something collided with her side, and Grace hit the ground hard, her body's momentum propelling her forward, sliding her across the rough surface.

She desperately groped for purchase, but there was

nothing to grab on to as she slid right off the edge of the building.

The fingers of one hand caught the lip of the roof and she cried out. Sucking in a breath, she swung up with her other hand and hung on for dear life. "Shit. Fuck."

Someone moved to the edge and looked down at her. "Hello, demon butcher. Nice to finally meet you in person."

She'd never seen the guy before, and with all her focus currently on not falling to her death, she was unable to reach out with her senses and feel what he was.

He crouched down and flashed her a grin. "As much as I'd like to pull you up, your crimes are too numerous for leniency. Termination is the only cure for your particular illness."

"What the hell are you talking about?" Her fingers were screaming, but she had a decent hold for now. She could easily swing herself back up if this asshole wasn't in her way. There was a fire escape behind her, across the alley, though. If she sprang off with enough force, she'd make it.

"You've traveled down the wrong path, little demon butcher, and now you're infected. A killer of your own kind, fighting against those who wish to be set free from darkness." He poked out his bottom lip. "He said to spare you if your powers were impressive." He shrugged and tilted his head. "Such a shame, you really are a hot piece of ass."

She gritted her teeth and lifted her feet, the soles of her boots gripping on to the rough concrete wall, and glanced behind her, preparing to spring back to the fire escape across the alley—

The male above her froze, nostrils flaring, his gaze boring into her. "Well now, what do you know."

The demon, because it was obvious that's what he was, grinned wide and reached out, like he was about to help her up.

His hand was midair when his head hit the rooftop and rolled to the side. There was a clatter of steel, then Chaos was suddenly there, gripping her forearm. "I've got you."

Next, she was in motion, lifted like she weighed nothing, pulled to her feet before she had a chance to swing herself up.

Those dark, almost charcoal eyes took her in from head to toe, assessing, searching for injuries. The neon sign across the street shone on his muscled forearms and huge, bulging biceps, highlighting his incredibly ripped bare chest and stomach. It also lit up the tattoo-like markings on his arm and the ink on the side of his shaved head.

She gritted her teeth against the connection between them, because even looking at her with emotionless indifference like he was now, just being in his presence, had her fighting the urge to squirm.

Gunner was crouched behind him, searching what was left of her attacker. "Wallet, phone." He threw a small switchblade down beside the other objects. "Extremely unmanly knife." Then he looked up at her. "All right?"

She scowled at the knight, pissed and humiliated. "Why wouldn't I be?"

Chaos snorted. "You're welcome."

"I didn't ask for your help. I sure as shit didn't need it."

Gunner's lips twitched, but he didn't comment. He thought she was full of it. Underestimated her like most other people. She'd survived this long without the knight's help, and she'd keep on surviving. That's what she did.

"You're reckless and goddamn stubborn," Chaos said. "You'd be fucking dead if I hadn't saved your ass."

"Wow, tell me how you really feel." She was going for light and unaffected but wasn't sure she pulled it off.

"Do you have a death wish, female?"

She rolled her eyes. "I *was* just about to jump to safety

across the alley. In case you missed it—though I'm not sure how since you can't seem to stay the hell away from me—I'm kinda good at that. But I was hoping to find out why he wanted me dead first." She glanced at the pile of ash behind them. "Say, why don't you tell me again how soft and cuddly some demons are."

He ground his teeth. "Not all demons are created equal."

"What about that one?"

Chaos wasn't the only one who'd tried to convince her of the same bullshit. Chaya had once told her what a super awesome guy her and Mia's demon father was, and Grace was ashamed to admit she'd pretended to agree with her friend to get her to work for her, was still lying to her. But Grace knew the true nature of demons firsthand, and nothing would change her mind.

"I'm wasting my fucking breath with you, aren't I?" Chaos said and crossed his arms over his wide chest, causing his monster biceps to flex. "From now on, use the sidewalk like everyone else. You're not superwoman, you're not super anything. You're a demi-demon with a hero complex. Stick to stripping and leave the fighting to the trained professionals."

"Chaos..."

Chaos cut Gunner off with a hard look. "She needs to hear this for her own safety."

Jesus, he really was a giant, egotistical asshole. "I didn't know you cared?"

"The only thing I care about right now is that you're wasting my time."

"Then please, by all means spread your wings and fly... preferably into the sun, but I'm not picky, a concrete wall would be okay as well. I can handle things from here." She shoved past him and stepped over the ashy remains of the creep who'd attacked her. Couldn't get much deader. "I really wish you hadn't killed him. I would've liked the chance to question him."

To ask why he'd paused, why it looked like he'd changed his mind and was about to help her back up.

"Did he say anything?" Gunner asked.

"Nothing important." She picked up the wallet and did a quick search. Nothing. Inwardly cringing, she slid her hand deep into his jeans pocket, then unable to help herself, glanced back at Chaos and winked. "Don't panic, I'm not searching for tips. I can't exactly use my feminine wiles on him in this condition." The male growled, and she shook her head. "You really are a humorless bastard."

"You have no idea," Gunner muttered, lips twitching again.

"How do you live with him?"

"It's not easy, but getting to beat on him during training helps."

A shiver came out of nowhere and traveled over her skin, raising goose bumps. That was some mental image. But instead of Gunner, it was her. She'd love to have a go at him, maybe make him lose some of that tightly held control, get him all sweaty and pissed off. Maybe he'd pin her to the floor.

She quickly shook the images from her head. The very idea had guilt twisting her insides. After what he'd done, how he'd let her people down, he was the last male on earth she should be lusting after.

She spotted something among the ashes and picked it up. A ring with a weird dragon birdlike creature engraved into black stone. The same symbol as the one on the cuff link she found in Tina's apartment.

"What is it?" Chaos moved beside her, and the hum of all that tightly leashed power radiated from his big body, calling to her on a purely instinctive level, making her want to rub against him, to take some of it for herself.

"Not sure." Not a lie. She had no reason to go into Tina's disappearance with the knight, not yet anyway. It could mean nothing, they could be members of the same lonely-hearts club or bought them from the same store.

"Have you seen this before?" she asked anyway.

He shook his head, ran a hand down his beard, then glanced up at her. "You can leave now. We'll clean this up."

She rolled her eyes again. "You sweet talker, you. Admit it. With charm like that, you're beating the females off with a stick." Then for some messed-up reason, she held her breath, waiting for his answer.

"I don't have time for females," he said without breaking eye contact. Was he sending her some kind of message? Like she might be desperate to get him between the sheets.

Wow. Grab a guy's dick once and he gets all kinds of ridiculous ideas. Arrogant jerk.

"Aww, even self-centered meatheads deserve to get off occasionally, big guy." She didn't know why she was pushing him, it wasn't like his sex life was of interest to her. Because it wasn't. She was just messing with him. Grace didn't care who he fucked. Nope.

Then why are you holding your breath again?

His gaze darkened and his tongue darted out to lick his lower lip, leaving behind a sheen that made it look even fuller than before. He leaned closer. "I wouldn't worry your-self about it. I assure you, I get off when I need to."

An image came unbidden, Chaos naked and wet in the shower, his fist wrapped around his cock, pumping the hard flesh with sure, firm strokes. She swallowed. "Well...good for you."

Good for you?

What the hell was wrong with her? Her face heated, and

she crouched back down, pretending to look through the dead guy's stuff again. Gunner's amused grunt didn't help her fight her embarrassment, either.

She got to her feet. "Can't find anything else."

"No," Chaos said. "And I can't see how that would have magically changed since you checked two minutes ago."

Bastard. "I'll head off, then." She hated that Chaos thought he'd saved her, that in his mind, she'd just proven all the unflattering shit he thought about her and her ability to fight.

"You sure you're all right, Grace? You want me to drop you home?" Gunner's wings snapped into place, the bronze feathers were stunning, gold flecks threaded through each one, picking up the light.

"What, you mean...fly?"

"Yeah."

"No," Chaos said.

She spun to face him. "Why not?"

He opened his mouth, then closed it. "We have shit to do. That's why."

As much as she would love to feel what flying was like, and pissing off Chaos would be an added bonus, something about going with Gunner didn't feel right. "I'm fine, thanks anyway."

Being this close to Chaos muddled her gray matter.

Made her crave things she knew she didn't actually want.

Needing to escape Chaos's burning gaze, she strode to the edge of the building, right where she'd been dangling a short time ago.

She turned to face him, and Chaos's eyes narrowed.

Grace gave him a one-fingered salute and dropped off the side, catching the lip with the tips of her fingers. Chaos yelled, followed by the sound of his boots pounding toward her. Before he could reach her, she kicked off the wall,

47

propelling herself into the air and twisting on her way across the short distance to the fire escape on the other side of the alley. Grabbing on, she swung through the bars and started climbing.

She turned back when she reached the rooftop, unable to hide the fuck-you smile on her face. Chaos stood across from her, the space she'd just jumped now between them. His expression could have been carved in stone. Grace laughed, spun, and ran for the shadows.

Underestimate me again, I fucking dare you.

She refused to think about him again tonight. She had more important things to worry about.

CHAPTER 6

CHAOS TURNED AWAY as Laz gently pulled Eve into his arms and said something against her ear before kissing her.

"Promise me you'll be careful?" she said.

"Always am."

Zenon and Kryos had walked into the control room without a second to spare, no doubt because they'd been dragging out the goodbyes to their own females. Chaos didn't want to intrude, but they needed to get going. When he looked back at them, Laz had Eve's dark, curly hair fisted in his big hand, looking into her eyes. "Love you."

She pulled him in close, and he leaned down so she could whisper something to him that made Lazarus pull her in tighter before he finally let her go. Chaos felt like a voyeur, but for some fucked-up reason he couldn't look away, swallowing thickly when his brother took his mate's mouth for one last deep kiss. When she walked away, Lazarus watched until she was gone.

Chaos cleared his throat, a weird feeling gripping his gut. "You ready?"

Lazarus rubbed a hand over his face. "Yeah."

"Everything okay?" Gunner asked Laz.

"Let's just go."

Gunner crossed his arms. "It's not like I haven't seen how loved up my brothers are before," he said gruffly. "I mean, I can feel puberty hitting all over again when I'm around Zen and Mia, and let's not get started on Kryos and Meredith."

Kryos grinned, and Zenon chuckled quietly. The sound was rusty, but it was genuine and something none of them had ever thought to hear from the Hell-born knight. They'd nearly lost him not long ago and Chaos thanked the fates every day that Zen found Mia, that she'd been able to save him with her power. Chaos never would've forgiven himself if they'd lost him as well.

Tobias's absence would always be felt. Always. And made Rocco's absence now all the more cutting. Zenon had talked to him, but he was staying close to the alley where he'd last seen Kyler, and refused to come home.

"Talk to us, Laz," Gunner added.

Laz gripped the back of his neck. "Eve's worried, scared every time I leave at night. It's gotten worse lately."

The grins dropped from Kryos's and Zenon's faces, and by the hollow looks in their eyes, Chaos guessed they'd had similar conversations with their own females.

Chaos rubbed at the sudden ache behind his ribs. But there was nothing he could say or do, to change any of it. "Right, let's head out." He hated how rough his voice sounded.

He lifted his chin at Gunner, who was staying behind, and strode to the balcony jutting from the control room. They unfurled their wings and took to the skies.

Splitting up, Kryos and Zenon branched off, heading for the center of the city, while Chaos and Laz made their way to the outer perimeter on the east side, where a lot of upmarket bars and clubs were located—including Revelry. But under no circumstances was he going in.

Not after the way his hackles—his demon—had reared to the surface when Gunner had offered to fly Grace home. Not when he'd nearly come out of his damned skin when she'd stepped off the edge of that fucking building. Every instinct he possessed had come alive like some dormant part had been doused in ice water, coughing and spluttering to the surface. He didn't understand it and had no intention of pursuing the feeling.

"There." Laz pointed to a building below. An empty bar. The owner had gone broke and closed a few months back and no one had taken over the lease yet. A demon male was at the rear of the building, and went in though the back door, towing a female demon behind him.

They could just be looking for a quiet place to fuck, and he sure as hell didn't need to see that, but it could be something else as well.

They landed a few feet away, and Laz motioned Chaos to go first. "After you, my liege."

Chaos shook his head, his brother had obviously had the same thought and would rather not have that shit burned into his retinas for all eternity. "So kind."

Laz shrugged, his gaze still weighted, worried about his mate.

Chaos pushed the door open as quietly as he could. Although they'd been joking around, he'd happily go ahead of any of his brothers, putting himself in danger first should things go wrong. They walked in and...nothing. They did a quick search and found the place completely empty.

Chaos reached out with his senses, but the invisible imprint he always felt when demons were, or had been, near, came back with a big zero on the demon-o-meter. "I can't sense them."

"Trap?" Laz said, alert, scanning the large open space.

Something was definitely off.

The sound of footsteps echoed around the room.

"What the fuck?" Laz searched the room wildly.

"Go." Chaos turned to get the fuck out of there, but it was too late as whatever had been cloaking the demons lifted.

At least twenty surrounded them, and the fuckers were rocking glazed no-one's-home expressions. They hadn't had an encounter like this for several weeks, but he hadn't been stupid enough to believe they'd stopped altogether, just that whoever was controlling the demons in Roxburgh had taken a time-out to strengthen their forces.

Laz being mated meant his powers were stronger, and he sent the ones directly in front of him flying against the unforgiving wall with a blast of power hard enough to leave a dent.

Chaos's were limited, and as always, his sword arm was his best bet. He fought, cutting through the demons as they rushed forward. Lazarus continued to blast them back, but whoever had control over these demons had them getting right back up.

Time and again, despite their screams of pain, broken bones, missing limbs, or the fact that several were gray from loss of blood, they kept coming.

Chaos and Laz quickly got into a rhythm. Laz would knock them back and Chaos would remove their heads.

He was panting and covered in blood when they finally cleared the room. Only one remained and Chaos closed in, grabbed the male by the throat, and pinned him to the wall. "Who did this to you?" The demon's mouth opened and closed like a dying fish, like he wanted to tell him, but whatever force had hold of him had control of his damn vocal cords. "This is pointless."

He pulled back and removed the demon's head. It instantly disintegrated, turning to ash like the others.

Lazarus planted his hands on his hips. "How did they know where we were? How do they keep finding us? Bigger numbers? We would've been screwed."

He wanted to know the answer to that as well. How did these fuckers know where they were patrolling? Chaos pulled his phone from his pocket and sent a text to Zenon warning them.

"They're toying with us right now. Testing their power." He ran his hands over his head. "Diemos is behind this somehow, but who the hell is pulling the strings here on Earth?"

"Marcus might have some ideas."

Marcus was a full demon, and for lack of a better term, Zenon's "father in-law." "I've already questioned him, he hasn't heard anything. Since his daughter hooked up with a knight, he's well and truly out of the loop."

Lazarus cursed.

A wall-shaking crash echoed through the room, the sound coming from the rear of the building. Jesus, now what? They raced for the exit and burst out the door.

Rocco.

Fuck.

He had his hand wrapped around a demon's throat. The fucker was probably a lookout. Their brother's eyes were flat black, his inner demon working with him as he held the smaller male in an unyielding grip.

"I'll ask you again, and this time you'll tell me the truth." Rocco grabbed the demon's wrist and slammed it against the wall. Blood leaked from him in several places and his index finger was missing.

The demon was fully alert and making a lot of noise, but not the kind of noise Roc wanted. Without hesitation, he sliced off another digit. The demon screamed.

"Roc, fuck. Stop," Lazarus said, coming up beside him.

"He won't tell me if she's all right. He won't..." Rocco punched the wall by the demon's head. "Fucking tell me!" he screamed in the male's face.

Chaos moved in, too. He'd never seen Rocco like this, this out of control.

"I-I don't know who y-you're...ah, talking about...I-I... was given sanctuary..."

"This isn't you, my brother. Step back." Chaos didn't miss the fear in his own voice. They'd all watched Tobias go through something similar, and they couldn't let Roc slip away as well.

Rocco reared back with a roar and took the demon's head off. He stumbled back, breathing hard.

Laz stepped up. "Roc...you need to come home, you..."

"Stay the fuck back!" Roc yelled, covered in demon blood, eyes bloodshot and hollow, face drawn and pale. "I mean it," he snarled, then he shifted and was gone.

"We're losing him," Laz croaked.

He was right. Rocco was slipping away, and if they didn't come up with a way to bring him back, they wouldn't only lose their brother, they'd more than likely lose the war as well.

They needed every knight at full power, with their heads on straight. The way things were going, there wouldn't even be a war, they'd get their asses handed to them well before it even got to that point.

If that happened, the Hell's Gate would bust wide open, suffocating everything in its path with unrelenting darkness, and nothing would ever be the same again.

CHAPTER 7

"You have to talk to him," Laney said.

Mark leaned against the wall, arms folded, expression grim. "I'll do it."

Laney shot him a dirty look before Grace could even answer.

Grace and Mark had gone down the friends-with-benefits road several years ago. A serious mistake on her part. She'd been lonely, wanted some company. Unfortunately, they'd had zero chemistry. But ever since, he occasionally got the misguided urge to protect her. She could kick the guy's ass from one end of the gym and back, but he'd had her under him a handful of times, so now he thought he needed to protect her.

Insane.

Infuriating.

And one of the main reasons she now avoided romantic relationships.

She fixed Mark with a hard stare. "No, you won't."

He bristled but shrugged. "Fine. Whatever you want."

"That's right." She may not always love being their leader

—the responsibility sometimes weighed heavily, especially when they lost someone in battle—but they'd needed someone, and for whatever reason, they'd chosen her.

Maybe it had been her determination—her hatred had shone the brightest, and they hadn't missed it. Someone needed to make the hard decisions, and that's what she did. So if anyone was going to talk to Chaos, it would be her.

As much as Grace hated...*loathed* the very idea, in the end, it was the best option, for everyone. There was a hellsgate demi in the hands of their enemy, who at any moment could gain her powers. Stopping that from happening was more important than her distrust and resentment toward Chaos.

"Any word from Tina?" Just saying her name made Grace's muscles tense. The sick feeling wouldn't go away. Tina wouldn't just run away and leave the city. Leave them.

Heads shook and muttered noes filled the room.

Something bad had happened to their friend. She knew it down to her bones. "If you can, question the demons before you kill them. Do whatever necessary to make them talk. Someone knows something. Right, let's get back to work before Vince pops an artery."

"You sure about this?" Mark asked when the room had cleared.

Pulling her phone from her back pocket, she glanced up at him. "No," she answered honestly. "But as it is, we're getting in each other's way. We should be fighting together."

"He won't go for it, and I don't trust him, Grace. And after what happened to your family, how the hell can you even consider this?" Mark shot at her, then walked out.

Grace stood stiff, the queasy feeling in her gut gripping tighter. Would Chaos even remember her parents? Had he been the one to train them when they were in the compound, young and new to their powers? Or were they just another face in a sea of faces he thought he was helping but instead sent out into the world to be slaughtered.

Pain sliced through her, tears prickling the backs of her eyes.

She shoved her fingers through her hair. He'd never agree to her idea if she came at him like she had been, all fury and hatred. She needed to find some freaking control. She could pretend she didn't despise him. She faked it here every night.

The coming war didn't give a shit about her pain or her past. It was going to rise up from Hell and devour everything in its path. There was no time to be angry and hurt. Not anymore.

Scrolling through her contacts, she hit Mia's name.

The phone rang twice. "Hey, Grace!"

"Hey."

"What's going on?"

"I need to get in touch with Chaos. Can you help me?"

Grace clapped her hands to get her class's attention. "Right, time for some one on one."

The advanced class she taught twice a week had a few other possible candidates to join her crew, but no one as good as Mia and Eve, who she noted were absent today. Mia hadn't said they were skipping class when she spoke to her, but it wasn't hard to guess why. And if she was honest, it stung a little.

She didn't force people to fight in this war. Helping someone gain the ability to protect themselves was one of the most worthwhile things she'd done, whether they decided to use their powers for killing demon scum or not.

She just hoped their overbearing males lightened the hell up and let their mates come back to her class. Because the truth was, the fight may come to their females whether they liked it or not.

"Okay, form a circle around the mat and we'll get started."

The door swung open.

Grace glanced up as Chaos strode in.

She straightened, every muscle in her body tightening, preparing to what? Attack? To defend herself? Run the other way? She had no idea, but she had no control over it.

Yeah, she'd asked Mia to get Chaos to contact her. But never in a million years had she expected him to show up at one of her training sessions.

The hulking half angel, half demon making her life difficult was wearing workout clothes—nylon shorts, a muscle shirt—and that ever-present grim expression. The cold determination in his dark gaze made her shiver and her heart speed up.

He was an oncoming storm as he prowled across the floor. Power snapped from him, reaching out to her. Did he know he was doing it? Could he feel it, too, or was her block strong enough to hide the volatile energy reaching out from both of them, trying to draw the other closer, clashing, intertwining?

Grace felt it. Every. Damn. Time.

But today, it was stronger than ever.

Snapping herself out of it, she straightened her spine. They needed to talk, but not here, not now. She started toward him and held up her hands. "This class is full."

He crossed his arms, emphasizing their massive size, and she found it a struggle to drag her gaze away from all that defined, deeply tanned skin.

Get it together, Grace.

He quirked a brow. "You can't squeeze in one more?"

Everyone was watching now. She couldn't exactly

demand he leave. "I don't think there's anything I could teach you here."

"Maybe, maybe not. Perhaps I could show you a thing or two." His voice had dropped so deep she felt it tug low in her belly.

What the hell was he doing?

She struggled for something to say, something to make him leave.

He lifted his chin, aiming his dark gaze over her shoulder. "We're holding up your class."

She glared and did the only thing she could, she turned her back on him and faced her students. "You're in luck. We have a special guest. Chaos is a combat and defense specialist, and he's going to show us some new moves."

His low growl rumbled behind her, for her ears only, and she didn't hide her smile when she crooked her finger for him to follow. All but a couple of her students were demi, so apart from the humans, everyone knew who he was and at one point had stayed and trained at the compound.

So it wasn't a surprise when many waved and greeted him by name, and though the guy was no charmer, the batting lashes and coy smiles didn't surprise her, either. What she *was* surprised by was her reaction to all the female attention thrown his way.

She didn't like it.

Which was freaking absurd.

This mate thing was no joke. She disliked the male intensely, had made no secret of it, but right then, the urge— the pure, raw, animal *instinct*—to drop into a fighting stance in front of him and let everyone know he was hers, was hard to resist.

No, her draw to him had never been so strong. She needed him out of there before she did something she could never take back. Something she'd most definitely regret.

He stood, legs braced apart, hands hanging loose at his sides, and a small superior grin tugging up his wicked, sensual lips. "Where do you want me?"

Between my thighs.

No. Nope.

He narrowed his gaze on her, dark and glittering, and drew in a rough breath before letting it go slowly, like he'd just read her wayward thoughts and was trying to gather his own failing control.

Clearing her throat, she straightened her spine. She had to be imagining things. He had no idea who she was to him, she'd made sure of it.

"Ready?" she blurted, much too loud.

His grin spread wider, and he flashed straight white teeth, like a shark about to take a bite out of his much smaller, much weaker prey.

"Careful, you might strain something," she muttered.

She'd never seen the surly bastard smile before, not like that, and yeah, he looked good when he did, and she wasn't the only one who thought so. Several females actually giggled for Christ's sake. She rolled her eyes even as her heart pounded harder.

More giggling.

She swung around before she could stop herself, aiming a cold stare at one of the gigglers. "Something funny?"

The girl's face turned an unattractive shade of red and her gaze darted back to Chaos. "I...ah...no."

"Yes, Chaos is all tall, dark, and...*bulgy*, but I'm sure he's not the first good-looking male you've ever seen, and I'm sure he won't be the last. Take a good look, get it out of your systems, then let's focus on what we're here to do, yes?"

The room went completely, *utterly* silent.

Fuck. Had she really just blurted that out loud?

Chaos stepped around her to address the class, thankfully ignoring the idiotic things she'd just said. "Let's get started."

He moved through his lesson at a steady pace. He was good, of course. His muscled body moving with speed and ease, something that should be impossible for a male his size. He wasn't a bad teacher, either. He was still bossy as hell, though, but the other females didn't seem to mind his heavy-handed approach. Nope, not one bit.

By the time the class drew to an end, his darkly tanned skin was covered in a fine sheen of sweat and his shirt clung to his chest and flat stomach, defining his bulging abdominal muscles. Her mouth watered, and God, she wanted to touch every bit of that sleek, muscled body. She wanted to *touch him.*

And she hated herself for it.

As the last of her students walked out the door, she knew she had to pull it together. They needed to talk about the coming war, about what was happening around the city. And she needed a clear head to do it.

"Nice moves," she said, trying to come across unaffected, but her husky voice told a different story.

He inclined his head. "Thanks. You're not bad yourself."

Her eyebrows hiked high. "Did you just compliment me? Has the world already come to an end?" Grabbing a couple bottles of water, she handed him one.

Something flashed across his handsome face, but then it was gone. "I've never said you aren't a good fighter, Grace."

He lifted the bottle to his lips and drank deeply, causing his throat to work in a distracting way that for some weird reason affected parts of her body that had no right to be affected.

"You did say I was incompetent, though." *You need to get him on your side, not pick a fight.*

He lowered his bottle. "I was angry. I shouldn't have said that."

Again, not something she expected him to say. She kept her surprise to herself this time. "But you think we should stay out of this war?"

His gaze dropped to her mouth, and his jaw tightened, before it lifted back to hers. "I think you don't know as much as you think you do. I think you and your people could be an asset to our fight if you would listen to what I've been trying to tell you instead of killing indiscriminately. Why did you want to see me, Grace?"

She shivered again at the sound of her name rumbling from the massive demon hunter and crossed her arms as well. "Fighting with each other is counterproductive. We should be working together. I have demi, a lot of them, trained and ready to fight. We're an asset you can't afford to ignore. Not anymore. There's a hellsgate demi in the hands of our enemy. We need to stop fighting each other and work together."

He tilted his head to the side, studying her for several long, intense seconds. "Is that right?"

His voice was doing that deep, almost hypnotic thing again, and suddenly she was being drawn in and had to fight her body's desire to move closer, to touch him.

"Yes."

He stared down at her, so much going on behind his dark gaze that she couldn't take it another second.

"Teach me a move. Not one you just showed the class, but one you use when you're fighting," she said into the tension-filled silence. She needed to move, to hit and kick, fight him before she did something else to him. Something a lot more pleasant.

His head jerked back slightly.

She swallowed hard. "You afraid I'll kick your ass?"

He grinned again, that shark smile. "Oh, I think I can handle it."

She shrugged, her belly a riot of nerves. "Well, then, what are you waiting for?"

To her surprise, he moved to the center of the room and crooked his finger at her like she'd done to him earlier. "Come here."

A throb started between her thighs. Maybe this wasn't such a great idea after all. She hesitated.

"Now, Grace."

Heat flooded her body at that low, rumbled demand, and desire, hot and hungry, hit her with force.

As much as she wanted to run the other way, she couldn't. This was her bright idea. She couldn't back out now. Tightening her ponytail, she shook out her arms and legs to stop them from goddamn quivering and stepped onto the mat with him.

"Watch me, then I'll come at you, yes?"

"Sounds good." *Sounds terrible.*

He ran through the moves and she barely saw what he was doing, too mesmerized by the play of all those bulky muscles, the incredible strength of his body, the graceful, brutal way he moved.

When he finished, he looked up at her. "Got it?"

"Yep." *Nope.*

She should get him to run through it again, but the idea of showing any weakness to this male had her grinding her teeth. Then it was too late, and he was moving in behind her. Close. So close. Too damn close.

"For this exercise, I'm going to take you from behind," he said, voice impossibly rough and deep.

Take her from behind? Seriously? He had to know how that sounded, the images it conjured.

"Right." Her nipples tightened. *Shit. Shit. Shit.*

He cleared his throat. "And you're going to try to stop me."

Grace braced, waiting for the attack, and even though she knew it was coming she could barely control the explosion of nerves erupting in her belly.

He waited, several seconds ticking by. His breath brushed the side of her throat, his breathing deep and even. He wasn't touching her, but she could feel every inch of his body. The immense heat radiating off his skin was like a physical touch, and it lifted goose bumps all over her.

When he finally attacked, she knew it was coming. His breath hitched, a tiny tell, but enough to give her a split second of warning, enough time to loosen her body and execute her defense.

She did as he'd instructed, somehow it had gotten through to her, and she grabbed his forearm, twisting away, running through the sequence of moves, fighting back.

He switched things up suddenly, coming at her from another angle. Grace spun and deflected his strike with her right arm, then swung back, her body spinning away, leg high. Her kick made contact with his side, but he didn't slow.

He kept at her, relentless, fully on the offensive. Not going easy on her, not even close. Not that she'd expected him to. She countered every move as best she could, adrenaline racing through her veins. He didn't let up, kept coming at her over and over again. Her lungs were screaming when he finally made a move to take her down to the floor. She hooked her leg behind his knee in retaliation, locking on, refusing to go down without a fight, and he went down with her.

She was about to spring back to her feet, but he moved quickly, one solid arm banding around her, keeping her down. How could he move so fast? It should be impossible.

He rolled and pinned her to the mat. Her legs tangled

with his, his body a heavy, unrelenting weight on top of her. She hissed and he grunted as they wrestled, as she fought him.

It was no use, she gritted her teeth and looked up at him. His gaze locked with hers, but there was nothing cold in their depths this time, no, they blazed. He'd loved every minute.

Her breath stuck in her throat.

Oh shit.

He was hard.

The impressive length of him was hot, unyielding steel against her stomach. And he wasn't trying to hide it.

"Is talking the only reason I'm here, Grace?" he said, voice like an earthquake rocking right through her.

He didn't know she was his mate, but he felt the connection, the pull, it was there in his eyes. "Christ, you're arrogant," she said instead of answering him, afraid that maybe, just maybe, a small part of her had been looking forward to seeing him again.

His gaze searched hers, sliding down, moving over her face. No doubt taking in her hot cheeks that she knew were bright red and not just from exertion.

She couldn't escape that penetrating stare as it grazed her parted lips, watching each of her panted breaths explode from her.

His nostrils flared.

No, she couldn't hide it or fight it. Her body's reaction to the male above her was right there to see. "I hate you," she said, a last-ditch effort to muster her self-control.

Heat darkened his features, and her nipples tightened in response. "Good."

Then his mouth came down on hers, hot and hungry.

She gasped into his mouth, the contact hitting like an electric current sending heat pumping through her veins, warming her limbs and making the pulse between her thighs unbearable.

Chaos grunted against her mouth, and didn't wait for an invitation, no, his tongue pushed between her lips, taking what he wanted.

She groaned at the taste of him—dark, exotic, intoxicating. His massive arms came around her, one sliding under her, down to her ass, the other going up to cup the back of her head.

She was caged in, his hard body surrounded her, vibrating with unbelievable strength, with power. If he chose to, he could crush every one of her bones like they were toothpicks. He wouldn't, though.

No, she knew he wouldn't hurt her. He wanted inside her. He didn't know why he wanted her so badly, but he did.

She knew all of this, because she felt it, too. She also knew it wasn't really her holding him back just as tight. It was something much bigger than both of them. Which was why she couldn't stop her hand from sliding under his shirt, seeking the heat and texture of his skin. It was like her body had a mind of its own, and right then, it wanted to get as close to Chaos as it could.

He ground against her, and she wrapped her legs around his waist.

Chaos growled and did it again, the hard, unrelenting length of his cock pressing down on her clit through her workout pants making her whimper.

She needed to tell him to stop. *She* needed to stop, but instead she lifted her hips and rocked against him. The big hand on her ass shoved down the waistband of her pants and his long, thick calloused fingers gripped her bare ass cheek. She needed to shove him off before it was too late. Before she let him yank down his shorts, tear down her pants, and slide inside her.

There would be no hiding who she was if that happened.

Grace gritted her teeth as he kissed and sucked his way up her throat, his beard tickling her skin, her nipples getting incredibly tight, aching so deeply she was on the verge of begging him to suck them.

The words were on the tip of her tongue to demand he take her. And they shamed her. With the way she wanted him, the confusing thoughts and feelings bombarding her the tighter he held her, the deeper he kissed her, she knew she was in serious trouble. Giving her body to him would be bad enough, but she couldn't live with herself if she developed actual feelings for him as well.

And with how strong the mating bond felt in that moment, she knew she was in real danger.

There was no way in hell she would ever be this male's mate.

"I can smell you, Grace. How much you want me."

She shook her head even as she nuzzled his jaw, sucking on his strong throat, grinding against him.

"Christ," he bit out. "I want to fuck you, angel. Let me fuck you."

Angel.

Grace squeezed her eyes shut. The hunger and grit in his voice only increased her own need. It throbbed through her body, making her shake, making her want to cry with how much she wanted him.

But she had to say no, she had to end this now. This was a huge mistake. If they had sex, he'd know, he'd know who she was, and then she'd be stuck. She'd be his, because that's the way it worked, that's the way he'd see it and he'd never let her go. He'd claim her, use her to increase his power, and she would rather let a demon slice her to pieces than belong to the male on top of her.

A male who caused the destruction of her family.

A male she needed to stop kissing and get the hell away from right goddamn now.

"We've been building up to this from the very start. You know it and I know it. Tell me I can have you." He lifted his head, his eyes black pools of liquid fire, so deep and dark and hot they burned into her, scorched her. "Say it," he said between clenched teeth.

It was a demand. He was demanding that Grace give herself to him, that she give him consent. This was a man used to getting what he wanted. He would never force her, but he also didn't like the word *no* when he wanted something.

He must have seen something on her face, in her eyes, because he growled.

"Grace..."

"No," she said, in as strong a voice as she could muster. "Get off me."

Chaos growled again.

"Now."

He released her instantly and climbed to his feet, pulling her up with him. Her body was buzzing like an electric current was arcing over her skin, pulsing and slick between her thighs, nipples hard, aching points desperate for his hands, his mouth. She had to lock her knees so she didn't fall on her ass.

He watched her, his massive chest laboring, his eyes, once again those of a shark, hard and cold, hungry, following her, not leaving her. There was no hiding his massive erection, he didn't bother trying. He stood with his hands at his sides, fingers curled into fists, legs braced apart.

"I didn't think you were the type to play games," he said, voice as icy as his unwavering stare.

She kept her spine braced. Ready if he came at her. The male wasn't all angel, he was half demon as well, and Kishi were barely more than animals. "Things got out of hand. I don't want you. That's not playing games. Obviously, your ego is too bruised right now to recognize the difference."

His nostrils flared and his lids lowered like a beast scenting the air for prey. "I can smell how wet you are, how much you want me inside you. Lie to yourself all you want."

"You're a pig."

He grinned, flashing those straight white teeth again. But there was no humor, no warmth. It was kind of terrifying.

"Yet, you still want me to fuck you."

"Get the hell out," she said, her voice embarrassingly unsteady.

He dipped his chin, turned, and strode from the room with an arrogant swagger that set her teeth on edge.

And she tried, so damn hard—but she couldn't look away until he was out of sight.

CHAPTER 8

CHAOS WALKED into his apartment and kicked the door shut behind him.

He would overcome this, this fucked-up need...this hunger for Grace. He had to.

Uncurling his fists, he yanked off his shirt on the way to the bathroom. He'd walked out of her gym an hour ago, and he could still smell her, taste her. Feel her lips on his, her tongue against his, hear the sound of her whimpering in his head. He was hard as stone and furious with himself.

What the hell had he been thinking? He hadn't been, and that was the problem. The female scrambled his brain as soon as he saw her.

Why was he so drawn to her? What was it about her that had him zeroing in on her whenever she was near?

He grunted, cutting off the idiotic thought that worked its way forward. No. Not that. He'd know it if was *that*. He hadn't felt her when she came into her power like Kryos had Meredith, or Zen with Mia. Lazarus had fucking collapsed during a fight when Eve hit his radar. No, it wasn't that.

She made his dick hard, that's all. There was nothing more between them. If there was, he'd *know*.

Which meant what he was feeling for Grace was lust, nothing more, and something he could most definitely overcome. He just had to try harder.

He shoved down his shorts and looked at his cock. It was harder than he'd ever seen it, veins bulging along his shaft, pre-come still leaking from the head.

Grace forced her way back into his head, the way she'd writhed under him, nails digging into his shoulders, hips moving restlessly against his, her pussy rubbing against his cock, so hot and wet he felt it through the fabric of her tights.

"Fuck." He cranked the shower to cold, finished stripping, and climbed in. The ice-cold spray sucked the wind from his lungs, lifting goose bumps all over his flesh, but did nothing to cool his blood or deflate his dick.

Quickly soaping up, he fought to ignore the throbbing need making him shake, making him sweat despite the freezing water pounding his skin. He needed to get her out of his head. It wasn't working. Nothing was goddamn working. Chaos was confused and constantly horny.

That wasn't him.

When he was hard, he fucked or tugged one out, then he moved on.

As for confused? He never had a reason to be. He knew what he was on this earth to do. His world was black and white. But Grace was a million shades of gray, shit, no—she was a goddamn rainbow of color. Chaos didn't see in color. He chose not to. He didn't have that luxury.

His anger rose, and he pounded his fist into the wall, cracking several tiles. With a vicious curse, he pressed his palm against the cool ceramic squares, supporting his weight, and wrapped his fingers around his dick.

The first tug had him gasping, that's how hard he was,

how much he needed release. He didn't fuck around, he squeezed his shaft, thrusting into his fist brutally.

Don't think about her. Don't fucking think about her.

But she was there, had never left, filling his head. Images bombarding his mind. Instead of leaving, he was tearing her tights down her toned legs while she pulled at his shorts, taking his cock in her hand.

He groaned low, the image so damn real. His hand was no longer his. It was Grace jerking him off, her squeezing and tugging his impossibly hard dick.

"Fuck me." Her voice echoed through his head, clear, like she was right there with him. Smiling up at him, leading his cock to her bare pussy, spreading nice and wide for him, holding him to her wet-as-fuck opening.

Yeah, definitely a fantasy. The female had never smiled at him like that, except maybe after she'd given him shit and called out some creative death threat. In his mind, though, her smile was soft, hungry. He shouldn't be thinking about her like his, but he couldn't stop now, there was no way he could stop.

So he stayed in that gym with her and grinned back as he lifted her hands over her head and pinned them down with one of his own.

Letting the taste of her, still on his tongue, fill his senses, he groaned. The press of her smaller body against his was imprinted on his flesh, and he let it roll through him, sinking deeper into the fantasy.

Leaning in, he kissed her soft mouth again and slammed inside her with one brutal thrust.

Her scream of pleasure rocked through him, echoed through his skull, and with a vicious growl, he instantly came. His release exploded from him with force, making it hard to breathe, making his knees weak. He could barely hold himself up as his hand continued to glide up and down his length, as the orgasm that didn't want to end flowed through him, making him grunt and growl, and dammit, want the real thing even more.

Want *Grace* even more.

Chaos leaned against the wall, forehead to forearm, taking a moment to catch his breath.

He gritted his teeth. He would overcome this. He would. He had to.

~

"You've talked to him?"

Zenon stood across from Chaos, yellow eyes hard, brows lowered. "He still won't come back."

Kryos cursed, shoving his fingers through his curly blond hair. "How did everything go so fucking wrong? We're failing, and honestly, I can't see a way out. There's no way to get Rocco's mate back that I know of, which means one thing: Diemos walking through the portal is not an if, it's a when, and we don't have the strength or the manpower to stop him."

Gunner aimed his pale amber eyes at Zenon. "What about Lucifer?"

They'd recently discovered that Diemos was Zenon's father. It rocked their brother's world, but even more insane, it meant that Lucifer was his grandfather.

Unfortunately, the former king of Hell had been AWOL for centuries. Nobody knew where he was.

Zenon's yellow eyes deepened, darkening to almost black. "What about him?"

"He's your blood, maybe there's a way to reach him?" Lazarus glanced at Chaos. "What about Willow? You think she could help?"

Willow was an extremely powerful witch. Her library of

the arcane, the histories of the immortal, of Heaven and Hell was extensive. "I'll talk to her."

"Why would Lucifer help us?" Zenon said. "He doesn't give a fuck about Earth."

Chaos shrugged. "We don't know that. We were led to believe he was locked out of Hell, but is that really possible? He hasn't attempted to go back through the portal, which makes me think that maybe he likes it here just fine."

Zenon jerked his head to the side. "Even if I could reach out to him some way, I don't want him anywhere near Mia."

"He might be our only hope," Kryos said.

"It's a risk, for sure. He could turn on us." Gunner crossed his arms. "But if there's a chance he could help, we need to find him."

Lazarus rested his ass on the nearest desk. "This whole conversation might be for nothing, he's stayed away this long."

"True," Chaos said. "But we need to try. If we can't find a way to fix this mess, we're all fucked anyway."

Chaos's phone chimed and he checked the screen.

Number unknown. "Yeah?"

"Who knew it would be so easy to talk to a knight, and the exalted leader no less."

Chaos straightened and put it on speaker. "You know my name, how about you help me out with yours?"

A chuckle echoed down the line. "I don't think that will be necessary."

Gunner was already at one of the computers, working to trace the call.

"What do you want?"

Several beats of silence. "This is a courtesy call, actually. I understand things haven't been going too great for you lately. Tobias is dead. Rocco is close to losing his mind, and the female who was to be his mate is in Hell." The male chuckled again. "Though, from what I hear, Diemos has grown quite fond of her."

The back of the chair Zenon was gripping snapped off in his hands.

"Again. What the fuck do you want?" Chaos ground out.

"Just delivering a warning."

There was no real point to this call, other than waving his dick around. Whoever this fucker was, he was feeling confident, too damn confident.

The phone groaned under Chaos's fingers as he gripped it tighter, trying to keep the reins on his temper. "What warning? If we don't back off, you'll talk us into an early fucking grave?"

Another beat of silence. "I just thought you should know that things are about to get worse for you."

The phone went dead.

"Got him," Gunner said, looking up from behind a monitor.

"Weapon up," Chaos snarled.

Chaos crawled on his belly to the edge of the building, Gunner and Zenon moving in beside him. They looked down at the Walmart parking lot.

Demons, at least seventy of them, stood in a large circle, eyes glazed and completely motionless. After his and Lazarus's fight with twenty of them in the abandoned bar a few days ago, he knew running in half-cocked was not the right move. They'd keep coming back, bleeding, broken, like a hoard of blood-lusting zombies. They were outnumbered.

It was late, the parking lot was deserted, but cars still drove by and no one even glanced at the large group of demons assembled there. Not once. They weren't exactly shrouded in shadows, either.

"What the fuck is this?" Gunner said, looking from the circle to the humans driving by.

Zenon shifted beside him. "Someone's blocking them."

Gunner scowled. "Why can we see them, then?"

"Because they want us to." Chaos twisted, looking around. "Our mystery caller wanted us to come here, wanted us to see this, whatever the fuck it is."

A sleek black car pulled into the lot, driving right up to the motionless demons.

"We can't just fucking sit here and do nothing," Zenon hissed through clenched teeth.

Fuck. "There's too many of them, and the way they are, the way they'll keep getting back up, it'll be like fighting three times as many."

The back door of the car opened and someone climbed out. Male, tall, concealed by a black hooded robe. Power radiated from him like a whip, lashing out, wanting to be felt.

Demon.

Chaos glanced at Zenon. "You recognize him?"

Their brother had been born and raised...and tortured... in Hell. He'd gotten up close and personal with many powerful demons while he was held there. Even without seeing this male's face, he would recognize his power.

Zen shook his head.

They watched as the male in black walked up to the closest demon and raised his hand. The robe's sleeve slid back, revealing a wicked-looking blade—

He slit the throat of the demon closet to him. It fell to the ground, and they watched as he moved to the next, then the next. He didn't bother to remove their heads completely, just left them there bleeding, unable to ash out.

Zenon froze beside them and a low, rumbling growl

escaped. "I've seen this before. They're summoning something."

Fuck. "What?"

"I don't know. Summoning can go wrong. They wouldn't bring Diemos through, not like this, it'd be too risky, but with how many he's sacrificing, I'd say something big or powerful." Zenon looked at him, his yellow eyes swirling, growing dark. "We have to stop them."

If they were summoning something from Hell, whatever it was, it was coming to cause destruction.

Chaos yanked off his shirt, his brothers doing the same, and each called their demons forth. Chaos's wings snapped from his back as he shifted into his Kishi demon form with a roar.

Shifted, they looked like giant gargoyles. Only their skin was deep crimson, almost black. Horns protruded from their heads, black and shiny, and long ivory fangs reached halfway down their chins.

What set them apart was their eyes and wings.

Chaos tilted his head to the figure shrouded in black. "Try to take him alive," he said, his voice now an inhuman rumble.

They extended their wings, catching the wind, and lifted off the roof.

Sword in his hand, Chaos flew straight for the demon trying to unleash Hell on his city. Zenon threw one of his twin fighting axes, the Li Kweis spun, an audible *thwump, thwump, thwump* as it whipped through the air, heading straight for their target.

But instead of immobilizing the fucker, it stopped several feet away, suspended in midair for several seconds before falling to the ground with a clatter.

The air around the circle of half-dead demons shimmered, light moving over an invisible surface, like rippling water.

"They're surrounded by some kind of force field. Some-one's protecting them," Chaos barked.

Gunner roared and clawed at the surface of the barrier. The demon in black ignored them, now chanting rhythmi-cally, the same words over and over again as he moved around his circle of demons, slitting throats, blood dripping from his fingers, his knife, soaking his cloak. There were only a handful of demons left.

Zenon took his axes to the barrier, Gunner and Chaos doing the same with their swords. It was like trying to cut through molasses. Every slice closed in the wake of his blade, repairing itself instantly.

The last demon fell, and the male in black moved to the side as blood flowed from the fallen, flowing to the center of the circle as if drawn there.

The ground glowed as his chanting grew louder. The asphalt shook beneath their feet, and they watched in horror as a hairline crack snaked across the surface, growing wider and deeper with every passing second.

"It's happening," Zenon barked.

Gunner stumbled back as the ground lifted in the center of the circle in big jagged, triangular-shaped chunks of asphalt.

A reptilian-looking red leg burst through, four shiny black claws tearing at the surface, each one twice the length of Chaos's sword. A high-pitched, ear-shattering roar came from below the surface, making the invisible barrier quiver and ripple.

Another scaled crimson leg appeared, claws sinking into the blacktop that was now bubbling around the glowing orange hole the Hell beast was dragging itself out of.

It roared again and used its massive, muscular legs to explode free, landing with a ground-shaking thud. The hole beside it began closing.

It was doglike except red and scaled and had two heads, one eye each. Its mouths hung open, lips peeled back, yellow teeth dripping drool. It shook its heads and twin holes, its nostrils, flared.

Both heads lowered, nosing a half-dead demon, then each snatched one up in its jaws. The sound of bones crunching, of flesh being torn filled the night.

"What the fuck do we do?" Gunner yelled.

Chaos glanced at Zenon, hoping like fuck he'd seen a creature like this in Hell. "Will cutting off its heads work?"

They watched the beast eat its way around the circle of death, filling up on the sacrifices littering the ground.

"They'll just grow back. You can't stab it in the heart, either. It doesn't have one, or any other vital organs. It's immortal."

There were only a few demons left, and the male in black had backed away, so the beast was between the knights and him.

The demon vanished.

Chaos growled. "Someone's cloaking him."

They didn't have time to worry about the demon, though, because the invisible barrier around the creature shimmered—

Then it was gone.

The beast picked up the last two bodies and tossed them down its throat.

Chaos and Gunner gripped their swords and Zenon swung his axes. "If we can hack it up, cut off its heads, its legs, maybe we can weaken it enough to lock it down. Keep it headless, buy some time to work out how to kill it or send it back," Chaos said.

His brothers dipped their chins.

The beast's heads swayed on its long necks, the movement snakelike as it turned to face them.

They braced.

The beast roared with so much force the ground shook and launched at the closest target. Gunner's battle cry rang out, sword gripped in both hands. Zenon and Chaos ran toward their brother, but the creature was fast. Faster than it looked.

It beared down on Gunner, jaws wide open. Gunner raised his sword.

But instead of reaching Gun, it collided with an invisible barrier, it's huge body hitting it like a brick wall before flying back.

Someone or something had stopped it.

The Hell beast screamed, loud and piercing, lifting goose bumps all over Chaos's skin, then turned and fled.

They took off after it.

It ran past cars, people on the sidewalk. No one paid it any attention. The beast bumped a car, sending it a meter from its original position, a store window smashing when it's tail whipped around. People stopped in their tracks, someone screamed, but they weren't seeing the beast, just the destruction it left in its wake.

The creature was still being cloaked.

They took flight, going after it, but somehow it vanished into the shadows.

Chaos turned to Zenon on his right, the wind whipping his hair, snatching the fury in his voice. "Where would it go?"

"It's full, and the summoning would have drained it of energy. Somewhere it can hide and rest."

"How long?"

"After feeding like that? A couple days at least."

They had some time. Not much, but it was something. "I want you to go after the fucker who did this, see if you can sense his power, he can't have gone far." Chaos turned to Gunner. "Try to find the beast. Don't engage it. If you can, lead it away from downtown. We don't want any humans stumbling across it. Whatever's making it invisible might only be temporary."

Gunner caught his gaze. "What will you be doing?"

Chaos cursed. They needed more eyes on the ground, more manpower to help find and contain the beast. They couldn't do it alone. "Getting some help."

CHAPTER 9

LANEY POKED her head around the door. "Vince wants you out front."

Grace looked up from lacing her boots. "I'm due on stage."

"We're swapping apparently. Oden's here again."

Great. He'd been here the night before as well, and he'd insisted on having her sit with him the entire evening. Despite her best efforts, she hadn't been able to get him to talk, and the creep hadn't left the club until 3 a.m.

Worse, he'd brought her a bracelet that she'd refused, but Vince had all but begged her with his eyes from across the room to accept it. Vince was definitely in some kind of trouble, but he wasn't talking. As much as she wanted to shake the shit out of him, he was family, and she owed him her life.

He'd provided her with protection and a place to stay when she had nowhere else to go. Had given her a way to make good money when she'd lost her family and had shown up with nothing but the clothes on her back.

Which was why she'd stayed at Oden's side, why she'd laughed at his jokes and stroked his ego. Oden was a man used to getting what he wanted. She'd talked to a few of her people, and heard more sick and twisted rumors. Like what happened to business associates who didn't let him have his way.

She needed to find out what Vince had gotten himself into.

He told her he had it under control, but she didn't believe him. So unfortunately, for now, that meant cozying up to Oden.

She shuddered. Having his revolting hands on her was an exercise in restraint. Because the urge to bust the creep's nose whenever he touched her was getting harder and harder to resist.

Ever since Chaos had come to her gym, since he'd kissed her, the idea of touching or being touched by anyone else had become almost unbearable.

She curled her fingers at her side and straightened. Every time she saw the knight, spent time with him, it grew stronger. She had to overcome this, work at strengthening her block, so she could resist the pull their bond was having on her.

The faces of her family—her parents, her brother—filled her head and guilt swamped her, along with an even stronger dose of self-loathing.

Christ, the fates had really screwed her over with this shit. First, the whole idea of mates, of being cosmically matched to some random guy, was supremely messed up. But making two random strangers meet and instantly want to fuck was totally twisted. And second, matching her with Chaos, of all males, was just plain evil.

The sheer power of the bond she was now fighting almost constantly, a bond she would happily fire a bolt at and smile while it twitched and bled to death at her feet, astonished her. Terrified her.

Since that kiss, she'd had to fight harder than she ever had before to keep her block up, to keep who she was to him, from him. She curled her fingers into a tight fist. After he'd swaggered out the door, a part of her, a *large part*, had actually wanted to go after him, to bring him back and finish what they'd started. God, since then she'd barely thought of anything else.

Goose bumps lifted all over her skin. Her body had no trouble remembering the way his weight had felt on top of her. His mouth on hers. The way he'd held her tight.

Stop it.

Pushing all thoughts of the pain-in-the-ass knight from her mind, she headed out into the club.

Oden wasn't alone this time; he had two other males with him. Vince was hovering beside them looking flustered. Oden glanced up as she approached, his dark gaze traveling over her in a way that made his feelings more than clear.

He wanted her.

And he wasn't a man used to hearing no.

This was a game for him right now, but she knew he wouldn't play nice when he decided he'd had enough of the chase.

"Oden, this is a nice surprise. Gentlemen." She smiled at his companions and rested her hip against his chair.

Vince smiled at her, his shoulders visibly relaxing. "See, here she is. I told you she wouldn't be long." The males with him took her in, assessing, unnerving.

"I was just about to go on stage," Grace said, resting her hand on Oden's shoulder, willing to do anything, even touch the bastard if it would help Vince. They'd be having a serious conversation after her shift, though, this couldn't go on. She did not pimp herself out, not for anyone.

Oden's gaze turned cold, and he pulled her toward his lap, like he had the right to touch her, like she belonged to him. She resisted, but his fingers dug into her waist, holding her too tight. "I think you can spare me a few minutes of your time?"

"Of course." She refused to climb into his lap, though, and instead draped her arm over the back of his chair and forced herself to relax when what she really wanted was to scratch his damned eyes out.

His hand roamed while the males talked business, barely avoiding her no-go zones, skimming the underside of her breasts, fingers brushing low across the tops of her thighs. She did her best to ignore it, to listen to the conversation. She was a decoration, the blond bimbo, too stupid to understand what they were talking about. But Oden's friends kept glancing her way. Whatever. It wasn't the first time someone underestimated her, and it wouldn't be the last.

As time ticked by it became obvious they were talking in some kind of code, but no matter how hard she tried to decipher it, she couldn't work it out. Her spidey senses were on high alert, and by the time Laney's dance had come to an end, she was ready to tear his wandering hands off his wrists and choke him with them. "I better head backstage. I'm up next."

She turned to walk away, but Oden grabbed her wrist, stopping her and tugged her back. He slipped his hand around her waist, just above her ass, and pulled her in close to his side. "Wear this." He stood and turned her to face the bar, lifting a necklace over her head. "I want to see you in nothing but my diamonds."

She lifted her gaze, and whatever she was about to say seized in her throat. Chaos stood leaning against the bar, pose relaxed to the casual observer. But she knew better. Behind his midnight gaze, rage burned, and when Oden gripped her hips roughly and dragged his nose along her throat, every muscle in his body went rigid.

She knew little about the instincts of knights and the females they were meant to mate with, but she wasn't stupid enough to think his reaction was anything more than that. Chaos may not know she was meant to be his, but he had to feel something, even if it was watered down through her shields.

Chaos was not a male to lose control easily, but right then she thought he was as close to it as she'd ever seen him, and that was saying something, considering she'd seen him brutally kill demon after demon with single-minded focus. It was confirmation that on some level he sensed their connection, there was no other reason for what she saw in his eyes.

Wrapping her hands around Oden's wrists, she moved out of his hold. "Thank you, it's beautiful."

"Go dance for me," he said roughly against her ear.

She chanced another glance over at the bar, but Chaos was gone. Scanning the place, she breathed a sigh of relief. Good thing. She wasn't ready to deal with him right then.

She hurried backstage and waited to be announced.

"Welcome to the stage, Miss Gigi Fury!"

The crowd cheered as she strode out with a set of large, pale-blue, feathered fans. The music started slow, a low throbbing beat, and she took her time moving across the stage. The lights were bright, and she couldn't see the audience very well. And like every time she danced, she blocked them from her mind and let the music move through her.

The song slowly changed, getting heavier, moodier. Using the feathers for cover, she removed several items of clothing to the music and after turning away from her audience, she bent low, placing the fans on the floor.

As the song changed tempo, the beat faster, she crawled across the stage on her hands and knees.

Rolling, she arched up onto her hands, head back, hair trailing on the floor behind her, thighs spread wide in only her underwear, stockings, garter, and bra. She lifted her head and did a little shimmy before undoing the delicate fabric supporting her breasts. She cupped herself, holding the fabric to her chest, and spun before lying back once more. After another sexy shimmy, she flung her bra away, giving the crowd her yeah-I'm-so-hot-I'm-writhing-here-all-by-myself treatment.

Jesus, men were easy.

Finally, she got to her feet, this time with her back to the crowed, moving with the music while the song came to an end.

The lights dipped, darkening the area round her, and the crowd cheered.

She took a couple of steps, about to walk off the stage—

Chaos stood a few feet away, legs braced apart, fists clenched at his sides, and an expression she had no hope of reading but made her heart pound and her pussy clench with need.

Quickly walked off, slipped on a robe, and headed to the dressing room. She didn't need to have the power to see through walls to know he'd be waiting for her.

When she pushed the door open, he stood there, arms crossed over his monster chest, volatile energy rolling off him in furious waves.

Neither of them spoke as he moved toward her, closing the space between them like a stalking panther. The room was empty, and with a glance at the door by Chaos, it flew shut, the lock sliding into place behind her all on its own.

His fingers curled around the necklace Oden had put on her. "Diamonds, huh? Never thought you'd fall for that shit."

"He wants to waste his money on me, who am I to argue?" she said, pretending that she didn't want to toss the stones in the trash, that having him put it around her neck like some kind of ownership had made her sick to her stomach.

"You're fucking him."

It took a moment for his words to reach past her haze of lust.

"No." She hated that she felt the need to explain herself but was powerless to stop. "I'm doing it for Vince...something's not—"

"I get it, Grace." His face twisted into a sneer, even as his hand lifted and his fingers gently, so incredibly gently, slid across her cheek and along her jaw. "No need to say another word."

But he didn't get it. He thought she'd fuck that bastard, that she'd sell herself for the diamonds around her neck. She could see it written all over his face.

Why the hell did she care? He could think what he liked. Honestly, it would be easier if he hated her—for a lot of reasons.

Crossing her arms, she straightened her spine. "Why are you here?"

His jaw tightened and his eyes grew even harder, so much ice she actually shivered. "Something happened tonight, something...unexpected. Things have changed."

Grace went on full alert. "What things?"

"A demon, he summoned a beast from Hell. Someone protected him, blocked us from getting to him." His entire body went rock solid. "We couldn't stop him."

She attempted to wrap her mind around what he'd just told her, the fact that he'd chosen to tell her. "There is some kind of...Hell beast loose in the city?"

The muscle in his jaw ticked. "At the moment, it's invisible to humans. I don't know if it's the same for demi. We need manpower, people on the ground searching for it. We need to contain it before it wakes."

Grace had to be hearing things. "You're asking for *my help*?"

"Yes," he said without hesitation.

"But you said—"

"I didn't want to involve demi in this war. How could I want that when I was created to protect *you*?" He gritted his teeth. "But we need help with this. We can't do it alone."

I was created to protect you.

Freudian slip? If he knew she was his mate, that's exactly what he'd want to do.

But that had to cost him, asking her for help. And honestly, she never thought he ever would. She'd truly believed he would rather lose this war than ask anyone for help. He'd surprised her.

"I think you and your people could be an asset to our fight if you would listen to what I've been trying to tell you instead of killing indiscriminately."

Then again, this wasn't the first time he'd surprised her. When he'd visited her at her gym, he'd almost admitted that he needed them then. She hadn't been willing to bend, to meet him halfway. Hating him was easier than thinking there was more to him than she first thought.

"You want our help to find this beast?" she said, voice huskier than she would have liked.

His eyes narrowed, gaze dropping to her mouth. "Yes," he said, again without hesitation.

"Did that hurt?" She couldn't stop herself from asking. They'd been fighting against each other for months, and now here he was asking for help. It was almost unbelievable.

He took another step closer, so close now she could feel the heat radiating from his rock-hard, tightly coiled body. "You hate me. I don't blame you. My intention was only to protect you and your people. But I see now we can't do this alone, not anymore. I may not always agree with you, Grace, but I respect you." He ran a hand over the ink on the side of his head. "Will you help us?"

She'd dreamed of this moment, many times, but torturing

him, making him beg—like she always imagined she would if he ever came to her—didn't appeal quite so much anymore. This was probably all some act, some kind of manipulation. She definitely wasn't going to drop her guard around this male. But there was only one answer. "Yes."

He dipped his chin, his Adam's apple sliding up and down his strong throat. "If you find the creature, you are not to engage. This beast won't be killed easily, or maybe at all. It regenerates lost limbs quickly, is without vital organs, our best bet is to contain it somehow."

He gave her the location of their last sighting, then held out his hand. "Phone."

She gave it to him and watched as he programmed numbers into it.

"My number. I've put Gunner's in there as well. He's still searching. Contact him when you're downtown, and do whatever he says."

"I'll gather my people and head out now."

"This thing will be looking for somewhere quiet and dark to rest. There could be demons guarding it. Follow any you see in the area. We'll question them at the compound."

"We can do that," she said, her belly feeling weird, skin prickling restlessly.

He said no more, just stood there, dark eyes locked on her. She had no idea what he was thinking, but it was hard not to squirm under that heavy stare. He leaned forward.

She swallowed, her body heating, recognizing who he was to her, and responding, betraying her. A pulse between her thighs started beating low and deep, and her heart gave a mighty *thump*. "I'll get changed and send out the bat signal."

He blinked like he was shaking off some kind of fog. "Yes, of course." He took a step back.

"Will you be joining the search?" she asked for some unknown reason. She refused to believe it was because she wanted to fight alongside him, that she wanted to see him in action again.

"Yeah, but first I need information on this creature that could help us fight it, if there is any."

"Good plan."

He dipped his chin again and took another step back, then finally turned and headed for the door. He opened it and was about to walk out, but instead turned back to her. "And, Grace?"

The way he said her name, dipped low, kind of gritty, had her fighting a shiver. "Yes?"

"Be careful."

Then he was gone.

CHAPTER 10

CHAOS WALKED out of Grace's dressing room, through the bar and growled when he spotted Oden still sitting at a table. He carried on out onto the street, refusing to look back.

Seeing Grace with that male, watching him put his fucking hands on her and drape diamonds around her slender throat had pissed him off; his demon sure as shit hadn't liked it, either. The monster inside him had twisted and clawed, trying to get free. When Grace had looked up, her mahogany eyes locking on his, everything inside him had seized, then lurched forward, as if trying to *drag him* forward, to get closer...to her.

He still didn't understand it. Yes, he wanted her. The kiss they'd shared had been on repeat in his head. But he'd never been this hung up on a female. And right now, Grace should be the last thing on his mind. Thinking about that female, having her entering his mind all damn day and night, didn't make sense, and it was causing a loss of focus, of control, he couldn't afford.

Ignoring the rage pumping through his veins at the mere thought of Oden's filthy fucking hands on her smooth, pale skin, he extended his wings and lifted off, flying a few streets over and landing outside a tiny black shop. The place was closed, but the witch who owned it was always close by.

Many years ago, Willow had created the spell that surrounded the knights' compound—a kind of repellent warning off human and demon alike. She helped them out occasionally, and had an extensive library and knowledge that had been passed down her line for generations.

Willow was under their protection, not that the female needed it. She was more than capable of looking after herself.

She and Chaos also fucked from time to time. No strings, no expectations. He hadn't been to see her in a while, but it wasn't like Willow would've sat around pining for him. She had several males she enjoyed on a regular basis, and that was more than fine with him.

The door of her little shop opened before he could knock.

Willow stood there, red hair wild, green eyes wide and curious. "It's been a while," she said.

And for the second time that night, he prepared to say four damn words he shouldn't have to. But he was failing, had failed the demi in this city too much already. He was born, created, to protect them, by whatever means necessary. Admitting he was wrong, that he couldn't do it alone, cut to the deepest part of him.

"I need your help."

Grace strode through the crowd, determined not to lose the demon moving quickly ahead of her. She'd been patrolling for hours and was desperate to get her hands on her fleeing target. Even now the creature that had been released from Hell could be waking.

She didn't know for sure if this demon had anything to do with it, but considering one of his buddies had just mauled a human male, eating the flesh off one arm to the bone, only a block from where the beast had been released instead of feeding somewhere more private, she thought he might.

It obviously didn't want to leave his post and risked discovery when it got hungry.

The demon lost its head, and the human lost his arm, but thankfully she and Mark had saved the guy before he'd been eaten alive. Mark had taken him to the hospital for treatment, while she continued her search for the Hell beast.

Tangling with a beast was preferable to spending time with Oden. He'd accepted her brush-off after Chaos left the club about as well as you'd imagine. Cold. Angry. But the way he'd looked at her, it was like he thought she was playing some sicko cat and mouse game with him, like the wait was part of some warped foreplay.

A shudder slid down her spine. The guy seriously freaked her out. She loved Vince, she did, but no way in hell was she sleeping with that sleaze. She'd drug him next time if she had to, anything to keep his filthy hands from pawing all over her.

Every time the guy touched her, she wanted to blow chunks. Oden wasn't ugly. Of course, the creepy, murdery, psycho killer-ish vibe brought him down a whole lot of notches on the hot-o-meter. But it wasn't just that. Her visceral reaction to the male had nothing to do with how much she loathed him. Because it wasn't just Oden. If any male touched her, even Vince—a barely there hand to her lower back, a brush of fingers against hers when she worked the bar—her body reacted like she'd just chugged a bucket of rotten fish guts.

There could be only one reason for that. And every time she saw Chaos, it got worse.

The demon ahead veered off the pavement and crossed the street. He carried on for a few meters, then ducked into Big Fred's Pizza. *Huh.* She guessed he had to eat something since he didn't get a turn to nibble on the human, but pizza?

The restaurant was bustling, and she stood at the door for several seconds, trying to spot her target. There. He'd just hit the hall that led to the bathrooms and glanced back, gaze bouncing around the busy room until it landed on her. He knew he was being tailed.

Shit.

Dodging several people, she ran through the restaurant and down the hall. There was a fire exit at the end, the door still ajar. "Dammit."

Shoving it open, she ran out after him, pulling her phone from her back pocket as she went. She hit Chaos's number.

"Yeah."

"Need backup. Behind Fred's Pizza on Claymont."

She disconnected, shoved her phone in her back pocket, and sprinted across the small, staff-only parking lot. The sound of the demon's heavy footfalls echoed as he ran, and she dug deep, pushing harder, determined to catch him.

There was an alley ahead, leading back to the street. She'd lose him in the crowd if he got that far. She leaped as she kicked off with her right foot, propelling herself into the air, and tackled him to the ground.

They struggled, and *holy shit* was he strong. Grunting and growling, he muscled her onto her back and leaned over her, his lizard-like tongue snaking out, tasting the air around her face. "Hmm, you smell good enough to eat."

Rearing up, she smashed her head into his nose. The guy roared and reared back. She throat punched him, knocking him to the ground, and jumped to her feet. He rolled and she brought her boot down hard on his back, then aimed two swift kicks where she hoped his kidneys or some other vital organ should be. His howl of pain told her she'd hit something important.

Pulling her knife from the sheath in her boot, she moved in. Feet either side of his shoulders, she crouched down, fisted his hair, and wrenched his head back, before pressing her blade to his throat. "What do you know about the Hell beast, asshole," she said, yanking his head back harder.

He hissed and struggled against her hold.

"Talk or I'll start slicing," she demanded.

"Fuck you," the demon cried as one of his arms flailed at his side.

"Either you talk to me, or I'll hand you over to the knights. I hear Lazarus gets off on making demons scream…"

Pain tore across her thigh.

She hissed, sucking in a startled breath. He'd scratched her with his claws. The stinging sensation instantly intensified, like acid burning deeper into her flesh.

"Can you feel my venom spreading, bitch?"

"What will it do?" She pressed the knife harder into his throat until black blood bubbled to the surface of his skin. She didn't know what he was, didn't think she'd ever encountered one of his species before.

"It's so you won't feel my teeth sinking into your flesh. So you won't be able to scream while you watch me eat you alive. In a few minutes your whole body will be paralyzed. You'll be at my mercy."

He could be valuable, but she could feel the venom working. She didn't have long. "My arms still work, shit for brains."

"It's too late." He laughed.

She slit its throat wide open but in her weakened state struggled to remove his head. It took more time than she had right then, the exertion probably spreading the venom quicker. But she couldn't leave him alive, where a human or another demon might find him and take him somewhere safe to recover.

The deed done, she fell back, curling on her side, crying out as the pain in her leg intensified. Dropping the bloody knife in her hand, she groped for her phone. She needed help. Now.

The fucker had wanted her to kill him, there was no other reason she could think that he'd tell her what was about to happen to her. Whoever ordered him to guard the beast was more terrifying than death if the knights got him to talk.

The sound of boots hitting asphalt echoed behind her.

She twisted around. Lazarus stood a few feet away, wings extended.

"You're injured." He crouched beside her.

She motioned to the pile of ash. "Got scratched. Not sure what species. Flesh eater, venomous. Paralysis before eating its victims alive."

"Fuck."

The asphalt thudded on the other side of her, and she didn't need to turn her head to know who it was, she could *feel* him. She kept her eyes trained on Lazarus. "Is there an antivenom?" She was starting to freak the hell out, could feel the poison spreading.

"What the fuck happened here?" Chaos's rough voice moved over her and she shivered, still refusing to look at him.

"Sounds like a venious demon," Lazarus said to his brother. "We need to stop the venom from reaching her heart."

"What?" Grace cried, then moaned in pain.

Chaos was suddenly in her face, teeth gritted, eyes wild,

big fingers wrapped around her chin, forcing her to look at him. "Where?"

Even pissed and slightly insane, the male was hot. "L-left thigh." Another wave of agony sliced through her and she screamed.

Shoving her to her side, he pulled a blade from his boot and cut through her leather jeans, exposing the scratches. "I need to cut you to get to the venom, then I can suck it out."

"You *what?*" She twisted her head toward Lazarus. "This is a joke, right?"

He shook his head.

Grace screamed again, this time because Chaos was slicing into the scratches in her leg, making them deeper. The knife clattered to the pavement.

Before she had a chance to catch her breath, Chaos's mouth came down on her thigh and he sucked, hard. A couple of seconds later, he twisted away and spat out the infected blood. Then he was back, lips latched on to her, sucking again.

Grace had never felt pain like it in her life. It burned like fire, searing through her veins, scorching her from the inside out. She screamed again, lost in the agony.

Lazarus held her down, while Chaos kept sucking.

She didn't know how long they'd been at it, time seemed to stand still, but the pain finally began to subside, and before long, every deep draw...*Jesus*...shot pleasure-pain through her body, making her twitch and jolt, until it was no longer about her leg.

Every time he sealed his lips on her skin—she felt it between her thighs.

She grew hot and wet and a groan slipped past her lips before she could stop it. Holy shit, if he kept this up she might actually orgasm, right here on the dirty ground. She was too weak to fight it. There were worse ways to die, she supposed.

Chaos stiffened beside her, those big shoulders rising as he sucked in a deep breath, then let it out on a low growl. He could smell her; how hot she was. The sucking slowed and his tongue and lips caressed her skin. Another groan rasped from her throat.

"I'm just gonna...I'll ah... You got this?" Lazarus said to Chaos.

Chaos didn't spare the other male a glance, just kept on sucking.

Seemingly at a loss for words, Lazarus extended his wings and shot into the sky.

Heat burned her cheeks. "Did you ah...get it all?"

One more swipe of his tongue, then he lifted his head—eyes bright with hunger and need—her blood coating his lips. She had the almost uncontrollable urge to flip him onto his back and ride him into the asphalt.

"Think so. Can you move your leg?"

She did and agony spiked though her again, like she was being cleaved in two.

Chaos cursed, gripped her thigh, and sucked hard again.

The pain kept building, so intense she could only thrash and scream.

Something snapped inside her.

Oh fuck.

Her block, it shattered completely, the walls she'd built to protect herself since she was a kid, the barrier she shored-up daily so Chaos would never find out who she was, crumbled, leaving her totally exposed, more vulnerable than she could ever remember being.

Chaos froze—then growled like a wild animal.

His weight suddenly came down heavily across her legs.

Fear exploded through her, and she gripped him, trying

to push him away, to shove him off as something powerful surged through her. Her fingers dug deeper into his shoulders, and instead of pushing him away she was unable to let him go. She opened her mouth, but no sound would come out as power like nothing she'd ever felt built inside her. It kept building, pulling more power inside her.

Then she felt it, felt *him*. Chaos was all around her. Yes, he was on top of her, but Christ, she could feel him inside her, flowing through her veins, his heart beating behind her ribs. She couldn't see. Her eyes were wide open, but there was only darkness and Chaos pulsing through her bloodstream.

"Stop! *Fuck*, Grace, you need to stop."

Chaos's voice echoed through the darkness. This was wrong. It was all wrong. Whatever was happening was too much, too strong. She couldn't contain it. But it kept coming, flowing into her.

It hurt more than the venom she'd had in her blood, more than anything she'd ever experienced in her life. Terror had her clutching Chaos tighter, and she screamed in pain, in fear, trying to get whatever it was out of her.

"No!" she cried, pushing it away with everything she had.

It left her in a rush, a tsunami flowing from her, pouring out, back to where it came from.

Chaos roared, his weight suddenly gone.

Grace lay there in shock. She couldn't move. She wiggled her toes, her fingers. Not paralyzed. Drained. Every bit of energy had been drained from her. She cracked her eyelids, turning when she heard a scraping sound.

Chaos was picking himself up off the ground, the brick wall behind him crumbled. He rose, wide shoulders covered in dust, and then his eyes came to her.

Black, his eyes, every part, was black as night. "What did you do to me?" he said, voice inhuman, blended with his inner demon.

She shook her head, scared out of her mind. But not of him, of whatever she'd just done. "That's never...I don't know what..."

He strode over and she struggled to sit, to scramble back, but she couldn't move. She was too dizzy, her limbs too weak and shaky to get her feet under her.

"Were you ever going to tell me?" he said, blinking down at her with those terrifying yet beautiful, black-as-night eyes. "Were you ever going to let me feel it?"

There was no point pretending she didn't know what he was talking about. Her block had collapsed. He knew all her secrets. She shook her head.

He sucked in a breath. "Fuck."

She curled her lip. "Y-yeah, you could say that."

He took a step back and ran his hands over his shaved head. "*Fuck.*" His gaze flickered, deep brown, then back to black "How long have you known?"

She shrugged. "Are you really so surprised?"

He didn't respond, instead he stared at her in an unsettling way, his chest pumping with each of his harsh breaths, the muscle in his jaw jumping. His beautiful dove-gray wings snapped out and instead of retreating he closed the distance between them and scooped her off the ground.

"What are you doing?"

"You think I'm letting you out of my sight now that I know the truth?" he said, all grit.

Grace watched, stunned as vicious-looking fangs grew where his canines had been, extending halfway down his chin, like his demon was trying to take over, like he was about to shift into his Kishi demon form.

But he didn't, instead he growled low, a purring sound vibrating heavily from his chest as he dipped his head to her throat and breathed deeply, dragging his nose along her skin.

"Mine," the demon and Chaos said together.

Oh shit. "Chaos. Just...just hang on a minute..."

He ignored her and took several deep pulls of the air with those massive gray wings, and they were in the air.

"Holy fuck." The adrenaline rush was enough to get her moving, and she all but climbed his torso, wrapping herself around his head like a python trying to strangle the life out of him.

The rhythmic inhuman sound that came from him stunned her. He was—laughing.

"Take me down, now," she said.

His muscular arms eased her back down his body, so he could breathe...and see...and held her tight to his chest. "I won't let you fall. I won't let anyone hurt you ever again."

She should be freaking out. He knew who she was, what they were. But instead, at his promise, she calmed, relaxing against him. And if she wasn't on the verge of passing out, she thought she might feel...exhilarated. She was flying through the air.

On some screwed-up level, she trusted this male, trusted that he would never intentionally hurt her, and that disturbed her more than almost being paralyzed and eaten alive by a flesh-eating demon.

She'd finally lost her mind.

CHAPTER 11

GRACE HAD GONE limp in Chaos's arms a short time after she'd calmed down. For a female who liked to leap between tall buildings, her fear when he'd taken to the sky had surprised him.

And in a twisted way, pleased him.

Grace was so strong and brave, so sure all the time, he wondered if she possessed any fear at all. Without a healthy dose of it, people tended to take stupid risks.

They tended to get dead pretty quick as well.

Electricity danced over his skin as he remembered the moment when she dropped her block, when he'd felt what she'd been hiding from him. It'd been so powerful, he'd fucking collapsed.

The signs had all been there from the start, though, hadn't they? He'd just chosen to ignore them, hadn't believed them because he knew that there should be more. Well, he felt it now.

All of it.

Christ, the way he'd found her, prone and bleeding. She could have died, another demon could have discovered her before he got there, paralyzed and completely helpless. Clawed fingers gripped the pounding muscle behind his ribs, and he tightened his arms around her.

She groaned but didn't wake. Chaos quickly loosened his hold, but she snuggled closer, gripping *him* tighter. His demon purred like a contented feline, and for the second time that night, he and his demon were one.

Chaos dipped his head and drew in her scent again, he couldn't get enough of it. She was covered in fuck knew what from the filthy alley floor, but her scent was stronger, and the vibrations of her power were like a siren's song designed only for him, drawing him closer, making him weaker and stronger at the same time.

Grace was his.

The idea of finding a mate had terrified him for centuries…and yeah, a lot about the whole mating thing still did. But fuck, it was like a limb or some vital organ—a piece of his goddamn brain—had been missing, and he hadn't even known it until now.

With Grace he could feel whole, for the first time in his life.

He landed on the balcony of the control room and was thankful when he found it empty. He strode through, out into the hall, and took the stairs down to the next level, where their living quarters were located. Grace had lost a lot of blood. She needed food and rest, time to heal.

"She okay?" Laz asked, coming out of nowhere.

Chaos shook his head. "Keep looking for the beast. I want any updates you have, otherwise I'm not to be disturbed." He strode into his apartment, kicked the door shut behind him, and throwing out a hand compelled the lock to slide home.

Grace stirred as he carried on through to the en suite bathroom. Dirt and grime covered her. Her pale blond hair was streaked with filth, and the scratches on her thigh needed to be cleaned. There was also an underlying scent of demon on her skin. Chaos needed to wash that off because every time his own demon smelled the venious who clawed her, he wanted to kill it. And since the fucker was already dead, that was causing some serious problems.

She was also cold, so fucking cold, and he needed to warm her up.

He carefully lowered her to her feet, but her knees buckled, which meant the shower was out. Holding her to him carefully, he turned on the water to fill the tub.

"Grace?"

Her eyes opened, lids heavy, mahogany eyes dull. "So cold," she whispered.

Fuck. "I know, angel. I'm gonna warm you up."

He grabbed the bottle of heavy-duty painkillers he had for when he was seriously injured and sat on the bathroom floor, cradling her to him. He gave her one. He usually took two or three, but he was a lot bigger than her and also immortal.

When he was satisfied she'd swallowed it, he stripped off her shirt and bra. Next her leather jeans. He was working them down her long legs when she whimpered. That sound of pain distressed him in a way he'd never experienced in his life. He sure as hell couldn't bear to cause her more of it.

Sliding the knife free from his boot, he carefully cut the jeans from her body. The pants were already destroyed, so he didn't think she'd care. He cut off her underwear as well, then realized he'd have to get in the water with her or she'd fucking drown.

He kicked off his boots and managed to get his shirt off while holding her. But his jeans, covered in demon blood and fuck knew what else, were a no-go. Reluctantly, he laid her on a towel, his gut clenching when she curled into a ball, shivering. She was pale, so delicate and fragile he couldn't fucking take it.

Stripping quickly, he turned off the water, scooped her onto his arms, and climbed into the massive tub with her. He rested her between his legs, against his chest. She hissed when the water hit her wound, and he winced, feeling fucking ill that he was causing her pain but knowing there was no other choice. This was the best way to clean out the scratches, to warm her up.

She thrashed in his arms until the pain obviously eased. She was barely conscious, and still she shivered almost uncontrollably.

He sunk down lower in the water so she was submerged to the base of her throat, willing it to warm her. Chaos held her like that for a long time, until the shivers fucking finally subsided.

It wasn't long after that she went rigid in his arms.

"Don't freak out," he said against her ear when he thought she was about to try and stand. "You lost a lot of blood, you were freezing and I needed to clean your wound."

"And you needed to be n-naked for that?" she said, voice raspy, no doubt from her screams.

"We were both covered in blood and you couldn't support your own weight."

She was silent for several long seconds. "Right. Well, thanks…for this, then, b-but I need to…" One of her hands went to the edge of the tub, attempting to climb out, but she was still too weak.

He tugged her back against him, not ready to let her go, even though he knew he needed to. "For once stop fighting me and let me do my job."

She tensed again. "What job is that?"

I'm your male, it's my job to take care of you in every way I can. To fulfill all your needs, to provide your comfort. He ignored the words ringing through his skull and said instead, "I'm a knight. Looking after demi is what I was born to do."

"And how many demi have you stripped naked and climbed into a tub with lately?" she said, her voice gaining strength and teeth no longer chattering.

He grinned. "Just the one."

More silence, then, "Okay, I'm just gonna say it. There's no point ignoring the elephant in the room...well, there's no ignoring its"—she wriggled against him—"trunk anyway."

He choked, then cringed. "Grace..."

"I've heard the rumors. The effect a knight's er...female has on him, especially when they first meet."

"Not sure what you're talking about."

"You know exactly what I'm talking about."

Yeah, he did, and he was currently fighting it like hell. Not that fighting it seemed to be working. She'd obviously felt his raging hard-on against her back, it was impossible to miss. But he didn't want her to think he was some creep or an animal that couldn't control itself. "Ignore it."

"Seriously?"

He cleared his throat. "We're naked and wet in a tub together. Any male would be hard. You have nothing to fear from me. I am actually capable of controlling myself."

More silence, and he noticed she didn't try to pull away.

"Chaos...we need to talk about what happened out there," she finally said.

"We will," he agreed as he encouraged her to tilt her head back so he could wet her hair thoroughly. He ran his hands through the soft strands, then started lathering it with soap since the shampoo was in the shower and there was no way he was moving from this spot.

"What are you doing?" she asked, sounding confused and a little shocked.

"Washing your hair. There's dirt in it from the alley." And not touching her right then was an impossibility.

"You don't need to do that...I can wash my own..." She tried to face him and whimpered again.

He cursed. "You're injured, in pain, and you stink like alley and demon. So just this fucking once, would you stop fighting me."

She grumbled something but did as he asked. She didn't relax against him fully like she had before, and he found he missed it.

What a fucking mess. Everything, all of this.

But it also felt so damn right.

He worked the soap into her hair, massaging her scalp with his fingers since there was grime along her hairline as well.

She resisted, holding herself away for a while longer, but in the end, she gave in and relaxed. He knew it was because she was weak from blood loss, but his demon started purring again, fucking thrilled at her closeness, that she was letting them take care of her.

Chaos tried hard to ignore the silkiness of her skin against his, how pale she looked against him, how small, the way her scent had grown stronger, filling his head, making him dizzy, like he was the one who'd lost blood.

He'd gotten his dick somewhat under control, until he gently scooted her down the bath so she could tilt her head back in the water and rinse off the soap. Over her shoulder, he could see her nipples just below the surface of the water. He swallowed, watching as the necklace she wore slid across her chest—not another male's diamonds—but two rings, both gold.

He wanted to ask about them but didn't think she'd welcome his questions, so instead he worked his fingers through the silken length of her hair, supporting the back of her neck with his other hand, massaging lightly.

She moaned.

It wasn't pain, it was all pleasure, and his body responded instantly. It didn't help that her long hair was kind of tickling his balls.

When Grace slid back up, her cheeks darkened. The female actually blushed.

Whether it was because of her response to his hands on her or to his physical reaction to her feeling pleasure, he had no idea, but there was nothing he could do about his cock now. Not with Grace pressed against him.

"Ignore it," he said again roughly, as he began running the soap over her shoulders, trying and failing to do what he was asking her to. Not easy when his throbbing cock was aching for her so badly his mind kept throwing up images of him cupping her ass and lifting so he could slide inside her.

There was no getting his dick back under control now.

She made a sound, a mix of astonishment and humor. "I'm not sure that's possible."

"Try harder," he said, oddly amused himself, despite the pain he was in.

"Your dick feels like it's pointing at me, like it's accusing me of something," she said, and her head lolled to the side.

A laugh burst from him. "What?"

"Why is your dick angry at me, Chaos?" she said, teasing and sounding drowsy. The painkiller he gave her was finally kicking in, and going by how out of it she suddenly seemed, he probably should have gone with half, not a whole one. "Doesn't surprise me. Your dick is as arrogant as you. *Heh.*" She giggled.

"You think my dick's arrogant?" She was funny and relaxed, and he wanted more.

"It probably scowls like you, too. Can penises scowl? I bet yours can."

She turned suddenly, easier, her side now to his front and she looked down at him through the soapy water. Trying to see his *penis scowling*? Yep, she was totally out of it now.

"I can't see," she said, frowning, then giggled again. "Maybe I can—"

Her fingers wrapped around him under the water. He jolted and hissed.

She looked up at him, eyes wide. "Yep, it feels angry, too." Then giggled some more.

"Fucking hell." Her fingers gripped him tight, and he was ashamed to admit that he was close to coming.

He reached down to dislodge her hand, but it slid lower, then back up, and his eyes rolled back in his head from the pleasure of it. When he finally managed to open his eyes again, she was looking up at him with that wide-eyed stare again.

"I thought it must be, but *damn*, it really is," she whispered.

"What?" he whispered back.

"Big. It's really fucking big, Chaos."

He quickly pulled her hand away before he disgraced himself. He stood, taking her with him. "Okay, time for sleep."

Grace shook her head. "No, I'm not tired. I need to go home."

He threw a towel over her and carried her from the bathroom.

She was out cold before he reached the bed.

Laying her down, he quickly dried her and tugged one of his shirts over her head, covering her naked body.

She wasn't going anywhere, not while she was so vulnerable, not until she'd fully recovered.

Maybe not even then.

CHAPTER 12

CHAOS COULDN'T MAKE himself move, hadn't left her side in three hours. He wanted to dress her wounds, but he also didn't want to disturb her. Grace needed her sleep. So he'd sat frozen beside her, his mind in turmoil, not sure what to do. Wanting desperately to look after her, yet knowing that whatever he did would cause her some kind of pain or discomfort.

He'd lost his fucking mind. Obviously.

He should be demanding answers from her. For instance, *what the fuck* had happened back in that alley? And he didn't mean the simple answers, like why she engaged a demon with no backup, or even the fact that she was his mate and she chose to keep that from him. What he really wanted to know was what the fuck that power was she'd used on him before throwing him clean across the alley.

Grace was full of secrets, and he wanted to know them all. Every last one.

She stirred and he was drawn closer, watching...fascinated by every subtle movement, the way her breathing had quickened, lips parting slightly. Her lashes were thick half-moons on her smooth cheeks, and they trembled before her eyes finally opened.

Rich brown irises locked on him and knocked the wind from his lungs.

She sat bolt upright and they narrowly avoided cracking skulls. He reached out to steady her and she brushed his hand away, her eyes on him but unseeing for several seconds.

"Grace?"

He saw the moment it all snapped back into place, what happened, where she was, why she was with him?

She shoved her hair back. "What time is it?"

"Four in the morning."

Grace looked down at herself and frowned at his shirt that she was wearing, then looked back at him. "Have you been sitting there the whole time?"

"Yes."

Her chin jerked back. "Why?"

Because I couldn't make myself leave your side. Because all I wanted to do was climb in bed with you and feel you against me. He shrugged, then stood. "Waiting for you to wake so I could dress your wounds."

He forced himself to leave her and grabbed the first-aid kit from the bathroom.

She eyed him warily when he walked back in, which pissed him off. No, he had no right to feel that way. He hadn't exactly worked to build her trust, had undermined and berated her every chance he got. Public relations weren't his strong suit. As far as he'd been concerned, Grace was getting in the way of him doing his job and putting herself at risk every time she went out in the field.

He'd been wrong, of course. She was a skilled fighter, determined, relentless. He'd just been too stubborn to see it.

Her eyes narrowed and hardened at his scrutiny. "I got

injured, it happens. I'm sure you've been injured a million times, so don't you even think about telling me not to fight."

He shook his head and dropped to his knees on the floor beside the bed, flicking back the covers to get to her injured leg. "I won't get in your way, not anymore," he said, even as his instincts screamed at him to keep her locked safely in his room and never let her out of his sight. But Grace was a warrior. Who was he to stop her if she wanted to fight? "You have every right to defend the demi in this city. I'm sorry I didn't see your side of things sooner."

Grace stared at him, astonishment written all over her face. "The catch?"

"No catch. You were right. We need to work together, knights and demi. It's the only way we can win this war. I know that now."

It felt wrong even saying it. But he had no right to lock her up and hide her from the world, no matter how he might want to.

"I'm not mating with you, Chaos," she said into the heavy silence.

"I know," he rasped, even as it cut him to the quick. He had no right to ask that of her, either. After the way he'd treated her, the things he'd said, he wasn't surprised she'd hidden who she was, that she would reject him.

Though, right then it didn't matter that they weren't mated, he *needed* to take care of her.

"Lie down, Grace."

"Whoa. Hold up. I'm not sleeping with you, either."

He deserved that, too. She didn't trust him, not one bit. "I want to tend to your injuries, that's all."

It was a lie, of course, he wanted inside her, to feel her wet heat wrapped around him so badly he throbbed from it, his blood so hot and thick with lust he burned and ached all over. But she'd made it clear that wasn't going to happen, and he'd have to find a way to live with it.

"Just get me something to wear, my leg's fine." She glanced down at her ravaged flesh, getting a good look at it for the first time and winced.

"Will you let me help you?" he said, close to begging.

She let out an agitated breath and nodded, reluctantly.

Thank fuck.

"Roll onto your stomach." The worst of it was on the side and back of her left thigh, and though he'd cleaned it, it would still need antiseptic to prevent an infection.

Her long legs were smooth, her muscle definition proof of her commitment to her training, and he guessed the dancing didn't hurt, either. He knew she wasn't wearing underwear and the urge to tug up the shirt and bite into that firm, pert little ass was so strong he groaned.

Grace glanced over her shoulder. "All right?"

No, I'm not inside you. He dipped his chin and crawled onto the bed, straddling her just above the knees, to keep her still. This would hurt. The cuts he'd been forced to make were deep.

Who was he kidding? The position wasn't necessary. Grace could handle whatever he was about to do, but it turned out he was a glutton for punishment. He needed to be close to her. Had to be. Fuck, his dick was rock hard and the heat of her body seeping through his jeans wasn't helping one damn bit.

"Are they bad?" she asked, voice nothing but a husky whisper.

"You'll live." He carefully applied the antiseptic.

She hissed. "You saved my ass out there."

He could think of a few other things he'd like to do with her ass and bit back another groan. "If you hadn't called in your location...if he'd managed to get the upper hand—"

She stiffened and growled, and her body jerked beneath him. "Who the hell's fault is that? If you didn't give sanctuary to every demon that gave you puppy-dog eyes, this wouldn't have happened in the first place."

He was so turned on, he almost missed what she'd said. "We'd never give sanctuary to a Venious demon. They're flesh eaters. Their nature will never change."

She made a scoffing sound, suddenly on the defensive. "You expect me to believe that bullshit? If you're not letting them in, then obviously, you need to up your game. Demons are crawling all over this city. How many do you let by when the portal opens?"

"None if we can help it. You know that yourself, Grace. You've been there," he said, trying not to bite back. He didn't want to argue with her. "But demons have been on this earth as long as we have. They are living and breeding among us. You're proof of that."

She was quiet beneath him, the muscles in her slender back tensing, her shoulders rigid.

He ran a hand down between her shoulder blades. "You truly believe I'd grant sanctuary to just any of them?"

"Why would I assume different? I've seen you give mercy when they come through, hands up in surrender." Her voice sounded desperate, confused.

"We also bring them back here to be interrogated. I'm not sure you know this, but Zenon is Hell born, that's how we know not all demons want to cause harm, some just want to live in peace."

"Hell born?" she choked.

"We only learned he existed when he stepped through the portal." Chaos didn't go into details, it was Zenon's story to tell, but he wanted Grace to understand why they didn't kill every demon who left Hell. "It used to be a lot harder to decide, which was why many didn't get a pass, but now that

115

we have Eve, we can easily learn their motives for wanting sanctuary."

"What can she do?"

"Read people's thoughts. Her power's grown a lot since she mated with Laz, though. She can block it out now, easily, thank fuck. Only listens to people when she has to. But she can do a lot more than that. I've seen her pull information from someone, riffle through their brain like a filing cabinet to get what we need."

Grace was quiet for several long seconds.

"Grace?"

"Can you get off me."

Something had upset her, he could hear it in her voice.

"Now. Get the hell off me."

Like fuck. "What's going on? You didn't know, now you do. Why are you freaking out?"

She struggled, her breath sawing in and out of her chest. "I said…Get. Off. Me."

Her thrashing increased, but this wasn't just anger, this was something else altogether, this was panic, fear. "Calm down, you're going to hurt yourself."

"You're lying. You're a damn liar. I don't believe you." Then she reached back and scratched at his arm.

Before he knew what he was about to do, he lifted his hand and brought it down on her ass. Hard. The *smack* of his palm against the thin fabric of his shirt covering her rounded cheeks was loud and rang out in the now quiet room.

She stilled instantly and twisted to look at him, eyes blazing with fury, but there was heat there as well. "You did not just spank me."

"You were throwing a tantrum." The scent of her need hit him hard, low in the gut.

She gritted her teeth. "Get off me."

Something had her spooked. If fighting with him helped

her deal with whatever it was, he'd give her what she needed. For now.

He raised a brow.

"Please."

He eased off the bed, not bothering to hide his massive erection. Why would he? When a male found his mate, fucking her, being ready to fuck her, was part of the M.O. Her gaze dropped to his dick and she sucked in a breath, followed by a whole lot more of her intoxicating scent filling the small room, driving him insane.

He bit back a vicious curse, suddenly frustrated and angry with himself for how he'd fucked all of this up so badly. He adjusted his dick before his jeans cut off his blood supply. "It's how I'm hardwired. I know who you are. My demon knows who you are, we can *feel* it. Making you our mate includes fucking, and right now, we want to fuck you. That's not going to change. So either ignore it, or give in to it."

"I don't want you," she hissed. "I will never give you that."

He had no idea where the animosity had suddenly come from. He'd thought things between them would improve after admitting she was a skilled fighter, after asking for her help. After saving her life. Apparently not.

His anger and frustration shot higher. "I can smell how much you want me, Grace. Lying is pointless."

Her eyes hardened, fire blazing from their depths. "I'm out of here."

"You're giving up immortality, you realize that?" A pathetic last-ditch effort, but he was that desperate. If immortality was the only reason she'd accept him, he'd take it.

She laughed. It was bitter, humorless. "I'm sorry, but playing house with you for eternity does not sweeten the deal, Chaos."

In other words, she'd rather be dead than with him.

Awesome. He drew in several steadying breaths and motioned to her thigh. "I've cleaned your wounds, but you need them properly dressed to stop infection."

"I'll do it myself, or get someone else to do it." Climbing off the bed gingerly, she brushed past him toward the bathroom, leaving him no choice but to follow.

Jealousy struck, fast and unexpected. "Who?"

"Who, what?"

"Who would you get to tend to you?"

She lifted her filthy and shredded clothes off the bathroom floor and cursed. "That's none of your damn business."

"Oden?" The green-eyed monster had taken over, and he had no control over the words spilling past his lips. "Now you've dropped your block and we can both feel it, it will be me you want when you're wet and aching. *Not him*," he all but roared. "It will be me you hunger for."

"Shut up..."

"I could tie you down, have you at my mercy, and you'd beg for it. You'd let me give it to you, too, give you what you need, because as much as you try to deny it, you will always want me. Only me. The fates made you for me, female. Every part of you was designed *for me*. No one will ever be able to satisfy you like I could. Protect you, take care of you like I would."

"Shut the hell up," she yelled. Then she came at him.

He held his ground as her fist connected with the side of his jaw with enough force to rattle his teeth. And sick fuck that he was, he'd never been more turned on in his life.

She got in his face. "You're a fucking bastard." There was pain in her voice, pain he didn't understand.

Yeah, you do. You just keep on hurting her.

He rubbed his jaw, taking a moment to get his shit together. Her pain was loud to him, filled the room. He'd caused it. He knew he had. But he got the feeling that something else was going on here.

He searched her eyes when she finally looked up. Disappointment, disgust looked back at him. He felt sick to his stomach.

She truly hated him. He grabbed for the doorframe. The blow of that reality hit harder than he thought possible.

She's never hidden how much she despises you.

His brothers thought he was a heartless bastard. And for most of his life, he'd lived up to it. But for some reason, he didn't want the female in front of him to see him that way. He wanted her to see him as something more than a cold-blooded, ruthless asshole.

Grace took a step back, then several more, and fear washed through her gaze.

Yeah, that didn't make him feel like a fucking prick *at all*. His mate not only didn't want him, she was now scared of him.

"Chaos?" she whispered and used the back of her hand to brush away a stray tear.

The tear sent another wave of fury through him. He'd made her cry?

"Are you going to go full Kishi on me?"

He looked down at his fingers wrapped around the doorframe. The wood had been reduced to splinters under his hand. "I hurt you. My demon doesn't like it. Neither of us do."

Her gaze darted to his destroyed doorframe and back to him.

"We would never hurt you." He wanted to put her mind at rest, wanted that look of fear off her face. "Now that I know who you are...hurting you would hurt me. I will never do anything to hurt you. But my emotions, what I'm feeling...it's volatile. I'm sorry I lashed out, got...jealous. You have to understand, Grace, there is a demon inside me that knows you should be his, ours, and that instinct is…strong." *Understatement of the century.* "Seeing you with another male for example…and things could get bad…for him."

"Is that a threat to control me?" she fired at him.

He shook his head. "It's instinct, pure territorial instinct."

"So basically, you've pissed all over me and no one else will come near me?" She crossed her arms, looking even angrier.

He took a steadying breath, trying to keep his shit together. "No. No one will know you're mine except you and I…"

"I'm not yours."

"I don't see it that way. I can't."

Her fist came down on the bathroom counter. "This is what I didn't want. What I was trying to avoid."

The words came out before he could stop them. "Would being with me be so awful? I know we've had our differences…"

"Yes, damn you."

Her words were another blow, hard and sharp. "I won't force you into something, not when it repulses you so much, but you have a power that you obviously can't control…"

"What? No…I don't have a power. I never have…"

"Grace, you drew mine right out of my body, and when you gave it back, it flung me across the fucking alley."

"I what… What did I do?"

"You need to stay here until you learn to use and control it, just like every other demi new to their powers."

She stiffened.

"Right now, you're a risk to others. You can leave when you can control it." Just saying it felt wrong.

He turned to go.

"I won't be pressured to mate."

He dipped his chin. What could he do? She didn't want him.

"You're doing this to punish me, aren't you? Making me stay here…with you."

Fuck. Ouch.

Her words struck like daggers, causing an anguish inside him he didn't know how to process. He turned back to her, and the truth came unbidden, a truth he barely understood, but for some reason needed her to hear. "I would never punish you, Grace. How could I when my every instinct is screaming out for me to drop to my knees and worship you?"

She looked at him, shocked, but said nothing.

Grace didn't want anything from him. *She didn't want him.* Maybe that was a good thing since he only seemed capable of hurting her.

He'd made her a promise to leave her alone. Now somehow he had to learn to live with it.

CHAPTER 13

ZENON SIPPED HIS BEER, and sat back, scanning the bar—people watching, humans called it. And the frail creatures in this shithole were watching him right back. Not meeting his eyes, though, never that. Nothing new. He had the same effect on humans as a hungry lion walking into a room.

It used to bother him.

Now it kind of amused him.

How Mia saw him was all that mattered. His mate didn't find him terrifying, she told him all the time he was "beautiful" or "insanely hot" and showed him daily. No one else's opinion of him mattered.

As for his brothers, things had improved there as well, and their mates had grown used to him.

The demi they retrieved and trained still weren't sure of him, so he left the training to his brothers, but you couldn't win them all.

The door across the bar opened and Silas strode in. At six and a half feet tall, and built like a warrior, the angel was seriously intimidating. Like always, he was dressed in black from head to toe. Add in the heavy black boots and thick dark lashes that ringed his silver eyes, so it looked like he was wearing eyeliner, the guy looked like some kind of devil-worshipping, goth, serial killer.

Silas spotted Zenon and shoved his fingers through his short, gold and black hair, and made his way over.

"This place is a dump," Zenon said by way of a greeting.

Silas took the seat across from him. "I thought it had a certain charm."

A waitress hustled over and put a glass in front of the angel and smiled. "Your usual."

"Thanks, Mandy." Silas took a sip and scowled at Zenon's raised brows.

"Your usual?"

Silas shrugged. "The noise, the realness of this place, helps me think."

"Isn't there some place in Heaven you can hang out? You know, a room full of angelic assholes comparing dick sizes?"

"Yup." His lips curled. "But the other angels got jealous, so I gave up. Besides, I much prefer humans."

Zenon took a sip of his beer. Despite the bar and the light chitchat, there was no missing the urgency in his own voice or the sharp tension in Silas's gaze. "You know why I wanted to meet?"

Silas lifted his glass and downed the rest of his drink, putting it back on the table with more force than necessary. He dipped his chin, jaw tight. "And I've been given strict instructions to keep my mouth shut."

"Why?"

"The usual fucking bullshit."

In other words, leave it to fate and butt the fuck out. "Do they get that Hell's about to bust free and either wipe out humanity or enslave it?"

The glass in Silas's hand exploded, glass shards flying everywhere. The angel jolted, looking down at his clenched fingers. He cleared his throat. "My hands are tied," he rasped, still looking at his hand like he didn't know who it belonged to.

Zenon couldn't believe what he was hearing. "You know the outcome?"

The angel shook his head. "I'm too close." He glanced back at Zenon. "Have become too...involved. They're preventing me from seeing."

"Can you at least tell me where to find Lucifer?"

Silas opened his mouth, then gasped in pain.

Zenon searched the angel's gaze, his eyes were glassy, bloodshot. "They're physically preventing you from helping us?"

"I'll lose my wings if I disobey, if I help you."

"They'll throw you out of Heaven?"

Silas shoved his fingers through his hair again. "I've gone against them before. They have good reason not to trust me."

They were keeping tabs on him, probably listening to him even now, to their conversation. Zenon didn't understand any of this. "What did you do?"

Pain lined Silas's face again. "I can't say." His fingers curled into a tight fist again and he snarled. "Follow your course..." he bit out and clenched his teeth.

"Find Lucifer, contain the beast?" Zenon asked, fury coursing through him when he saw the blood vessels in Silas's eyes had all burst, the whites now completely red.

Silas stood suddenly, staggering to his feet, and held out his hand. Zenon took it, and the angel clasped it tight, giving him a subtle nod. "I have to go. Take care."

Then he turned and walked out, swaying like he'd downed a bottle of whisky. Zenon cursed and stood as well. Something caught the light, glinting brightly on the floor. He crouched down.

A feather of spun gold, long and delicate, lay by Zenon's feet.

The angels weren't fucking around. Silas had done something to piss them off, and they were punishing him for it. They were punishing them all.

Grace was doing her best to ignore Chaos. He stood across from her in one of the training rooms, and the way he was watching her was making that extremely difficult.

She forced herself to focus on James and what he was saying. James, a demi as well, lived permanently at the compound and helped the knights train their people when they were brought here, freshly transitioned and desperate to control their powers. He was also one of her crew. Something Chaos and his brothers did not know.

James was an amazing fighter dedicated to the cause. He was also loyal to the knights, loved them like family, but he'd gotten sick of seeing them and his people suffer and not being able to help.

So he'd sought her out after the knights found out about her. She'd been wary at first, worried that he was a spy, but in the end he'd proven himself more than trustworthy.

And right now, she was finding it hard to focus on what her friend was saying with Chaos watching them so intently.

He stood with his arms folded over his massive chest, thighs braced apart, and a look on his face that she was sure would've wilted a great deal of the demi who had stood in this room before her.

She was determined to master her power, though. True to his word, Chaos had not let her leave the compound, and she was going out of her damn mind. At night, he and his brothers left to hunt the beast, and she was forced to stay behind. She had people counting on her, one of them still missing, and a freaking job. Still, Chaos refused to budge.

Three nights she had spent in his bed. Three nights in his apartment filled with his things, his maddening scent—*him*. He'd given her the bed, had insisted on it, while he'd taken the couch. It was pure torture. The more time she spent in his presence, the louder the bond between them called. She was in a constant state of arousal, and with Chaos in the next room, she couldn't even get herself off. The whole situation was making her seriously cranky.

She needed out of this place and away from Chaos before she did something she could never take back.

He dropped his hands to his sides, veins and tendons roping them, his strength evident in every inch of his body, in every move he made. The male was all warrior, honed to perfection. Lethal.

And if you asked him, he'd drop to his knees and worship you.

Dammit, she needed to stop thinking about that. Unfortunately, it was *all* she could think about. The words he'd said to her kept playing over in her mind. To have any kind of control over the male in front of her seemed ridiculous. But instinctively, she knew if she became his, if they mated, he would do anything for her. Anything. Like having her own personal guard dog.

Yeah, no, that was too tame. More like a guard dragon.

But tying herself to another being for the rest of her life was not something she would ever do. Especially not to a knight. It would be a betrayal of the worst kind. Her parents would be disgusted with her for even being in the same room as him.

"Can we get this over with already?" The fact she had a power she never knew about had blown her mind, but she was confident she could control it. It felt…natural. They'd trained the last three days, and she'd managed to do what she had with Chaos in that alley to James twice. She'd also managed to use James's power like it was her own, before she'd given it back.

Chaos glanced at her, and Grace shifted in place as he sent James away.

James grinned and gave her a double thumbs-up behind Chaos's back before he disappeared out the door. Smart-ass.

"What's going on? I thought we were training?" she said, trying not to show how much being alone with him affected her.

Chaos stepped closer. "We are. But today you'll be using me."

The way he said that sent a shiver dancing down her spine. Her blood instantly heated and her mind conjured up all the ways she could *use* him. "Why?"

He started toward her like a prowling animal. "We know your power is strong, let's see just how strong."

Without thought, she took a step back. "But in the alley… with you, it was too much, you were too powerful."

He ignored her retreat and closed the gap between them. "The whole point of this is to learn your limits. Until you can do that, you won't have full control over it."

His voice was deep and rumbly, gliding over her skin like velvet brushing between her thighs. Curling her fingers into a tight fist, she forced herself to ignore it. "Fine, let's get this over with."

He grabbed her shoulders and turned, changing positions, so his back was to the padded wall.

She raised a brow.

"My instinct will be to pull away. This way, I can't."

He took her wrist, his rough, thick fingers, hot and strong, curled firmly around skin and bones that seemed far too fragile all of a sudden. She'd only ever felt that way with him. She hated it, but also craved it. He could easily crush her if he chose to. But he held her like she was delicate, as break-able as she felt right then, precious, and lifted her hand to his throat, holding her fingers against his skin.

They were close, too close. His unwavering dark eyes were aimed down at her, so intense, like he couldn't look away from her.

Dangerous.

This is dangerous.

She forced herself to look away, to ignore how his skin felt against hers, how the muscles under his shirt rippled every time he moved, the way his breathing had grown heav-ier, the way he still held her wrist like he didn't want to let go, and focused on what she had to do.

Closing her eyes, she did what James had taught her. She thought about where her power manifested, where she'd felt it that first time. In her chest.

The more she thought about it, focused on it, the emptier she felt, the bigger the space inside her grew, yawning wider.

Just like that, it came to her. Natural.

"Ready?" Her voice sounded soft, husky—needy.

Chaos shifted slightly. "Take it."

She began drawing his power into her, slow and steady, more controlled than she had the first time. Her skin began to tingle and prickle. James's power was nothing compared to Chaos's. And the more of it she took, the dizzier she got. So much, there was so much. She felt him pouring into her, filling her. But this was nothing like the first time, and nothing like it was when she trained with James.

Chaos's breathing had grown even heavier, his breath brushing her temple. She had her eyes closed, but she knew he'd leaned in, his face almost close enough to touch hers.

Oh shit, it felt...good, even when she was sure she couldn't take anymore.

"Take it," Chaos growled. "Take everything."

She didn't think he was talking about his power anymore. Her skin was flushed and tight, tingling, nipples hard and aching, between her thighs throbbing and wet.

"I...I can't take anymore," she said, on the verge of something so damn good, she whimpered.

"Keep going," he gritted out.

She gasped. "I can't, I can't take anymore."

His body pressed against hers. "Then stop, Grace. Stop, and give it back."

She did, and a sob escaped before she moaned helplessly. Her hands moved over him in a restless way, sliding from his thick powerful throat to his shoulders, then down to his biceps and back up.

This time, the release, as she sent his power back, left a sensation of euphoria in its wake, firing through her body. She cried out, shaking uncontrollably.

Chaos ground his teeth as his power flowed back to him, filled him. His hands clamped on her hips and he tugged her closer.

When there was nothing left, when she'd given it all back, she sagged against him, unable to stop herself. His heart was hammering against hers, his fingers flexing and releasing at her hips. Grace struggled to catch her breath, to gain control over her body. It screamed for him, for what she knew he could give her.

She wanted to shove him to the floor, yank down the front of his shorts, and ride the massive erection pressing into her.

One of his hands finally came up and he took her chin, tilting her head back. His nostrils flared. "Okay?"

"Yes."

"Fuck, angel. You're so damn strong, so fearless," he said as he brushed his thumb over her jaw.

He wanted her closer, she could see it in his eyes, and

right now, after what just happened, her body cried out for the same thing.

His words echoed around her head. But she didn't feel strong, she felt weak.

Her control dissolved into dust, and instead of pushing him away, she fisted the front of his shirt and tugged him closer, then sliding her arms around his neck, she jumped, wrapping herself around him.

Chaos caught her, his strong arms banding around her, one under her ass, the other across her back. He cupped the back of her head a moment before she slammed her mouth down on his.

The heat and strength of his body against hers was almost as addictive as his kiss. He fisted her hair and tilted his head, taking over the kiss, thrusting his tongue between her lips before spinning them and pressing her into the padded wall behind her.

More. She wanted more. And like he'd read her mind, he gave it to her. Gripping her ass, he thrust his heavy, hard cock between her thighs, dragging its weight over her pulsing, wet flesh. She wanted to tear their clothes away and take him inside her. She wanted him to slam her against the wall and thrust hard and deep, filling her, taking her—

Someone knocked at the door.

Grace stilled.

"Don't pull away from me, Grace," Chaos said hoarsely against her lips. "Don't do it."

Goose bumps lifted over her skin at the aching need in his deep voice.

"Please, angel," he rasped, shudders moving through his body, his hand still massaging her ass, the other fisting her hair tighter. "We both want this."

The knock came again. Harder.

"Let me go."

"Grace…"

"Put me down, Chaos."

He growled, low and vicious, even as he put her down like she was the most delicate thing in existence. He spun away, strode to the door, and yanked it open. "What the fuck do you want?"

Kryos was standing there, body almost vibrating.

"What is it?" Chaos said, seeing the other male's anger, his impatience.

"We got one. Laz's getting Eve. Thought you'd want to be there."

Chaos lifted his chin and Kryos strode off.

He turned back to Grace. "Coming?"

"What's going on?"

"They brought in a demon for questioning." He strode out of the training room.

Was she coming? She wouldn't miss this, no damn way. Trying and failing to shake off the lust still riding her, she rushed after him.

CHAPTER 14

CHAOS FELT Grace at his back as they strode down the hall to the elevator. He could *feel* her, so in tune with her very existence, it was like her hands were still moving over him, her mouth still under his, her moans filling his head.

They climbed in the elevator and the urge to pull her against him, press her into the wall, and take her swollen lips all over again almost won out.

Chaos gritted his teeth against the waves of lust still riding him. The scent of Grace's need filled the small space, making his head spin. Her body wanted him, even if her head was telling her she didn't, or shouldn't.

Christ, he'd pleaded with her. Begged her to take him, to let him have her. He'd never done that with any female in his life. The females he'd bedded made it more than clear they wanted him, and if they didn't, he found someone else. Simple. Uncomplicated.

Problem was, he didn't want anyone else. Willow had offered herself to him when he'd been to visit her, but he couldn't do it. He'd fucking willed himself to get hard. But he didn't want the witch like that, not anymore. There was only one female he wanted.

Only one female he'd want for the rest of his existence.

He'd promised to leave her alone...and he kept his promises. But this one...he wasn't sure if he could. How could he when all he wanted to do every moment of every day was be near her, touch her, talk to her—fucking mark her. It was primal—a driving, animal need—and he wasn't sure how much longer he could fight it.

And after what happened in the training room, the way Grace had climbed his body, wrapping herself around him, kissing him like her life depended on it, he hoped like hell she'd eventually give in, that she would give them what they both needed.

"Where are we going?" Her husky voice broke the silence between them.

"We have..." He had to clear his throat. "Holding cells below the building."

The elevator doors slid open, and she followed him down the concrete hall to a room at the end. He pushed the door open and walked in.

Kryos was just inside, while Lazarus stood over the demon in the center of the room. Eve was at her mate's back, and the knight had a hand curled around the demon's throat, and his other arm, behind him, wrapped protectively around his female's waist, holding her to him.

Eve's hands were against Lazarus's back, her eyes closed. "I see it." The curvy female gasped, and her eyes snapped open. The blue of her irises glowed and swirled before they rolled back in her head.

"What's happening?" Grace whispered.

Being this close to a demon, one they knew was hostile, Chaos had to resist doing exactly what Lazarus was and tug

Grace behind him to protect her. She wouldn't welcome that, not from him, not from anyone, and despite his instincts roaring at him to do just that, he also knew she didn't need that from him. His female could take care of herself.

He leaned in, speaking quietly. "When Lazarus first brought Eve in, she could only hear others' thoughts. Her power has slowly and steadily increased. She can now see images, memories, can manipulate a mind to feed her the information she needs. She can hear others' thoughts easily, if she chooses. But for her newer powers, she needs touch. Until she's strong enough to do it from a distance, Laz acts as a kind of conduit."

"That's impressive." She glanced up at him, lips quirked up on one side. "You really are okay with demi getting involved, huh?"

"Yes. What I'm not okay with is uncontrolled situations. This is controlled."

"Which is why you want us to work together?"

"Yes." *And because I'll get to spend time with you.*

"There's a house," Eve said, her power coming through in her voice. "Surrounded by trees."

"Can you see a road name, sweetheart?" Laz asked her gently.

"He's nervous, excited. There's four of them in the car. They're on the freeway, heading east. There's a sign up ahead. They took the exit onto Conway."

The demon hissed and struggled.

"The trees are getting thicker. Forest. The excitement in the car is thick…they're close. Another sign. Cannon Lake."

The demon roared. "I'll fucking kill you!" Birdlike claws exploded through its shoes and from the ends of its fingers. The demon's hands were tied behind its back, but Laz was close, and it managed to drag the razor-sharp talons on its feet down the front of his leg.

Laz hissed, but the demon's scream was louder, pitched so high that Chaos's ears rang. The demon's head suddenly slumped back, black blood oozing from its ears.

"Shit," Kryos muttered.

Grace frowned up at Chaos. "What just happened?"

"Another side effect of her increased power." He shrugged. "Laz was threatened. Someone fucked with her mate, so she ended him. Basically, she put the fucker's brain through a meat grinder."

"She can kill with her mind?" Grace asked, looking horrified and impressed at the same time.

Chaos dipped his chin.

"I'm sorry," Eve said, turning to Chaos, eyes wide. "I couldn't stop. He hurt Laz and I just...I..."

Chaos shook his head and gentled his voice. "You did good, Eve. We got what we needed."

Lazarus pulled her into his arms. "It's okay."

"But there could have been more." She leaned back, looked up at Lazarus, then at Chaos. "Something important, but I...I lost control."

Chaos moved in, wanting to reassure her. He sucked at this type of thing, but he knew how much Eve, Mia, and Meredith wanted to help. They saw their mates come home battered and bleeding every night. The strain this war took on them. "No one blames you for protecting your mate, Eve." Now that he knew about Grace, he understood how strong the urge to protect was—and that was without him and Grace actually mating. "The information you got. You saved lives tonight."

Laz gave him a look of gratitude, and Eve pulled away from her mate and stunned Chaos when she wrapped her arms around him and gave him a tight hug before looking up at him.

"You're my family, all of you. I want to help. I'll master this power, I promise I will," she said.

"I don't doubt it," he said and watched as Laz led her away.

Kryos walked over and, pulling his blade free, removed the demon's head so it would ash out.

Grace moved up beside him. "Do you use Eve a lot?"

"We do now."

She nodded, throat working. "When demons seek sanctuary?"

"Yeah."

"I didn't realize...before." She actually colored.

They hadn't talked about it after she accused him of giving sanctuary to any demon who asked for it. "How could you?"

She crossed her arms, her expression closed off. Not that the female had ever actually let him in. "Right...well, I need to go. I'm needed at Revelry. My people will be worried, and I have a good grasp on my power now."

She was right. His excuse to keep her here no longer existed.

Kryos wordlessly walked by them and left the room, obviously sensing the conversation was about to get personal.

The idea of her leaving made his fucking gut ache. He gripped the back of his neck. "You don't need to leave."

"Yes, I do," she said, frowning. "Why would I stay?"

She looked genuinely confused, and the part of him so desperate for his mate felt her rejection like a sharp jab to the sternum. "You kissed me, Grace."

"You know why I did that," she said. "It wasn't me. It was the...this thing between us. I don't want it, Chaos. And I don't...I don't want you."

"Your scent tells me something else." He closed in, unable to stop himself. "I can smell it, Grace, whenever you're with me."

"And once I'm away from you, it won't be a problem anymore."

He dipped his head, breathing deeply as his hunger for her roared back to life. Not that it had ever left. No, his hunger for her was always there now. Always. Distance would not diminish it.

"Give in, Grace," he pleaded, desperate for another taste of her lips.

She planted her hand on his chest. "Not happening."

"Grace…"

"I said no." She turned from him and walked out the door.

Chaos stayed where he was, unable to move. He had to let her go because he wanted her too much. If he kept her here and couldn't touch her, he would eventually lose his mind.

No, he would never stop wanting her, but maybe some distance would make it a little bit easier.

He fucking hoped so.

Grace leaned across the bar so she could hear the guy shouting his order.

She didn't usually pour drinks, but Hannah had left a message with Vince that she'd be away for a few days dealing with some family drama and would be back when she could.

There was absolutely no reason for Grace to worry, but she couldn't help it. With Tina still missing, Grace was seriously on edge.

She handed the guy his drink and spotted Oden stroll into the club. According to Vince, he'd been absent the last few days, while she'd been stuck at the compound, and her oldest friend was nearly coming out of his skin.

Vince rushed from his office now to greet Oden, all nervous smiles and sweaty brow, and she didn't think his reaction was excitement at having the male back in his club. She was so done with that asshole's bullshit. She wanted the powerful demi gone, but until Vince told her what the male held over him, she wasn't sure how to accomplish it.

Brushing Vince aside, Oden strode toward her, eyes cold and determined.

Here we go.

He planted his hands on the bar. "A bottle of champagne to my table," he said to her, his weird blue-black eyes unwavering, his lips tight.

The male was pissed.

"It's nice to see you again, Oden." She leaned forward, and his gaze dipped, looking down the front of her top. Her stomach lurched.

"Is your phone broken?" he asked.

He'd messaged her more than once while she was with Chaos, and she'd stupidly ignored them. "Sorry, I've had a crazy couple of days…"

"I've had some important business matters of my own to deal with."

She smiled, doing her best to soften him up since Vince looked near passing out. "Anything interesting?"

He leaned forward as well, close enough that his breath brushed her lips when he spoke next. "You're a stripper, the finer details would only confuse you."

He'd delivered what he hoped would be a verbal slap, but she'd stopped feeling the sting of barbs like that a long time ago. All he saw when he looked at her was a female who took her clothes off to pay the bills. A whore who was playing hard to get. His male ego had been bruised when she didn't respond to his messages, and now he wanted to return the favor.

She smiled wide, too wide. "You're probably right. I've never had much of a head for business."

His thick fingers wrapped around a hunk of her hair and he tugged her forward. "But you're not just a stripper, are you, *Gigi?*"

Her stomach dropped, fell right through the floor. Did he know what she really did every night? Somehow, she knew that knowledge would be dangerous in this man's hands. Widening her eyes, she stared at him with what she hoped conveyed innocent confusion. "No?"

He shook his head, that eerie dark gaze locking on hers.

"What else am I?" she asked.

His lips curled cruelly. "You obviously tend bar as well, yes?"

He was trying to rattle her, and she hated that it was working.

"And I think...you also help Vince with this place, far more than he would admit?"

Thud. Her heart fired back to life, pounding behind her ribs. He was trying to find out if she knew what Vince was mixed up in. If she knew what he and Oden discussed when they locked themselves away in Vince's office.

"I do staff rosters and make sure the bar's stocked, so yeah, I guess you're right." She smiled again, like he'd paid her a massive compliment.

He tugged a little harder on her hair and brought her closer. "Yes, I think you're a very clever girl. Far more than you let on."

More with the goofy grinning. "Why thank you. That's one of the nicest things anyone's ever said to me."

"I doubt that very much." His frigid gaze didn't waver. It

was a stupid move on her part, but the fighter in her refused to break eye contact first.

He broke first and the pissed-off vibe he'd been projecting rose to volcanic territory. She'd made a huge mistake, had revealed too much, and worse, added another bruise to his fragile ego.

To a male like him, she'd just thrown down a challenge.

"You want some company?" She angled her head toward the table his champagne had been delivered to. Sitting with him was the last thing she wanted, but if she didn't make nice, Vince might end up paying for it.

He was also hiding something, and she wanted to know what it was.

He shook his head and crooked his finger at one of the other dancers. Jemma's face lit up and she swung her hips as she walked toward Oden.

Well, he wouldn't have to work for it with Jemma, she gave it away freely, and often. Which was fine, but now any chance of Grace getting information from the male was over.

He wrapped his fingers around the back of Jemma's neck and leaned in, whispering something into her ear, then he turned to Grace again, a smug look on his face. "Make sure you answer next time." Then he led Jemma away.

Okay, maybe not all hope was lost. He was trying too hard to ram home how unimportant she was, that she was replaceable. He still wanted her. Why, she had no idea, but his ploy to make her jealous had backfired.

Now she knew just how much power she held over him.

She glanced over at his table, and sure enough, he was watching her.

Game on, asshole.

Her shift dragged, and ignoring Vince's worried glances and playing the injured female for Oden's benefit was exhausting. Oden eventually left, and much to Jemma's dismay, he left alone, which was unexpected and a little worrying. Did he think he was doing her a favor? Did he think she owed him now for not fucking one of her coworkers?

Just when she thought she had the guy figured out.

By the time she went upstairs to her apartment, she wanted nothing more than to climb into bed and fall into a dreamless coma, but catching some shut-eye wasn't an option.

For one, there was a Hell beast still on the loose in the city.

And when she walked into the quiet of her small apartment and looked at her bed, all she could see was Chaos. His enormous body pinning her to his bed at the compound as he cleaned her wounds, the way he smelled, the deep rasp of his voice.

The way he'd tasted when she'd lost control and kissed him.

It'd only been a day since she'd seen him, but instead of relief, she felt like a junkie in desperate need of a fix.

Every conversation between them had been playing through her mind. For the most part, he'd been…reasonable. He'd actually asked her for help. She was still struggling to believe it had happened.

She shoved her fingers through her hair and paced her room. She'd seen him fight. The male put it all on the line, every time. He left each and every battle bloody and exhausted.

She'd seen him with his brothers. He cared for them. Chaos made the hard decisions, even when it pissed off the other knights.

Grace sat heavily on the end of her bed.

Everything he did was all for a greater good, honoring what he was, what he was born to do.

Yes, the male could be stubborn, misguided. Even thick-headed. But she couldn't deny that everything he did, he did to protect the demi he was created to protect, to keep this city safe.

Her mother's and father's faces flashed through her mind. Her brother.

Was it really the knights who had failed her family?

All these years, she'd hated Chaos, had blamed him and his brothers for failing to protect them, had trusted them so little that she'd trained hard to became a fighter in her own right.

Had she been wrong about everything?

Really? Now you're blaming your family for their own deaths?

Guilt slashed through her and she squeezed her eyes closed. She wasn't thinking straight. The bond with Chaos was screwing with her head.

Standing, she paced across the room. She needed to get the hell out of her own head, where everything she believed suddenly wasn't black and white anymore, and her emotions were a jumble of twisted and confused feelings and memories.

Changing quickly into leather jeans and a long-sleeve, black T-shirt, she strapped on her weapons, tugged on a jacket, and climbed out her window.

The old iron fire escape protested as she climbed the ladder to the roof. The wind slapped her in the face and she sucked it back, trying again to clear her head. And once again, before she could stop herself, she looked up into the night sky.

Looking for dove-gray wings glinting in the darkness.

Stop it.

The guilt clawing at her intensified.

No. She didn't want him—the *thing* fate had put inside

her did. It was a deceitful attraction, a false connection, fraudulent lust, and she wanted no part of it.

Being around Chaos for several days had screwed her up, leaving her confused. Her emotions had been on lockdown for so long, she didn't even understand her own thoughts or feelings anymore.

The wind changed direction and a stale, sickly sweet scent hit her. The smell was unmistakable. Death. She looked around, expecting to find a dead pigeon or a rotting stray cat.

Instead she saw a hand stretched out from behind an air-conditioning duct on the rough concrete rooftop.

Please no.

Scanning the area around her, reaching out with her senses, Grace searched the shadows for movement, but she was alone. Her heart was in her throat as she rounded the duct, sucking in a harsh breath, when her fears were realized.

Tina lay on the hard roof, her hair fanned out around her pretty face, her body laid out like a sacrifice. Her skin was gray, emaciated, like something or someone had drained the life right out of her. She'd been missing for two weeks, but the condition she was in...it wasn't decay, this was something else. Her skin looked leathery, taut, like it had been vacuum sealed to her skeleton.

Grace crouched beside her friend and ran the backs of her fingers across one cold cheek. "Who did this to you?"

Why?

What the hell was going on?

Tina stared blindly at the stars overhead, and Grace gently closed the female's eyes, fighting back tears. They were friends. Tina had worked and fought beside her for the past two years, and like most demi, she'd suffered a lot of shit early in her life, only coming into her own after gaining her powers and learning what she truly was.

She didn't deserve this.

No one deserved this.

Grace stood and searched the rooftop again. Whoever did this to Tina had wanted Grace to find her. *Demon butcher.* That's what the demon on the roof had called her while she'd dangled off the side of the building.

Someone wanted her to stop. And she had a feeling this was only the beginning.

CHAPTER 15

Grace watched as her team carried Tina off the roof. She shook as rage pumped through her, fierce and hot. Whatever happened next, whatever the knights had planned, she would be a part of it. For Tina. For all the demi who had suffered—were suffering right now—at the hands of their enemy.

Yanking her phone from her back pocket, she hit the number Chaos had programmed into her phone, a number she seriously didn't want to use.

He answered almost immediately. "Grace?"

She locked down the violent emotions rampaging through her before she spoke. "You found the house yet?"

"Something's happened."

How could he know that? *How?*

She hadn't bothered telling him about Tina, why should she? Another dead demi? Big deal, right? The knights had bigger things to worry about. They wanted to win the war, but they didn't give a shit about the casualties. Even as she thought it, her belly gripped tight, guilt slicing through her. Because she knew different. Because she knew Chaos, and that wasn't him.

Christ, she had the sudden urge to cry. Instead, she held tight to her anger, the only thing capable of holding back her tears.

"You asked for our help. We're coming with you. You need to concentrate on containing the beast. We'll hold back the demons guarding it," she said, ignoring what he'd said.

A pause. "Okay."

"Okay?" The word slipped out, sounding as stunned as she felt.

"You expected me to fight you on this?"

"Yes." She'd expected his anger at the mere suggestion, despite telling her he wanted them to work together. Trust didn't come easy. She'd been waiting for him to take back the offer since he made it.

"You don't know me as well as you think you do, Grace."

His voice dropped when he said her name, and she squeezed her eyes closed, doing her best to ignore how deeply that affected her. "Text me the address."

More silence.

Her phone beeped.

"Done," he said, in that insanely deep, soul-shaking voice.

Grace disconnected without another word, afraid of what she'd say, and followed the rest of her crew. Right now was for saying goodbye to Tina.

~

Grace walked up to the burly shifter manning the entrance to Toxic, and he let her straight in with a wink.

The Roxburgh sex club was the last place she should be right now. She should be with her crew getting ready for the battle later, or going through their game plan for tonight with the knights.

A weird feeling fluttered through her belly and she

146

squashed it. It was easier to tell herself she was here because Chaya worked with her, that she might have some important intel that could help them tonight, or that Grace needed to let her know what was going on.

Never mind that Mia would have spoken to her sister already, possibly Zenon as well.

No, she wouldn't allow herself to actively think about her real reason for coming here, that she couldn't ignore the niggling thought growing in the back of her mind another moment.

She spotted Chaya and Brent instantly, they were sitting in a booth by the bar. Chaya was dressed in skintight leather and Brent was at her side wearing one of his slick suits. The little Domme had her hand possessively on her husband's thigh as he stared at her intently, nostrils flaring, heat and longing written all over his face. God, hungry as hell for his wife.

Grace sucked in a breath, envy spiraling through her when Chaya gave him a little nod and Brent all but pounced, kissing her so thoroughly even Grace's knees went weak.

A certain huge, confusing, sexy, dominant male entered her head, and her body heated instantly.

Grace approached them, passing couples in various stages of play. Some out there fucking for all to see. Brent had always kept the serious play behind doors, but a lot had changed since he and Chaya had married.

Chaya pulled back as Grace reached their booth, and Brent actually growled in frustration. Chaya's eyes narrowed at him and she made a *tut-tut* sound. Someone had obviously been misbehaving, no doubt on purpose knowing Brent.

Chaya smiled warmly. "Grace! Come join us."

Brent turned to her, a pained look on his face. "Hey, sweetheart, what's going on?"

If anyone else called her sweetheart, she'd break their

nose, but Brent was far too charming for his own good. Grace slid into the booth across from them and Brent signaled someone to bring them drinks.

"You heard about Tina?"

Chaya nodded, eyes getting glassy. "James told me."

"And I take it Mia and Zenon filled you in on everything else going on, what's going down tonight?"

"You need our help?" Chaya said.

Brent leaned forward. "I spoke to Laz, he told me about Roc. Shit's getting critical. You need another fighter tonight?"

"Always," she said.

He dipped his chin as Chaya threaded her fingers through her husband's, gripping tight. He glanced at her, something moving between them, communicating with just a look. His gaze came back to Grace. "I'll be there."

A male delivered their drinks and Grace waited for him to leave before she spoke. "I want anything you can get on Oden. There's something seriously off about that male. Anything, it's all important."

Chaya reached over and gave her hand a squeeze. "You got it. I'll put the feelers out."

"Thanks." Grace took a sip of her drink.

Chaya scrutinized Grace in a way that made her shift in her seat. "But that's not the only reason you're here? What's going on?"

Grace glanced at Brent. She knew he wouldn't repeat anything she said, but Chaos and the other knights were his friends. Talking about any of this in front of him was kind of awkward.

"I'm just going to check on, ah…something," he said, reading her look easily.

He turned to Chaya, the heat returning in his gaze. "I'll await your summons, Mistress."

Chaya watched her husband walk away, a possessive, loved-up expression on her face that Grace actually envied.

Then she turned back to Grace. "Right, get talking. You're acting all twitchy and weird, and I don't even know where to start with your emotional state."

"I am not twitchy."

"Tell me your leg's not jiggling under the table as we speak."

Grace stilled her leg, heat crawling up her neck.

Chaya chuckled.

"Seriously, sometimes I think you're a witch."

"Nope, but your emotions are all over the place. Reading them is actually making me dizzy to the point of nausea... also horny. It's a freaking odd mix."

"I'm making you want to puke and fuck?"

"Yep. So spill already before shit gets messy."

There was no hiding from Chaya, maybe that's why she came here, because she'd be forced to talk about it with someone. Instead of bottling it up inside.

That's exactly why you came here, and you know it.

Grace released the breath she was holding. "I wanted to ask you something about Mia."

Chaya frowned and sat up straighter. "What about her?"

Grace forced herself to continue. She hadn't gone to Chaos with this because it would only give him the wrong idea, same with asking Mia directly. She still wasn't sure what she planned to do with the information if the answer Chaya gave her was what she thought it was going to be. "Her power, did it increase after she mated Zenon?"

Wariness rearranged Chaya's features. "Why do you ask? You know there's no way Zenon will let her fight."

"It's not that."

Chaya leaned forward. "Then what?"

Grace cursed. "Chaos is my...mate..."

"What?" Chaya shrieked.

"We're not *mated*," she rushed out. "I don't want that, I *really* don't want that. But I guess I wanted to know what I'm missing out on?" There was more to it than that, but she wasn't ready to think it, let alone voice it yet.

Chaya frowned. "What you're missing out on? Have you seen Zenon and Mia together?"

Grace shook her head. But the knight made sure everyone knew Mia was his. He had her name tattooed in bright blue on his stomach.

"Mia is *literally* everything to Zenon. *Everything.* And he is everything to her. Her power's the reason he's still alive. No joke. The connection between mates reaches levels the rest of us will never understand. In Mia and Zenon's case, being together was literally vital to his survival. If you mate with a knight, there's more, there's always more."

Grace swallowed hard, heart racing.

"But to answer your actual question? Yes, her power grew stronger. Like *whoa* stronger. Honestly, I can't see a negative. Why the hell would you resist it?"

Grace curled her fingers around her glass. "I just…it's not for me."

Chaya's gaze softened, her head tilting to the side, no doubt reading her volatile emotions again. "Okay, but I'm here if you ever need to talk."

The small house on the outskirts of Roxburgh was fucking grim, the kind of house the local kids avoided in a horror movie. The only light source came from a single streetlight halfway down the block and a small bulb burning above the back door.

Mark and Laney took the right, and Grace and James

took the left. The remaining members of her crew had surrounded the place and were waiting for Chaos's signal to move in.

Zenon was by the back door, and he glanced up a moment before Chaos landed lightly at his side. They were talking, but it was too dark to read their lips.

Then Chaos turned her way, somehow finding her among her people concealed in the shadows. His dark gaze locked on her and he shook his head.

He wanted them to wait.

"Hold," she said to James.

He repeated her command using his power of telepathy to communicate to the rest of their team. James could transmit words with his power, and it was seriously strong. He'd once screamed *stop* telepathically to a demon trying to escape them and it had slammed on the brakes so fast they'd nearly run right over it.

There was a small shed at the back of the yard that had caught Grace's eye, and she signaled to James that she was going to check it out. Crouching low, she ran for it.

The thing was covered in grime, and she brushed away the cobwebs clinging to the window, trying to look inside. Nothing. Up close, she realized the glass had been painted black. She checked the door. It was locked with a padlock. She quickly picked it, trusting James to have her back while she concentrated on the task.

The padlock was shiny, new, and clicked open smoothly. Gripping the edge of the door, she pulled. The well-oiled hinges moved freely, the heavy wood swinging open soundlessly.

The fetid air hit her instantly, and she jerked back, lifting her arm to her nose and mouth. The stench coated her tongue, hitting the back of her throat. Retching, she turned and spat onto the ground behind her, barely stopping herself from throwing up. She pulled a small flashlight from her back pocket and lit up the interior. "Jesus." She stumbled back a step.

The floor was littered with human remains, most of the bones picked clean.

James moved up behind her. "Holy fuck."

They'd seen some disgusting things over the years, but nothing like this. This jumble of bones and gore and rotting flesh had once been someone's mother, father, sister, child. Somewhere, someone was missing them, wondering where they were, what had happened to them.

A wave of emotion hit her and she struggled to swallow. She never let her emotions get the better of her, but all this thinking about her family lately…then Tina, it was messing with her head.

This was how they were feeding the beast, keeping it full and sleepy, docile until it was needed. Lazarus landed beside them, looked into the shed, and cursed under his breath.

He stilled suddenly, his head twisting, his gaze slicing to James. He quirked a brow at the smaller male.

James squared his shoulders. "This is where I belong, Laz."

The corner of Lazarus's mouth curled up, then he was gone, joining Chaos and Zenon.

"Fuck," James muttered under his breath.

"You okay?" she asked him.

"Yeah, I mean, I prepared myself for this, for whatever happened tonight after they saw me." He lifted his hand and crossed his fingers. "Here's hoping they don't throw me out on my ass."

She patted his shoulder and tilted her chin to the knights. "I need to know what is going on over there." She was done waiting on the sidelines.

Her people looked to her, and she would not let them go

into any situation blind. So ducking low, she sprinted across the yard and joined the knights gathered by the back door of the house.

"It's under the house." Chaos motioned to the adjoining two-car garage. "The floor's been dug out. It gets in through the garage. We're going to try to tie it down." Each of the knights had heavy chain looped over their shoulders. "We can sense demons in the house." His gaze stayed locked with hers. "No idea how many. Can you hold them off while we contain the beast?"

"Yes," she said without hesitation. "Those chains, will they be strong enough to hold it?"

"Honestly, I don't know. They've been charmed by a witch. To most creatures they would be unbreakable. I've no clue if it'll work here. But we have to try."

She nodded. "We'll move in on your signal...and, Chaos?"

His gaze locked on hers, and God, it telegraphed so much. There was no missing what he was thinking. *I believe in you. Take the fuckers out. Be safe.* But what came through the loudest? *I want you. You are mine.* She suddenly found it hard to breathe.

"Good luck," she rasped.

He dipped his chin, those eyes not wavering from hers, and she forced herself to walk away, which was way harder than it should have been.

She and James followed the knights to the front so she wouldn't miss the signal, and her blood began pumping thickly through her veins, adrenaline quickening her breath.

Brent moved up from the edge of the yard, standing at her side. He gave her a chin lift and bumped fists with James.

"Ready?" James asked as the knights moved to the garage's entrance.

She nodded, not taking her eyes off Chaos.

Chaos turned to her, then and dipped his chin, then he was gone.

"Move in," she said.

James repeated her order, and they rushed for the house.

"Let's give the bastards a surprise party they'll never forget," Brent said, an evil grin on his face and a wicked-looking knife in his hand.

Grace rushed the front door and kicked it in with a grunt. James, Brent, and several other demi moved in behind her, while the rest of her crew came in through the back. They ran through the small house, feet pounding, weapons drawn and—

Nothing.

The house was empty.

A roar filled the air from below the house, so loud the ground shook beneath their feet and several windows shattered. The knights were fighting the beast.

Grace spun around. "This doesn't make sense," she yelled. "They wouldn't leave it unguarded."

A shriek came from the other end of the house.

Grace gripped the knife in her hand, ready, the space was too confined for her bow.

Demons appeared out of nowhere, swarming the house, climbing up from beneath the floorboards, dropping from the ceiling. "Take them out!" she yelled.

Moonlight filtered into the house, the only light to see by. The demons came at them, some with vacant gazes, some with glowing eyes full of excitement. The sounds of fighting and the roar of the beast below echoed all around them. Grace moved in with a cry of rage, engaging the first demon that came at her, ducking his fist and following through with one of her own to his throat. Spinning, she kicked it in the chest, and he staggered back toward James. James grabbed its hair, face twisted with rage, and dragged his blade across it's throat, removing his head with quick efficiency.

The next moved in, and at the same time a weird sensation moved across her skin, like someone had plugged the place into an electrical socket, lifting the hair on her arms. The demons began to vanish, then reappear all around the room, making them impossible to follow.

One appeared in front of her, knocking her knife from her hand. She swung, but it vanished. She spun, looking for it. Suddenly he was back in front of her. Before she had a chance to react, he plunged a blade into her right side.

Crying out, Grace looked down in stunned disbelief at the knife lodged between her ribs. All around her demi fought, engaging wildly, confusion on their faces as demons popped in and out of the room.

With a hiss, Grace clutched the knife in her blood-slicked hand and pulled it free. When the demon appeared in front of her a second time, she brought the knife down in an arch, catching it and spraying her and the wall with the demon's blood. She didn't know where she'd injured it, or how deep, but it was not enough to incapacitate it because it came at her again. This time pain shot up her thigh. The fucker bit her.

"Backs to the wall!" she yelled.

At least that way the demons couldn't reappear behind them. Christ. They couldn't fight this. Her people would be slaughtered.

The floor began to shake, then the floorboards in the kitchen exploded, giant splinters firing across the room like daggers. A scaled claw broke through.

"*Get out now! Now!*" she cried.

She stumbled but managed to right herself, starting to feel weak from blood loss. Demons were still popping in and out of view, ruthlessly attacking. She forced herself to stick to the walls so at least her back was covered.

She'd almost made it to the door when another blow came from her left, a fist to the jaw so hard she almost blacked out.

More of the floor exploded, demons and demi falling through to the Hell beast's cavern below. Demi scattered, the rest escaping through the door.

One of her people fell on the floor a few feet from her, badly wounded.

Fighting consciousness, she stumbled to him, gripped him around the waist, and hauled him up with every bit of strength she had left. Brent grabbed his other side, and the three of them all but threw themselves out the door.

"Where's Mark?" she called out.

A sob burst from Laney. "He didn't... Grace, he didn't make it."

She wanted to scream, to rage, to cry, but demons would erupt from the house at any moment and there was no way they could outrun them. All they could do was brace for the attack—

A roar ripped through the night sky, and the house literally exploded in front of them. Grace scrambled back as a beast, it's skin scaled and crimson, emerged from the wreckage. Its heads shook with force, its eyes—one in each head—wide with fury. It's fang-like yellow teeth dripped as it snapped at the knights surrounding it.

The warriors circled the beast, each holding the ends of their chains. The thick lengths were wrapped around the body, but it fought viciously against the five males struggling to hold it.

"Help them!" Grace cried.

Somehow, she made it to Chaos's side, the other demi joining in, grabbing the chains, helping to hold the beast down. The creature vibrated, its skin pulsing and glowing as a scream tore from its mouths and the chains surrounding it shattered like they were made of glass, sending them all flying across the yard.

Grace winced, waiting for the pain as she hit the ground, but Chaos had surrounded her, cradling her in his arms, cushioning her landing and holding her close.

His head shot up as soon as they stopped rolling, his eyes scanning the area. "Fuck. It's gone."

Some of the demons they'd been fighting stood motionless, that vacant look back in their eyes, and the rest ran, escaping into the night.

"What the hell is going on?" Laney said beside her, backing up several steps.

"It's like the warehouse a few months back, like the abandoned shop. They're just standing there like zombies," Lazarus said, voice low and rough.

"They were forced to fight, unlike the ones who ran," Chaos said in a low, terrifying voice that made her shiver. "Finish them. Most of them are already fucking half dead."

Grace clutched her side and felt the blood oozing through her fingers. "We need to find Mark. I'm not leaving him here."

Chaos gripped her shoulder, looking down at her. "Mark?"

Black spots danced across her vision. She'd lost too much blood.

Lifting one of her blood-slicked hands, she gripped the side of his throat, needing him to listen, and groaned as another gush of warmth pushed past the fingers of the hand still clutching her side. "My people, my dead, wounded…"

"Grace, you're hurt."

She grinned. "I'll live." If she got to a hospital in the next fifteen minutes, anyway.

He cursed low and long and leaned back carefully, scanning her body. "Jesus."

"Please, I need to get my wounded to a hospital," she forced out.

The sound of his voice was muffled, and she knew he'd turned to bark orders at someone. "Cars are on the way," he said when he turned back.

They'd be okay, they had to be. Chaos would make sure of it.

Then her thoughts scattered as the black spots invaded her vision and her legs turned limp. Fucking typical, she'd gone all this time with barely a scratch and now both times she'd been badly injured, it was in front of him. He'd think she was weak, and that pissed her the hell off. She didn't want him to think she was weak.

Semiconscious, she was aware of someone moving in, one of her people, trying to take her from Chaos.

Her knight growled, the viciousness of it lifting goose bumps over her skin. "Don't touch her," Chaos said, his voice all demon.

Her knight? Where had that come from?

But she was glad he didn't hand her over—she wanted to stay where she was, with him.

Grace tried to open her eyes again. *Nope.* Not happening. Damn, she hurt, so much. She wanted to get closer to Chaos, needing him. His warmth, his scent, his comfort.

"Let me take her to the hospital," someone said urgently, and attempted to take her from Chaos again.

"Put your fucking hands on her *one more time* and you'll lose them." No mistaking who'd said that.

Chaos started barking orders. He was looking after her people. They were safe now.

She relaxed into him, felt his arms get tighter around her, possessive, sure.

Then her belly plummeted and wind whipped through her hair. They were flying.

"I'm tired," she said against Chaos's chest, the rapid beat of his heart somehow soothing.

"Stay with me, Grace. You fucking stay with me. You hear me?"

She was cold and tired. She pressed closer, to take more of his warmth, but her limbs wouldn't work anymore. Her arms slipped from around his neck.

He cursed several times, and shook her lightly. "Grace!"

Then everything went black.

CHAPTER 16

CHAOS LANDED on the control room balcony with Grace limp in his arms. Her skin was cold and clammy, her breathing weak.

He didn't need to take her pulse to know her heart rate had slowed. He could *feel* her slipping away. She was dying, her life's blood running right out of her body. He'd kept pressure on the wound at her side, but it didn't matter, she'd already lost too much blood.

Fear like he'd never experienced slammed down on him. Shoving open the steel doors, he strode in.

"Where's Jack?" he said when Eve came rushing forward.

"Your quarters. Do you need help?"

"I've got her."

Eve let him rush past, not pushing. Good thing because he was walking on a razor's edge and the last thing he wanted to do was bark at the female when she was only trying to help.

Jack was a doctor, a demi who worked at a human hospital and was called in to treat his people when "unexplainable injuries" occurred, like demon attacks or powers gone haywire. Chaos had asked Gunner to call him before he'd taken flight.

There were demi all over the city in important and high-powered positions, and there were also a good number in the health sector. Grace's were on their way to a human hospital since demi had the same internal makeup as humans. But Grace needed the best. And that was Jack. Plus, a hospital could mean leaving her side, leaving her unprotected while they worked on her, and right now he physically couldn't do that, not without losing his mind completely.

Her breathing turned shallow and labored, and his panic rose. He took the elevator and when it opened on his floor, jogged the remaining distance, clutching her to him tightly, trying not to jostle her.

He burst through the door and Jack was waiting, his living room set up like a makeshift ER. Jack had the ability to see inside a patient, like a living, breathing X-ray machine, and he could speed up the healing process. He motioned for Chaos to place her on the gurney he had by the couch.

Reluctantly, Chaos laid her down.

Jack lifted each of her eyelids, flashing a light over each one. "Name?"

"Grace."

"Hi there, Grace, I'm Dr. Jack Connors. I'm going to take a look at you, okay?" She didn't move, gave no indication that she'd heard a word he'd said. Jack glanced up at Chaos. "She's your mate?"

He swallowed hard. Just hearing the other male say the words set off his possessive and protective instincts as well as calling his demon to the surface. "Yes." His voice sounded like a wounded animal. "But we haven't...finalized things yet."

Yet.

Suddenly the idea of not making her his was intolerable. Unacceptable. *Grace was his.*

The doc gave him a brisk nod. "I'll let you cut off her clothes, then. I need to see what I'm dealing with."

The guy was no idiot. The barely controlled flood of emotion swimming though Chaos's head and pumping through his veins was no doubt written all over his face. *Touch her and die.*

Pulling his blade free, he cut through her shirt first. "Fuck."

The cut to her side was narrow but deep and still oozed blood. While he worked on cutting off her leather pants—the second time he'd done it since he'd met her—the doc started doing his thing.

Placing his hand over the wound, Jack closed his eyes and went completely still. After several minutes, he turned to Chaos. "She's lucky, the knife missed her major organs."

Thank fuck.

Her leather pants fell away, and his gaze slid over her, taking in every inch of her pale skin. Her beautiful, strong body was covered in faint scars. Battle scars. His mate was a warrior. A tough, ruthless, intelligent, smart-mouthed warrior. Pride filled him even as the sight of those scars twisted fear in his gut.

How the hell had she survived this long? Grace seemed to have a death wish, threw herself into every fight like it was her last. Like she didn't care if it was.

That thought did nothing to calm the hurricane of emotions inside him.

The near-fatal scratches she'd received on her thigh not long ago were still healing, and now her other thigh didn't look much better. Teeth marks decorated it, and although it had stopped bleeding, the surrounding skin was severely bruised. He lightly brushed his thumb over the abused flesh.

Jack walked into the room carrying a chair. Chaos hadn't even noticed him leave.

"Sit down and rest your arm on the bed," Jack said calmly. "She needs your blood."

Her skin had turned gray and her lips were going blue. "But my blood, it won't match..."

"She's your mate, even if you haven't finalized things. I have to assume your blood will work on Grace, like Kryos's does on Meredith. There's no time to find anyone else. It's the best chance she has right now."

Chaos didn't need any more convincing, he sat down and offered up his veins. With quick efficiency, Jack fed a line into the artery on the inside of his wrist, then into one of Grace's veins. Chaos sat as still as he could as Jack went around to the other side of the gurney and placed his hand over the stab wound in her side. He closed his eyes again, using his powers to give her natural healing abilities a kick start.

Her color improved almost instantly.

"That's an impressive power." It wasn't the first time Chaos had witnessed what the male could do, but it always amazed him. Knights had the power to heal quickly on their own. They stitched each other up if shit was bad enough. But they called Jack in when the demi in their care needed him.

Jack shook his head. "That's not me; that's your blood. And with your quick regeneration abilities you should be able to give her a pretty good amount before you feel the effects."

"She can have as much as she needs." She could have it all, every last drop.

Jack's mouth kicked up in the corner. "I don't want you passing out. If you start to feel light-headed, tell me."

After Jack had stitched her up and dressed her wounds, he removed the transfusion tube and packed up his equipment. "You can move her to your room, she'll be more comfortable in her own bed."

Jack's assumption was a natural one, and for some unknown reason, Chaos didn't correct him.

Grabbing one of his jackets off the back of the couch, he covered her near nakedness. Now that the doc had finished patching her up, he didn't like the idea of another male looking at her like that. "What happens now?" Chaos asked.

"It's a waiting game, I'm afraid. She'll make a full recovery, but her body took a beating. Despite the transfusion, the blood loss will have taken its toll." Jack's gaze met his. "You need to prepare for..."

"What? Christ, what aren't you telling me?" Chaos barked.

Jack gave him an exasperated look. "...some side effects," he finished.

Chaos's heart kicked against the back of his ribs. "Like?"

"With the amount of your blood we had to give her, and because your blood's so potent, her body will take a few days to process it properly. She might be aggressive, irritable, or become highly..." He cleared his throat. "...er, amorous."

Chaos's spine went ramrod straight. Yeah, that got his attention. "You're telling me when Grace wakes up she'll be pissed off and horny?"

The doc actually blushed. "That's exactly what I'm telling you."

His dick stirred, filled. He really was an asshole, getting a hard-on while Grace lay unconscious in his living room. But shit, he wasn't made of stone, despite what everybody else thought. "Right, I'll watch for that." He ran a hand over his head. "And is it advisable to *treat* her, ah...symptoms?" Jesus, he never thought in a million years he'd be having this conversation.

Jack grinned. "Well, that's up to you and your mate. But I'm guessing it would definitely help with the irritability. If you do, you'll have to be careful. I don't want her stitches torn. I'll be back in a week to take some blood. I'd like to make sure it's integrated into her system like I expect it to."

Jack left, and Chaos carefully scooped Grace into his arms and carried her to his bedroom. He laid her on his bed and pulled the covers over her. Again, she didn't stir, and he found himself leaning down and placing his ear to her lips, listening to her even breaths, feeling its warmth against his skin.

She'd scared the living crap out of him. He could honestly say that on the flight to the compound, when she'd gone limp in his arms, he'd never been more afraid in all his life.

He pulled up a chair and took her hand in his. Her skin had warmed and was no longer clammy.

Brushing her long, blond hair away from her face, he studied her still features. So beautiful. And she was tough as shit. He couldn't have asked for a better mate if he'd dreamed her up himself. Why had he ever thought resisting this was a good idea?

Still, with or without her, the coming war had to be his first priority, he knew that. Yes, she was a distraction when he was with her, but she was more of one when they were apart. He'd discovered that the hard way.

What if you lose her like Tobias lost Scarlet, like Rocco lost Kyler?

Could he afford to risk it? With so much at stake? Any day now, Rocco's female could gain her power and open the gates of Hell. And the way Grace risked her life every damn night—could he allow himself to get attached to her?

He stared down at her so still and fragile. She'd hate this. Hate feeling weak.

Who are you kidding? You're already attached.

～

A warm hand to the back of his head woke him. The finger-nails lightly grazing his scalp sent pleasurable tingles all over his body. He lifted his head from the mattress. Grace was awake.

Thank fuck.

She looked up at him, her beautiful brown eyes were filled with worry, and anger.

"Laney, James, the others, are they okay?" Her voice was croaky.

He took her hand because he couldn't help himself and passed her the glass of water by the bed. "Your injured are in the hospital. I called James, you had only one fatality. The rest are going to be fine."

Somehow James had kept his involvement with Grace and her crew a secret from him and his brothers. It stung that he didn't feel he could share that with Chaos, they were family, but fuck, he understood it as well. Up until a short time ago, Chaos would have lost his shit if he'd know James was fighting with Grace.

Now he just respected the male even more.

She took a sip of her drink and passed it back. Her hands balled into fists. "One fatality is one too many." A tear rolled down one cheek. "I can't believe Mark is gone."

Oh fuck, she was crying.

Seeing that tore at his chest. He reached for her.

He reached for this mate.

CHAPTER 17

GRACE SCOOTED BACK, away from Chaos's outstretched arms.

"Grace..."

She held up a hand to ward off whatever he'd been about to say. "Don't. I'm fine." It was a complete lie. Pain and rage wrapped around her, growing with every breath she took until she could feel nothing else. She didn't want to feel anything else.

So many demi had died at the hands of demons, suffered even now as slaves to their kind, kept as play things. No, this wasn't new, losing her kind to those evil fuckers. But losing Tina and Mark, it was just...it was too much.

"Is his body still at that house? He deserves a proper burial." She bit her lips to stop an angry sob from breaking free. "I just...I can't believe he's gone, that I'll never see him again, never talk to him." She glanced up. "He was a good man. It shouldn't have ended like that, not for him."

Chaos's thick forearms rested on his thighs, and his dark gaze locked on hers, like he was assessing her mood, her mental state. "You're pretty cut up about this guy. You two were close?"

She made a strangled sound, fighting back her bellow of rage. "Jesus fucking Christ, Chaos. What the hell is wrong with you? Cut up? Of course, I'm cut up. We've been fighting together from the very beginning. He's family."

Tension flowed from him and washed over her. "Were you lovers?" he asked.

"Are you actually jealous of a dead man?"

His jaw tightened.

She'd always believed she was in this on her own, that she could never truly trust anyone. She finally understood, and now it was too late to tell Mark, to tell Tina how much she cared about them. How important they were to her.

"Apologies," he said quickly, before she could form a reply. "I have no control over the possessiveness. It was shitty of me to ask." His voice was tight with regret.

"Yes, it was."

He shifted in his seat. "I know that pain, and it fucking sucks. Use it, let it fuel your rage on the battlefield, but don't let it eat away at you. Mark knew the risks, Grace. Every soldier does. You go to war, there's always a chance you won't come back. He knew that, and he chose to fight anyway."

He was right, deep down Grace knew it, but that truth didn't make it hurt any less. "Can I have my phone? I want to call the hospital and check on my friends."

"They're fine, you're not. You need to rest."

Her body throbbed and ached, but it was only then that she fully took stock. Her injuries had been treated and she was only wearing a pair of panties. There was a dressing on her ribs, and if she moved quickly, pain shot through her side. There was also a deep, constant throb coming from her thigh where the demon had bitten her, and a Band-Aid on the inside of her elbow.

She glanced at Chaos. He looked exhausted, lines etching

his handsome face. "Who treated me? The last thing I remember is flying." *And how good it felt to have your arms wrapped around me.*

"I had someone come to the compound and treat you. You'd lost a lot of blood, passed out on the way here. I was so..." He cleared his throat and rubbed his hands against the denim covering his massive thighs. "The doctor gave you a blood transfusion. He's a demi and used his power to kick-start your body's natural healing."

"A blood transfusion? From who?"

He pointed to a Band-Aid matching her own on the inside of his wrist.

He'd done that for her? He'd taken care of her people, had rushed her to safety and given her his blood. He'd saved her life. Probably the lives of some of her crew, as well. The more time she spent with him, the more she realized he wasn't the man she'd believed him to be.

"You've been with me the whole time, haven't you?"

He shifted again, like the question made him uncomfortable, and when he avoided it all together, she knew it did. "Thank you, Chaos. For taking care of me. For taking care of my friends."

He shrugged like it was nothing.

But it wasn't nothing. It was huge. And a bone-deep weariness, a kind of disappointment she didn't understand creeped in.

Because she'd learned repeatedly through her life that nothing came for free. Not even when it came to the people who were closest to her. "I'll repay you, somehow. I promise."

His body stilled in an unnatural way. "What?" His voice held an edge she hadn't heard from him in a while.

Suddenly, she couldn't meet his eyes. "You saved my life. I owe you. I won't forget it."

"You *owe* me?" More with the scary voice.

She forced herself to look at him and nodded. "Of course, I do."

He stood abruptly, hands on hips, and studied the ground for several long seconds. When he looked up again, she knew she'd fucked up.

"You don't *owe me* a damn thing. You don't need to... Jesus, Grace." He shook his head, the muscles in his jaw tightening, then took several steadying breaths. "You hungry?"

Okay, it seemed they were changing the subject. Fine with her. "I could eat."

"Don't move." Then he walked out the door.

She looked around his room, all neat and orderly. No wonder the guy kept his head clean shaven, a hair out of place might send him over the deep end. Not that it wasn't hot, because it was. She squirmed. *Shit. Stop thinking about his hotness.*

She sat there, restless, not sure what to do with herself. When he returned, she couldn't stop her gaze from roaming over him as he walked toward her. All tall and hard-bodied, and grumpy, like he wanted to spank her again. *Stop it!*

Chaos passed her a plate. He'd made her a sandwich. She lifted the top to check out what was in it.

"Sorry, can't cook worth shit." A blush darkened his cheeks.

Her mouth went dry, and she found she wanted to put him at ease. "Neither can I. Good thing I love PB and J." She smiled, but knew she failed.

The grief and anger inside her wasn't going anywhere, and now, thanks to the sexy bastard taking care of her, she was also hot under the collar. So messed up. Two of her friends were gone, and her traitorous hormones were prodding her to jump Chaos.

He frowned. "With all the fighting and training you do, you really should be eating a high-calorie, high-protein diet."

She swallowed the bite she'd taken and rolled her eyes. "I do eat other stuff as well."

He dipped his head, clearly pleased with her answer.

"You up to telling me what happened in there tonight?" Chaos asked, looking as if he was unsure whether or not to ask the question.

The food turned sour in her mouth. But if there was some small detail she'd picked up in that house that would help track down whoever was controlling the demons in Roxburgh, she'd go over every horrific detail until she was blue in the face.

She gave him a blow-by-blow of everything that happened after he'd given the signal to go in. "I've never seen anything like it. They kept vanishing, then reappearing. I can't believe the rest of the team walked out alive." She yawned, there was no stopping it, and he took her plate from her.

"Lie down and get some rest."

"Christ, you're bossy."

He grinned.

"Fine." She slammed her eyes closed, locking out that gorgeous smile before she gave into her hormones and pounced.

Grace woke with a scream. Images of monsters, of beasts flying through the portal, of demons slaughtering her people, had invaded her mind.

Drenched with sweat and heart racing, she struggled to breathe. They could lose. Hell could win.

Sitting up with a groan, she glanced around the room. Chaos's room. She was alone. It was dark and silent. A stab of disappointment took her by surprise.

She glanced at the chair he'd been sitting in earlier. It was closer to the bed, like he'd been watching her sleep. To someone on the outside looking in, they'd think it was because he had feelings for her.

He didn't, not really. It was the bond between them, nothing else. And that was okay. She didn't need him to care about her. She didn't want him to. Because dream Grace had come to a realization that awake Grace should have figured out for herself by now—especially after what they'd been through in that house of horrors. The demons sure as hell weren't playing fair, they'd do anything to win, and after losing another one of her people, one of her friends, she knew she had to be just as ruthless.

She didn't have a choice in this.

There never had been one.

What she wanted, what Chaos wanted, wasn't important. Winning this war was the only thing that mattered. She always believed she'd do anything to win, but when faced with the truth of who she was to Chaos, who he was to her, she'd fought against it. Denied it. Hidden it.

It was selfish and cowardly.

She was done fighting fate.

Pain twisted in her belly. Maybe if she'd given in to it sooner, Mark and Tina would still be here.

She knew what she had to do, but she wasn't going to do it while lying in his bed looking weak and pathetic. It was far too important... She needed to be on an even footing with him. It was the only way.

Pulling back the covers, she gingerly slid her feet out of the bed and stood. Not too bad. At least not as bad as she'd expected to feel right then. She made her way to the bathroom. It was fairly big, all white and black tiles and shiny chrome. She remembered being in the tub with Chaos the last time she was there, his massive body cradling hers, and shivered, her entire body clenching as pleasurable tingles danced across her exposed skin.

There was a stack of fluffy gray towels by the sink and shampoo and body wash in the huge shower.

She turned the water on and climbed in, careful not to get her stitches too wet.

The shower had excellent pressure and felt so good, the heat working to ease her aches and pains. So good.

She clicked open the body wash and sniffed. It smelled like Chaos. She'd gotten up close and personal with him enough times to know how his skin smelled. A low, deep ache started between her thighs.

Her body heated, and her breasts grew tight and achy. How the hell could she be horny at a time like this? Then again, when Chaos was around, she was always in a constant state of arousal.

Something that wouldn't go away if they didn't mate, right? Another reason to give in and stop fighting. Being turned on almost constantly was too much of a distraction. At least they could scratch that itch and get on with their lives.

She realized she still held his body wash pressed to her nose. How pathetic could she get?

One sniff and she was ready to start dry humping the first thing she could get between her legs. What the hell was wrong with her?

She ran her hands down her warm, wet, slippery skin, and shivered. The ache deep inside increased, and her nipples actually hurt they were so tight.

She was so desperate to get off, she shook, her skin heating and prickling, her breath coming harder, faster. Widening her stance, she slipped her fingers along her slit, and a moan broke past her lips.

Oh yeah, that felt good.

Even better when she brushed over her clit. Maybe she could get herself off quickly, take the edge off before Chaos got back, before they talked.

Leaning against the wall for support, she closed her eyes and started circling her clit, brushing over it, and when that wasn't enough, rubbing it in earnest. But after a few minutes, she bit back a desperate curse. It wasn't working. She was so desperate for release she whimpered, tears of frustration prickling the backs of her eyelids.

The water turned off suddenly.

Grace's eyes flew open. Chaos stood there, gaze burning with hunger. He held up a towel. "Step out, Grace."

Heat slashed her cheeks. "Don't you know how to knock?"

"I heard a moan and thought you might need help." His hungry gaze traveled over her naked body. "I was right."

CHAPTER 18

GRACE'S GAZE was heavy with lust as she looked at him. Her skin flushed pink, a result of the hot water and her turned-on state, and shit, it suited the hell out of her.

She didn't try to cover herself, and Chaos took advantage to the fullest, his gaze moving over every gorgeous inch. Sleek and strong. Pert, round ass; narrow hips; those perfect-handful tits, nipples tight and pointed. His mouth watered, desperate to taste every inch of her beautiful body.

"Step out, Grace." For once, she didn't argue. She stepped into the towel he held, and he rubbed it over her skin carefully, making sure to avoid her injuries.

"What do you think you're doing?" She sounded a little bewildered, but mostly needy as hell.

Always so sure and confident, it was good to see her a little off balance for once. Because that's how she affected him, and he couldn't help but push her a little more.

He pressed his lips to her ear. "I know how much you need release. *Jesus fucking Christ*, the scent of you, it's the sweetest, most intoxicating thing I've ever breathed. You

SHERILEE GRAY

have no idea what it does to me." She trembled. "And I intend to get you there."

She shivered as he pulled her long hair back and squeezed out the moisture, then turned her to face him, her little panted breaths rushing past her full lips, fire lighting her eyes. "That's presumptuous."

"You want it."

She blinked up at him, then her jaw tightened. "You're so fucking arrogant."

"The males you've had in your bed…" He bit back a hiss, the very idea of anyone else touching her made him want to douse his brain in bleach. "None of them could ever do for you what I can. No one will ever make you as wet, or come as hard."

Her chin lifted, her eyes flashing. "Really? You talk the talk, but I doubt—"

"We were made for each other, Grace. No one else can ever compete with that."

She stilled, trembling under his hands. Finally, she licked her lips. "Chaos…"

"You will always be bound to me, we'll be bound to each other, whether you want it that way or not. It's just the way it is." He didn't know what it meant for either of them, but just saying the words, expressing the way he'd been feeling, brought a sense of calm he hadn't felt since he had set eyes on her.

"What if I say yes?" she said, voice strong but shaky.

Now it was Chaos's turn to still. "What?"

She lifted her chin. "What if I agree to mate with you?"

His heart raced. "You truly want that?"

Determination shone in her mahogany gaze. "I want to win this war. I want the power mating will give us. Eve's power has grown. Chaya told me Mia's has as well, maybe it'll be the same for me."

"What are you actually asking for?" His voice sounded rough as hell, and he stood frozen as he waited for her response.

"We mate, then carry on living our own lives. There's no affection between us—this is not some love match. I won't be tied down. I can't give you that. It's not who I am. I don't need someone to protect me, and I won't stop fighting. I won't leave Vince or the demi who trust and believe in me, either. But I will give you this, this part of me, to make you stronger, to make me stronger, so we can have a better shot at winning this war."

Why did her words feel like a knife to the sternum?

She was right, of course. It made perfect sense. Increased power and an outlet for all the hunger they stirred in each other, without all the confusing emotional garbage. They were programmed to want this, to need it. She held no affection for him, and didn't want it from him in return.

But if she thought she could just walk away after they mated, he needed to clue her in. "We're going to fuck, Grace, but you need to know, it won't just be today. That's not how this works. I'm hardwired to want you, and that will never change. Do you understand?"

She nodded. "That's fine, as long as you understand why I'm doing this, that it will never be more than that."

"Yes," he said, even though that single word felt torn from him.

She grazed her nails down his back, and he shuddered. She liked that, seeing his tiny loss of control. He could see it in her eyes, the way they flashed slightly.

He leaned in, nipped her bottom lip. "I promise you, I won't ask you for more..." He held her gaze. "I'll never ask for more than this." He ground his erection against her tender flesh, and she gasped. Unable to stop himself, he leaned in and gently bit down on the tendon straining beneath the skin

177

at the base of her neck, sucking hard enough to leave a mark, then trailed his lips along her jaw to her ear. "And FYI, when we fuck, I'm in control. That's the way I like it, and so will you."

"Is that right?"

"Yes."

"So. Damn. *Arrogant.*"

Despite her protest, the way she trembled told him she wanted it, wanted to hand over that control to him. "You like that, too."

She growled under her breath, and he chuckled.

"You're still asking for a lot," she finally said.

"I know, but that's how it has to be." He cupped her breast and squeezed lightly.

Her breath grew heavy. "What do you actually want from me? Before we go any further, I need you to spell it out as well."

What was he saying? He barely understood it himself. So he told her the truth. "I'm not sure, but I do know I'll need more—more of your time, more of your attention." He cupped her between the thighs. "And more of this hot, tight pussy."

She moaned and her head fell back. "I'm...*ahhh.*"

"You still want me inside you?"

"Yes, I...I can't think. I'm so hot, I need..."

"I know what you need, and I'll make you come as many times as you can take." He lifted her in his arms carefully and carried her into the bedroom, his head spinning from what she'd just told him, what she'd agreed to.

Grace rubbed against him, lost to her need, undulating in his arms...then let out a small cry of pain.

He smoothed her hair back from her beautiful face. "*Shhh,* I'll take care of you, but you have to be still or you'll hurt yourself."

"What's wrong with me? *Ahh*." She squeezed her thighs together, legs scissoring restlessly.

"It's my blood, it's strong and you needed a lot. The doc said this could be a side effect."

She groaned. "How long?"

"A day or two." He placed her on the bed carefully, and she reached for the front of his jeans, tugging open the button. He pulled back out of reach. In his current state, if he took her, he'd hurt her and he'd rather cut off his own arms than do that.

"Please," she whimpered and spread her legs. "Fuck me, Chaos. I need you. Make the ache go away."

Jesus. Fucking. Christ. She was bare and swollen and so damn wet.

His dick was a steel rod in his pants, so hard he could barely walk, and Grace lay sprawled on his bed, open and begging for his cock. His restraint was as close to snapping as it ever had been. "I'll make it better," he choked.

Her hands went to her swollen breasts and she squeezed, groaning. "Hurry, please."

Yanking his shirt over his head, he crawled up between her thighs and drew his tongue through her cleft. Her hips lifted off the bed and she cried out, a combination of pleasure and pain.

"Shit." He needed her to be still, or she could tear her stitches. Using his shoulders, he spread her wide and took her narrow hips in his hands, pinning her down, then pressed his mouth to her slick pussy again.

As soon as he tasted her, his mind went blank, fucking short-circuited. Grace was the only thing that existed. Hunger, fierce and wild, washed through him and he gave in to it. He licked, sucked, and kissed her tender flesh, but still he couldn't get enough.

Fuck, she was hot and wet, tasted so damn good, that

scent driving him wild. If he didn't rein in his shit, he'd come in his pants just from having his mouth on her.

It took less than a minute and she was screaming and convulsing against his mouth. He didn't stop, though, no, he continued to eat her perfect pussy until she came a second time. When the tension in her thighs eased, he lifted his head. "Better?" His demon was right there in his voice with him.

But she rolled her hips again, and a groan of frustration escaped her throat. "More. I need you inside me."

Inside her was where he wanted to be as well. He'd wanted it for so long that he dreamed of it every night, fantasized about it most of every day, but he was terrified he'd hurt her.

He wanted to take her hard and fast, fuck them both into oblivion, and it would take all his self-control to go slow and easy. The female lying on his bed, begging for him to ease her pain, to bring her pleasure, was *his*, and he realized in that moment, he would always find a way to give her what she wanted.

He slid down the zipper on his jeans and shucked them off. His dick jutted from his body, leaking from the tip. Grace thrashed on the bed, moaning every time she squeezed her thighs together.

"Roll on your side, angel." She did as he said and he moved in behind her. "That's it. Now lift your leg over mine." Her skin was on fire. Wrapping one arm across her chest and the other over her hips, he pinned her body against his so she couldn't move.

"Ready?" he muttered against her ear.

She stiffened. "No, hold on." She reached back and undid the chain around her neck that she always wore and placed it on the bedside table.

He stilled as well. "What is…"

"Nothing."

It wasn't nothing. "Grace…"

"Goddamn it, just fuck me." Then she stiffened again, just a little.

He should push, find out what was bothering her, but he wanted her so bad he could barely think straight. It was nerves, that's all. He got it. "Relax, Grace, we're fucking, not mating, not yet. Not when you're injured."

She nodded and held her breath, pressing back as he tilted his hips, positioned the fat swollen head of his cock to her slick-as-fuck opening, and finally…fucking *finally*, slid deep inside her. He pulled out and thrust back in instantly.

He groaned and Grace cried out as she reached back, one of her hands going to his hip, nails digging in, trying to hold him to her, to make him move harder, faster, but he kept the pace nice and slow.

She pushed her ass back. "More…I need more."

"Trust me," he said against her ear. "Let me take care of you. Let me show you that I know exactly what you need."

She went still in his arms, then after several painstaking moments, stopped fighting him. Fuck, that pleased him. He released a shuddering breath. With the way she shook in his arms, he knew it wasn't easy for her to give up control. But she did anyway, giving herself over to him, trusting him. He was determined to show her that she could. With her body, with all that she was.

Every muscle in his body had gone rock solid, and sweat beaded his skin as he restrained himself, ignoring his natural instincts to pound into her. He kept that slow and easy pace, making them both insane. His balls were tight, and sparks of pleasure shot down his spine and lower belly, along his shaft to the head of his cock. He gritted his teeth and slid a hand between her slick folds, circling her stiff little clit.

Oh fuck. He saw it then, the delicate thread, the connection that proved what they both already knew, that she was his mate. "Fuck, I see it. I can see it."

He fought to ignore it, how bright and strong it was, how easy it would be to reach out and grab hold, to make her his mate, but he resisted. He didn't know what would happen when he finally did, but he knew from what his brothers told him, his control would be shot to shit.

He would not hurt her. Could not.

Her body was strong and tight, and slick with sweat, and as they slid against each other, every damn nerve ending fired to life, heightening each touch, each movement.

Then her inner muscles grasped at his dick, squeezing hard, knocking the wind from him. She cried out, "Do it."

"I don't want to hurt you."

"Goddammit, Chaos, I can take it. Make me your mate. Do it now."

"Fuck," he snarled, already zeroing in on the gossamer thread in his mind's eye. "You sure?"

"Yes," she panted. "*Do it.*"

He couldn't resist any longer, and grabbed hold of that delicate thread and let it take him, both of them over the edge. Chaos roared as pleasure engulfed him like nothing he'd ever experienced, a feeling that could only be described as euphoria pushing through his veins until he was full to overflowing.

His vision went dark and his ears rang. He thrust into Grace, his mate, harder and faster, lost to her completely.

Grace flew apart in his arms, screaming, nails digging in to his hip, holding him tighter. Her pussy milked him, made him come harder than he had in his entire life. He planted his cock deep inside her, filled her, ground against her perfect ass, until they were both trembling.

It was a long time before they could talk, before the last tremor moved through her, before she stopped gripping him and setting off zings of pleasure through his entire body.

Finally, she relaxed back against him and chuckled breathlessly. "Holy shit."

Holy shit didn't even come close. "I didn't hurt you?"

She shook her head. "You were gentle." She was quiet a beat. "I'm healing fast, thanks to you."

Silence filled the room, heavy and thick. They were mates, were bound for life, and neither of them had any idea what to say or do.

"Was it…is that how you expected it to feel?" she whispered.

He cleared his throat. "Better."

"What happens now?" she said just as softly.

"I don't know." Why was there this weight on his chest all of a sudden? Why did he feel unsatisfied? *Because my mate is probably already thinking of an excuse to leave my bed.*

He should probably get out, give her some space, but he couldn't bring himself to do it. He needed to be right where he was, with his female. *Shit.* "I finally got a taste of you, got to slide deep inside you. Fuck, I came so hard I couldn't see straight. My vote would be fuck some more," he said, trying to keep things light.

It was unconscious he was sure, but her hand had slipped over his, and she was playing with his fingers. It was such a simple action, but he felt it in the center of his chest. His inner demon fucking rolled to his back in ecstasy as desperate for her touch as Chaos was.

Grace stilled. "Are you…is that…what is that sound?"

"My demon likes you. It's the demon version of purring."

"How often does it…do that?"

"This is the third time, I believe, and each time was when we were with you. He's never been this calm, this content, in my whole life."

"Will he stay like that now? Calm?"

"Let's just say we now have more of an understanding."

"What was it like before?"

He'd never spoken out loud about how it felt, and he had to clear his throat before he could talk. "Like a never-ending battle...and darkness, so much of it, always trying to suck me under."

She curled her small, delicate fingers around his much larger hand and squeezed, comforting him, telling him without words that she was glad it was finally over.

The quiet stretched out again, and he ran his hand up and down her side, pressed his nose to her hair and breathed her in. He wanted to hold her so tight that she could never leave his side.

He realized in that moment that fighting his demon had been nothing compared to fighting his instincts where his female was concerned. He'd royally fucked himself.

"So, uh...I was kind of demanding before," she said, breaking the silence.

He wished he could see her face, wondered if she was blushing. She didn't do it often, but he heard something in her voice that made him think she was. "I like you demanding." He nuzzled the back of her neck, drawing in her scent again. "It turns me on."

"From what I can tell, you only have two emotions: pissed off or horny. I'm hoping, if I'm really lucky, I'll eventually get them both at the same time."

There was humor in her voice, but for some reason he didn't like that she thought that about him, that she thought he was cold, some kind of unfeeling machine.

He must have given something away because Grace tightened her fingers around his. "I was joking, you know. I know there's more to you than that."

Did she? He desperately wanted to believe that. He

glanced at the bedside table, the chain she wore still lying there. "The rings, why do you wear them?"

Silence. "That's not something I want to share."

The *with you* went unsaid, but he heard it loud and clear.

It was ridiculous to expect her to suddenly share everything...hell, anything with him, especially with their history, but he still hated that she wouldn't. "I should go, let you get some rest." He forced himself to say it, even though it was the complete opposite of what he wanted.

"Oh no, you don't. I haven't finished with you." She rubbed her soft ass against his already achingly hard cock. "I need you to fuck me again, but harder this time."

Relief washed through him. "Are you purposely being demanding again?"

She laughed, a light, raspy sound that was sexy as hell. "It turns you on, doesn't it?"

"Yes, but everything my mate does turns me on." He thrust into her again.

In seconds, he was totally absorbed in the feel of her wrapped tightly around him, the sounds she made, her intoxicating scent, and the words slipped past his lips of their own volition. "Stay here. Move in with me."

She stilled. "What?"

"For now, at least." Until he got her out of his system. He ground into her deeper this time and nipped her ear. "Well?"

"Mmm-hmm."

That was good enough for him.

CHAPTER 19

GRACE CRACKED her lids and groaned when she realized where she was.

The windows of the compound were boarded up, but she knew it was past morning.

Shit.

It was probably cowardly, but she wanted to get out of there before Chaos woke. It was for the best, really, she needed to assert her independence in this fucked-up *relationship* from the start.

She needed to make it clear that she did what she wanted when she wanted, mated or not. She'd seen how possessive his mated brothers were, and that wouldn't fly with her.

But man, Chaos was *right there*, hot and hard, pressed up against her, holding her to him like he knew she planned to escape. She hadn't meant to fall asleep, but neither one of them had been in their right minds last night, and getting enough of each other had been an impossibility.

Her skin heated all over again.

And then he'd told her about his inner demon, that

mating with her had calmed it. His admission had reached into her chest and squeezed her stony heart.

She couldn't imagine what that had been like for him, how finally having control of that part of himself would feel. He'd been fighting his entire life, not just against the demons in this city, but against the one inside him.

The male already had her twisted in knots, had her second-guessing too much about her own life. Learning more about him would just complicate things.

Her feelings for Chaos had turned from hating his guts to grudging respect, and she was still trying to get her head around that. They'd mated, were working together, but that didn't mean she was suddenly his biggest fan. The guy was arrogant, he pissed her off more than not—he also hit every one of her hot buttons.

The husky, filthy commands he'd whispered to her last night filtered through her mind and she shivered. Okay, almost every word pissed her off, the rest turned her the hell on.

So. Damn. Messy.

But one of the main reasons she needed to get out of there ASAP, was she wanted him again. Even with how sore her body was from her injuries, and after all the screwing they'd done, she wanted more. Her cheeks heated. God, she'd begged him to fuck her, repeatedly, and she knew he'd never let her forget it.

She wriggled, but the big bastard surrounded her, one massive arm slung around her waist, its dead weight pinning her to the bed in a way that, alarmingly, was not unpleasant. He smelled fantastic, too. Panic over her wayward thoughts, accompanied by an overwhelming urge to snuggle closer, almost had her lashing out and shoving him away. She did not freaking snuggle.

I need to get the hell out of here.

He made a grunting sound and rolled forward a little. All that smooth bare skin, pressing heavier against her back, radiating masses of bone-melting heat, the kind she wanted to rub up against.

Get out of the bed. Now.

Grace attempted to lift his arm, but he grunted again and dragged her closer. Wincing when her stitches pulled, she squirmed around onto her belly and, ass in the air, crawled backward, wriggling out from under his arm.

Free.

Finally.

Unfortunately, she made the mistake of looking back at him. He was sprawled on his stomach now, the sheet so low she couldn't help but admire the top of his very fine, muscled ass. Disturbingly, it was taking way more effort than it should to resist crawling back into that bed, rolling that big, muscular body so he was on his back, and taking advantage of what she knew would be some seriously impressive morning wood.

Scowling, she turned away and went to his dresser. Since her clothes were destroyed, she riffled through his drawers. His T-shirts were all the same, black. Everything was perfectly folded and in its place. She got the feeling that was how he liked his life here at the compound, orderly, especially since all other aspects were so fucked up.

That was probably why he'd agreed to her sex-only condition before they sealed the deal. A mate would mess with his organized, regimented life, and we couldn't have that.

And that suited her just fine. She grabbed a shirt and found a pair of his workout shorts. Gray, instead of black. Amazing. More like the store had been out of black that day. The guy didn't have clothes, he had a uniform.

She quickly dressed. The shirt was a tent on her, and she

had to bunched up the extra material of the shorts at her waist and tie it with her hair tie. She finished off her stunning ensemble with her combat boots. The only piece of clothing that had survived her visit from the doc were her panties, but right then she had no idea where they were, so she was going commando.

"Where're you going?"

She straightened at the sound of Chaos's sleep-roughened voice and turned to face him. "I need to leave."

Chaos had rolled to his back, one arm bent behind his head, a hand on his abs, and was watching her. There was no missing the huge erection tenting the sheet.

He gave her a head-to-toe and smiled. "Nice outfit."

That smile did things to her, things she didn't need to be feeling, not then, not ever. "Right, well, I have to take off."

"You're still recovering. Get back in bed."

He flicked the corner of the sheet back for her, like he expected her to follow his every command without question. Which was exactly why she wasn't staying.

"I've been in bed long enough. I feel fine." Plus, if she got back in there with him, she didn't think she'd have the strength to ever get out again.

"You haven't exactly been resting." A sleepy, sexy grin tugged at his lips.

She made herself ignore it. "I'm rested."

"You're not. Get back in."

She ignored him, and put her necklace back on, grabbed her phone and wallet off the bedside table, and shoved them in one of the giant shorts pockets.

The bicep behind his head bunched, and he rubbed the other hand over his chest, lower, over the swirling scar on his ribs, his angels brand. "Stay."

She watched, mouth dry, as he dragged his hand over his rigid abs, never taking his eyes off her, and slid it under the covers. She couldn't exactly see what he was doing, but it was pretty damn obvious that he'd wrapped that big mitt around his dick and was now stroking himself, slow and easy.

She took a step back.

"Grace."

Do not give in. If she did that now, it would be a slippery slope. He'd think he was the boss of her. That he only had to click his fingers and she'd obey. Or in this case, wave his gorgeous dick and she'd jump on it.

Resisting was the right thing to do. Still it took every bit of self-control not to peel off her clothes and get back into bed with him. "No."

His gaze darkened. "Get back in bed, Grace."

She took another step back. "Not happening." She motioned to the bed and his delicious nakedness. "I know this will be hard for you to understand, but fighting and fucking isn't the only thing I do. I also have a job. You know, so I can eat."

His gaze went dark and menacing. "You don't need to earn money. Not anymore. I'll give you all the money you need, give you whatever you want."

Anger shot through her, hard and fast. "I don't want your money. What we agreed to, what we have, essentially boils down to fuck buddies. I'm not the little woman, Chaos. I don't need or want you to take care of me. I make my own money, have my own place, fight my own battles. The only difference between our relationship now and twenty-four hours ago, is that from time to time, we'll fuck. That's it."

His expression went from soft and sexy to hard and pissed off. "That's not what we agreed to."

"You promised me you wouldn't ask for more."

"And I haven't. I *offered* more." His voice was so low, he sounded more animal than man, and frankly, kind of terrifying.

"Well, I don't want it."

He flicked the sheet back all the way and climbed out of bed. Her pussy clenched. He stood in front of her, muscles straining, abs tight, all solid, barely restrained power. His hand was still on his heavy cock and he stroked it slowly, gaze fixed on her. "You want me, Grace. You want me inside you again. You can't hide it from me."

She did, and that was the problem. Her body wanted to obey him, more than willing to overlook the risks. Her body wanted to follow his harsh, low commands and didn't get why her brain was trying to convince it to behave differently.

Which was her cue to get the hell gone.

"I guess I'll be in touch." Then she turned to leave.

"Let me get dressed and I'll go with you." He moved to his drawers and yanked one open, scowling at her when he saw what a mess she'd made of his clothes.

"That won't be necessary. I'll call a cab."

He crossed his arms over his massive chest, giving her another display of flexing, rippling muscle. "I had your car brought here."

"Why?"

His body relaxed and he shrugged, a small smile playing at the corners of his lips.

Yeah, that just pissed her off more. "What the hell are you grinning about?"

"Irritability. It's another side effect of my blood."

Was he serious? "Go to Hell."

"Not a great idea."

"Why?"

"I'll die."

That sucked the wind out of her. "Right, well, I'd forgotten that."

"I hadn't."

He was still grinning like he was loving every damn minute of this. "Stop it."

"Stop what?"

Looking so damn sexy. Being all happy and weird and confusing. "Being annoying!"

He laughed, and dammit, that just made him hotter. She clenched her thighs together. "Bye."

"You had a knife buried between your ribs yesterday." He stilled and his fists clenched at his sides as a shadow moved across his eyes. "You can go, but only to pack."

Uh, what now? "Pack?"

"Once you've done whatever it is you need to do, call me and I'll help you with your shit."

She looked at him like he was high. "What are you talking about?"

The relaxed attitude flew out the window, vanishing completely with her question. He stood up straighter and his jaw did that clenching thing it did when he got super pissy.

His gaze sharpened. "You, moving in here with me for a while. That's what I'm talking about."

Her knees turned liquid. "You were serious?"

"Yes."

Her gut clenched because she knew in that moment that she'd made a mistake, a huge fucking mistake. "That was a heat-of-the-moment thing. I didn't think you were serious."

"Yeah, I'm getting that."

She crossed her arms. His stare was predatory, hard, unyielding. The same look he had in his eyes before he went into battle. "Why would you even want that?"

His heated gaze moved over her. "Isn't it obvious? Until things die down, it's only practical."

Die down. Her hackles rose. This was all about convenience for him. Having a place to plant his dick whenever the mood struck him. Nice.

"I'm not moving in here with you," she said.

He scowled again. "You agreed."

She snorted. "I didn't agree to shit."

He took a step closer and she took another one back. "I said, 'move in with me, at least for now' and you said, and I quote, 'Mmm-hmm.'"

"You had your cock inside me." Dammit, her voice sounded all husky and needy. He took another step closer, and she planted her feet, refusing to retreat another step.

"So?"

"So, I wasn't...thinking." Yeah, shit, that gave away too damn much. Her flight instincts kicked into high gear.

He ran his hand over his head roughly, obviously fighting for control. He turned from her suddenly, pacing away, then back, then away again—

She took her chance while his eyes were off her and rushed out the door. She'd made it to the elevator down the hall when Chaos came barreling out after her looking furious. He'd at least pulled on some jeans.

The elevator doors closed before he could reach her.

Grace let out a breath as she watched the numbers tick down to the garage and sighed in relief when the doors slid open and she saw her car waiting.

But her relief vanished when she stepped out.

Goddamn it. Facing the inhabitants of Hell would be preferable to the two knights currently standing beside her Toyota. Fucking perfect.

The walk of shame was bad enough, but in front of these two? She knew she looked like crap, or like someone had well and truly fucked her brains out. Which was damn close to the truth. And she wasn't ready to admit the truth to herself, let alone these two.

Gunner and Zenon both eyed her as she approached.

"So it's your car," Gunner finally said.

"Yup…" Her words died in her throat when Zenon moved closer, his long, dark hair hanging forward, eyes narrowed as he leaned in. The big, terrifying, inked-up male sucked in a breath and his eyebrows shot to his hairline. She refused to blush. Not happening. "Did you just... Are you sniffing me?"

"Yes," he said, low and gritty.

Shit.

Gunner shook his head. "Jesus, just when I think you're starting to act kinda normal."

Zenon scowled and flipped him off.

The elevator *pinged* and they all turned as Chaos came storming out. His jeans were undone, hanging low on his hips, and the muscles in his chest and stomach flexed as he strode toward her. He looked insanely sexy and pissed as hell.

"Something you want to tell us?" Gunner said to his brother, a low rasp to his voice that had Grace turning to look at him.

Gunner's gaze looked hollow, his smile not reaching his eyes.

Chaos just growled and stormed up to her, backing her against her car, effectively blocking her escape. "We're not finished."

"Yeah, we are." Her voice sounded strained, almost unrecognizable to her own ears.

He leaned in closer, and he didn't look himself, not at all. "Get back in the elevator, Grace."

"What the hell is your problem? Back the hell off." Okay, now she was kind of scared. This wasn't him, at least she didn't think it was. Whoever he'd morphed into was freaking her out big-time.

"We had a deal," he said in that voice that was a combination of demon and angel.

"Are you shitting me?" she said, pleased when her voice

came out strong instead of as shaky as she felt. "You'd drag me back upstairs and *make* me have sex with you because of some deal you *think* we have? I told you, I'm not moving in. That will *never* happen."

He flinched, the dark shadow in his gaze starting to lift. "I'd never force you."

She swallowed hard. "I agreed to mate with you, and I also told you I couldn't give you anything more. You need to accept that."

His fingers slid around the side of her throat, up into her hair, fisting it lightly. "Grace..."

"No."

"Just, you need to...*fuck*, just listen to me—"

"Let her go." Zenon's gritty voice cut through the tension, low and filled with warning. "Your female said no."

There was so much weight behind Zenon's words. She had no idea what it was, where it came from, she was just glad for the unexpected support.

Anger and shock transformed Chaos's expression, and he twisted his head to face his brother. "You don't know what's going on here, Zenon. This isn't what you think, I would never—"

"Fuck, man, she's afraid of you," Gunner said, voice harsh. "Mate or not, she asked you to back the fuck up."

Chaos frowned at his brothers. "No, she's not—"

"Look at her," Zenon gritted out.

Chaos turned back to her, his eyes clashing with hers, and he stumbled back. And just like that, all emotion washed from his face.

His expression went blank. "I was out of line. I'm sorry."

The transformation was so sudden, the difference in his mood so abrupt, she just stood there, waiting for him to say something else, to fire some other pissed-off comment her way. But none came.

Dipping his chin like she was someone he'd just met, he turned and strode away.

She watched him go, her face heating with humiliation as he climbed into the elevator, staring woodenly ahead.

"Okay?" Gunner asked.

She planted her hands on her hips, tying to appear unaffected when she was anything but. "What the hell was that? What's wrong with him?"

Gunner gave her a look that said more than words could. She knew what it was. Chaos was a mated male. She was his mate and she was walking away.

"You should probably go," he said.

"Right." She glanced at Zenon. "Yeah, um...thank you. I know he'd never hurt me...like that, but this is all new." And she did, deep down on some visceral level, she knew he would never hurt her, but he would run right over her if she let him.

Zenon gave her a stiff nod. "We know he wouldn't." He glanced at the elevator as if he expected Chaos to burst back through at any moment. "But letting you leave right now, especially so soon after mating, is going against every one of his instincts."

Why did she suddenly feel guilty? Kind of...sad. Dammit, Chaos had agreed to this.

"Grace," Gunner said, opening her car door.

She didn't need to be told to get lost twice. She climbed in and fired the engine to life.

She drove up to the gates to leave and glanced at the cameras mounted there, waiting to be let out. They shuddered instantly, then slowly slid open.

Was Chaos watching her from the control room?

The pain in the center of her chest intensified, and she peeled out onto the road and did not look back.

Time to refocus her thoughts back to the war.

An image of Chaos sitting beside his bed when she woke after being injured, the worry in his eyes as he stared down at her, stormed her mind.

Gritting her teeth, she shoved it back out and planted her foot on the gas.

CHAPTER 20

DESPITE THE QUICK HEALING, thanks to Chaos's blood, her ribs still throbbed like they'd been used as a punching bag.

Too bad, no rest for the recently stabbed and bitten. The club was short-staffed, Hannah was still away with her family crisis, and there were demons and a two-headed beast loose in the city.

Grace felt hobbled, and it was not a feeling she enjoyed.

She glanced up from behind the bar, looking toward the main door. She'd been doing it all night, half expecting Chaos to come storming in and drag her upstairs to pack all her stuff.

Who the hell did he think he was, anyway?

Yeah, he'd been messed up from mating with her, but he'd been so completely out of line. Did he truly believe she'd turn her world upside down, *move in with him*, just in case he got a hard-on in the middle of the night? The more she thought about it, the angrier she got.

Actually, she'd been angry all day, snapping and bitching at the staff. Maybe Chaos had been right about the effect of his blood. It had definitely affected her libido.

An unwelcome shot of pleasure zinged through her belly. Her traitorous body kept remembering every touch they'd shared in his bed. He'd been gentle, mindful of her injuries, when she'd all but begged him to fuck her harder. But that iron-clad control of his had never slipped once.

Of course not.

Well, not until they had…done what they had.

Mated.

What would her parents think? Her hand went to her stomach as familiar pain sliced through her, because she knew, didn't she? They'd be disgusted with her, feel betrayed. "Shit." She slammed a glass down on the bar.

She didn't want to think about that, or about Chaos.

Thankfully, over the next couple of hours, the bar filled, keeping her occupied, but her side now ached like a bitch and her thigh was throbbing again.

Vince should have made an appearance by now so she could take a break.

But another half hour ticked by and still no sign of him.

She was serving one of the regulars, a sweet old guy who tipped well and she suspected only came in because he was lonely, when Gunner strode in, spotted her, and headed her way.

Great. Now Chaos had sent his brother to check up on her. What was this? High school?

"You can tell Chaos to back the hell off," she said as soon as the knight stopped in front of her.

He lifted both hands in surrender. "I wasn't sent here by your mate." His top lip had a jagged scar through it on one side that you could see even through his short beard, and his mouth twisted on one side in a barely there smile. "But I'll be sure to pass on your message."

"Don't bother." She sounded like an asshole, but right then she didn't give a damn.

Concern covered his rough features. "I'm surprised to see you up and about."

"I'm fine. You want a drink or something?" Her ploy to divert the conversation did not go unnoticed, but he didn't call her on it.

He rested his forearms on the bar, and she couldn't help but admire the beautiful ink covering them. She also noticed the small cross that dangled from a chain around his neck. It was gold, delicate...feminine. It looked completely out of place on the big male. "Yes, but I won't."

"How can I help?" God, she wished she was out on the streets hunting tonight, her aggression levels were off the charts and she needed to beat the shit out of something.

There are other more pleasant ways to burn off some steam.

She shut down those thoughts as quick as they came.

"You seen Oden tonight?" Gunner asked.

Just the mention of that male's name was like a bucket of ice water. "No. Why are you looking for him?"

Gunner shrugged. "He's a powerful demi. We keep an eye on a lot of people."

The guy was being cagey on purpose. He wanted her to bite, so she did. "You got something to say, then spit it out."

He was watching her like he didn't trust her worth shit, and that did nothing to improve her current emotional state.

"You sure you haven't seen him tonight?"

"Are you deaf?" she fired back.

"No, and I'm not stupid, either, so cut the shit. Oden was here about half an hour ago."

She rested her hands on the bar, kind of freaked that she could have missed him. "It's been busy most of the night, he could have slipped by without me seeing him."

"He left through the front of the club. I followed him, then *poof*, I couldn't sense him anymore."

She stilled. "Fuck." They both knew what that meant. He

was involved in the war, deeply involved. In her gut she'd known. The male hadn't just been hanging around to get in her pants.

"You know where he might have gone, how he was able to do that? Has he ever shared anything like that with you...during your time together?"

Was he actually questioning her loyalty? She gritted her teeth, fingers curling into fists on the bar. "I gave the prick a lap dance, Gunner. I'm a stripper, that's what I do. So, no, he didn't share his plans for world domination with me. He let me bounce around on his dick for a bit, shoved a twenty down the side of my G-string, and sent me on my way like a good little whore."

Gunner's eyes darkened. "I don't think you're a..."

"Sorry, my bad. You just think I'm a liar, and someone who would betray her people for some asshole with a fat wallet and a little power. Don't you think I'd be with Chaos right now if that was the case?" She turned away before she threw a bottle at him and served a waiting customer.

Gunner waited for a while, but she ignored him until he finally gave up and left.

She'd feel bad for the attitude she'd given him, if he hadn't all but accused her of colluding with the enemy. She needed to talk to Vince. Now. Jesus. That disappearing act Oden did was proof he was a traitor to his people, that he was thoroughly tied up in the war.

Grace got someone to cover for her, and rushed to Vince's office.

No one answered when she knocked, and when she opened the door, the room was empty. Dread spiked through her belly, and she raced upstairs to his apartment. She knocked several times, but there was no answer. Racing to her place next door, she grabbed the spare set of keys she kept for him and let herself in.

The place was trashed. "Vince?"

A groan came from the bathroom. She rushed in. Vince lay on the floor, clutching his side. She pulled his hand away and lifted his shirt. There was a massive bruise, the mark was unmistakable. A boot print. He'd definitely broken some ribs. His face was a mess, broken nose, split lip. But he was alive. "Oden did this?"

"L-leave it, Grace," he groaned.

She helped him up, basically dragging him off the floor, and felt her stitches pull painfully. "We need to get you to the hospital."

"No. I don't want anyone to know about this. I can't go to the hospital... Shit." He gasped in pain.

She helped him to the bedroom and onto the bed, making him as comfortable as she could. "I'll be back. I know someone who can help." Well, sort of knew them—she'd seen his handiwork, anyway.

Striding back to the living room, she pulled out her phone. The doc who'd patched her up had left his number in case any problems arose. She had a problem all right, just not one he might be expecting.

He answered after two rings.

He didn't sound thrilled when she explained the situation, but seeing as she was Chaos's mate he'd be there in fifteen.

Vince was shivering when she walked back in, no doubt going into shock. She pulled the covers over him and brushed his hair away from his forehead. "You owe him something. Money?"

"Y-yes." He coughed, then cried out in pain.

"You sure it's just money, Vince?"

He stared at her through bloodshot eyes. "Yes."

"You'd tell me if there was more, wouldn't you?"

"Of course," he choked out.

She wanted to believe him, she really did. But as much as

she loved Vince, he'd made some dumb decisions before. Especially when it came to powerful demi like Oden.

Vince grabbed her wrist hard enough to bruise. "Promise me you'll stay away from him, Grace."

"Vince..."

"Promise me. He's dangerous, into some serious shit. I'd rather hand over the club than..."

"Than what?"

He shook his head.

She grabbed his shoulders, suddenly feeling ill. "I know he's involved in the war, Vince, on the wrong fucking side. He's colluding with demons, isn't he? Are you involved?"

He shook his head wildly. "No. I would never betray our people, never."

"Is he trying to pressure you to join him?"

He closed his eyes, looking pained. "I won't do it, Gracie, I won't."

"We'll stop him, Vince. I promise you that."

A gasp came from the door, and she spun around. Cate, a new dancer, stood there gaping. *Shit.* Grace jumped up to block her view. "You need to leave, and keep this to yourself, do you understand?"

She didn't move, frozen at the door. Grace reached out and grabbed her arm. Her power flared out of nowhere, shot to her sternum, then fired down her arm. Cate cried out, eyes wide with terror and pain.

The other female shrieked and slapped Grace's hand away, stumbling back. "What did you just try to do to me?"

Grace grabbed on to the wall for support. "I-I'm sorry. I didn't mean to."

Cate spun around and ran from the room.

Shit, with her injuries, her emotions all over the place, finding Vince beaten, she'd dropped her guard.

"What the fuck was that?" Vince said from behind her.

"Nothing."

Vince watched her, a weird expression on his face. "That wasn't nothing, Gracie."

"It's…it's new, okay." He was the only person who knew she'd never had a real power, until now anyway.

"What is it?"

"I can…draw others' powers into me, use them."

He smiled, pride shining from his eyes. "I knew you had it in you, Gracie. I always knew you were destined for great things."

She sure as hell didn't feel great right then.

CHAPTER 21

CHAOS POUNDED his fist into the punching bag, blow after blow until his bare knuckles were split and bleeding. He hadn't been near Revelry or Grace in four days, and it had done nothing to ease his need—she was still there in his head, constantly on his mind. She'd moved in and redecorated his gray matter, and there was no going back.

He couldn't sleep, could barely eat. This whole thing was a major fuckup. On top of that, Rocco was still AWOL. If Chaos couldn't get through to him, they would lose him just like they'd lost Tobias. That couldn't happen.

Not to mention the two-headed nightmare hiding somewhere in the city. It was only a matter of time before it went apeshit and started eating humans in plain sight.

His world was crumbling around him and yet all he could think about was Grace.

He slammed his fist into the leather one more time, the force of it hard enough to jar his shoulder. He would conquer this.

Winning this war had to come first. He had to find a way to force her from his mind, forget the way she looked naked on his bed, the way she'd felt beneath him. Even the way she joked around and teased him. A smile came to him unbidden.

He'd thought things had changed between them, but he'd been wrong.

He'd been accused of being heartless, ruthless, single-minded by his brothers, by Grace. Well, he needed that single-mindedness now. He needed the ruthlessness, that *control* back. Right. Fucking. Now.

His powers had increased, the surge buzzing through his veins, and that's what he needed to focus on. Not the infuriating, sexy female who'd taken up residence in his head.

Sweat slid down his chest, soaking into the waistband of his shorts, but he continued to pound the bag, even when it got to the point where he had trouble lifting his arms.

Gunner came out of nowhere. "Chaos."

He swiped sweat out of his eyes. "What?"

"Where the hell were you? I've been calling your name for the last five minutes."

Get it together.

"It's one in the morning. I wasn't expecting company." He snatched up a towel and wiped himself down. "What is it? Rocco?"

Pain flashed through his brother's eyes. "No. Just a trail of dismembered demons. He doesn't even bother taking their heads now."

"Shit."

Gunner rubbed his hand over his short beard. "Oden did a vanishing act tonight, I saw him. He's working with the demons. But I couldn't track him, the male's smoke."

Every muscle in Chaos's body seized. "Where?"

"Revelry."

His demon twisted inside him and snarled. "Alone?" The roughness of his voice gave away too much, but he had no control over his reaction.

"Yeah." Gunner didn't have to say anything more, it was written all over his face: bewilderment, confusion...pity. "Why don't you just go and apologize. Move her into the compound. It's where she belongs."

A longing, deep and fierce, gripped him by the throat. "Didn't ask your opinion, so keep it the fuck to yourself."

Gunner glanced down at Chaos's cracked, bleeding knuckles. "Yeah, 'cause your way of handling it seems to be working out great for you."

"Grace and me...we're not like Laz or Kryos or Zen and their mates. Neither of us wanted it."

Shaking his head, Gunner let out a sigh. "You trying to convince me or yourself?"

Why the hell were they even discussing this? "You don't know what you're talking about." Chaos cracked his neck, hoping to release the tension riding him. "We're in a goddamn death roll, time's running out, and if we don't find a way out, we're gonna drown. I can't afford to let this shit with Grace get in my head. We're mated, it's done. That's all we needed."

"This isn't something you can just ignore," Gunner said.

Chaos was suddenly weary as hell. "You think I don't know that? Shit, our brother losing his mate has fucked more than Rocco's head. It affects us all. As much as I didn't want it, I knew when the time came, if we were all mated, we'd be at our strongest. We might have stood a chance. That's not happening for Roc now. We've lost Tobias. That just left you and me without mates. I had to do it—we needed the strength—and now I have to learn to fucking live with the consequences."

Gunner dropped his gaze and let out a shaky breath. "She's not out there for me."

His voice was strained, rough, a tone Chaos had never

heard coming from the male before. "Zenon thought that once, too. So did I. She's out there."

Gunner's features shifted, a combination of self-loathing and pain stared back at Chaos. "I know. I fucking know, all right? She's not out there, not anymore."

Chaos froze, really looking at his brother. He hadn't been the same since Lazarus and Eve mated. Her power had fucked with them all, and Gunner had ended up locked in the cells, afraid he'd lose himself to his demon completely. He refused to talk about it. "Gunner..."

"Don't," he said, making it clear he wasn't going there, then his eyes locked on Chaos. "You're making the wrong decision," he rasped. "You think you have a good reason, some noble crap, no doubt, for denying yourself. Fuck that. You will regret it if you try to keep her at a distance. I promise you that." Then he walked out of the gym.

Chaos knew he should go after him and press for more information, but it was obvious Gunner didn't want that, and who the hell was Chaos to offer advice when he'd made so many mistakes of his own?

The silence of his apartment was oppressive when he walked in later, and for the first time that he could remember, he hated it. When he walked into the bedroom, his eyes immediately landed on his perfectly made bed. Nothing in his room, his apartment, was out of place, it was like it always was—like some emotionless robot lived there.

He stared at the pillow beside his, where Grace had lain tucked in tight against him. He hadn't changed the pillowcase. Why? He didn't know. He just knew it calmed him, calmed his demon, and every morning he woke with his face buried against it, like her scent drew him to it while he slept.

A fantasy of her cuffed to his headboard, body hot and straining, skin flushed, legs spread wide, her telling him how much she needed him, wanted him, filled his head.

Unable to get up and leave him again.

At his mercy.

Sinking into her like that, tight and so damn wet.

The sound of her voice, her cries, her panted breaths echoed through his mind like she was right there with him. His dick filled and lengthened. God, how he hungered for her.

The demon inside him clawed to the surface, making his skin itch, feverish need pummeling him from all directions. Without thought, instincts fully in control, he crawled across the bed and buried his nose against the cool cotton, drawing in her now fading scent.

Rolling onto his back, taking the pillow with him, he groaned and shoved down the front of his shorts, freeing himself. He wrapped his fingers around his painfully hard length and squeezed.

This was what he'd been reduced to, sniffing a fucking pillow so he could jerk off. Pathetic. But no other female could slake his lust. Other females no longer existed to him.

Only Grace.

He slid his hand up and squeezed the head, then back down. Letting his eyes drift closed, he allowed images of her to flicker through his mind, the way she'd come hard around him, nails scoring his skin, the sounds she'd made.

In minutes, he was teetering on the edge.

Increasing his strokes, faster, rougher, he came with a shout, hot come splashing his stomach and chest. Breathing ragged, he shoved the pillow aside and stared at the ceiling for several minutes, each exhale loud in the deafening silence.

He'd fucked everything up.

He'd failed the males that trusted him most, missing what was going on in his own fucking house. He'd lost Tobias, blind to the pain that had consumed him at the loss of his mate, and he hadn't even known Rocco had found his, and now it was too late.

They'd trusted him, chosen him to lead them. He was leading them straight to Hell.

Climbing off the bed, he got in the shower to wash off the remaining traces of his latest loss of control. He was dressed and strapping on his weapons when there was a soft knock at the door. Desperate to get out of there, to hunt down some demons, make them fucking talk, fight off some of this frustration, he yanked the door open with a growl. "What?"

And froze. Grace stood there, legs braced apart, hands loose at her sides. Trying to appear relaxed when she was anything but.

"Sorry, I should have called." She glanced back down the hall. "Maybe I shouldn't have come." She looked back at him and bit her lower lip.

He felt it in his balls. "It's fine," he choked. "What's going on?"

"Can I...come in?"

She wore leather pants, the kind she fought in, and a black tank that clung to her gentle curves. His mouth went dry.

"I was just leaving." He needed his focus back, his unwavering control, and just being in the same room with his female in front of him turned him into a male he didn't recognize, a male he couldn't afford to be, not now.

She placed a hand on his abs and stared up at him. "Please."

Something was off. There was something different about her, and it was the only reason he stepped back and motioned her in. "What is it?" He crossed his arms to stop from reaching for her.

She moved in, until they were only a foot apart. "I, uh...I

thought you might like some company?" She did some more lip biting and stared wide-eyed at him.

Sex. It was written all over her face and in the way she held her body.

His dick instantly went hard and his breathing choppy. He didn't move. He knew if he did, he'd tear off her clothes and pounce on her. That's how badly he wanted her. She could destroy his resolve with a single look.

Leaning in, she pressed her forehead against his chest, nuzzling into him, and slid a warm hand up his bicep, the other fisting the shirt at his waist.

"What do you say?" Her voice was different, not the way she sounded when she'd been in his bed, all husky and full of need. This was something else. Grace was trying to seduce him, but she didn't want him, not right then. There was a thread of something he didn't understand.

Then it clicked into place. This was the persona she wore when she worked, the voice, the expressions she used when she was at Revelry. It was Gigi Fury begging him to fuck her, not Grace.

He forced himself to take a step back. "What are you doing?"

"What does it look like?"

Then she fucking batted her lashes at him. "Desperation."

She flinched, and the mask dropped, revealing a whole lot of pain and vulnerability. He'd be lying if he said it didn't get to him, because it did, but he held his ground. "What's with the act? What is it you really want?"

Grace turned and walked away, and he was about to go after her when she sat heavily on his couch. "I need your help." She looked up at him. "One of the girls from Revelry, one of my fighters went missing. She showed up dead on the roof above my apartment a week ago. And her body...a human didn't kill her."

Shit.

"Then Hannah didn't show up for work. She'd called in, said it was a family thing, but when I called to check on her tonight, her family said she wasn't with them. James went to her apartment, and she hasn't been there in days. No one's heard from her since that first night." She stood and paced to the other side of the room. "It's Oden. He has something to do with it, I'm sure."

Grace had come here to manipulate him, to soften him up because she needed his help? She'd assumed that before an information exchange could happen, she had to give him something first.

That's what she truly thought of him? Yeah, that cut in a way he wasn't prepared for. It also pissed him the fuck off.

"Just an FYI, you don't need to offer up your pussy as some type of bribe to get me to do my job. I agreed to work with you because I respect your abilities, not for what you'll give me in return."

It didn't stop him from wanting her, though, but the fact she was willing to let him fuck her to get what she wanted, yeah, that did not sit well with him, not at all. He didn't deal in that type of currency.

She stared at him, face flushed with embarrassment, eyes sharp, bright.

He planted his hands on his hips. Fuck. How could he get through to her? How could he get her to trust him? "Okay, yeah, we have an unusual arrangement...but, Grace, you need to *hear me*, because this is the important part. You. Are. My. Mate. There is no get-out-of-jail-free card here, this is it, you and me for as long as we live. That's a fucking long time." His hands dropped to his sides, fists clenched. "So no matter what's going on between us, no matter where you are, even if you're on the other side of the fucking world, if you need something, anything, you come to me. You reach out to me, trust me, and I will be the one to give it to you. Because that's my job, my privilege. I don't need payment, there is no barter system between us. I give to you and I'll keep on giving to you because I want to, I need to. Understand?"

She sucked in a sharp breath. "I made a bad call, okay, I'm sorry but…"

"Do you understand?"

He could see in her eyes that he'd said too much. He was asking for blind trust, and that wasn't something she gave easily or lightly. She depended only on herself, had for a long time, and now he was asking her to put her faith in him, to trust that he wouldn't misuse it. She wasn't ready to give it to him.

"Not really. No," she said, confirming it.

"Don't worry. You will. Let's go." He grabbed his jacket, shrugged it on, then headed for the door.

He didn't want to talk anymore. Right now all the things on the tip of his tongue were better left unsaid, for both of them.

CHAPTER 22

ZENON STRUGGLED TO BREATHE, his skin crawling, and his chest pumping so hard the bed shook.

Somehow Diemos had found a way into his head, his dreams, and was trying to call to Zenon's inner demon. The nightly visits hadn't let up and he wasn't sure how much more he could take.

He rolled Mia into his side and soaked up the warmth of her body, her soft hair tickled his skin, her addictive scent easing the hurricane building inside him. She made a sweet little sound and wriggled closer, and his heart literally ached with how much he loved her.

She was his everything. His reason for every breath he took.

Diemos was in his head. Not in this room with them, nowhere near his precious mate—still that was too close for Zenon. Far too fucking close.

He struggled to control his breathing, not wanting to wake her. Mia hadn't been sleeping well either, worried about the future, worried for him. He would do anything to relieve her fears.

Burying his nose against her thick red hair, he squeezed his eyes shut and breathed her in, desperately seeking calm.

But even though Diemos resided in Hell, he wouldn't leave him. His face, his presence bounced around Zenon's head. His father had found a way to reach him, just like he'd promised, and the sickening, suffocating sensation wouldn't leave him alone. It was oily and dark and thick. Made him want to scrub his fucking skin raw.

Zenon didn't want that evil anywhere near Mia.

Gently removing her arms from around his waist, he climbed out of bed, tucked the covers around her, then shoved on a pair of jeans and left their apartment. He needed to clear his head.

The control room was empty when he walked in, which was a good thing because he didn't want to talk about this, not yet.

Pushing through the doors, he strode outside to the balcony and gripped the railing. He filled his lungs with night air, and his wings sprung from his back, ready to take flight. A short one, just to shake this feeling.

He saw movement in the shadows and spun around…and stilled.

He knew who it was instantly, the male who stepped from the darkened corner and into the moonlight. Knew deep in his soul.

Zenon took in the other male. They were around the same height, and he had black hair like Zenon's as well, only the male watching him closely had his buzzed at the sides and longer on top. It was slicked back, revealing pale yellow eyes, also like Zenon's, only lighter. The male wore a black T-shirt with Prada printed across the front—he obviously had a sense of humor—and his skin was covered with ink, except for his face, which was ink-free. Well, mostly ink-free. Something was written in sloping script above his

215

left eyebrow, which was arched as Zenon's gaze met his again.

They looked roughly the same age by human standards, mid-twenties. Could be brothers with the similarities.

"Lucifer," Zenon said, still not moving, not fucking blinking.

A smile curled the former king of Hell's lips. "No hug for Grandpa?"

Zenon remained still as Lucifer came closer, as the older male circled him slowly. It was pointless doing anything else. Lucifer could click his fingers and turn Zenon to dust if he chose to.

"Your wings," Lucifer said, hand lifting almost cautiously. "They're kickass. Can I?"

Zenon's wings were not like his brothers'. They weren't feathers; they were leathery, like a bat, all demon. Nothing about them said he was half angel. Inside he recoiled at the idea of letting anyone but Mia touch them, but he found himself dipping his chin, granting Lucifer permission.

He gritted his teeth as Lucifer reached out and gently brushed his fingers along the edge.

"You don't like it being touched," Lucifer said and tilted his head.

Their eyes met, and Zenon felt the moment Lucifer took a peek inside his mind, saw the other male flinch when he got the full 3D version of Zenon's shitty life loud and clear.

Lucifer pulled his hand away, curling it into a fist.

"Don't touch me again," Zenon said without heat.

"I won't. Despite what people say, I'm not a total dick." He tilted his head again, gaze intense. "Silas told me where to find you," he said, answering Zenon's unasked question. "The dude likes you a lot, piqued my curiosity."

Zenon knew that was bullshit. "Your interest was piqued before that, though, wasn't it? Diemos told you about me when Helena took me from Hell. You came after me, and he took his chance and warded the portal, blocking you from reentering so he could claim your throne." Helena had been his master in Hell and on Earth, she'd owned him from the age of fourteen. Until Mia had saved him. Freed him.

Lucifer smiled and slid his hands into his pockets. "Honestly? I'd never been prouder of the little shit."

"Why not come to me before now."

"You didn't need me." His gaze moved over Zenon's wings again.

"You took Diemos's wings. Why?" Zenon asked before he could think better of it.

Lucifer's intense yellow stare came back to Zenon. "I was protecting him from himself. My boy wasn't satisfied just being my heir. He wanted more. But Earth's not for him."

"He sees it differently."

Lucifer gazed up at the sky. "He's like me in a lot of ways, but unfortunately, he gets his temperament from his mother. A thaneous demon. Bitch had four arms, and like six boobs. Volcanic in the sack, was in to some seriously kinky shit, but man, was she *crazy*."

Zenon blinked, opened his mouth, closed it again. Nope. Not touching that.

"Diemos and I, we're both risk takers. We want something, we go after it. Our motivations, though…" He shook his head. "In that we're total opposites." His gaze locked on Zenon's. "He thinks he can control you, that the demon inside you will obey its king. My son doesn't understand what pure love—the truest kind, the kind that fucks with your head and has you walking around with a boner twenty-four seven—can accomplish. He won't understand why he can't control you, those kinds of feelings are beyond him. You thought mating Mia is what leashed the demon inside you." He shook his head. "Nah, it was love, being

217

loved. There is nothing more powerful than that shit. Nothing."

Hearing Lucifer say Mia's name, knowing that he knew she existed, made his gut tighten and his skin prickle with unease. Despite the casual banter, the guy was terrifying. Darkness hovered around him like a black cloud. "You can stop him," Zenon said. "I know you can."

"Yeah, maybe. But the fates will be pissed if I mess with things. We're all pawns. We need to let this game play out."

Zenon cursed. "This is not a game, this is fucking Armageddon."

"No shit." Lucifer grinned. "I can help you with one thing, though." A chain appeared in his hand, thin and gold. "The beast Diemos sent for me, this'll hold it."

"For you?"

"He doesn't want any obstacles when he comes to Earth, including me."

"You mean when Rocco's female gains her powers."

"Yup."

"Can you stop it from happening?"

"Dunno."

Goddammit. Lucifer was about as helpful as Silas had been. "Can you bring her home?"

"No."

"Fate?" Zenon was so filled with pain and rage for Rocco, for his female, he had to grab the balcony railing.

"Fate."

"Can the beast kill you?

Lucifer shrugged. "If it caught me at the wrong...right? Moment. Like when I'm getting busy or taking a dump or whatever, maybe, I guess." He held his hand out again, holding up the chain.

Zenon frowned and took it. It was no bigger than the one Mia wore around her neck.

Lucifer chuckled. "It's a grower not a shower. It'll do the job when the time comes."

Zenon shoved it in his pocket. "We can't do shit if we can't find it."

"Next time Diemos reaches out to you in your dreams, go with it. Let him think he has you. He'll lead you right to it. You're the key, kid. Through you, the beast can find me. One taste of your blood and it can track mine."

Zenon grunted. Diemos said he might have a use for him. Turned out he was dinner. What he wouldn't give to take the fucker's head. "I'm bait."

Lucifer smirked. "I wouldn't take it personally."

"Kinda hard not to."

He chuckled. "Well, the chain will hold that ugly two-headed fucker until I can send it back."

"You can do that?"

"I need to gather a few things to prepare. But it isn't all that complicated."

Zenon narrowed his eyes. "I thought you couldn't inter-fere with fate?"

The smile returned. "I can't, but I don't see the harm in offering a little help here and there."

Obviously, fate could go fuck itself if it involved a blood-thirsty monster trying to hunt down Lucifer and tear him to shreds.

"How will I contact you, when we have it locked down?" Zenon expected an "I'll just know" or "think of me" or some other all-powerful bullshit.

Instead, Lucifer pulled his phone from his pocket. "Number?"

Zenon rattled it off and watched as the once king of Hell, his grandfather, added him to his contacts.

"Texting you now so you got my digits as well."

Zenon's phone beeped in his pocket.

They stood there then, the silence stretching out. Lucifer's eyes locked with Zenon's, and the urge to drop his gaze, like he had always been expected to do when he was in Hell, when he was with Helena, was hard to ignore. But he didn't. He stared back, unflinching.

"If I'd known when you were born, if I'd known that you existed, I would have doted on you, loved you," he said roughly and stepped forward, lifting his hand again. He didn't touch this time, just let it hover beside Zenon's cheek. "I would have protected you."

Zenon didn't know what to say to that, had no words.

"I'm proud of you, Zenon," Lucifer said, then vanished.

Zenon looked down at his phone, at the text Lucifer had sent him.

A devil emoji grinned back at him.

CHAPTER 23

THE CLUB WAS BUSY, but Grace knew the minute Chaos walked in the door. Like low-level electricity, tingles traveled over the surface of her skin. Need zinged through her belly. Lower.

Humiliation hit her face, remembering his rejection the night before. He'd figured her out almost instantly. Jesus, she'd never felt smaller. Asking for help didn't come naturally or easily to her.

Since she'd been on her own, she'd worked for everything she had. Nothing had ever been handed to her. She'd expected Chaos to take what she'd offered without question. Instead, he'd shot her down, and in that moment, she'd never felt more pathetic.

"Just an FYI, you don't need to offer up your pussy as some type of bribe to get me to do my job. I agreed to work with you because I respect your abilities, not for what you'll give me in return."

Those words had played on repeat in her head since he'd said them.

She hadn't expected that. That seemed to happen a lot with Chaos. She'd spent the last twelve years hating him, blaming him, expecting nothing but arrogance and stupidity, but then she'd met him, and yeah, the male was arrogant, but he also gave a shit about her people, about this world. About all of it.

Grace busied herself collecting glasses as Chaos and Lazarus walked across the floor, headed straight for the office. After she'd shown him where she'd found Tina's body the night before and shared everything she knew, he'd told her he was coming in to speak with Vince.

Naturally, her boss would be their first stop—Tina and Hannah had both worked at Revelry—and going by the expression on Vince's face, he wasn't happy about it.

Both knights towered over him, and with an extremely unhappy glance her way, Vince led them to his office. She would have joined them, but Vince didn't know about her and Chaos, or that they were working together. He had enough going on without her adding to it. Chaos would fill her in later if there was anything she needed to know. Her surety of that surprised her.

He would, though. She had no doubt.

"What are Chaos and Lazarus doing here?" the new girl beside her asked. Grace still couldn't remember her name, and she'd been told twice.

"No idea."

Excitement lit the female's eyes. "I was so sad to leave the compound after my training. They're all so smokin' hot."

Grace's hackles rose in an instant, and the urge to reach out and smash the poor unsuspecting female's face against the wooden bar was almost irresistible. "They're both mated."

She pouted. "Too bad."

"Yeah, too bad." Grace's hands curled into fists as an emotion she didn't want to name reared its ugly, unmistakably *green* head. "You okay here on your own?"

"Sure."

"I'll be back after my dance."

The poor girl hadn't done anything wrong. She was right, they were hot, all of them, and their newest staff member had eyes in her head. Why the hell should Grace care if the girl was mentally undressing Chaos and all but drooling down her chin?

But dammit, she did.

And right then she needed to get the fuck away before she succumbed to the rage building inside her chest and accidentally on purpose tripped the girl, then stomped on her.

The changing room was empty when she walked in. Good thing, no one needed to be around her at the moment. And if Grace was honest, the anger growing inside her with every passing second had nothing to do with the female behind the bar, not really.

Chaos being kind of distant, perfectly professional, last night after they'd left his apartment, and again tonight when he'd walked in here, should please her. But it didn't. It felt… wrong. She was trying to work out her jumbled emotions, and since she was seriously struggling with that, anger had become her default. Anger she was used to. Knew what to do with.

Grabbing her favorite black leather corset, the one that made her small tits look much bigger than they were, and sheer lilac panties that were feminine and delicate with ruffles on the butt, she quickly changed. Her stockings and garters had black satin bows and her heels were spiked but cute. She'd had several outfits made, different themes to match her moods. But this one, the mix of vixen and virgin always earned her fantastic tips.

That was the only reason she was desperate to get out on the stage for her performance tonight, right?

It had nothing to do with the way her skin still tingled,

telegraphing loud and clear that Chaos was in the building. Of course not.

Pulling her hair back, she secured it into a tight bun, then slid on a pair of black-framed glasses and the finishing touch, a gray, houndstooth pencil skirt and fitted jacket.

One naughty librarian coming up.

When she walked past Vince's office, the door was open and the room was empty. Before she knew what she was doing, she'd closed her eyes and reached out, searching for Chaos. She wasn't even sure it would work. It did. Oh God, she felt him. The tingling across her skin intensified.

Since the mating, her body hummed and burned when he was close.

He apparently could turn it off at will.

After a few words to John, the lighting and sound guy, she stood back and waited for him to introduce her. Moments later the lights went low and silence engulfed the club.

John introduced her and she walked out slowly, the click of her heels ringing out, drawing everyone's eyes her way.

A spotlight hit her, revealing her to the crowd, and the opening notes of her song started. She strutted to the chair waiting on the other side of the stage, and dragged it with her, hips swinging, to the middle of the floor.

She was going for slow and sensual to start with. The tease began with unbinding her long blond hair and letting it fall down her back. Moving around the chair, she sat and arched against it, sliding her hands from her throat, down over her breasts, stomach, and thighs, then fisting the hem of her skirt, she dragged it higher.

Lifting her hand to her mouth, eyes wide, she spread her legs slightly, giving just a peek of her panties. "Oops." With the skirt still hitched up, she spun and bent over, rolling her hips.

A dark, volatile wave of emotion washed over her, stealing her breath, but not in a bad way.

Chaos.

He was watching her.

The wave thickened, wrapped around her like a sensual haze, and for some insane reason, she let it take hold, embracing it. With her back still turned, she let her jacket slide from her shoulders and pulled off the glasses, dropping them with the jacket.

The skirt went next, right as the music picked up pace, going from slow and easy to moody. Heavier. It pumped through the big speakers on either side of the stage, and she let it move through her, her hands drifting lower, then sliding between her thighs.

Chaos's mood changed, she sensed it brushing over her skin, rolling through her. Anger, jealousy, and lust blasted her from all sides, that iron-clad control of his was slipping and he didn't like it one bit. She craved his surrender to it in a way she didn't understand.

The corset and panties stayed on, for some reason she couldn't bring herself to take them off. And as the final notes of the song died away and the lights dimmed, no longer blinding her to the audience, she looked out. She didn't have to search hard.

He stood close to the stage, looming in a way that warned every other male in the room to stay back, staking a claim he didn't have a right to, not really, not with their agreement. Still, a thrill of excitement shot through her.

His dark eyes were trained on her, unwavering, predatory, filled with heat and fire...promise.

She spun around, giving him her back, and stalked off, hoping like hell her legs would hold out with her knees suddenly shaking.

In the dressing room, she quickly slid on a pair of jeans,

but left on the corset, then headed back out to the club. Like she'd promised, she headed back to their newbie at the bar. And as she moved, she could feel Chaos's eyes on her, burning into her the entire way.

Do not look at him.

He'd see it in her eyes that her dance had been for him, only him. "You getting the hang of things?" she asked the female when she reached the bar.

The girl stared at her, eyes wide, and Grace realized just how young she was, maybe nineteen, twenty, and her chest squeezed.

"How did you learn to dance like that?" she asked, awe in her voice.

Grace forced a smile. "Someone taught me when I was about your age."

"Can you teach me?"

Had she ever been this naive, this innocent? "You'll make decent tips waiting tables, you don't need to rush into anything."

The girl frowned at her, more than likely assuming something else was behind her motives in discouraging her. "I'd be good. I know I would."

Grace rested her hand on the younger female's shoulder. "I don't doubt it. You still want to dance in six months, when you've been here a little longer, I'll teach you, okay?"

The girl's eyes slid from Grace's, moved behind her, and the frown vanished, her mouth dropping open.

Grace knew who was standing behind her before she turned to face the leader of the Knights of Hell. A warrior. A protector of her people. Her mate. She'd felt him stalking her like prey from a distance since she'd walked back onto the floor.

She'd relished every second.

"Let's go," he said before she could get a word out.

Her heart pounded in her chest. "I'm working, Mr. Personality, and despite what you think, the world doesn't stop turning because of you." She didn't know why she was fighting this, why she was grasping on to that last bit of the anger she carried from her past.

Because your anger is all you have left of your family.

The muscle in his square jaw jumped. "I've cleared it with Vince."

"What? How?"

He shrugged his massive shoulders. "Knight business."

"Really? And what business is that?" Though she knew exactly what it was. Lust flowed from Chaos to her in a relentless ebb and flow of intoxicating waves, building ever higher.

He leaned in, his lips brushing her ear. "I'm going to give you what you want, what we both want. What I wanted to do to you last night." He lifted his head and held her gaze. "That little performance. You wanted me to lose control, yes?"

She swallowed hard. She'd told herself she could turn him on, then turn him down, like he had her. It was utter bullshit. She wanted him so badly that she trembled. "Maybe."

"You got your wish."

Then her hand was engulfed in his and he was leading her through the club and out the back to the internal stairs that would take them to her apartment. His long legs took the steps two at a time, forcing her to scramble beside him. Before she could pull her key from her back pocket, he lifted a hand and used his powers to unlock the door.

It shut behind them with a bang, and he turned, gripped her hips, lifted her off the ground, and slammed her against the door. His mouth came down on hers, hot and hungry a second later, his tongue sliding against hers, his erection between her thighs, grinding hard.

She wrenched her head to the side. "We shouldn't do this."

As much as she wanted him, she knew everything would change if they did this now. Everything.

Pinned to the door by the hips, she had nowhere to go, and he didn't back off. She didn't think he even heard her, until he pulled back with a growl and stared down at her.

"You're lying to yourself if you think either of us can walk away now." He did some more grinding and she groaned. "Am I wrong?"

She didn't want to think about it, didn't want to talk anymore, didn't want to admit how much she wanted this, not to him, not to herself. So she stopped protesting, wrapped her arms around his neck, and pulled him back down, kissing him, hard.

Gripping her ass, he carried her to the bed and threw her on it. He came down on top of her, covering her with his body. His mouth came back to hers, opening wide, forcing hers to do the same, his head tilting to the side, fucking her mouth with his, owning it.

"You wanted me to tear those pretty little panties off, didn't you, Grace? Knew that would be all I could think about when I saw them." One large, hot hand moved down between their bodies and he worked the zipper on her jeans, shoving them down her legs and off, tossing them to the floor.

He flipped her onto her stomach and jerked up her hips so she was on her knees, face in the blankets. He covered her sheer lilac underwear with his hand, his rough and calloused fingers snagging on the delicate fabric as he pressed two fingers against her swollen clit with a hiss. "Drenched, like I knew you would be. Gonna eat that wet pussy now," he growled, then tore the panties from her body and flung them aside. "Spread nice and wide for me."

She didn't try to fight it, didn't want to. She spread her knees wider, offering herself up to him. Right then he could have done whatever he wanted to her and she wouldn't have protested.

His shaved head prickled her skin a second before his hot mouth covered her pussy and his tongue slid over her clit. She arched her back, lifting her ass higher, seeking more, and he gave it to her, working her sensitive flesh until she was writhing and begging.

She came hard against his mouth, fisting the sheets as deep, rumbling groans vibrated through her, making it that much more intense.

He reared up behind her, making a sound like a hungry lion. "Love the way you taste. Could eat you all night and never get enough. But if I don't get inside you right fucking now, I'll lose my mind, angel."

So would she.

His T-shirt landed on the floor beside the bed.

She was flipped over again, and he loomed above her as she slid her hands down his ripped chest and abs. She'd never seen a male as beautiful as him, and she wanted to touch him.

He lifted up to his knees. "Free my cock."

She ran her hands down over his cut abs, hard and tight like hot stone, around to his hips, then brought them to the front to pop the button open. She bit her lip and looked up at him.

He cursed, and she smirked.

Brushing her hands aside impatiently, he tore the front of his jeans open, shoved them down, and freed his beautiful dick. Grace bit her lip and moaned as he wrapped his fingers around it. Was he trembling?

She watched in hungry fascination as he slid his fist up and down the hard length several times.

"You want this?" he asked.

Would he make her admit it? Could she?

"You want my cock, Grace?" he asked again, so deep she felt those words move through her.

"Is your ego so big I have to spell it out for you?" She was stalling, and he knew it. She also knew that his ego wasn't the actual reason he was making her say it.

He squeezed his dick and moaned softly. "Need to hear you say it." His free hand moved up her body and tugged her corset down so her nipples popped over the top. He ran a finger around an aching tip, then pinched. "Tell me."

"Argh...all right. Yes. I want it. Happy now?"

He grinned all wicked and arrogant.

Before she could open her mouth, she was back on her stomach, ass in the air, and he was moving in behind her.

Grace pushed back, arching against him. The fat, blunt head of his cock notched against her opening, then he was pushing in, spreading her wide. God, he felt even bigger like this. She dropped her head to the mattress and groaned as he filled her, steadily, barely giving her a moment to adjust, to catch her breath.

His hands went to her hips, and she was forced to hang on as he immediately started pounding into her, hard and so damn deep.

"Fuck yes," he gritted out.

He took her like a man deprived, a man consumed with his need. A need she thought that perhaps only she could satisfy. And dammit, the feeling was mutual.

"God, harder," she groaned.

Chaos cursed and gave it to her, bodies slapping, skin slick, feeding their out-of-control hunger for each other.

Suddenly, he pulled out and flipped her again. He shoved his thighs between hers, eyes latching on to her own, then he slammed back in.

Grace cried out, clinging to him as he came down on top of her. He wrapped his arms around her, one hand going to the nape of her neck, holding her where he wanted her as he took control of her mouth again. The other went to her ass, gripping her flesh tight in that big, rough-skinned hand.

His massive body strained, rolled, thrusting into her, not an inch of space between them. She'd never felt anything like this, this good. Being with Chaos was darkness and light. Dirty, yet somehow tender. Ravenous hunger and the deepest satisfaction all at the same time.

She gripped his hard, muscled ass as he thrust into her, encouraging him to fuck her even harder.

He was all she could feel against her skin, filling her over and over again, and her next orgasm was already building. His dark eyes stayed focused on her, seeing everything. She couldn't take the intensity and squeezed her eyes closed, turning away.

"No. Look at me," he said. "I want to make sure you see me when I'm fucking you, that you know it's me making you come."

Did he truly think she could be anywhere but right there with him?

He growled, the sound so raw and animalistic she wondered if his demon had joined them, but his eyes were still a dark, rich brown. His thrusts got harder, like he was punishing her, like making her come right then meant something she couldn't fathom.

For some reason, the idea that he thought she wanted someone else, was thinking of someone else, wasn't something she could bear, so she kept her eyes open and locked on his. Even when the pleasure moved through her, so intense she had no hope of holding back her cries. And when it finally became too much, she arched her head back and let sensation take over, focused on the feel of his big cock thrusting in and out of her. The way her inner muscles tightened around him. The sounds of his grunts and growls.

"That's it. Fuck, that's it, Grace. Give it to me. All to me."

She couldn't think about those words, the meaning behind them, not when he planted himself deep inside her and came with her, growling low.

"Tell me you won't deny me this anymore, Grace. Please, don't deny me you," he said against her throat.

CHAPTER 24

GRACE STILLED BENEATH HIM.

Fuck.

"Grace?"

She was quiet for the longest time, then finally, she sucked in a breath. "Deny you anymore? What the hell are you talking about?"

Fuck, he'd said it out loud, hadn't he? *Fucking idiot.* "I didn't mean...I don't know what I'm..."

He did not stutter or stumble over his words. He sure as fuck didn't get flustered. Ever.

She shifted under him. "Spit it out, Chaos."

He ignored how good that subtle movement felt. How her silky skin and those long, sexy legs moved against him. How hard she was making him all over again, and worked at sorting out what he needed to say. Honesty would probably be a good start, because this wasn't working for him.

The truth was undeniable.

He couldn't live like this.

For some reason it was hard, holding those beautiful brown eyes. This female, shit, she made him feel unsure, vulnerable. Again, not something he was used to. He sure as fuck didn't like it.

He cleared his throat because his vocal cords were so damn tight. "This mating thing, it's a fuck of a lot stronger than either of us realized. You feel that, too, yes?"

Please say yes.

He held his breath, only letting it out when she slowly nodded.

"Sex is a big part of it, and I..." *Shit.* However he said this would make him sound like an asshole. He pushed on. "I haven't...I can't be with anyone else." *I don't want anyone else.* "When you mate, you're supposed to live together. What we're doing...it's not natural, and it's...it's messing with my head, my control." Admitting that was a hit to his ego, especially since she obviously wasn't suffering the same problem. Yeah, she wanted him, but not like he did her, not in a *tear-the-walls-down-with-her-bare-hands-to-get-to-him* kind of way.

Her fingers flexed against his ribs, and he realized he hadn't restrained her like he'd planned to. Then he remembered the way her hands felt on his body while he'd fucked her, the way she'd clung to him, how much he'd liked it. His dick got even harder.

"You want to live together? We've already been over this."

That's exactly what he wanted, but going by the horror in her voice, in her eyes, that wasn't an option.

Her chest rose and fell in an agitated way, and he wanted to lean in and taste her smooth skin, draw one of those aching little buds into his mouth and take away whatever she was feeling right then.

He stared down into her beautiful eyes and fought the urge to kiss her again. "You won't bend on this?"

"No."

He wanted to fall asleep after being inside her every

night, wanted to wake up to her every morning, to her soft warmth, her drugging scent, and take her all over again.

Since that wasn't an option, he had to try to make her understand what he needed from her. "The connection we share, it can't be explained away, it can't be manipulated or suppressed. It just *is*. I know that now."

Her gaze searched his. "What are you saying?"

"I need the animosity between us to stop. And I need access to you when…" How the hell did he put this without sounding like a fucking sleaze?

She turned to stone beneath him. "You want unlimited access to my body. Is that what you're saying?"

The way she said that and the look on her face made him fucking ill. He searched his mind for the right words, for anything that would make what he was asking of her okay. He was grasping at thin air. "The sounds you make, the way you move beneath me, I know you like the way I fuck you, Grace."

Her nails dug into his skin. That only turned him on more.

"Your ego really is out of control," she bit back.

He slid out of her tight pussy a little, then back in. The soft moan that escaped from between her lips told him she most definitely liked what he was doing. Right then he needed that confirmation more than anything. The alternative wasn't something he could stomach. "You want me to stop?" he choked out, throat tight as hell.

Planting a hand on his shoulder, she pushed.

He fell back, rejection flooding his body. She was going to deny him, was going to climb off the bed and leave him there, desperate for her, on the verge of goddamn insanity.

But she didn't, she straddled his hips, gripped his cock, and took him back inside her, and rode him—slow and easy.

A vicious curse exploded from him, and his eyes rolled to the back of his fucking head when she squeezed down hard.

He didn't do this—he never let females top him—he was always in control.

His hands automatically went to her hips to halt her, to flip her underneath him and take over, but she slid down his length, squeezing her pussy tight again as she rolled her hips and he lost the ability to move.

"Fuck!" His vision actually blacked out for several seconds.

He was torn between his need for control and watching her ride him.

His gaze was drawn to the sexy spitfire riding his cock. The way her skin had turned pink the more aroused she became. The sway of her perfect breasts, those pretty pink nipples so tight and desperate to be sucked. The way her strong thighs flexed as she moved on top of him. The way her abdominal muscles clenched and released as she rolled her sexy hips. And all that blond hair, wild around her face.

Beautiful. Every inch.

Her wounds hadn't healed yet, and the white gauze against her skin had him biting back a snarl.

There was no taking his eyes off her, not for a moment.

What had she done to him?

Her bottom lip was red and puffy from his kisses, from the way she bit it the more turned on she became. His female was perfection in every way, and watching her like this was more than he knew what to do with.

His hands moved to her tight ass and he gripped it, holding her in place, and began to thrust up when he couldn't take it anymore. Needing to go deeper. Needing more.

"Is that a yes, Grace?" he rasped. "You'll give me this, we'll give each other this when we need it?" He was almost afraid to hear her answer, but he was starting to believe that she might actually need him as much as he did her.

She planted her hands on his shoulders, sunk down his cock, and ground harder. Her breath hitched. "Like a booty call?"

Fuck, he hated that term.

But if she said no, he didn't know what he'd do. It turned out, being inside her, just being near her, was the only way he could function now. Until things settled down between them at least.

"If that's what you want to call it." His hands tightened on her hips as if holding her to him could make her say yes. He thrust up again, deeper this time. She cried out. "Well?"

Leaning in, she slid her cheek along his jaw, her hair falling like a silken curtain around them both. "If I agree, it doesn't mean I suddenly answer to you. I still go where I want, with who I want, whenever I want, understand?"

If that was a deal breaker, he was fucked. "I don't share, Grace," he said, rocking into her. "I need to be the only male that you're fucking."

Her eyes narrowed as her fingernails scored his chest. "And will I be the only female?"

"Yes," he answered instantly. He didn't want anyone else.

She looked down, gaze locked on his, something moving deep in her eyes. "I never slept with him, you know. With Oden. If you think I would do that, could do that...I can't..."

He jolted beneath her, a rough breath exploding past his lips. Relief washed through him even as he knew it to be true. "I know. I do, Grace." He was a jealous fucker, but he knew she would never be with a male like that, not for any reason.

Her lids lowered, eyes bright. "Okay then, yes."

"Yeah?"

"Yeah."

Thank God. The last few days without her had been hell.

He'd never in his life felt more out of control. He'd thought staying away from her would help him maintain the self-discipline he lived by, but the mating had messed with him in far more ways than he'd anticipated. Grace was the only thing keeping him sane.

Then all thought scattered because she was moving faster, her beautiful body undulating on top of him, taking what she wanted, using his body to give herself pleasure. He hungrily ate up the sight of her, satisfaction filling his chest. Watching as she came for him, clamping down hard on his cock, throwing her head back, her long hair brushing the tops of his thighs.

Fuck, she was magnificent.

The feel of her body gripping his became too much, and though he wanted to drag this out longer, he didn't fight it. He came hard, pumping his seed deep inside her.

She collapsed on top of him, and he loved the way her thighs trembled and her panted breaths brushed his throat. His arms came up and wrapped around her, unable to resist holding her close. But she pulled away and slid to the bed beside him. It took all his willpower not to pull her back into his arms and hold her tight to him.

He turned to her and her eyes were closed, a small smile on her swollen lips. A female well and truly satisfied. His chest swelled along with other parts of his anatomy.

How could that be possible? He liked fucking as much as the next guy, but this was something else. He was a starving man, and Grace was an all-you-could-eat buffet. He ignored his cock and asked the question that had been plaguing him since the moment he met her.

"Why do you hate me, Grace?"

Her eyes flew open, and a shadow moved across them when she turned to him. "I don't hate you."

The *anymore* hovered between them. "Grace…"

"I need to get some sleep. You should go." Her gaze darted to the door.

A cold wash moved through him. Grace trusted him to fuck her to multiple orgasms but not share the secrets that weighed her down. Secrets that had shaped her into the female she had become. Beautiful, strong, sexy, a fucking warrior.

Secrets that obviously involved him.

As her mate, he should be the one to make it better for her, to bring her peace from whatever caused her distress, bring her happiness. But that's not what they had. Instead, he'd somehow hurt her, and he needed to know how. "Please, tell me."

She rolled away from him and got out of bed, uncaring of her nakedness, and dammit, he wanted her again, badly. She grabbed a T-shirt from her dresser and pulled it over her head. It was worn and faded and had "Linkin Park" scrolled across the front. It barely skimmed the tops of her thighs.

"Can you just let this go?"

He sat up, leaning against the headboard. "You made it clear how much you hated me from the moment I met you. But now we work together. Sleep together. Grace, we need to clear the air for this to work. And honestly, I need to know what the fuck I did or I'll lose my damn mind." He forced himself to relax, to appear as nonconfrontational as possible. "I think I deserve to know what I did, don't you?"

Grace paced away, then back, a look in her eyes that wrenched something deep inside him. Christ, what the fuck was it?

He felt her distress and pain like it was his own. But he didn't say that, didn't want to freak her out. Their connection was growing every day. A constant torment. He could feel her, but he couldn't touch her when he so desperately wanted to.

239

Finally, she sat on a chair in the corner of her room and pulled her legs up, crossing them and tugging the shirt down at the front with one hand to cover herself. It was on the tip of his tongue to tell her to let the shirt go, to not hide any part of herself from him, but he kept his mouth shut.

The silence stretched out, and he didn't think she was going to talk, but then she looked up and the pain in her eyes cut him to the bone. Her other hand lifted the gold rings she wore around her neck, and she gripped them tight. "I had a family once."

His stomach dropped and dread crawled up his throat instantly.

"My mother and father were both demi. Did you know that? I'm a second-generation demi-demon. I also had a younger brother, Curtis."

No, he hadn't known that.

She gripped the shirt tighter, and he knew instantly it had belonged to her brother. And the rings she always wore had been her mother's and father's.

"Our parents blocked us, kept us safe. Neither my brother nor I had gained our powers, but we felt it, knew there was something there, you know? I guess it's a second-gen thing? None of the other demi I know experienced it. Whatever it was, because of that, we were able to train to block ourselves even before we got powers, so we could go to school and have actual lives." She glanced up at him. "That's why I'm so good at blocking. I've been doing it since I was a kid."

He swallowed hard, knowing what he was about to hear next was going to be bad. "What happened, Grace?" The waves of pain coming off her intensified, making his own chest ache. He wanted to go to her, but she had closed herself off. She didn't want his pity or comfort.

"We'd both been homeschooled until we were strong enough to hold a secure block. My brother was fifteen when he was able to go to school. He'd made some friends, had a girlfriend." She bit her lip, her eyes closing for several seconds. "We'd just gotten off the bus and were walking home. We were talking, not paying attention to our surroundings, and Curtis got clipped by a guy on a bike. It knocked him over and he landed weird, breaking his arm badly and hitting his head. He was in a lot of pain, unable to focus on anything else. I felt it...his block dropping. I tried to cover us both, but I was still young and didn't have my powers. I wasn't...I wasn't strong enough."

Her eyes were haunted. Seeing her in pain was torture.

"I got him home as fast as I could. I knew once we got there everything would be okay. My parents could cover him." She looked up at him, agony and rage in those beautiful eyes. "Demons. They followed us home."

Fuck.

"My dad, he fought, but they were too strong, even against his powers. My mother had a healing power and was defenseless once they killed him. All three of them were slaughtered in front of me...and I... I just ran. I put up the strongest block I could, and I ran." A single tear slid down her cheek, and she brushed it away. "I survived."

Fuck, so much worse than he thought. He remembered them. Her family. "Angel..."

She glanced up again, but she wasn't really looking at him, she was looking inward. "I went back the next night. I was in denial, didn't want it to be true, and...you were there."

Chaos stilled.

"You were with Lazarus and Kryos, and I heard you talking. You blamed them. You lifted my brother in your arms, and you were so angry. You said it was my parents' fault Curtis was dead, that if my father had brought his family to you, they'd all still be alive." She gripped the fabric of her shirt tighter, her knuckles going white. "My father had lost friends and loved ones to demons. He hated you for that. Convinced himself it was your fault for letting demons into the city. He didn't trust you or the knights and told us not to, either. And when you blamed my dad, I hated you even more. I convinced myself that it was your fault as well. That they were dead because of you."

He wanted to go to her so damn badly. "Grace…"

"Vince eventually found me on the street, hanging around the club, and offered me a job cleaning. He looked after me, gave me a place to live, protected me."

His thigh muscles tightened and bunched, wanting to launch himself out of bed and pull her into his arms.

"That's why I hated you. I blamed you for their deaths. In my mind, it was your fault that I had no one left." She shook her head. "And I stayed angry at you, even when I could see you cared for us demi. When I saw you put everything on the line every time you fought, because I didn't want to believe it. Believing it would mean letting some of my anger go… letting *them* go. And I…I didn't want to be angry at my dad. I didn't want to blame him—hate him for taking everything from me." She clenched her teeth.

He moved then, couldn't stay away another second and strode to her, crouching in front of her chair. "I'm sorry, angel. I'm so fucking sorry." What else could he say?

She was shaking her head. "But it wasn't him, either. My dad loved us. Did the best he could. And you're right, I've been hostile toward you because I used you to feed the rage in me. Directing that anger at you was easier than the truth. But I know it wasn't your fault, Chaos, it wasn't the knights that failed my family." Her gaze lifted to his, hollow, broken. "It was me. I wasn't strong enough. If I'd been strong enough, if I'd practiced more, like they were always nagging me to… If I'd been able to block us both, my parents would still be here. Curtis would still be here."

"No." Grace jolted at his sharp tone, but he couldn't contain it. Now he understood why she fought so hard, why she was so single-minded when it came to killing demons. "You did nothing wrong. Nothing. Baby, you were a kid. Too young and inexperienced to hold that kind of block. Neither you nor your parents could have anticipated what would happen that day. The blame sits squarely on the demons who killed them. No one else." He took her face in his hands and held her haunted gaze. "What happened was not your fault, do you hear me?"

A small shaky smile tugged her lips. "So damn bossy."

Her skin was smooth and warm beneath his fingers, and he brushed away the single tear that streaked down her cheek. "You should listen to me more. I'm never wrong."

"Uh-huh. And modest, too."

She didn't believe that it wasn't her fault, not yet, but he wouldn't give up until she did. He brushed his thumb across her lips but resisted leaning in and kissing her. "So you don't hate me anymore?"

"I don't hate you anymore." Her grin turned wicked, though still wobbly. "But you're still a pain in the ass."

He couldn't help it, couldn't resist another moment.

He leaned in and kissed her.

CHAPTER 25

GRACE WOKE SURROUNDED BY CHAOS, his massive arms bracketed her body, holding her tight to his chest like he was afraid she'd run away in the night.

He'd taken her to the compound after they'd spent most of the night hunting the beast. And as soon as they walked through the door to his apartment, they had torn off each other's clothes and fucked on the floor before finally making it to the bed.

The intensity of it scared her. But she couldn't stop it. She was a Chaos addict.

The male had gotten under her skin; there was no denying it anymore.

She snuggled into his warmth and shivered, remembering how Chaos had asked her with quiet intensity why she hated him. Jesus. She'd spilled her guts, had told him all her deepest, darkest secrets. Had spoken her fears, her true ones that had lived deep inside her for so long. Why had she done that? Shared with him things she'd never told anyone, not even Vince.

He hadn't looked at her like the coward she'd always

believed herself to be, running to save herself when her family had been slaughtered. No, he'd comforted her, and after he'd wiped her tears, he'd carried her back to bed and taken her again, hard and demanding. His dark eyes had been locked on hers the whole time, like he was trying to will her to believe that it hadn't been her fault.

Chaos hadn't treated her like she was some fragile female whose emotions made her weak. He treated her like an equal.

Later, she'd woken alone, his scent on her sheets, but no sign of the male himself. She'd hated it.

Not this morning, though. This morning she was in his bed, and he seemed reluctant to let her go.

Goose bumps prickled over her body despite the heat radiating from his skin. It was too much. *He* was too much. Everything about him overwhelmed her, overpowered her emotions.

He'd made it clear he hadn't liked her dancing in front of a crowd when she'd performed for him. The possessive mated male inside him refused to share her with anyone else, not that she wanted anyone else right now. But she was terrified that if she let him have his way, if she let him take parts of her little by little, there'd be nothing left.

She'd lose herself. She'd become Chaos's mate. There would be no more Grace Paten. Before long he'd ask her to stop working at the club. How long before he wanted her to stop fighting?

Chaos made a rough sound and his hold on her tightened, his warm, bare skin pressed against hers, one heavy thigh shoved between hers.

She squeezed her lids shut.

Be strong. You have to be strong.

He pressed his hot lips against her ear. "What's going on in that head of yours?"

"You're awake." Stupid question, he was obviously awake, but he'd taken her by surprise.

He nuzzled the back of her neck, and she heard him draw in a breath. "Love the way you smell...fuck, it turns me on."

He was hard and hot against her ass. She wiggled her butt against him and chuckled. "No shit."

A growl rumbled through his chest against her back. "Don't test me, female."

"Or what?"

"I'll give it to you like I'm fucking desperate to."

Her stomach swooped. "You haven't already?"

"Been gentle with you so far," he rasped.

Her stomach clenched. "You think I can't handle you? I'm tougher than you think."

His hand dipped between her thighs. "Oh, I know you are. But I didn't want to scare you away."

"I'm not scared of you," she said. "I can take anything you can dish out."

She turned in his arms, and he instantly pinned her to the mattress, his eyes black and glittering. "You ever been tied down, Grace? Fully at someone else's mercy, putting your pleasure totally in someone else's hands?" His gaze dropped to her mouth and his nostrils flared.

Her heart raced faster. Could she do that? Could she give him that kind of power over her? He watched her, unflinching, all brutal demon warrior.

His phoned *pinged* and he glanced at it on the bedside table and cursed. He kept her pinned under him as he snatched it up and put it to his ear. "What?" He grunted unhappy. "Now?"

Another string of curse words, a lot more creative this time, and looking so put out and surly by the interruption it was almost comical.

Suddenly Grace had to bite her lip not to giggle. She

never giggled. Like ever. Maybe it was the release of nervous energy that was saturating the room. Whatever it was, she couldn't hold it in.

Chaos ended the call and looked down at her, jaw tight. "Something funny?"

She shook her head. "Nope."

His eyes crinkled at the corners, an almost smile, but then he sat up abruptly and swung out of bed, tagging his jeans off the floor in one fluid movement.

She rolled to her side, resting her head in her hand, and took in his beautiful, powerful body, his shaved head, the tattoos, all that smooth skin. Lethal was the word that came to mind. The male was a deadly weapon all on his own.

He turned back to her, and she licked her lips when he shoved his jeans on, took his erection in hand and tucked it in, wincing as he zipped up.

Lethal...and stubborn.

Chaos was pissed off. He had plans for her this morning, and they'd been interrupted.

"So sulky," she said, smirking. "Someone's used to getting his own way."

He rubbed a hand over his chest, his abs tightening, and he frowned, looking sexy and grumpy at the same time. "I don't sulk."

Was he trying to make her insane on purpose? Her smirk turned into a grin. "I'd say you were seriously close to throwing a full-on tantrum."

He fished a shirt out of his dresser and tugged it on, and when he turned back, she swallowed hard at the determined look in his eyes.

"Female, you have no idea what I want to do to you right now. None. Laughing at me for being forced to get up and leave you in my bed, wet and unsatisfied, has just earned you a punishment."

Holy shit. Her thighs snapped together, and she had to squeeze them tight. "Punishment?"

Every bit of his hot-blooded focus was on her. "I promise you'll like it."

Her inner muscles throbbed and her nipples tightened to the point of aching. She opened her mouth, closed it. What the hell could she say to that?

"Zenon called a meeting. I won't be long."

Her stomach rumbled.

"I'll bring food back," he called over his shoulder. "Don't fucking move."

Grace lay there stunned as he walked out, but not so stunned that she didn't admire his backside as he did. The male looked damn fine in those worn jeans.

She flopped back on the bed and groaned in frustration, while her belly did somersaults. God, she thought she might want that, to be punished by him. What the hell was he doing to her?

Ignoring her bossy male's orders, she climbed out of bed and strode to the bathroom.

Her male? Nope. Not thinking about that little slip.

She needed a shower, needed to clear her head and leave Chaos's bedroom before he hypnotized her with sex and punishments and she forgot her old life and never left this room again.

She was drying off when her phone rang. Grabbing it off the bathroom counter, she checked the number. *Unknown.* It could be anyone. One of her people. Vince was always changing numbers. But the tingle at the back of her neck told her it was someone else.

"Hello?"

"Grace?"

She curled her free hand into a fist. "Mr. Oden."

"Come now, why so formal?"

Asshole. "What do you want?" There was no point pretending anymore. He knew who she was, had just used her real name. He knew what she did to demons at night, had more than likely always known, and she knew he'd chosen the wrong side.

"Straight to the point. That's why I like you so much."

"You flatter me." If he picked up on the sarcasm dripping from her voice, he didn't let on.

He was in hiding. Had disappeared after beating the shit out of Vince. The knights had been looking for him. But finding the beast was the priority, and because of that, he'd managed to stay hidden.

"I require your presence this evening, Grace. And it would be in your best interest, and the best interest of those you care about, to attend." All the easy charm was gone, replaced by an edge that sent a shiver down her spine.

"Where are we going?" she asked, refusing to let him know he'd rattled her. They both knew she had no choice but to do as he asked. He'd already hurt Vince, could hurt more of her people, and no one could stop him—not when Oden was in bed with whoever had control of the demons in the city.

"I'll have a car pick you up at eight thirty outside Revelry. Dress formal." The phone disconnected.

Fuck.

Her mind raced, coming up with a plan. She could ask Chaos to follow the car when she was picked up, and if something went south, he'd be there to get her out. Wherever Oden was taking her, rushing in ready for a fight wasn't the right move, not yet, not until they knew what they were dealing with. He was in deep with a demon who'd summoned a beast and had the ability to control large numbers of demons at once. Fuck knew what else he was capable of.

249

He'd asked her to dress formal, which she had to assume meant there would be other people with them. Safety in numbers, right?

As long as they're not all demons.

Shit.

Wrapping a towel around herself, she pulled the door open—

Chaos was sitting on the bed, dark gaze on her. "I told you not to move."

She arched a brow. "I wanted a shower. And heads-up, I'm not your dog. I don't sit and stay on command."

His nostrils flared. "Who were you talking to?"

Possessiveness rolled off him like a thundercloud.

She'd given him an inch, and what do you know, he'd taken a mile.

She also knew instinctively that he wouldn't let her go tonight, definitely not on her own. The mated male in him wouldn't allow it. And she needed to go. Oden could lead her to the beast, could lead her to the major players working for Diemos. "Laney just checking in."

He watched her closely, and she wanted to squirm.

"Yeah? How is she?"

"Good." She sat beside him and took the plate he held in his hands. "Is this mine?"

He dipped his chin.

"Peanut butter and jelly. Your specialty."

A low chuckle rumbled from him and she forced herself to control her racing heart.

He watched her while she ate, a satisfied expression on his face as she chewed the last mouthful.

"Better?"

"Yes. Thank you. I worked up an appetite." She looked up at him. "Are you hunting tonight?"

"Yeah, Zen has a lead."

He was keeping something from her as well, she could see it in his eyes. She wanted to question him, but considering what she was about to do, she refrained.

She was used to keeping things to herself, but right then, she wanted to lean on someone else. It wasn't that simple, though, nothing ever was. And especially not with Chaos.

"You'll keep me updated?"

His gaze dropped to her lips. "Of course."

If he wondered why she hadn't demanded to go with him, he didn't say. Whatever Chaos had going on tonight was important and he was glad she wasn't part of it. More reason to keep her meeting with Oden to herself.

The mated male in him was in full-blown protection mode. He didn't care about her credentials on the battlefield, he was following his instincts to keep her safe. Her stomach clenched painfully. This was exactly why they would never work, why she needed to hold back and not let herself get attached.

He reached out and brushed her hair behind her ear. "You coming here when you're finished for the night? Or should I come to you?"

"No." Keeping her tone even and her expression neutral, she smiled at him. "I'll come to the compound. Bring stuff for a night or two." Distracting him with the prospect of two more nights of sex would hopefully stop him from questioning her about her plans for the evening. She felt guilty, dishonest, but what else could she do?

More intense staring. "Why the sudden change of heart?"

The male never let her get away with a damn thing. "Can't a girl change her mind? And it's just a couple nights. I thought you'd be pleased."

"I am. Very." His voice had dropped several octaves, and he brushed his thumb across the hollow of her throat. "Text me when you get here if I'm not back. I want to know you're okay."

"Why wouldn't I be okay?" He wasn't even trying to hide it anymore. "Have you forgotten that before we mated, I spent all of my spare time relieving demons of their heads? Chasing the fuckers down and beating their asses until they cried for their mamas? I managed just fine without a big, bad knight to watch over me." It was a desperate attempt to make him stop acting like an overprotective asshat.

"Grace, do you have to argue with every damn thing I say?" There was no anger in his voice. "Just humor me, would you?"

"Fine, whatever."

"You made them cry for their mamas, huh?"

"I spanked those little bitches."

He tilted his head back and laughed, deep and rumbly and so sexy she had to stop herself from climbing onto his lap and kissing him silly.

When his chuckles died down, his gaze went back to her lips, like he was thinking, wanting, the same thing.

Grace cleared her throat. "But I might be late tonight. I'm going to visit Laney and check on the others." Her heart pounded behind her ribs at the lie. It unsettled her to lie to him, when he'd been nothing but good to her.

His fingers glided down her arm, then wrapped around her fingers, and he tugged her closer. "Be careful, yeah? You're still healing. Those wounds could open back up."

He pulled the key card to his room from his pocket and handed it to her. "Now kiss me before I go."

Jesus, he was chipping away at her defenses bit by bit. After everything that had happened—Vince getting beaten up, Mark's and Tina's deaths, Hannah still missing, then the call from Oden—she didn't think she could survive that kind of intimacy from him.

"I don't think that's such a good idea," she said playfully and glanced down at the obvious bulge behind his zipper.

Ignoring her protests, he lifted her and planted her on his lap so she was straddling him. "Not in the mood to be teased, Grace. Give me your mouth."

"Chaos..." His big hand gripped the side of her throat, fingers delving into her hair, and he moved in, taking her lips in a hard kiss. He licked her lower lip and she opened for him without any more thoughts of resistance, hungry for a taste of him. His tongue surged into her mouth, mating with hers. Heat spiraled through her belly and pulsed between her thighs.

A growl rumbled from his chest and he gripped her ass, hauling her closer. Fisting her hair tighter, he held her in place and dominated her mouth. And God, she loved it. His cock was hard between her thighs and she squirmed as his other hand squeezed her ass.

She rolled her hips and he lifted his head, breaking the kiss.

"Don't stop." There was no missing the pleading note to her voice.

He chuckled, raspy and low, dirty as hell. "When I get back tonight, I'm gonna be so fucking hard for you."

He licked his lips like he was imagining all the things he was going to do to her, and she pressed against him to ease the ache, inwardly growling at her own lack of willpower.

"Angel, I can smell how wet that pussy is for me. Fuck...do you have any idea how much I want you right now, how hard I'm going to take you when I finally get to sink inside you?"

"I'm good with now," she said.

He chuckled. "Zen and Kryos are waiting for me."

She slid her hand under his shirt, across his abs, and he shivered. She loved that she had that effect on him. "You don't play fair, you realize that, right?"

His fingers in her hair tugged lightly, tilting her head back, while the other grabbed her wandering hand, stilling it. "As soon as I'm done tonight, I'm coming for you. Be ready, because there won't be any warmup, nothing except me stripping you down and fucking you until you scream, do you understand?"

She licked her own suddenly dry lips.

"Do you understand, Grace?"

"Yes?" she whispered.

He gently set her aside, gave her one last, hard kiss, then walked out the door.

Butterflies went nuts in her belly.

No wonder he was acting all protective; she was behaving like some pathetic damsel, all gooey-eyed and pitiful.

Forcing herself to pull her shit together, she stood and tugged on her boots. She may not want to tell Chaos about tonight, but she needed backup. Someone who could get her out of there fast if things got ugly.

She just had to go find him.

CHAPTER 26

EVERY MUSCLE in her body was tight and on edge.

She was braced to fight, to defend herself.

Oden would arrive at any moment, and she wouldn't be dropping her guard while she was with him. Not a chance. Chaos would be pissed when he found out what she'd done, but she couldn't let this chance slip through her fingers.

She looked up at the night sky and saw the outline of a dark figure far above her, shadowed white wings extended, their silver tips catching the light every now and then as he coasted on the breeze.

Chaos might not be going with her, but she wasn't dumb enough to go alone.

She could have asked her crew, but after losing Tina and Mark, emotions were high and she didn't trust them to just sit back with the fuckers responsible within killing distance. They'd get themselves killed, too.

There'd been only one obvious choice.

There were demi living and working all over this city, a whole network of eyes and ears that she called on frequently.

There'd been sightings of Rocco around the city, of course. But mainly he seemed to be sticking close to the portal.

Her heart squeezed, remembering what happened the last time the portal opened, when his female was dragged through and taken to Hell. His agony had saturated the air around them, and it was now etched into his face, in his eyes, lining his features. The male was in constant pain.

He hadn't needed much convincing to watch her back tonight, not with how desperate he was for any information on Kyler. Maybe someone tonight might know something? God, she hoped so. Grace curled her fingers into a fist. Just looking at the male shredded her. Rocco was a shadow of himself. She knew from Chaos that they'd been trying to get him to come home, but seeing him tonight, she knew that wasn't going to happen, not willingly.

The club was filling behind her, music spilling out onto the street.

She checked her phone again. Her ride would be here any minute. She ran her hands down her dress. Formal wasn't exactly something she'd ever needed before. And there hadn't been time to go shopping. The below-the-knee, black satin sheath dress would have to do. At least it was stretchy and allowed her to move freely.

Whatever this was, wherever Oden was taking her, she needed to be ready.

Something would go down tonight, she was positive of that, and she wanted all the intel she could get.

She'd seen what they'd done to Tina, what had more than likely happened to Hannah. She damn well wouldn't let that happen to any more of her people.

Yeah, Chaos would be angry with her, but she'd been fighting this war since she was sixteen years old. Was the same age when she killed her first demon, when she stood over its ashes and vowed to do whatever it took to stop the abduction, exploitation, abuse, and murder of her people.

She mated with Chaos for that very reason, he knew this. Her power, though still new, had already grown stronger. She didn't need to be cosseted and protected. She didn't want that. Never had. Never would.

A shiny black car pulled up in front of her and the driver climbed out. "Hands against the car."

She did as he said and gritted her teeth as he slid his hands over her body, searching for weapons. She hadn't bothered with any. There was no way Oden would take her into his pit of snakes if she was packing. The male looked inside her clutch after feeling her up, and surprisingly let her keep her phone.

He opened the door for her, and Grace climbed in. The car was empty. "Are we picking up Mr. Oden next?"

"He'll meet you at the venue." Then he shut the door, trapping her inside.

A feeling of intense claustrophobia came from nowhere and suddenly she found it hard to breathe. Grabbing her phone, she keyed in a quick text to Chaos. *How's your night going?*

Her phone beeped a few seconds later. *Just ruined an ibwa demon's night. Jealous?*

Chaos's reply instantly had her heart rate slowing down, and the feeling of being suffocated vanished. She didn't want to think too closely about his effect on her, or the reason she'd immediately sought his comfort.

You know I am. Have fun x. She sent her reply, then blinked down at her phone. Why the hell had she ended it with a *kiss*. Shit, she was going soft, either that or losing it.

His reply was again quick. *Looking forward to kissing you for real later. Remember. Text me when you get to the compound.*

She felt her face heat and shoved her phone back in her purse. What was she doing? Did fuck buddies end texts with kisses? Because essentially, that's what they were. Texting for a booty call? Yes. Texting to ask how your fuck buddy's night's going because you had a mini freak-out? No.

But her mind remained so full of Chaos, she was surprised when the car pulled to a stop outside The Esquire, a towering skyscraper of luxury apartments.

The door opened and the driver motioned her toward the entrance. She knew Rocco was still with her, but didn't dare look up.

"Penthouse suite," the driver said and handed her a plain white card with a four-digit number on it. He grinned, all teeth. "Have a nice evening."

She made her way to the elevator and keyed in the number on the card. Nerves started up in her belly and she ruthlessly squashed them. She couldn't afford nerves, had to be ready for anything.

A variety of unpleasant scenarios flashed through her mind. Being this high up made for a more difficult escape—unless there was access to the roof.

The elevator glided to a stop and the doors slid open.

When she stepped out, she was greeted by a male demi. He led her to a set of doors and pushed them open.

The place was enormous, and gorgeous. She didn't know what she'd been expecting, but the tasteful surroundings and elegantly dressed people milling around, talking and laughing while a female in the corner played the piano for a little mood music, was not it. A high-stakes poker game or a mass orgy, maybe. Not this.

"Impressive, huh?" said the demi holding the door, and she realized she was still standing there gaping.

"Uh...yeah." He chuckled lightly and closed the door

behind her. A waiter swung by and offered her champagne. "Thanks." She took a glass, with no intention of drinking it.

"Grace, you made it," Oden said, moving toward her, those cold black eyes glittering.

Like she'd had any other choice, but she could play his game. She just wished she knew what the rules were. "Of course. So what are we celebrating?"

"You'll know soon enough." He took her hand, lifting it to his mouth and kissed her fingers. He was wearing a ring. Heavy gold and with the same symbol as the one she'd seen on the cuff link she'd found at Tina's apartment, the same ring the demon who attacked her on the roof wore.

She barely resisted the urge to yank her hand away and punch the asshole.

"Just an FYI, there's no cell service here, at all. In case you wanted to contact anyone?" His lips curled up in a tight smile. "Come, let me introduce you to some of my associates."

Now she knew why they'd let her keep her phone.

Over the next hour, Oden paraded her around the room like some trophy wife, introducing her to several males, all powerful. She could literally feel it rolling off them, and for some reason they were all more than a little excited to meet her. Like they had some secret joke going on, and no one had bothered to fill her in.

Finally, he took her to the far side of the room, where a couple stood. The male was tall, his features unusual but handsome in a weird way. The female at his side was about Grace's height but with some serious curves. Dressed like a Gothic princess, she was striking with her pale skin, violet eyes, and black makeup. Her only splash of color was the red stripe of hair down one side of her face. The male at her side had his long fingers wrapped around the back of her neck in

a possessive hold, but it was more than that—this male dominated her, and not in the sexy way.

He wanted to make sure she knew who was boss, who
was stronger...who was in control.

Grace itched to take the fucker's head off.

Oden stopped in front of them and dipped his head like
he was addressing royalty. "Sir, I'd like you to meet Grace.
The female I was telling you about."

The taller male leaned in and whispered something in
goth girl's ear. The female tensed. It was slight, but Grace
didn't miss it or the tight, forced smile she aimed at him
before he released his hold on her. Her unusual violet gaze
darted to Grace before she walked away.

The male didn't give his name, just stared at her, his
hawk-like gaze moving over her from head to foot.

Grace forced a smile. "Nice to meet you."

That almost black gaze finally landed on hers and held.
The hair lifted at the back of her neck, and every single
instinct she possessed went on high alert.

Demon.

A full-blooded disciple of Hell, and he had his hand
extended, waiting for her to take it. She had no choice, and
when he clasped his fingers around hers, he tugged her a
little closer. Those black eyes didn't leave hers, and she was
positive he could see inside her, see everything. She pulled
her hand back, but he held firm.

"It's lovely to finally meet you, Grace. I've heard so much
about you."

His voice was impossibly deep and grated down her
spine. "I wish I could say the same." If this creep had been
granted sanctuary, she'd eat her left boot. No way would
Chaos, or any of the knights, let this fucker out and keep
breathing.

A small grin tugged at his thin lips. The effect was terrifying. "Oh, we'll soon be very well acquainted." He released her hand, and she had to stop herself from rubbing her palm against her dress. He looked over her shoulder to Oden. "Well done. She is everything you said and more."

What the fuck was this?

Oden took her elbow and, after making their excuses, bowing his head and backing away like a simpering rodent, he quickly led her away, a shit-eating grin spreading across his face. "Good girl. You've pleased me tonight."

Like I give a shit. She spun to face him. "Why am I here, Oden?"

They wanted her, she knew that. Did they want her for Diemos's army? More than likely. They were constantly trying to grow his numbers here on Earth. Demi were regularly abducted for their powers and kept as prisoners by demons. She was well aware that hers was unique. Had one of them sensed it?

He ran the back of his knuckles down the side of her face and she jerked out of reach.

"There are things I can't divulge just yet. But I can tell you that every person in this room is working toward the same goal, or will be soon."

"And what goal is that?"

"A better world for our kind, and you get to be a part of that, be at the forefront of change, a catalyst for a whole new and exciting world."

She forced her breathing to remain steady, while her heart hammered in her chest. "Oden, what are you..."

"I wish I could stay and..." His stare slid down to her breasts, then lower before coming back to land on her mouth. "...keep you company, but I have a lot to do tonight. Stay and enjoy the wine."

"That's it?"

"Hmm, so eager?" He brought her hand to his lips, but instead of kissing her, he slid his tongue across her knuckles. Her stomach lurched. "I'll see you soon, Grace, I promise."

He wanted her to believe she was free to go. But she knew otherwise.

She watched him walk away. This was worse than she'd thought. What they were doing was bigger, more horrific than she could have imagined. How many demi were they keeping captive? How many had they slaughtered? How many were here tonight unaware of what was going on?

She pretended to take a sip of her drink, glancing around the room. She didn't know what the hell was actually going on, but she had to fight every instinct in her that screamed for her to get the hell out. The place was full of demi, but there were other demons as well, she could sense them now, like toxic gas polluting the room.

She glanced at the door. Several large males stood in front of it, blocking the way out.

Lifting her drink to her lips again, she forced herself to remain calm, and when the opportunity finally presented itself, she slipped down a hall at the back of the room. Maybe they had Hannah here? Others held against their will?

She searched several rooms, finding nothing. It became obvious that no one lived here. It had probably been rented just for tonight.

She walked out of another empty room and bit back a curse.

A male stood just outside, hands in his pockets, head tilted to the side and a small smile curving his lips.

Grace smiled back and curled her fingers into fists at her sides. "I was just looking for the bathroom?"

He took a step closer. "Remember me?"

"Uh, sorry, I'm terrible with faces." His mouth twisted, and that's when she noticed the flat, black emptiness of his eyes. Demon. *Fan-fucking-tastic.*

"Oh yeah, we've met. You even gave me a little present. How rude of you to forget." He pulled the collar of his shirt to the side and revealed a nasty-looking scar. "An arrow through the shoulder isn't as fun as you'd imagine."

Awesome. She offered up a wide-eyed, confused expression. "An arrow? I don't know what you're talking about."

"Yeah, you do." The smile dropped, and he grabbed her arm, hauling her across the hall.

Grace had no choice but to go. She didn't want to draw attention and knew she had a way better chance fighting this guy one-on-one. She didn't know who in this penthouse knew about her, but she guessed being a demon killer in this crowd was a pretty big no-no.

He pushed her into one of the bedrooms and shut the door behind them. "I volunteered to deliver you to your new home, but I thought we could have a little catch-up first? What do you think?"

"New home?"

"You didn't really think you were leaving here tonight?"

No, she hadn't. And she'd been ready, anything to get to the truth that would stop this war. And this place wasn't where they'd find their answers. Thankfully, Rocco wouldn't let her out of his sight. If they moved her, he'd follow and would gather the troops to take down these fuckers. That couldn't happen if this dickhead killed her before she got delivered to the next destination—and what she hoped was their main headquarters.

"What's it like? My new place? Will I have roomies?"

He frowned, momentarily thrown, then scowled. "I really would like to end you, torture you for a while first, but unfortunately that's not an option. But I will make you pay for what you did to me."

She'd backed up, giving herself some room. Leaving a pile of ash would be a pretty big giveaway, so she couldn't put this animal down. She had to incapacitate him. She glanced at the window. They were twenty stories high; he sure as hell wouldn't be yapping after a fall like that.

He moved toward her and she held her ground. She needed to knock him out, and to do that, she had to let him get close. He raked her with a stare equal parts lust and pure hatred. "How do you like it, demon killer? I like it hard and rough." He grinned wide. "I also like to bite. Every time you look in the mirror, you'll see my mark on your skin, like the one you left me. I'll make sure you never forget our time together."

He pounced, and she let him take her to the ground, but he was stronger than she'd expected, making it hard to fight him off and reach the pressure point in his neck.

He shoved up her skirt, exposing her thighs, and licked his lips. "I'm going to enjoy this."

As he came down on her, she had the opening she needed. Fisting his hair in one hand, she brought up her knee, nailing him in the balls, while she pinched the nerve on the side of his neck with the other.

The guy gasped and shook in agony, trying to struggle, but she refused to let go. A hot, tingling sensation began to move through her—her power. She didn't know what would happen with a demon, but she didn't stop it, she let it flow out of her into the fucker flailing in her hold, then started pulling it back inside her.

She could feel him, feel the darkness he held inside, then a surge of power exploded through her, power that was not her own, and she gritted her teeth so she didn't cry out as it filled her.

He went limp, and she released him, slumping back, his dead weight pinning her to the floor. She'd taken whatever power the demon had, and now she could feel it inside her, morphing and changing, becoming one with her own and making her own ability stronger.

Had mating with Chaos made this possible? More than likely.

The door opened and Grace shoved the male off, jumping to her feet.

Goth girl stood at the door, her pale gaze looking down at the dead demon. "Fuck," she hissed.

Not good, not good at all. Grace eyed the other female. She really didn't want to hurt her. She was a demi, but also something else, something Grace didn't recognize. The female had also suffered, there was no missing it in her haunted eyes.

"It was self-defense," Grace said.

"Oh, I don't doubt it." Goth girl shoved the guy with the toe of her boot. "Greg is a sick, twisted asshole." She glanced back up at Grace. "But we need to get him the fuck out of here before someone comes looking."

Grace held her gaze. "You expect me to trust you?"

"Nope. But you don't have much choice. Take his shoulders. I'll get his legs."

She was right, Grace didn't have much choice.

The other female checked to make sure the way was clear, then they carried the heavy bastard down to the kitchens via a back staircase.

An elderly male was standing at a counter and looked up when they walked in. His brows shot to his hairline, then he cursed. The female shook her head. "Don't say a damn thing, Spencer. Just help us get out of here."

The old guy hustled to what Grace assumed was the servants' elevator. "Up or down."

"Up," she said.

The doors slid open and they carried their mostly, but not quite dead demon inside.

"If the master asks after you?" the old guy asked.

"Tell him I'm having one of my headaches and I've gone home."

They dropped the demon on the floor to give their arms a rest. The elderly male looked concerned, afraid, but not for himself. His next words confirmed it. "He won't be happy."

"I'll be fine."

Grace didn't want to see her get into trouble. "I can take it from here."

Her pale eyes slid to Grace. "Hold the door." She raced out, grabbed a kitchen knife, and came back. "Not without this you can't. And you'll need help carrying him."

The door slid closed. "Thank you...for this," Grace said to her.

The other female looked down and sneered. "I hated that motherfucker. You've done me a favor."

The whole thing was surreal. Usually Grace would be on full alert, waiting for the female to turn the knife her way, but for some reason she knew that wasn't going to happen.

The doors slid open and they lifted the demon, carrying him out, then muscling their way through the steel door that led to the open roof.

"What's your name?" Grace asked. This female was helping her dispose of a demon after all.

She shook her head. "It's better you don't know." She gripped the knife. "Do you want the honors, or shall I?"

Grace held out her hand. "It's my mess." Then again it would be more beneficial to take him to the compound for questioning, but then she saw it, something in the other female's eyes as she looked down at the demon. Her stomach gripped tight. "Unless you want to?"

Goth girl stood motionless for a moment, then glanced up at Grace. "I've never done it before. Will you help me?"

Yeah, goth girl needed this. It was the pain and hatred in the other female's eyes that Grace recognized, but so much more, so much worse. If killing the monster at their feet helped the other female to heal in some small way, Grace was determined to help, she owed her that much at least.

Grace kicked off her shoes and goth girl snorted.

"Hey, they were expensive, I don't want this asshole's blood all over them." Grace glanced up with a grin, then fisted the unconscious demon's hair before dragging her finger across the demon's throat. "Through here. You might have to saw at it a bit, that knife doesn't look very sharp. Demon beheading 101, use a sharp knife."

Goth girl's lips twitched, then she dipped her chin and started slicing, or more hacking because yeah, the blade was blunt as hell. Grace pretended she didn't hear the gasps of rage, the desperate sob that escaped goth girl as she killed one of her tormentors. Because Grace had no doubt that's what was happening here.

The head finally came free and the demon ashed out.

The knife clattered to the rooftop by the other female's feet. She was breathing heavily, staring in both shock and relief at the pile that used to be a demon. "Thank you," she finally said.

"My pleasure." Grace offered her another smile. "Killing demons like him is kind of a hobby of mine."

Goth girl chuckled, then stilled suddenly and looked up, her sights trained up to the night sky. "You came with backup?"

"Of course."

"I need to go."

Grace held out her hand. "Come with me."

The female's eyes went flat. "I can't."

"I'll send help. We'll close this down, whatever it is."

"You won't find them...us, if you come back. It'll be like we were never here."

"What about the other demi in there? I can't just leave them."

"I've got it covered," she said, then spun and ran, disappearing back the way they'd come.

Boots meeting concrete brought her head around. Rocco stood a few feet away, arms crossed over his wide chest, flat gaze on the demon's remains. "What happened?"

"He recognized me." The wind would remove the evidence overnight.

His gaze pinned her to the spot. "Anything?"

He was asking about his mate. About Kyler.

She shook her head.

His throat worked several times. "Chaos is gonna pop an artery when he finds out you came here."

"Yeah, probably. But I don't answer to him. I don't answer to anyone. He knows that."

Rocco shook his head, not looking convinced, and glanced at the steel door goth girl had disappeared through. "Who was that?"

"A friend."

The sound of sirens filled the night.

Goth girl worked fast.

Rocco walked over and swung Grace into his arms. "Let's get you to the compound. I need to get back and tear this shit apart."

It wasn't hard to miss how much weight he'd lost. His skin was pale, his eyes sunken. He looked sick. This was the physical effects of a knight after losing his female, and Rocco and Kyler hadn't even gotten the chance to properly mate before she was taken from him. Grace's stomach gripped tight, an uneasy feeling taking hold of her. She ignored it and looked up at the big male. "Are you coming back...to the compound, I mean?"

He shook his head, eyes flashing between black and deep blue.

"They'll need you. The demon I met in there, he's powerful, Rocco."

"I'll come back when I have to and not before."

She wanted to hug him but didn't think he'd welcome it. "Can you take me to my apartment instead? I need to get changed first. I'll drive to the compound."

His massive white wings snapped open, the silver tips glinting under the starlight. "I wouldn't waste time getting there, Grace."

She rested her hand on his chest. "Chaos will be fine."

He looked down at her hand, then back at her, and an expression that looked very much like pity crossed his hard features. "Whether you like it or not, he would die protecting you."

"I don't need him to do that..."

"He has no control over it. He won't be okay with this. He can't be. It doesn't matter how capable you are. He's a mated male and you are his female. Losing you is his biggest and only fear now, no matter what he's said to you."

Deep down she'd known it. She just hadn't wanted to believe it. "Shit," she muttered.

Rocco actually smiled, it was small and didn't reach his eyes, but she was glad to see it, despite being fleeting. "He's going to lose his shit, I have no doubt about that, but maybe you could...I don't know, try to cut him some slack? He's new to this, like you are. His angel half wants to protect you at all cost, and the demon inside him would lay waste to this city to do it."

Fire trucks and police cars filled the street below, and they watched as people from The Esquire swarmed out. The false alarm goth girl had pulled to get the demi out wouldn't protect them forever, they'd all been marked, like Grace had, for whatever twisted role they would play in the coming war, but she'd bought them some time.

Then they were airborne, and all thought disintegrated while she hung on for dear life.

CHAPTER 27

THE THUD of Chaos's boots thumped against the carpeted floor as he paced his living room, checking his phone for the millionth time in ten minutes. This was how it felt to lose your mind. He still hadn't heard from Grace. Where the fuck was she? Why wasn't she answering his motherfucking calls or texts?

Every kind of scenario had been going through his head, and currently his mind had settled on the one where Grace was lying facedown in a damn ditch, skin gray and emaciated.

He'd tried to be cool and let her do her own thing like she'd demanded. But everything was different now. She wasn't some faceless, masked vigilante. She was *his*. His mate. His female. His to protect.

"Fuck this." Shoving his phone in his back pocket, he pulled his short sword off his bedroom wall and started for the door—

The sound of a lock disengaging reached him.

His heart gave one heavy *thump* in his chest, then lodged in his throat.

It opened and Grace stepped inside.

He dragged in a rough breath when he finally had her in his sights. She was safe...alive. Christ, his knees went weak.

His demon roared to the surface, right there with him as he tracked her movements. *Take. Claim. Mine.*

There was only one light on, and he was standing on the other side of the room in shadow. She didn't see him right away, and he drank in the sight of her, trying to soothe his frayed nerves.

It didn't work.

She wore jeans and a black tank top that showed a lot of creamy skin and finely honed muscles. Her long blond hair was down and he had an incredible urge to twist it around his fist, pull her into him, and make her promise to never put him through that ever again.

His independent female wouldn't appreciate that, though.

She hadn't seen him yet, and glanced up to the wall where his sword should be and released a relieved breath.

He gritted his teeth to stop the growl from ripping past his lips, then gave up and let it free.

She jumped a foot in the air, but instead of freaking out, she landed crouched in a battle pose. His dick instantly got hard.

"Jesus Christ." She scowled, straightening. "You scared the crap out of me."

His gaze tracked her, stalking her, his blood pumping. He carefully placed his sword on the table behind him and turned back to her. Christ, he was positive he could hear her pulse race faster all the way across the room.

"You remember what I said when I left you earlier?" His voice was nothing but rusted steel.

She nodded, her delicate nostrils flaring.

"You know what's about to happen?"

Her face flushed, the scent of her arousal already reaching him. "Yes."

Chaos had no control over what happened next.

In minutes she was naked, her clothes tatters at her feet, and his cuffs were locked around her wrists. He'd hoisted her up in his arms.

"What are you doing?" she asked on a shaky exhale and licked her lips.

He didn't answer as he carried her across the living room. There was a hook in the ceiling he used for a heavy bag occasionally, and he headed for it.

"Arms up," he said, all monster.

She did as he said, her pale skin flushing darker and her breath quickening.

He secured the cuffs over the hook above her head, and she had no choice but to lock her long, sleek, bare legs around his hips. *Fuck, yes. This* soothed both him and his demon. He was in total control. She was bound. Couldn't get away from him. For a short time, he had her here, with him. Safe.

He could feel her heat, how wet she was, through his shirt against his stomach.

With a hiss, he tore open his jeans, freeing his cock. "I've wanted you in my cuffs for so fucking long, Grace, you have no idea." He dragged the fat head of his cock through her drenched folds. "But every time this perfect, tight-as-fuck pussy distracts me, and all I can think about is getting inside it."

She whimpered.

He nipped her jaw. "Gonna fuck you now."

Her tits shook with her ragged breaths. "Get on with it, then."

He gripped her tight ass and slapped it. "Do not test me, female."

She gasped, then opened her mouth to fire back some smart-assed comment, but he slammed up inside her, filling her with every hard inch.

She screamed and instantly started coming, shaking and squeezing down on him, clutching at his dick over and over.

Chaos leaned back, hands still on her ass, holding her where he wanted her, and pounded into her, hard and fast. Her body jarred with every thrust, face dark, eyes heavy, those long legs holding on to him tight. Satisfaction dripped from her, her cries of more filling his head, and as much as he wanted to lose himself in her, he couldn't.

Fucking each other into oblivion was easy. He wanted more. All of her.

This moment was a turning point. He had to show her that he could give her everything she needed, that she could let go with him like she hadn't with anyone else. That she could trust him to take care of her the way she truly needed.

So gritting his teeth, fighting his own urgent need to blow inside her grasping, wet heat, he fucked her until she was about to come again—then quickly withdrew.

Grace cried out, shaking, cursing.

He nipped her puffy lower lip. "You don't get to come again, not yet."

She hadn't replied to his text messages, and then she'd fucking sneaked in, looking guilty as hell. What was she going to do, pretend she'd been here waiting for him for hours when he got home? She didn't trust him. He fucking *needed* her trust, and he was going to earn it, starting right now.

He dug his fingers deeper into her pert little ass. "It was nice of you to finally show up." He leaned in, sucking one of her tight, pointed nipples into his mouth and glanced up at her as he released it. "Your phone broken? You lose it? Hey, maybe the dog ate it?"

Fire blazed behind her eyes, her chest rising and falling rapidly, pretty little tits shaking. "I was driving...and then I was here, so..."

He yanked his shirt off with one hand and pressed up against her. He needed to feel the heat of her skin against his so badly he shook. Every labored breath she took caused her peaked nipples to graze his chest. He wanted to slam back inside her, desperately, but he wanted to get through to her more.

He leaned forward and breathed her in, filling his lungs with her sweet scent—and stilled. "Demon."

She tightened her legs around him and rammed her bare pussy against his cock now trapped between them.

"Yup, remember, I kill them sometimes." Her lips parted and her tongue darted out to swipe over the lower one, and he swore he felt it across the head of his cock.

"What aren't you telling me?"

Her brow scrunched, her legs loosening around his waist, and she groaned. "Look...fuck. Okay, but you're going to be pissed. It had to be done. And I got good intel..."

"What did you need to do?" Dread filled him.

"Oden invited me to a little get-together." Those long legs tightened again when he took a step back. "He threatened to hurt my people if I didn't go."

"You were with Oden?"

"Yes."

Was she serious? A growl, loud enough to shatter windows, erupted from him. He took several breaths to calm the fuck down.

"Grace." Her name came out more a groan than anything, and spoke volumes about his current state of mind. This female would be the death of him.

The sweet scent of her arousal surrounded him, and he muttered a curse. Did she have any idea what she did to him?

His gut was in knots. Every part of him constantly ached to touch her, to just be near her.

The female turned his brain to fucking mincemeat. She confused him, excited him, drove him insane.

Her fingers clenched and unclenched above her head and her eyes flashed. "It was fine. I was fine." She glanced up at the cuffs. "Can you...you know, let me down for this conversation?"

"No. Obviously this is the only way to keep you from fucking off and doing shit behind my back." He rolled his hips, his cock sliding through her slick folds, grazing her clit. She shuddered and ground down on him. He held her still. "Talk."

She scowled. "It was a kind of party, I guess. Really, they were parading demi in front of a room full of demons so they could sense our powers. Including mine. Who knows how many demi they're already holding prisoner. This is bigger than we thought. There was a demon there, Chaos, he was so damn powerful, and Oden would have crawled up his ass given the chance. This demon, he has to be behind everything that's going on in the city. I'm sure of it."

"Where?" he bit out.

"I told Gunner when I got here. They're already checking the place out."

He ground his teeth. "You were in a room full of demons?"

"I knew what I was getting myself into."

"How?"

Her eyes narrowed.

"How did you know what you were getting yourself into?"

She took an agitated breath. "Oden took an interest in me. I knew he wanted me for something, and after Tina and

Hannah went missing, then discovering his involvement with the demons, it wasn't hard to figure out why he wanted me there."

"You went alone? You put yourself in danger?"

"Rocco followed me, knew where I was at all times."

"What?" He couldn't believe what he was hearing.

"I knew you wouldn't let me go. I needed to go, Chaos."

He was, yep, he was actually losing his fucking mind. He unhooked her arms and lowered her to the ground, undoing the cuffs and tossing them aside.

She watched him warily as he yanked up his jeans. "How did you get out?"

"A demi, she's not there because she wants to be, but I couldn't get her to come with us. She made sure the others in the building got out and helped me dispose of...ah..." She snapped her mouth shut.

She was still trying to keep shit from him. "Finish what you were going to say."

Her spine straightened. "A demon, okay, one I'd apparently fought before. He was supposed to take me to wherever they're holding our demi."

"He attacked you?"

She walked up to him and pressed her beautiful naked body against his. "I knocked him out, and the demi I met helped me get him to the roof. We ashed him there. There was no cell service in the penthouse or I would have called you. I'd planned to if I wasn't..."

She bit her lip, stopping herself again. This time he finished for her. "If you weren't captured?"

Grace dipped her chin.

"You went in expecting you would be." Not a question.

"If I hadn't been forced to kill that demon, they would've taken me where they're keeping my people. Rocco would have followed, called you all in, and we could have set them free."

She shook—from anger, not from fear. Not Grace. Nothing scared her, and yeah, that terrified him.

"You could have been killed," he said, feeling close to the edge, so damn close.

"They want me alive. I'm no good to them dead." Her chin came up, and she looked stubborn as hell. "You think Oden could best me? You've seen me fight."

"Yeah, I have." And he couldn't stop himself from adding, "Scares the fuck out of me." He smoothed his hands over her bare shoulders and gently gripped the side of her throat because he had to keep touching her. "Turns me the fuck on as well."

She sucked in a shaky breath and his heart stuttered. He loved the way she reacted to him. How she seemed to crave him almost as much as he did her. But tonight she was playing with fire. "Don't do that again, Grace. If you ever willingly put yourself in a dangerous situation like that again, if you ever keep something like this from me again, I *will* punish you." It wasn't the first time he said it to her, and he meant it.

Her gaze darkened. "You'll *punish* me?"

"Yes." He'd said it now. And he wouldn't take it back. And despite the way Grace had slightly snarled the words, he knew she didn't want him to, either.

"You told me you'd never punish me, that you couldn't," she said, testing him, throwing his own words back at him.

The smile he gave her was sinister and dirty as fuck. "Oh, you'll like this punishment."

"How is that a deterrent?"

"It's not, but it gives me an excuse to tie you down and do whatever the fuck I want to you."

She stood there naked, heat blazing in her eyes and looking like his own personal wet dream. "What are you going to do? Hang me from the ceiling and fuck me again?"

Her voice shook, broadcasting how much she wanted him to follow through with his threat, but was too afraid to ask for it.

He shrugged. "Among other things."

Her eyes were bright with defiance, with desire. "That was fun and all, but I don't answer to you, to anyone." There was no anger in her voice, just conviction.

"I'm not anyone. I'm your mate. You don't lie to me. You don't keep shit from me. You treat me with the respect I deserve as your male."

Her eyes flashed. "And do I get the same respect?"

"Yes," he said without hesitation.

Surprise crossed her beautiful face. "Will you admit the information I got was helpful."

"Yes."

"That it was important."

"Yes."

More surprise. "So you're not angry with me? We're cool?"

"I'm not angry, I'm fucking furious." His breathing had become labored, and his erection throbbed like fuck. His control was slipping again, the more he thought about what could have happened tonight. "You are mine, Grace. And you *risked* what's mine. Christ, you were prepared to sacrifice yourself. How the fuck could you ever think I'd be cool with that?"

"Chaos…"

"You know I'm going to punish you now, don't you, angel?"

She blinked up at him, eyes wide, heat flashing through

them before she bit her lower lip and glanced up at the hook in his ceiling again. She squeezed her thighs together.

Yeah, she knew. She'd sensed it. Knew he needed more from her, and she was going to give it to him, because she wanted it, too.

CHAPTER 28

HAND SHAKING, Chaos cupped the side of her face. "You know that I won't hurt you. I would never, could never hurt you?"

She nodded, and it eased something inside him.

"The anger I feel, it will never touch you, or be directed at you. It comes from fear, from a feeling of hopelessness. That I could have lost you. But anger has nothing to do with what we're about to do."

He needed her to understand before this went any further.

"Okay," she whispered, lips parted, cheeks flushed.

"What do you want, Grace?" he said, voice all demon now.

Her chest was rising and falling rapidly. "To touch you." She looked up at him through her lashes, and he didn't miss the vulnerability there, the need…and not just physical.

Shit, this female could bring him to his knees with just one look.

"Please," she whispered.

That desperate plea nearly did him in. "On your knees."

She did as he said, and her fingers trembled as she parted the front of his jeans and took his hard cock in her hand. He had to fight not to thrust into her soft grip.

"Did I say you could touch yet?"

"You want me to," she said, looking up at him. "I know you do. Let me give you this."

She was decimating his control, trying to take it from him at the same time. His female was so damn strong. He cupped her jaw and tilted her face up. "Do you know how much I want that mouth on me?"

She shook her head and licked her lips.

He'd been inside her a short time ago, hot and wet and so fucking snug, it had been torture to pull out, to not lose himself in her. He needed to feel the wet heat of her mouth wrapped around him now. "Give it to me, then, show me how good you can suck me."

A shiver moved through her, and she shoved his jeans down to the tops of his thighs, took his dick in her hand, and looked up at him as she darted her tongue out, licking the head of his cock, tasting herself there, driving him wild. She made a little sound of pleasure.

He hissed.

She gripped the thick base and wrapped her lips around the head, sucking gently. Her other hand slid from his hip down to cup his balls, and he thrust forward, stuffing her hungry mouth full.

He let her have her way for several more painstaking minutes, let her think she'd won the control she thought she needed, enjoying the show as she sucked and licked him like she couldn't get enough. It was going to kill him to pull away again, but she wasn't going to get her way, not tonight.

He was walking a razor's edge, and when tingles shot up from the base of his spine, he knew he had to make his move. "Stop."

She shook her head and sucked harder, taking him deeper.

He snarled, nearly blowing down her fucking throat. Gripping her upper arms, he dragged her to her feet.

"Why did you stop me?" She grabbed his dick and pumped his iron-hard flesh in her fist, and fuck if he didn't thrust up, working himself against her tight grip.

She got up on her tiptoes and he couldn't deny her the kiss she was asking for. He leaned down, letting her suck and lick his lips, letting her kiss him.

"Please, don't say no. I need this...I need you," she gasped out, the last closer to a sob. Her words sliced through him. Christ, deep down she still believed he was a fucking monster, that he would mistreat her some way, *deny* her.

He cupped her beautiful face, brushing his thumb over the smooth skin of her jaw. "You think I would leave you wanting?"

She shook her head, too quickly, her cheeks rosy, hair wild around her face. She truly thought he was that much of a bastard.

He held her gaze. "When my mate needs to come, I make her fucking come. I would never leave you unsatisfied, understand?"

"Glad to hear it."

She was holding on, still trying to top him, his little warrior. But he knew she was faltering, that tremor to her voice told him how much she needed what he was going to give her. How much she needed to hand control over to him.

He slid his thumb along her pouty lower lip and gave her what they both desperately wanted, even if she didn't understand it yet. "But because you're being punished, how and when you get there is up to me."

Her little white teeth sunk into that sexy, puffy lower lip.

Chaos's gut gripped tight, and he lifted her off the

ground, carrying her toward the bed. She wrapped her legs around his hips and rubbed herself against his aching dick.

He grabbed her hips, stilling her.

She growled in frustration, and he had to bite back a smile.

He planted her in the middle of the bed. "Lie back."

Christ, he needed to find some fucking self-control, and fast. Not easy when his female lay in the middle of his bed, every bare inch of her smooth, tanned skin revealed to his ravenous gaze.

He had to lock his knees so he didn't fall into the bed with her and take her like a male possessed.

"Grip the headboard and spread your legs. Show me how wet that pussy is." She did as he asked, and he bit back a growl. She was drenched and puffy from his cock and so fucking beautiful. "You feel empty, don't you, angel?"

Her back arched and she closed her legs, pressing them together, like his gaze between her thighs was a physical touch. She squeezed them tighter and rolled her hips, the scent of her need spiking.

Jesus, she was killing him. "Legs apart and keep them that way," he demanded and stroked his achingly hard cock.

Her eyes followed his movements and her lips parted on another moan.

"Now, Grace."

She did what he said, perfect tits shaking from her panted breaths, lips full and red from sucking him.

"Good. That's good." He wanted inside her so badly his balls were drawn up tight as hell. "You need to stay just like that. If you move your hands, I'll stop. If you touch me, or yourself, I'll stop." *Or I'll fucking lose it.* "Yes?"

"You're loving this, aren't you?" she said, eyes flashing, a mix of anger and desperate need.

"Yeah, I fucking am, and so are you."

She didn't answer but let out a shaky breath, making those pert tits jiggle again. Her nipples were dark pink and tight. Hard little peaks aching for his mouth. Shit, he'd never had so much trouble keeping it together. He had to draw on every ounce of his control not to cover her body with his, slam inside her again, and own her pussy until she screamed. "Watch me," he demanded.

Her gaze slid over him and she gripped the iron bars of his headboard tighter, fucking writhing against the mattress.

Fuck me.

He kicked off his boots before he shoved his jeans off properly. Naked, he climbed onto the bed, crawling up between her spread thighs.

Taking her in, so fucking beautiful, he licked his lips and pressed four fingers to her soaked cleft, pressing down, spreading her pretty lips, her juices.

Her hips bucked off the bed and she slammed her legs closed again, holding his hand there. From the sounds she made, she was close to coming just from that barest of touches.

He pulled his hand free and shoved her legs open again. "You don't get to come yet, Grace."

"Sadist." Her voice broke.

He slapped her pussy, not hard but enough she'd feel it, and she cried out, her hips bucking.

She gasped, her thighs trembling. "*Oh my God.*"

"If I was a sadist, I wouldn't have let you come once already tonight." He shook his head. "You closed your legs again without my permission. Next time, I'll restrain them."

His fingers were coated in her arousal, and with the way his dick was leaking constantly now, he sure as fuck wouldn't need lube to fuck his fist. "I was about to fill you with my cock, but since you disobeyed me, you can watch me get myself off instead."

"You can't be serious. Chaos, please…"

Taking both of her ankles in one hand, he held her legs straight up, exposing her tight ass and sweet pussy. *Christ.* But instead of thrusting into her, he moved in closer, so his knees were spread, pressing against either side of her ass and sat back on his heels. "Eyes on me," he said and draped her legs over his thighs, forcing hers wider and keeping them that way.

With glazed eyes, she took him in, watched as he fisted his cock and started stroking. She gasped, her slim hips rolling again, nostrils flaring. "Please, dammit, I…I need you inside me."

He nearly came right then. He wanted to give her the fucking moon. Make her come so hard and so thoroughly that any male from her past would cease to exist in her memories. And he would. He'd show her tonight that he was the only one who could give that to her.

His cock was so hard, it stood up straight. He leaned forward, pressing it down, dragging it against her weeping pussy, sliding through her sweet lips, getting his shaft nice and wet, covering himself with Grace and growling at the sounds she made as he did.

"Keep your eyes on me. Do not look away."

She cursed as her gaze moved over him like she'd never seen anything she wanted more. He loved it, her eyes on him, the way it made him feel.

He sat back on his heels and started stroking again, faster, squeezing and pulling on his cock with fuck-all finesse. This was all about getting off as quickly as possible and it wasn't hard with Grace watching what he was doing between her thighs. With her naked and laid out for him. With her scent filling his head.

His balls tingled and he felt his orgasm at the base of his

cock. "Let go with one hand only. Use your fingers to spread yourself wide for me."

One of her hands released the bar and slid between her thighs, doing what he asked, exposing herself for him. The sight of her, along with her gasps and moans, were more than enough to tip him over the edge.

He fucking snarled as he pumped his cock hard and fast, coming all over the beautiful, delicate, pink, glistening flesh she'd displayed so prettily for him, coating her with his seed.

Grace panted, hips rolling, face flushed, a sound of frustration, of the deepest, sweetest kind of need coming from her on an agonized whimper.

Not even allowing himself to catch his breath, he took her hand from between her thighs, lifting it above her head again, and pressing her into the mattress with one hand to her chest, so she couldn't thrash around. He coated his fingers in his come and shoved two deep inside her.

She groaned long and low.

Rubbing his thumb in what he'd just decorated her with, he slid it across her clit, and fucked her with his fingers hard and fast.

Flinging her head back, she cried out, hanging on to the bars over her head, opening her legs wider, asking without words for him to go deeper harder, begging him for more.

He gave her more until he felt her tightening around his fingers, until she was right on the edge, about to come—

He pulled his fingers free.

Grace screamed, her beautiful body shaking hard, glistening with sweat, right there, right on the edge. And Chaos planned to keep her there a while yet.

She moaned. "P-please, Chaos."

He felt her plea right behind his ribs. "I know you want release, angel, and I promise you're going to get it."

Her fingers had turned white from gripping the bars of his headboard and her thighs were trembling so hard he knew she was desperate to slam them shut. She could if she wanted to. He hadn't restrained her again for that very reason. She could get up and go. He wasn't forcing her to do this.

This was all her. And when she finally let go for him, when she flew, he wanted there to be no doubt that it was exactly what she wanted. How she wanted it.

Grace played by her own rules, he knew that better than anyone, and right now, she wanted this. She wanted what only he could give her. Badly.

"Do you do this with all the females you fuck?" she rasped.

He covered one of her breasts with his hand, squeezing, teasing her tight nipple. "They don't exist. Not anymore."

Her mahogany gaze shot to his, her body shaking harder.

He didn't remember what he did with any other females before Grace. It didn't matter. Grace was all that mattered. "Don't move." He strode to the bathroom, grabbed a washcloth, and when he walked back in, Grace was still in the same position, hands gripping the bars of his headboard, trembling legs spread wide.

Gorgeous.

She had no idea how much that pleased him. In this moment, this brave, strong female—*his* beautiful, relentless little warrior—trusted him with her body, trusted him to give her what she needed.

Her gaze tracked him.

He sat beside her and took his time cleaning her off, wiping his come from between her legs, toying with her as he did it, watching as she writhed and whimpered, skin flushed and slick with sweat. She was still riding that edge but unable to take it where she needed so desperately to go, not without his permission.

Grace needed this, maybe even more than he did.

Tossing the washcloth aside, he climbed onto the bed again, sliding up between her thighs, and licked his lips. She stilled, chest heaving, her gaze locked on him as he nuzzled his way up her inner thigh. She'd waited long enough, had been so damn perfect. His female deserved to come, and come hard.

Chaos covered her pussy with his mouth—no more teasing, not anymore—and sucked and licked and ate her like she was his last meal, groaning at the soft, silky texture, the sweet addictive taste of her.

Grace tasted like heaven and was so close to coming apart already that when he pushed his tongue inside her, he felt the first pulse of her inner muscles. He wanted her heat squeezing his cock when she finally came, though. He wanted her eyes locked on his, wanted to feel her come apart for him.

Right before she toppled over the edge, he rose above her, covering her.

Grace cried out, tears glistening in her eyes, and her beautiful strong body quivered so hard her teeth chattered. God, she broke him, in every way.

"Shhh," he said against her lips as he looked down at her, as he took her hands from the bars above her head and curled them around his neck. "I've got you." Then he slammed into her so hard and deep she screamed.

Her nails dug into his back as she clamped down on his cock so tight he was lost, bucking and pounding into her while she came for him, crying out his name over and over.

He wanted more of her, all of her, all the time. More than he'd ever wanted anything in his entire life.

And when she came again, he let himself go with her, pumped her full, marking her with his scent and relishing the marks he knew she'd left on his skin. He hadn't lied, there was no one else before her, they were gone, washed from his memory. Grace was everything. All he needed.

He dragged his nose along her skin, nuzzling and kissing the spot between her shoulder and neck, sucking and kissing his way up along her jaw, then lifted his head and watched as she caught her breath and slowly opened her eyes.

"That was...I've never...holy shit," she whispered.

He couldn't speak for several seconds, not without saying something that might freak her out and send her running.

Reluctantly, he slid from her body, and she let out a lusty sigh.

He didn't know how it was possible, but she'd never looked more beautiful than in that moment. "Making you scream my name is my new favorite thing to do," he said to lighten the moment, ignoring the weight in his chest, the words on the tip of his tongue.

She laughed, low and husky, and his cock started getting hard again. "Who knew such a serious male could be so creative?"

He grinned at her, and he knew it looked deviant as fuck when her eyes widened slightly. "You haven't seen anything yet."

She reached out and traced her finger over the markings on his arm, the tattoo-like designs that all knights had, telling the story of what he was and where he came from. "I'm sorry I worried you. I'm not used to relying on anyone else... Since my parents, no one's ever—" She shook her head.

His heart jumped against his ribs. "I know it's hard for you to understand what this is, what we are, but you can trust me, angel. I will never...fuck, could never, hurt you."

She still looked uncertain. "This whole thing, it's just so confusing."

"I know, but we'll work it out. We just need to talk to each other. You can ask me anything, tell me anything, yeah?"

She nodded, but again didn't look totally convinced.

It cut him deeper than it should. They were mated, but they still didn't know each other, not really. It would take time to earn the total trust he so desperately wanted from her. He forced himself to climb out of bed and pulled the sheet up, tucking it around her. "You should get some sleep."

He stood to leave the room. The way he was feeling, some distance from her might be a good idea. She wasn't where he was. It was hard to accept, but pushing for more would only push her farther away.

"Chaos?"

"Yeah?" He couldn't bring himself to look at her as a wave of need washed over him so fierce it took all his strength not to turn around, get into bed, and hold her like she was the most precious thing in his life.

"Why do you call me angel?"

He swallowed, a lump forming in his throat. "Because you're what I imagined one would be like when I was a little boy...fierce, intelligent...breathtakingly beautiful."

She was silent several beats, and he worried that he'd said too much.

"Your mother was an angel," she said softly. "How is it you'd never seen one?"

He turned back to her and the way she looked, all rumpled and soft, made his gut ache. "They had their servants take care of us until we were old enough to train."

"But your mother..."

"I have no idea who she is."

Sadness filled her eyes, *for him*. He turned to leave again, before he kissed her, kept on kissing her.

"Chaos?" she said again.

"Yeah?"

"Are you coming back?"

The uncertain way she'd asked, giving away a piece of

herself in that moment, was something he'd been worried he'd never get. Fuck, just dropping her guard, that tiny bit of vulnerability, and it made him feel...shit, full, warm—whole. "Yes."

She relaxed, and until that minute, he hadn't realized how tense she was, afraid that he wouldn't come back to her? That he'd leave her after what they'd just shared, like it meant nothing? Jesus. He watched as she snuggled down under the covers and closed her eyes.

Fuck it. He'd talk to his brothers about what they found in that penthouse in the morning. He didn't want to leave her, not even for a second. He switched off the lights and climbed back in beside her, then wrapped her in his arms.

Grace didn't freeze up or pull away, no, she sighed in pleasure and pressed closer, like she was seeking comfort from him.

Along with the sound of his name on her lips when she came, it was the most satisfying sound he'd ever heard.

CHAPTER 29

IN A DUNGEON AT AN UNKNOWN LOCATION.

A whisper of sound jarred the male awake. His eyes flew open, but in the intense darkness he couldn't see a thing. All that nothingness matched the darkness in his mind. An empty void, that no matter how hard he searched, gave up nothing.

There was nothing.

Except *her*.

He clung to memories so vivid, it was like she was there with him.

Cold, unyielding manacles around his wrists and ankles clattered against the stone wall at his back, and the sudden movement caused the jagged steel to cut into his flesh.

A scraping sound came from his right. He didn't know how they entered his prison or if they were always here, living in the darkness with him. But the creature would cause pain, unspeakable pain, before it finally left him alone.

But first it would stalk, torment, until it became too much

and the screaming would begin—his own screams ringing in his ears, echoing off the walls until his throat bled.

A claw sharp as a blade sliced across his stomach, then was gone just as quickly. Warmth ran down his thighs and dripped on his bare feet. The next slice was to his shoulder, then his side, until all he heard through his heavy breathing was the steady dripping of his own blood hitting the stone floor.

It finally struck, latching on to his shoulder. The creature wasn't in the mood to play with its prey today.

He threw his head back and screamed.

Light suddenly flooded his cell, so bright and warm it stole his breath and burned his eyes.

The creature shrieked and retreated. He strained to see, but he'd been in the dark too long. The creature screamed, kept screaming until it wasn't able to anymore.

He blinked against the light. A shadow crossed him, the outline of a male filling a doorway. The doorway out.

"You were hard to find."

"Who am I?" he rasped. "Who are you?"

The big male closed the distance between them and placed his hand on his shoulder, the touch was gentle, kind, warm. He'd been so cold for so long.

And with that touch, it all came rushing back. Every painful, horrific, awful memory.

He didn't want them. He wanted them out of his head again, it hurt too much. They hurt too much.

"What the fuck do you want?" he asked thickly, because he knew who this male was now.

Who *he* was.

"I have a deal for you, and I think you'll want to hear it."

CHAPTER 30

GRACE SCANNED the quiet streets as she, Chaos, and Gunner followed Zenon through an industrial suburb at the edge of the city. Kryos and Lazarus flanked Zenon and both sported worried expressions.

She didn't blame them. Nerves were assaulting her belly as well and there was no controlling it. Not after discovering that Zenon was not only the son of Diemos, but also the grandson of Lucifer. *Freaking Lucifer.*

Well, apparently, Grandpa had told him how to find the beast, or was guiding him to it, or something—she didn't totally understand. But whatever was happening, the knight didn't look like he was fully aware of what was going on around him. His eyes were vacant, like no one was home, or at least someone else was in his driver's seat.

What she did know was the beast wanted Zenon's blood. Chaos had told her that through Zen, the beast would be able to track its true target: Lucifer. Basically, Zenon was bait to draw the monster out—

Zenon stopped suddenly and turned, head tilting to the

side like he was listening to someone. His back arched and his eyes rolled up so all you could see was the whites.

"Jesus," Laz muttered. "I don't fucking like this."

"Yes, sire," Zenon said in an echoey, demonic voice, then he looked at Chaos, face contorted, every vein and tendon straining against his inked skin. "The old steelworks building across the street," he said through gritted teeth. "I can't..." He took a step toward the looming building, all shadows and sharp angles. "Let...go..." He took another step.

"Hold him," Chaos barked at Laz and Kryos.

The two knights dove on Zenon, trying to hold him back. But it was like the male had tripled in strength. Gunner joined in, but Zenon fought even harder.

Zenon couldn't enter that building in the state he was in. He'd offer himself to the beast and would get himself eaten. Grace had heard Chaos promise Mia when they left that he would bring her mate home safe, whatever it took. But right now, even with Chaos joining the fray, they were still having trouble holding back their brother.

A male dropped from the sky, seemingly out of thin air, landing in a crouch in front of them. His gold wings snapped in tight to his back before vanishing completely. His silver eyes slid to Chaos. "I've got him."

The velvet roughness of his voice lifted goose bumps across Grace's skin.

Chaos stiffened. "You sure about that?"

The male dipped his head, gaze unwavering.

The knights released their brother and the tall, golden-winged male wrapped his inked arms around Zenon, holding him easily as he whispered something that caused him to still.

"Who is that?" Grace asked, unable to look away.

Chaos looked troubled. "Silas. An angel. He'll keep Zenon safe."

Her mate started toward the old warehouse, and they all jogged along with him. Gunner pulled the door open, and a roar filled the air, echoing off the iron walls.

"That's either the beast or one of Gunner's exes," Kryos said, pulling the Glock free.

Lazarus chuckled, and Gunner flipped them off.

Chaos swung around to her, his dark eyes trapping hers. "Call your people in." He cupped the back of her head and planted a hard kiss on her lips. "And stay back until we have it restrained."

She nodded, and for once didn't think about arguing. Tangling with the monster lurking in the dark was the last thing she wanted to do. But she could most definitely help with the demons she felt around them. Her people were hanging back awaiting her instruction. She quickly sent a text to James, telling them to move in.

The lights came on and the creature hissed.

It stood on the other side of the warehouse, and as soon as it saw them, it charged.

Bits of old and rusted machinery littered the huge area and demons began to crawl out of the shadows.

Her people moved in, facing off against the army of demons protecting the creature, as the knights ran toward the beast.

The demons attacked, all hell breaking loose. The demi were outnumbered, but Grace knew without a doubt her people were better fighters. She gripped her blade in her right hand, slashing at the demon that lunged at her, slicing a deep cut through its chest. Another came at her from the left, and she pulled her Glock from her thigh holster and blew a hole through its shoulder.

It flew back, hitting the ground. James, wielding an axe, removed its head as Grace swung around to engage the next one. Teeth elongated, drool sliding down its chin, the demon charged and she spun, kicking it in the head. It stumbled back, and she advanced, fisting its hair and dragging her blade across its throat. Its mouth gaped, its teeth biting at thin air. She hooked its leg and it hit the ground. James was there a second later and hacked off its head, turning it to ash.

No tricks this time, no vanishing and reappearing demons. They'd managed to take them by surprise.

The sound of growling suddenly filled the air.

Hellhounds, huge and black, with fur sticking up along their spines and eyes glowing red, surrounded them, then flew into the fray. Chaos had told her they were coming, that he'd made a deal and they'd agreed to help, but she'd never seen anything like them in her life, and she'd seen a lot of weird shit.

They tore into the demons, giant mouths filled with jagged teeth crunching through skulls, ripping off heads with deft efficiency.

She was covered in demon blood, muscles screaming as more demons came at them. She took her place beside the hounds, fighting, hacking her way through the ones still standing.

The sounds of the knights roaring echoed through the warehouse, the beast along with them. But it had retreated into the deep shadows, and she couldn't see what was happening.

A handful of demons ran from the building, escaping into the night, and her people and the hounds finished off the rest. Grace dragged her arm across her face, wiping away the blood splattering her skin and in her eyes as a huge hound moved toward her, sniffing at her feet and pawing at the ground.

It shifted.

A naked male close to seven feet tall was now towering over her. A pair of jeans flew at him, and he plucked them out of the air without even looking. His eyes stayed locked on her as he tugged them on, his sinewy, muscled body flexing as he did. His hair was shaggy and matted with blood, scruff covering his strong jaw.

"You're Chaos's female?" he said, eyes boring into her, nostrils flaring.

The male's voice was deep and so rough she had to force herself not to wince. She dipped her chin, not even trying to deny it. That's exactly what she was. There was no point pretending otherwise. She realized right then that she didn't want to.

Eyes the palest of gold moved over her. "You're good with a blade."

A vicious roar came from the beast.

Grace spun around as it stumbled forward again, and her heart leaped into her throat.

The knights were in their Kishi demon forms, clinging to the beast with their claws, trying to slash it with their swords, desperately trying to weaken it.

The creature shook like a wet dog, throwing the males clinging to it across the room. A blast of power filled the cavernous space, so strong Grace stumbled, and it lifted the hair on the back of her neck.

The huge male beside her growled out a curse, lips peeling back, eyes glowing red again as he scented the air.

Grace stared up at him. "What the hell was that?"

He ignored her, barking out an order to his pack. They stopped what they were doing immediately and closed in.

Her gaze flew back to Chaos as he flew at the beast again, wrapping himself around one of its thick necks. Laz was up next, Kryos right behind him, they ran back at it—

But hit the air around it like it was made of stone, their big bodies jarring to a halt. It was like an invisible wall had been lifted in front of them.

And Chaos was locked behind it, alone with the beast.

"Let's get the fuck out of here, Warrick," another male growled behind her.

All the hounds were in their human forms now, and the male beside her, Warrick, gave him a look that was utterly terrifying. "Stand your fucking ground."

Grace had no idea what was going on. She didn't care. Chaos was trying to fight that creature alone, tearing at its throat with his claws, biting into it with his fangs. But the beast was too strong and tossed him off again. Chaos hit the wall with a sickening crunch.

"Do something!" Grace cried as the beast stalked her mate.

Gunner roared and sprinted at the invisible wall, his brothers beside him, trying to slam through. But they couldn't, no matter how hard they tried.

Two huge jaws lined with razor-sharp teeth opened over Chaos, picking him up before he could get away and tossing him in the air like a rag doll. Grace screamed, flying at the invisible wall, pounding with everything in her. Chaos landed hard. One of his wings was bent wrong and blood pooled around him. She pulled her gun and fired, but the bullets were absorbed into the barrier, like she'd fired into a wall of molasses.

The creature moved toward Chaos again, and Grace cried out, smashing her fists so hard she drew blood. "Chaos! Get up! Move!"

The beast lowered its head, about to tear into him. It would kill him this time.

Chaos's arm shot out, and something gold glinted in his hand, it flicked out like a whip, wrapping around one of the beast's necks. Chaos yanked on it, hard, slamming the beast's head to the ground, dazing the creature, and then staggered to his feet. He tossed whatever it was he was holding and it looped around its second neck. Chaos gripped the end of the golden rope again, tugging as hard as he could. The two heads slammed together, and Chaos swung out, tangling it around its thick legs.

The beast shrieked, swaying as it fought for balance, so loud that they had to cover their ears. It thrashed and toppled over, hitting the ground so hard the building shook.

Chaos slumped down beside it, bleeding and battered, unmoving on the ground.

The room went deathly silent. No one spoke. The invisible wall remained, preventing Grace from reaching Chaos, keeping him trapped.

Zenon stood beside her now, Silas with him. She hadn't even seen them come in. Zenon pulled his phone from his pocket and typed something out, then shoved it back.

"We need to get him out!" Grace cried on the verge of a total meltdown as the pool of blood around Chaos grew.

"We will," Zenon rasped, but he looked as worried as Grace.

A moment later, the door crashed open behind them, followed by the sound of boots hitting the concrete floor.

They turned.

A dark-haired male with features unmistakably similar to Zenon's was moving toward them.

"Who is that?"

Zenon shifted but said nothing, his yellow gaze locking on the male walking toward them, bracing, waiting...for what?

The sound of those boots grew louder as the newcomer approached. Someone walked behind him, head bent. Grace couldn't see his face past his dirty blond hair hanging forward. Three females followed them both, all dressed in tight black leather from head to foot—one brunette, one with hair like spun gold, and the third with vibrant red hair and eyes so bright a green they seemed to glow. She was scowling, eyes narrowed. All three held wicked-looking blades, and the redhead spun hers as she walked, like she was ready to let it fly at a moment's notice.

The hounds bowed their heads, the knights going still, watching warily as he approached. The filthy male behind him, dressed in ratty jeans, shuffled after him, not looking up, not saying a word.

"Lucifer," Silas said when he reached them.

Lucifer?

Holy fucking shit.

He nodded to the angel and gave Zenon a chin lift.

No one moved, and she realized when she attempted to, she couldn't.

Lucifer kept walking, lifting his hand as he approached the invisible wall. It dropped instantly, and he kept on walking until he was right beside the beast.

He clapped his hands loudly and rubbed them together, grinning. "Right, let's send this ugly fucker back to Hell."

Lucifer crooked his finger to the silent male beside him, and the guy shuffled forward on shaky legs. Lucifer cupped his cheek and carefully brushed his hair back.

Startling pale-blue eyes glowed like neon from his dirt-streaked face. Zenon sucked in a breath beside her as the dirty male's gaze shifted to the knights in the room.

"T?" Lazarus choked. "Tobias?"

The male looked back at Lazarus.

"Your eyes. Fuck, brother, your eyes." Lazarus's voice broke on the last.

Grace didn't understand what was happening, but she knew Tobias was their brother. She thought he was dead, and going by the reactions in the room, so did everyone else.

Unmistakable regret filled Tobias's startling blue gaze. The knights in the room struggled to break free from the invisible binds holding them in place. Chaos moved slightly, doing the same, and Grace almost fell to the ground and wept with relief that he was still alive. But like the rest of them, it was obvious he was frozen to the floor.

A knife appeared in Lucifer's hand.

"No!" Gunner yelled.

Lucifer ignored them. "You will be rewarded for your sacrifice," he said to Tobias. "I promise you that."

Tobias looked to the knights again, his gaze settling on Lazarus. "I'm sorry, brother," he rasped.

Lucifer dragged the blade down both of Tobias's arms, deep and long, and tilted his head back, lips moving in a chant as blood pooled on the floor below Tobias's feet.

A dark, gaping, swirling hole opened in the ground beneath the beast, sucking it through. Tobias's gaze slid back to Lazarus again, not looking away as he was sucked through as well.

Lazarus bellowed.

The portal closed.

Grace's feet were free, and she ran to Chaos, hitting her knees beside him as the knights stared at the spot where their brother had vanished.

"Chaos?" He didn't respond. "Answer me, please, answer me." She searched for a pulse. It was weak.

Zenon went at Lucifer, and the former king of Hell didn't try to stop him as Zenon landed a brutal punch to his jaw.

Lucifer smiled, blood coating his teeth. "Ouch."

Zenon fisted the front of his shirt and shoved Lucifer against the wall. "You had T this whole fucking time?" he snarled.

Lucifer shook his head. "No, I rescued him from his prison."

"And then you sent him to fucking Hell."

Lucifer shrugged. "I offered him a deal. He willingly

accepted." He spat blood on the floor. "He felt he owed his brothers. He did it for you."

"What fucking deal?" Lazarus bit out.

Lucifer ignored him and kept his gaze on Zenon when he answered. "That is for Tobias and me to know and for you to find out."

Zenon shoved away from him.

"And you're welcome," Lucifer said, straightening and heading for the door.

The females with him followed, and the redhead slid her hand over Silas's back before she patted him on the ass. "Yum," she said and strutted away.

Silas cursed.

Chaos's pulse grew weaker.

"Help me, someone please help me!" Grace cried.

The knights snapped out of it and rushed in, lifting her mate and carrying him from the warehouse.

CHAPTER 31

Chaos lay naked on his bed, his body covered in dark bruises and puncture wounds across his abdomen and thighs. He was so still, his gray wings, one badly broken, inky and glistening from his own blood, were spread out beneath him.

He was pale, so damn pale, bloodless. Every bit of power he had left now going into repairing his body, healing all those wounds.

Jack had been called in because this was way more than the knights could deal with themselves. Gunner stood beside the bed, two fingers pressed deep inside one of the wounds low on Chaos's stomach, staunching the blood from a main artery that had been nicked by razor-sharp teeth.

Jack cursed under his breath as he worked around Gunner's fingers, desperately trying to soak up the blood pooling around the wound so he could see what he was doing.

Everyone seemed to be moving in slow motion, the silence so oppressive, Grace thought she'd lose her mind if someone didn't say something. Chaos was dying, and no one was saying anything.

She couldn't lose him. *She couldn't lose him.*

She'd only just allowed herself to accept it, what throbbed behind her ribs whenever he was near, what had been there a while now. The respect, the admiration, God, the awe, she'd felt as she'd gotten to know him—the affection, the *pride* that he was hers—it was *more*. What she felt for the male in that bed, *her mate*, was so much more.

He was everything.

Guilt over her parents had clouded the truth. She'd stupidly fought it, had been afraid of what was so clearly in her heart.

Afraid to let him in because she couldn't bear to lose him as well.

Right now, her heart lay bleeding on that bed. Cold and broken, battered and barely beating. She loved him.

She loved him so much.

They hadn't gotten the chance to learn everything about each other. She didn't know his favorite color, his favorite meal, his favorite TV show. Did he even watch TV? She didn't know that, either. He was her mate, and she *didn't know*.

"Shhhh, it's going to be okay. He's going to be okay," someone said close to her ear, and the room seemed to spin back into reality, time snapping again into full speed. Jack barking orders at Gunner. Chaos's brothers all around her, fear etched into their faces.

"Don't fight me, Grace, come on, I don't want to hurt you," the same voice said. "We gotta let the doc do his thing."

Fight?

That's when she realized strong arms were wrapped around her, gripping her wrists, stopping her from going to

Chaos. And that sound she could hear, that agonized whimpering like a wounded animal, that was coming from her.

Rocco didn't let go, even when she stilled.

He looked down at her with hollow eyes, so dark that the blue irises looked like shadows had bled into them. "I've got you," he said.

His cheeks were sunken in, worse than when she'd last seen him. But he was here, for his brother. She didn't reply, couldn't. She didn't try to pull away either because she needed someone to hold her up. If he let her go, she thought she might free-fall into nothing.

So she stayed where she was, collapsed against Rocco's chest, his strong arms stopping her from falling.

Finally, Jack stood back, wiping his blood-stained hands on a towel. "I've got the bleeding under control. He'll live, but he'll be out for a while. He needs to regenerate the blood he lost, and his body will already be working overtime to heal his other injuries. I'll line up the broken bones in his wings so they'll heal straight, but that's all I can do." He looked up, his eyes meeting Grace's. "Time is what he needs. Having his mate close will help." He shrugged. "In my experience, with any beings, it always does."

"He can have my blood," Grace rasped.

"It doesn't work that way, unfortunately. Besides, your blood wouldn't be strong enough. The only option is to wait."

Rocco finally released her, and Grace rushed to Chaos's side. She had to touch him, to reassure herself that he was actually there, that he hadn't left her. She gently cupped his face, his bearded jaw scraping against her hand. "I'm here," she whispered. "I'm not going anywhere. You're stuck with me; do you hear me? I'm staying right here."

He'd fought, had been prepared to give his life for this

war, to keep the demi and humans safe in this city, and he almost had. He'd almost died.

How could she have ever doubted him?

Lazarus and Eve came up beside her, and Grace looked up at the male. Eve was plastered to his side. She gave Grace's shoulder a reassuring squeeze, but her focus was on her mate and the pain he was obviously feeling.

Laz looked down at Chaos like he was willing him to open his eyes. But that wasn't the only thing causing him pain. What happened with Tobias in the warehouse had cut them all deeply, but especially Lazarus. The exchange between them before he was sent to Hell had made that clear.

"He'll be okay," Laz said gruffly to her. "Lazy fucker just needs to sleep it off."

Eve squeezed her shoulder again. "I'm here if you need me, for anything, any time of the day or night, okay?"

Grace nodded but didn't take her eyes off Chaos. She was almost too scared to look away from him.

Laz and Eve left and she was aware when Rocco, Kryos, and Zenon followed. Mia and Meredith leaving with them after they gave Grace a tight hug.

"Can I clean the blood and dirt off him?" Grace asked Jack as he packed up his things.

"Of course. He'll feel you close, your touch. It'll help him, knowing you're with him."

He left a short time later, and Grace reluctantly left Chaos's side to get what she needed. She filled a bowl with warm water, grabbed the soap, a towel, and several face cloths.

"Let's get you clean," she murmured as she sat on the side of the bed and dipped the cloth in the water.

She leaned over him and, careful of his wings, started on his shoulders and chest, so broad and strong, so powerful. God, he was beautiful. Every part of him. And not just the outside. He was stubborn and surly, could be short-tempered and blunt, but it was because he cared. Because he lived and breathed the fight.

Not sure what to say, Grace hummed softly as she rinsed the cloth, then gently slid it over the bruised skin on his pecs and down over his ridged abdominal muscles, careful of the white gauze dressings he had on his stomach and thighs.

Jack had thrown a sheet across his lap when everyone had crowded the bedroom, and she removed it so she could get every bit of blood. Her hands shook as she stroked the cloth across his skin. She couldn't bear to see one trace of his blood smeared on his perfect body. She worked her way down his thick, muscular thighs and long legs, cleaning his feet as well.

Using the towel, she ran it gently over his body, drying him off. Her gaze moved to his wings, dove-gray feathers that were streaked with dirt from the warehouse floor, some parts blood-soaked, making some feathers so deep a crimson they were almost black.

Her heart clenched as what had happened in that warehouse replayed in her head. The snapping of the monster's jaws, the sound of Chaos's body breaking as he was flung across the warehouse. It echoed through her mind, stealing her breath.

She couldn't leave his beautiful wings like that.

Grace replaced the water, grabbed another cloth, and climbed onto the bed beside him. She'd never really touched his wings. When he'd picked her up and carried her, when they'd flown through the skies, her fingers had only brushed them when she'd wrapped her arms around his neck.

They looked like velvet.

She brushed the tips of her fingers over the long, wide feathers. They *felt* like velvet.

Working her way over the one that was most damaged

first, she brushed the cloth over it, with barely there strokes, removing as much of the blood and dirt as she could. She was terrified she'd hurt him.

She moved to the other side and started again. Getting it as clean as she could. This side was basically undamaged, besides some missing or broken feathers. The wing arched high, and she slid her hand along it with the gentlest of touches.

Goose bumps broke out all over Chaos's skin, and he shuddered. Her gaze snapped to his. His eyes were still closed, but there was some color back in his cheeks.

Did he like it? When she touched his wings?

She did it again, nuzzling his jaw, pressing her mouth to his ear so he would hear her. "I'm here, baby. I'm here."

He shuddered again, his fingers twitching at his side. His eyes stayed closed, but one strong hand grabbed her wrist, tugging her closer and knocking her off balance. She fell beside him, landing on his wing, and tried to scramble away, but his grip tightened. Even unconscious, his instincts reached for her. He wanted her right where she was.

Grace was on her side, and she pressed into his, not giving him any of her weight but letting him feel the warmth of her body, the beat of her heart. The grip on her wrist finally eased and he relaxed.

"You scared me in that warehouse," she said, even though he still wasn't conscious, hoping that the sound of her voice would help like Jack said. "Don't ever do that again. You're mine, do you hear me, and I'm not losing you yet. I can be just as stubborn as you, and you don't have my permission to leave me."

She pressed a kiss to his throat, and started humming again, a tune she hadn't thought of in so long she was surprised she still remembered it. The words of the song her mother had sung to her when she was small came back to her, and she sang them to her mate, a sweet little song about love and family.

The wing she was lying on, his uninjured one, lifted, curling around her, cocooning them both in warmth and softness. She glanced up, but his eyes were shut, his face relaxed in sleep.

Grace didn't move. She stayed right where she was, where Chaos needed her to be.

~

Chaos blinked several times, trying to shake the fog from his head. He was hot, his skin tight, and there was a familiar ache down to his bones. His body was working to fix the damage that had been done.

A soft sound had him glancing down.

Grace was plastered to his side, her face against his ribs. One of her hands was curled at her side, the other arm under her head. Her brown lashes rested against her cheeks, and there were dark smudges under her eyes.

Memories came flooding back, or maybe they were dreams?

No, he still felt her touch, could hear her soft voice. It had happened, all of it.

Grace had washed him, had talked to him, *sung* to him. Fuck, his gut clenched. No one had ever done anything like that for him in his long life. Taken care of him like that.

She wriggled, made a small sound, then her eyes snapped open, like she sensed him watching her.

"Chaos, oh my God, you're awake."

She didn't move. It was like she was afraid to, like she'd been still for so long, it was instinct not to.

So she didn't hurt him.

311

"Grace…" His voice was raw, like he hadn't used it in a long time.

"Shhh." She lifted her hand carefully, and then gently, so very gently cupped his jaw, thumb gliding over his beard, while staring into his eyes. "Don't try to speak."

"How long have I been out?" he croaked.

"Five days."

He couldn't believe what he was hearing. "That long?"

"You lost a lot of blood…you were so…broken. Your body had a lot of work to do."

"You've been here with me the whole time?" He knew it was the truth, remembered coming in and out of consciousness now. Remembered her slight weight there beside him, always beside him.

Her cheeks turned pink. "I mean, I got up to eat and use the bathroom when you'd, uh…let me."

"Let you?"

"You held on to me, curled your uninjured wing around us."

He looked at her, took her in properly. Her cheeks were pale, her hair loose and a little wild, like she'd showered then let it dry lying right here. She was wearing one of his T-shirts, and when she carefully slid an arm around his waist, looking up at him with concern, he could see she was thinner. He curled his arm around her waist as well and hauled her up and on top of him.

She cried out, trying to wriggle away.

"You won't hurt me," he said gruffly. "Besides a few bruises, my bones have repaired themselves." He held her to him, his hands moving over her narrow hips, her now more prominent rib cage. "You stayed with me, beside me, for five days?"

She nodded.

"Angel," he choked.

312

She cupped his face again. "I was where I was supposed to be, where I wanted to be."

"You haven't been eating. I can feel your fucking ribs."

"I ate."

She couldn't eat, because he'd barely let her move.

He sat up, relieved that except for a few aches and pains and a bit of dizziness from lack of food, he felt fine. He planted Grace on the bed and pulled the IV feeding fluids into his body free.

"Where are you going, you're still recovering?" Grace was about to follow him, but he planted a hand against her belly and stopped her. "Stay here."

"Hang on a minute..."

"Promise me, you will not move?"

Her eyes narrowed, but she dipped her chin.

Chaos pulled on a pair of sweatpants, and after a quick bathroom break, because he needed to piss big-time, he headed to the kitchen. He made her a couple sandwiches—and ate two himself while he was at it. Then he poured her some juice and downed a glass himself.

Grace was still sitting in his bed when he walked back in.

He handed her a sandwich. "Eat it all," he ordered.

"What about you?" She held it back out for him.

He'd laugh if he wasn't so focused on seeing her eat the damn food. "I had mine." When she didn't make a move to take a bite, he said, "I promise. I ate in the kitchen."

Finally, she took a bite, her eyes closing and a little moan slipping free as she chewed. He sat watching her until she was done. "Now the drink."

She dutifully finished that as well.

As her throat worked, liquid making her lips glisten, he felt his body tighten and his cock grew hard.

"I'm supposed to be the one taking care of you," she said.

"You did, angel." He held out his hand and she took it instantly.

Yeah, he liked that. So fucking much. He stood, tugging her with him gently.

"Where are we going?" she asked, sounding kind of amused.

The food had helped, the weakness sliding from his bones. "Shower."

He led her to the smaller room and turned on the water. When he turned back to her, Grace had removed his shirt that she'd been wearing. She tossed it in the hamper, followed by her underwear. She wasn't wearing a bra, and he ate up the sight of her, his mouth going dry. Fuck, she was perfect. Small, high breasts, narrow but nicely round hips. Thinner yes, but still so damn gorgeous.

Grace took a step toward him, and all those lean, hard-won muscles flexed as she moved. So fucking strong. Inside and out.

"Beautiful," he rasped.

God, so beautiful.

He wanted to kiss her, badly, but he'd been out cold for five days. "Climb in."

"Are you getting in with me?"

"Try to stop me."

She grinned and climbed in.

Chaos quickly bushed his teeth, and she laughed softly, though her chuckles died when he turned back toward her and she got an eyeful of his cock.

He was impossibly hard. Somehow, he resisted giving his dick a stroke and climbed in behind her. Though the sight of her all wet and slick, the feel of her, just made his condition worse.

But right then, he wanted to take care of Grace, like she had him.

"Back to me, angel. Tip your head back."

She turned, arching back in a way that stole his breath, her tits, tight little nipples right there. Again, he resisted and ran his fingers through her hair, getting it nice and wet. When she straightened, he curled his fingers around her hips, pulling her closer, and lathered shampoo through the thick blond strands. Grace made little humming noises, sighing as he massaged her scalp.

Finally, he got her to tilt her head back again to rinse it out.

She sighed again as he ran a soapy cloth over her body, cleaning her like she had him.

"You don't need to do that…"

"I want to," he said, voice gruff. "Taking care of you makes me feel…"

"Content?" she said softly. "Satisfied in a way you never knew was possible? Whole?"

"Yes," he said.

She turned in his arms, looking up at him. "I would've taken down anyone who tried to take you away from me these last five days," she said earnestly. "And nothing, no one, could make me leave you."

Chaos's heart beat faster at her words, his eyes searching hers, fuck, getting lost in them. "Yeah?" It was all he had, all he could get out with everything he was feeling right then.

She slid her hands over his chest. "You're mine, Chaos. All mine."

He was suddenly struggling for breath. "You truly feel that way?"

Grace smiled, soft and a little self-conscious, but that stubborn chin of hers had lifted. His mate wasn't afraid of anything. "What I feel for you, it's not just this…this thing inside me, not anymore. When I thought I could lose you, when I saw you battered and bleeding and I couldn't get to you, everything came crashing in. I couldn't fool myself anymore. I didn't want to." She cupped his face, her thumb sliding over his whiskered jaw, and looked deep into his eyes. "You're the best male I have ever known. How could I not fall completely, hopelessly in love with you?"

His breath hitched. How could it be true? How could he be this lucky? He cupped her face as well. "You love me?"

"We were made for each other, how could I not?"

Chaos shook, the full force of his love for the female looking up at him, his female, throbbed through his veins, pumped in his chest. There was no stopping the wide, goofy-as-fuck smile from spreading across his face.

When she smiled back, he leaned in, and finally, *finally* kissed her like he'd been desperate to since he woke and found her lying beside him.

Her soft lips were heaven, her taste filled his head and made him fucking dizzy.

She loved him.

~

Chaos kissed her for a long time, until her lips felt swollen and tingly, and between her thighs was aching and slick.

Finally, he lifted her out of the shower and ran a towel over her body, drying her off. He dropped to his knees, running it down her legs, but stilled suddenly and wrapped his massive arms around her waist, holding her to him.

Throat tight, she looked down at her big, strong male holding her like she might break, like she was the most precious thing he had in his world.

She ran her hand over his shaved head. "Chaos?"

He looked up at her. "I didn't know how much I needed you, how much my life sucked without you in it. Christ, Grace, the thought of being apart from you. My world was black and white until I met you. Now I see in color, every fucking day." He shook his head, voice deep and rough and earnest. "Angel, I want to stay right here, at your feet, worshiping you for eternity. And still that wouldn't be enough time to make you understand how much I love you."

Grace had to blink rapidly as tears filled her eyes, as he leaned in and kissed her belly, nuzzled his way lower, gently pushing her so she was leaning against the wall.

"I need to make you come," he said gruffly. "I need to make you feel good."

Grace's head dropped back, as he lifted one of her legs over his shoulder and pressed his lips against her core. He grunted and slid his tongue between her lips, teasing her clit, making her quiver with need.

She gave herself over to the pleasure her mate was giving her, unable to stop herself from holding the back of his head and rolling her hips, seeking more. Chaos gave it to her. He slid a thick finger inside her, pushing deep and dragging it back out as he sucked on her clit again, harder this time.

She broke apart, calling his name.

He quickly pulled his finger free and pressed his mouth there instead, thrusting with his tongue, tasting her as she came.

When she finally collapsed back, he rose and wrapped her in his strong arms. Yes, he was looking a little like Rocco after a week of not eating, but he was still the most beautiful male she'd ever laid eyes on.

"I need you inside me," she said against his lips after he hungrily kissed her again.

He lifted her, and strode into the bedroom. They were on the bed a second later, and he was looming over her, muscled thighs sliding between hers, forcing hers wide.

She wrapped her arms and legs around his massive body, and his eyes seemed to glow as he looked down at her. He didn't say anything, just kept his gaze on hers as he reached down, positioned himself, and slid inside her to the hilt.

His eyes rolled up and he groaned. "Fuck, angel, I dreamed of this."

Grace smiled, which wasn't easy with how perfect he felt inside her, how desperately she wanted him to move. "You had a five-day wet dream?"

He chuckled, in a pained kind of way that made her laugh as well.

"No, I dreamed you were mine, and I was yours...in every way."

Not just sex. She'd convinced herself that was all she wanted with him, but she'd been so very wrong. "You are mine and I am yours," she said, gripping the side of his thick neck and holding that dark, intense gaze. "In every way."

He trembled at her words, his hips snapping forward. They both gasped. How could it be this good between them? This perfect? How could she ever have thought she didn't want this, that she didn't want him? She couldn't imagine her life without him now.

"You're my male, Chaos. Mine," she said on a growl of her own and rolled her hips. "And I will kill anyone who tries to hurt you, who tries to take you away from me."

The lust in his eyes turned molten. He loved hearing her stake a claim over him.

"Bloodthirsty female," he said so roughly goose bumps rose all over her skin.

"You love it," she teased and groaned when he thrust in deep and twisted his hips.

"Fuck, yeah, I do."

He moved faster, slamming deeper, taking her harder. He sucked on her skin, and she dug her nails into his back, teeth in his shoulder. They were marking each other, claiming each other.

Chaos gripped her to him and rolled to his back, staying buried deep, but giving her what she wanted. Planting her hands on his massive shoulders, she rolled her hips faster, harder, unable to take her eyes off his beautiful body straining beneath her, the feel of his eyes on her as she took him like he was taking her.

His hips slammed up as she came down, and her orgasm rolled through her. She cried out and her muscles gripped him tight, clutching and releasing over and over again.

Chaos gripped her hips and slammed up one more time, holding her there as she helplessly ground down, as his orgasm shot hot and hard inside her, drawing hers out even longer. Until she could only collapse against him, kissing and biting and sucking at his chest, rocking against each other until they were both spent.

Grace stayed like that, on top of her mate, one of his big rough hands on her ass holding her to him, his mouth pressed to the top of her head, while the other rubbed over her back, petting her, loving her.

This was where she belonged. With him. And he belonged with her.

For the first time in a long time she was more than the relentless anger that had been simmering inside her since she was sixteen years old. More than the agonizing pain she'd had to learn to live with. And more than her rabid thirst for revenge.

For the first time in so very long, Grace was happy. Truly happy.

Because of Chaos. Because of what he gave her, what they gave to each other.

He made her stronger. He made her whole.

And she was never letting him go.

CHAPTER 32

GRACE STOOD in the middle of her apartment. She'd lived here for so long, had been through so much within these four walls.

And now she was leaving.

Moving in with her mate. A shiver of pleasure zipped through her.

In just a matter of weeks so much had changed. Her whole world had been tipped on its head, and she wouldn't want it any other way. How could she? The man she'd thought of as her mortal enemy turned out to be the love of her life. She sure as hell hadn't seen that one coming.

"So you're really leaving?" Vince said, startling her.

He leaned against the doorframe to her apartment, an expression on his face she couldn't read.

"Are you going to be okay?" Oden had dropped off the face of the earth. No one had heard from him or seen him since he'd handed Grace over to demons at that sick, twisted party. Not surprising. The knights were on to him, and she couldn't imagine his demon friends had much love for him, either.

But she didn't like leaving Vince on his own.

"Of course. I'll be fine."

He wouldn't meet her eyes. "Is everything okay?"

"You're leaving me," he said simply.

"I'm not planning on disappearing off the face of the earth. I'll be back so much you'll get sick of me."

His lips curled up on one side, but he looked kind of nervous, twitchy. "Sure, you will."

Something was wrong. "Have you heard from Oden?"

He shook his head. "But you'll know if I do, promise. You're mated to a knight now, it's like having my own personal bodyguards."

Grace chuckled. "I wouldn't let Chaos hear you say that."

"And where is your mate tonight? Is he picking you up?"

Grace scooped the clothes from the last dresser drawer and shoved them into a bag. "Nope. He's with his brothers. He has some things on his mind, so I thought I'd surprise him."

She wanted to make Chaos happy, and she knew moving her stuff into his apartment would accomplish that.

After he'd been injured, Rocco had returned. Chaos had hoped his brother was back for good, but Rocco had taken off again. Chaos and his brothers were out looking for him, they wanted him home. Grace wasn't so sure they'd be successful, Rocco wasn't ready to come back, and that would devastate her mate.

So if moving all her worldly possessions into his apartment got her even a small smile, or that look that said his world hadn't been right until she was back in his sights, she'd do it. She'd basically moved in already; the thought of spending even one night apart caused an ache behind her ribs. Over the last week most of her clothes had ended up there, but she knew he'd appreciate the gesture.

"I'll miss you," Vince said, eyes bright.

She walked over and pulled him into a hug. "If you get all sentimental on me, you'll make me cry, and you know I hate crying."

"I've only ever wanted the best for you, you know that, don't you, Grace?" he rasped. "That's all I've ever wanted, what I'll always want."

"Of course." She lifted her head. "You saved me."

His hands went to her shoulders and he squeezed. "That's right…" He shook slightly. "I knew you were destined for bigger things. That one day you'd fight for a better future for all of us."

"You do know I'll come back," she said, trying again to reassure him. Vince was family, but she'd never seen him this visibly upset. "Hey, I'll even cover shifts if you need me to."

He gave her another squeeze. "Come on, I'll walk you to your car. I'm sure you want to get home."

Home.

She liked the sound of that.

But when she went to leave, her car wouldn't start. The engine not turning over at all.

"I'll give you a ride," Vince said. "I'll get someone to come fix yours in the morning."

"Would you?"

"Of course."

Vince's car was parked in the alley between Revelry and the pizza place next door. Grace put her bag in the trunk and Vince got in and started the engine. When she climbed in beside him, Vince was busy texting someone.

"Something wrong?"

He turned to her, the glow from the dashboard lights washing his face with muted blue. His eyes were wild as he lifted his phone, hand shaking, and showed her the screen.

Hannah.

Grace looked at Vince, then back at the screen. What the

fuck was this? Hannah stared into the camera, face bruised, crying. Her terrified eyes met Grace's. "Help me, Grace," she sobbed, her voice tinny and distant, echoing through the phone. "Please."

Vince's wild gaze met Grace's again. "Block yourself, or she dies."

Someone gripped Hannah's hair and she cried out, her frantic gaze locking on Grace again, begging her to do as Vince said.

She had no choice. Too many lives had been lost already, and this was Vince. Whatever he thought he was doing, this wasn't him. It wasn't. It couldn't be.

"Oden's making you do this."

Vince said nothing as he reversed out of the alley and headed down the street.

He gripped the steering wheel tighter. "I'm so sick of being nothing, Gracie, of having nothing. We...our kind, should own this city, instead, we hide our powers, we cower. We let the knights kill our people."

"The knights would never hurt demi."

"I'm not talking about demi. Goddammit, Grace, we are demons. We have demon blood pulsing through our veins. I'm sick of being treated like some fragile fucking human."

Grace stared at Vince, the male she thought of as a father, in utter shock. "You're helping them? The demons behind the attacks?"

"This should be our city, and when that demi in Hell gains her powers, we'll be free. We'll ascend to the heights we always should have been." He glanced at her. "I know you think you have feelings for your knight, but in time you'll get over it, you'll realize it wasn't real."

He'd lost his mind. "You've been handing innocent demi over to the enemy?"

"They're not the enemy, Gracie. They don't want to hurt

us. They want to work *with us*, work together for a greater good."

"They killed Tina and Mark. They use their own like fucking puppets to attack the knights, not caring how many are slaughtered. They don't care about you, Vince, about any of us. We're a means to an end, to help them gain power, for them to take the city. You think Diemos will keep us around once he's free?"

He was shaking his head. "You don't understand, but you will. And Tina only died because she fought. If she'd done what she was asked, she'd be there to greet you when we arrive. She only has herself to blame."

"You killed her?"

He shook his head again, white-knuckling the steering wheel. "Your block, Grace. Put it up now or they'll hurt Hannah, they'll hurt the others."

Vincent wasn't a killer. He wasn't a fighter, either. The male she'd loved like family was a coward. So damn greedy and desperate for power he had betrayed his own people.

Pain sliced through her. How could he do this?

"Why me?"

"Because you're special." He glanced at her. "They know it, too. They want you in Diemos's army, and they'll kill all the demi they're holding to get you there. One by one, if they have to. Do you want to be the reason they die?"

Her gut twisted.

They sped to the busiest part of town, where the clubs and bars were in full swing for the night, and the car swerved off the road and into an underground parking lot. If by chance one of the knights were flying above them, they have to follow on foot.

"Put up your goddamn block. Now!" he yelled.

She had no choice. So she did what he asked as they drove out of the garage and into the bustling street.

Vince visibly relaxed when he felt her power wash over them, when he knew she'd blocked herself from Chaos.

But Chaos would feel it, would instantly know something was wrong when he couldn't sense her anymore. Knowing that he would worry, would be terrified that something had happened to her, caused her physical pain.

But she would find her way back to him. She refused to believe that fate would be so cruel, that they would give her Chaos only to take him away so soon.

Grace shoved down the emotions raging inside her, centering herself to focus on the fight ahead. She'd learned to rely on herself a long time ago. She was on her own in this. Nothing new about that.

When she was a scared kid living on the streets, she'd had nothing to hope for, nothing to fight for. When you lost everyone you loved, you stopped caring what happened to you.

Grace had felt that way until Vince found her and gave her a home. Now, looking back with fresh eyes, she wondered if maybe he'd planned to exploit an emotionally scarred kid from the start.

Well, she wasn't going down without a fight. She had someone who loved her, someone waiting for her to come home.

Even if it turned out to be her last fight, Chaos would know she did everything to get back to him.

That his mate loved him enough to never give up.

Chaos sucked in a breath and grabbed for the brick wall beside him, his legs turning to Jell-O.

She was gone. Grace was gone. He couldn't feel her anymore.

The absence of her was like being stabbed through the heart, like he was bleeding from the open wound all over the dirty concrete beneath him.

Yanking his phone from his pocket, he called her. It went straight to voicemail. He called Eve next, but Grace wasn't in their apartment or the gym, fucking anywhere at the compound.

His mated brothers could trace their females easily, the connection between them that strong. The only way to stop him from finding her was if Grace was purposely trying to block him out. And the only way to sever it completely was...

He couldn't even think it.

He fired a text to his brothers and took flight, heading to Revelry. He stormed through the main doors, searching the place, asking the other demi who worked there if they'd seen her. He rushed up the stairs to her apartment two at a time. The place was empty. All her things were gone.

Climbing out the window, he went to the roof and tried again to reach out, to pick up any trace of her.

Zenon and Rocco landed beside him.

It didn't surprise him Roc was there as well. He'd come back for Grace.

"Anything?" Zenon asked.

Chaos shook his head, throat too tight to speak.

"The others are searching. Laz and Kryos are meeting with her crew. Gunner's gone back to that penthouse, to see if he can pick anything up."

Chaos shook, rage and fear pulsing through his body with such force it made him fucking dizzy. "What if we're too late? What if..."

"Stop," Rocco said. "We're getting her back, tonight."

His brother's eyes were nearly black, and there was death and pain etched into his features. He realized this was how Rocco felt constantly, that he lived with this pain twenty-four seven, and getting Chaos's mate back meant a fuck of a lot more to him than helping out his brother in his time of need. Because if they lost Grace…what hope did they have of getting Kyler back.

"Grace is tough, a fucking warrior. She won't go down easy." Zenon's even tone, his assurances and faith in Grace's abilities helped lock down Chaos's fear.

He was right. Grace was a warrior. A fighter.

But that didn't stop the terror pounding through him. He had no idea where his female was, who had her, what they were doing to her. Demons were behind this, powerful ones.

The fear grew to unbearable levels, and his demon stirred inside him. He didn't fight it, and let the monster within break free.

He roared as he shifted, taking his Kishi demon form. Dark crimson skin, razor-sharp fangs that extended to his chin, and black shiny horns that sprouted from his head. He knew he looked like the devil himself, and he reveled in the darkness flowing through him. There would be no mercy for anyone who laid a finger on Grace.

He looked to his brothers. Rocco had already shifted, and the way the other knight's eyes glittered, the way he licked his fangs like he already tasted the blood of his enemies, made it clear he was more than ready to tear anyone who got in his way into tiny pieces.

Zenon shifted as well, his leathery wings extended at his back, ready to take flight. "We won't stop until we find her."

They lifted off, taking to the skies.

CHAPTER 33

Vince tossed a scarf at her. "Put this on."

"I'm not really in the mood to accessorize, Vince." The guy was on edge, sweating profusely and twitchy as hell.

"Please, Grace, just put it on." His gaze softened. "You'll come around, you'll see, once you talk to them, once they explain."

"Come around to what? If you think I'll turn on the knights, that I'll willingly help demons take this city, you've lost your damn mind." It was getting harder and harder to keep her tone reasonable and not beat the shit out of him. The only reason she hadn't was Hannah and the other demi being held against their will.

They'd changed cars a little while ago.

She and Vince were in the back and there was a mother-fucking demon in the driver's seat. He kept glancing back at her in the rearview mirror. The disgusting vermin was wiry and well-muscled, and she didn't think he'd go down easy if she attacked. She also didn't know what weapons he had stashed in the front with him.

"I wouldn't talk like that if I were you," Vince said, gaze darting to the asswipe driving.

"What the hell is wrong with you?" She searched Vince's features, looking for any sign of the male she'd believed him to be all these years, but there was nothing. A day ago, hell, an hour ago, she never would have believed he could do something like this. She knew he wanted power, that he wanted to be important, but she never believed he'd do something like this to get it.

"How could you do this? How could you hand over your people, your *family*, to these monsters?"

Anger flashed in his eyes. "You don't know what you're talking about. *I'm doing this* for my family, for the greater good, and in time you'll come around to our way of thinking."

The greater good? "Who are you working for?"

"You'll find out soon enough. Now put on the damn scarf, Grace, or our friend here will make you."

The demon behind the wheel grinned at her in the rearview mirror.

He shifted in his seat, and she knew their demon chauffeur was hoping that he'd get the chance to deal with any problems that might arise. And by problem, she meant her.

Her options were limited. Jump out of a moving vehicle and leave Hannah and the other demi to die, or face whatever evil was waiting for her at an unknown destination. Not much of a choice.

Securing the scarf over her eyes, Grace remained silent the rest of the drive, trying her best to remember the turns they took, the distances between each one. But the longer they drove, the more impossible it became.

They seemed to drive forever before finally coming to a stop. By that point, she'd lost all concept of place and time. When the car door was opened, she was pulled roughly from the vehicle. No doubt by the demon driver, whose fingers dug deeply into her arm, trying to cause pain. She listened hard. They weren't in the city, not anymore, because the sound of traffic, of car horns and sirens were muted, distant.

"Let's go," a gruff voice said close to her ear.

Walking blind was not fun, especially since she expected the guy leading her to attack at any moment, or at the very least steer her into a wall or two. The ground beneath her feet was smooth asphalt. The sound of a door opening came next.

"Keep moving."

"This is all very cloak-and-dagger," she said in as dry a tone as she could manage over her pounding heart. She dropped her block, testing, but the light electric current licking over her skin told her that someone else was taking care of that now, was blocking the demi held here against their will. "I think someone's been watching too much human television."

"Cut the shit, demon butcher, or I'll *cut* it for you," he breathed right against the shell of her ear.

She gritted her teeth. It was the same name the demon prick who'd shoved her off the side of a building had called her, and the asshole who'd attacked her at the penthouse—and they certainly hadn't been fans of her work. This new development did not bode well, not at all.

He shoved her into a chair and then took great pleasure, she was sure, in tying her to it securely. So securely it caused pain. "The chains were forged in Hell, your powers are useless," he said, a smile in his voice. "We wouldn't want our special guest to get away now, would we?"

Fuck, he'd tied her tight enough that there would be no getting free. Bastard. She straightened her spine. "Good to see a demon actually taking pride in his work."

The slap that came was sudden and hard enough to send

pain spiking through her jaw.

Oh yeah, that rung her bell. Blood filled her mouth, and she spat it out, in what she hoped was his direction. When he hissed out a curse, she knew she got her target.

Adrenaline buzzed through her, firing her up. She would kill this asshole the first chance she got. "And here I was thinking we were friends," she said, and grinned.

She braced, knowing the second hit was coming. This time he skipped the backhand and went straight for a closed fist. Her head snapped back when it connected with the side of her jaw, and this time she saw stars.

A door crashed open. "What the hell are you doing? She's valuable, you stupid asshole. More valuable than you."

Vince was attempting to protect his prize. How sweet.

"If the master doesn't want her, I'm calling dibs. I want to make this bitch scream," the demon said.

She turned her head to where she thought he was standing and spat out more blood. "You make a lot of females scream?"

He leaned in. "You know it. Can't get enough of me. I'll make you scream for more in my bed, then for your life when I'm done."

"The only way a female would scream in your bed, weasel dick, is if she's faking it. Screaming in desperation to get the hell away from you, though, I would completely understand."

There was a crash, the guy no doubt lunging for her, followed by the sound of scrambling feet and some grunting. "Take him the fuck out of here," Vince said.

So there had been more than just the two of them in here, then, because Vince sure as hell wouldn't have gotten physical with the prick.

"I'm gonna have fun killing you, asshole," she called when she heard the door open.

She reached out with her senses, trying to pick up the

presence of others in the room, but felt nothing, not even Vince's familiar vibes. Someone was most definitely blocking them. "There's some kind of protective ward here, right? I can't sense you." Her words came out slightly slurred past the swelling on the right side of her face and mouth.

The scarf was lifted, and Grace blinked at the sudden brightness, and then realized one of her eyes was swollen almost shut.

Vince stared into her one good eye. "Something much better than that, more effective, too." His grin was fucking ear to ear.

"Sounds cool and all, but can you untie me now because I can't feel my hands." The cool and calm act was getting harder and harder to pull off, especially when she was bruised and bleeding, and with every passing minute, she knew her chances of getting out of here alive were decreasing. "Where's Hannah?"

He ran surprisingly gentle fingers down the uninjured side of her face. "I can't untie you yet, Gracie, not until I explain why you're here." He grinned and looked fucking insane. "If you agree to join our cause, you'll reap the rewards, have the privilege of helping to create a whole new world, a world where our kind will no longer live in fear of discovery, of demons. We will live together in harmony."

She snorted. "Sounds like some kind of hippie commune. Considering a demon just used my face as a punching bag, you'll have to excuse me for being a little skeptical."

"I think we both know why he might be a little pissed at you. But they'll get over it eventually."

"I doubt that."

He shrugged. "Hopefully our leader will agree that your nocturnal activities will work in our favor. A warrior to fight for our cause...and with your new power..." Excitement lit up his whole face. "You could be very powerful one day, so incredibly valuable to us."

"And what about Oden? What's his part in all this?"

Vince tilted his head to the side. "I owed him, but that debt was paid when I provided him with what he needed."

Her throat was tightened, and she struggled for breath. "Tina...Hannah."

His mouth twisted. "I didn't like doing it, Grace. But I knew it was for the best...for them, for all of us?"

"Do you still think it was the best for Tina?" She sucked in a pained breath and let all the hatred she felt right then show on her face. "You're a fucking coward."

Anger replaced the guilt in his eyes, but then he shook his head and dropped to his knees, cupping her face. "You don't understand, not yet. I want this so much, and you owe me, you know you do. I saved you, you said it yourself. You just have to do this for me, please do this for me."

She wrenched her head out of his hold. "What does Oden do with them?"

Vince shook his head. "He's just a courier. They use the demi for their powers. They'll help us with this war. And the ones that won't conform, well, you can siphon their powers. You can do what they won't."

"No."

His expression changed to one a father might use on a petulant child. "You'll come around. You just need time." He looked excited. "They have big plans for you. With the way you can take powers into yourself, you could be an army all on your own. And the way you look, no one will suspect you might have the power to tear their world down around them. You'll be the perfect weapon, Gracie."

They wanted to make her a freaking demi of mass destruction. "And if I don't? What if I refuse to do it? What if I like the world we have now?"

His expression turned troubled. "Then they'll make you."

"I'll end up like Tina, you mean."

He flinched. "No, not you, they promised not to kill you. You're too valuable, your power too rare."

"How many have suffered like Tina, how many of us have died for this greater good you speak of? Who does it benefit? Because from where I'm sitting, it's not us."

"Unfortunately, like any war, there are casualties. But when Diemos is released from Hell and takes his rightful place here, we'll be rewarded for our service to him." He rubbed his fingers over the gold ring he was wearing, one she'd never seen on him before. It was the same as the one Oden wore. That same symbol.

A phoenix rising, she suddenly realized. Diemos, rising from the fires of Hell.

She felt sick to her stomach. "Why did Oden kick the shit out of you if you're cult buddies?"

"I went behind his back, went straight to our leader and told him about you. Even before I knew about your power, I knew you were valuable. You've always been special. I saw that from the start. But Oden wanted to be the one to bring you in, to get the reward. To please our leader." He chuckled. "He actually thought he could make you fall for him, that's why he kept coming into the club. He thought if you were in love with him, you'd be his, his to control, his to command. It suited me to let him believe it. Idiot."

Jesus. "Until he beat you. Then you wanted me to stay away from him, would have been happy if I'd ended him."

Vince shrugged.

"And that's why Oden took me to that party? So he'd be the one to get the pat on the back?"

"Yes."

"But I got away. He must have been pissed?"

"Furious, and so was our leader. I can't wait to see his face when I bring you in."

Grace let him see her disgust. "That's all you really care about—power. You don't give two shits about me. I thought we were family, Vince."

He shook his head frantically. "We are, which is why I want you on the right side of this war. If you do as I say, you'll be fine."

"You've lost your mind. You realize that, right? What makes you think they won't kill you like the other demi who were no longer of use?"

"I can provide them with what they want. I'm valuable. And I have you. You belong to me. I found you on the street, I took you in. I own you, which means you are mine to offer."

"I don't belong to you." No, she belonged to a controlling knight and he belonged to her. Body and soul, she was his, would always be his.

Pain sliced through her just thinking about Chaos. What he must think right now. He'd be freaking out, thinking the worst.

"I've given you a lot of information, but we have a couple of days until you're brought before anyone. By then you'll have come around to my way of thinking."

"You're just going to leave me here?" Wherever the fuck *here* was.

"I have a business to run, remember. I'll be back with food later." Then he walked to the door and stepped out, shutting it behind him.

She was screwed.

CHAPTER 34

THE BUILDING WAS windowless and huge, all concrete and iron.

Grace had no idea how long she'd been there. God, forever. Vince had come back like he said he would, had removed her chains so she could use the bathroom, but kept her hands tied in front of her, a gun pointed at her head. She could have taken him out, he wouldn't kill her, but she needed him to find the others. And she refused to risk their lives until she could get them free.

She'd been trying to come up with a plan since he'd arrived.

He was currently helping her eat a cheeseburger and she'd just taken a sip of Coke, that she would have spat in his face if she wasn't so thirsty, when the door on the opposite side of the room opened and Oden walked in. He had one of his goons with him.

Vince stilled, looking pissed. "If you think you're taking her from me..."

Oden ignored Vince and the gun in his hand, walked

right up to Grace, and gripped her chin, tilting her head back roughly. "Miss me, baby?"

Grace smiled. "Like herpes, thimble dick."

He flushed, going red with rage and backhanded her.

Her head jerked back from the force, and when she looked at him again, she laughed, ignoring the pain radiating through the side of her face. Anger like she'd never experienced before pounded through her. These assholes had no idea who they were dealing with. They saw a female, one who took her clothes off for a living, and stupidly forgot the part where she spent the rest of her time kicking ass.

The moron had also missed that their magic Hell chains were lying on the floor beside her. Her powers weren't suppressed.

Yes, she was outnumbered, but she wasn't fucking helpless. She didn't think they'd kill her, not over Oden; like Vince said, she was too valuable, and if she got to do anything before they took her down, it would be to kill the son of a bitch looking down at her. "You don't like females who fight back, do you, Oden? That's why you killed Tina. She didn't want to join your little army of shit stains so you threw a tantrum."

Oden shook with rage, that unnerving black gaze boring into hers. "I didn't kill her." He grinned, eyes glistening with fury and glee. "I choked her until she passed out, then handed her to one of our demons. He savored her, slowly sucking the life out of her. It took days...*then* she died."

Grace slammed her head forward, connecting with Oden's nose with a satisfying crunch, and before he could react, she fisted his hair with her bound hands and jerked him forward, throwing him to the floor. Spinning, she avoided his goon, spun back, grabbed the gun he had at his hip, and shot the piece of demon shit in the head.

Oden, who had gotten back to his feet, kicked the back of her knee before she could point the gun on him and she went down, the gun flying across the floor. Oden advanced and she rolled, swiping his feet out from under him. He went down hard and she dove for him, fisting his hair as she wrapped her thighs around his neck and squeezed. He punched the side of her legs, the only place he could reach while kicking and flailing.

Grace squeezed tighter. "You don't get to hurt anyone else, you fucking prick."

He went red, then started going blue, his struggles slowing. Grace gritted her teeth and squeezed even tighter, putting more pressure on his throat, cutting off his oxygen supply. She closed her eyes, letting her power build, letting it flow from her into Oden before drawing it back to her like a wave, taking his power from him and giving it to her. He screamed, expending the last of the oxygen in his lungs, and finally stopped moving.

Kicking Oden aside, she crawled to the demon with the bullet hole in his head. It hadn't been enough to finish him, unfortunately, so she grabbed the knife she could see peeking from his boot. It took effort, but she managed to saw the asshole's head off, which was doubly difficult with her hands tied in front of her.

When he was ash, she climbed to her feet, advancing on Vince, who had stood by and did nothing while she killed two of his crew. Probably happy she'd gotten rid of the competition. The fucking attention whore.

Vince backed up. "Hang on a minute, Gracie—"

The door behind her flew open, the one across from her as well, and more demons ran in. A lot of them. There was no way she was getting out of this in one piece. There were way too many, but she wasn't going down easy.

She heard Vince yell for them not to kill her a moment before she attacked.

The clatter and groan of steel as Chaos landed on the fire escape outside Grace's apartment was loud, but he didn't give a shit if the thing snapped off the side of the building. He didn't care about much of anything except finding Grace and bringing her home.

He was losing the battle with his sanity at this point, his demon right there with him. She'd been missing for twelve hours—and they'd found *nothing*, had exactly zero leads. Grace could be injured…she could be lying in a gutter, gray and cold and lifeless like her friend.

A roar exploded from him, helplessness burning his lungs.

"Breathe. You need to kept your shit together." Zenon stood beside him, his leathery wings tucked in close to his back, huge-ass fangs down to his chin, his yellow eyes bright against his dark crimson skin. Chaos looked much the same, apart from the eye color, and it was a good thing they were invisible to humans in their Kishi forms or there'd be people running around screaming in terror.

"What if it's too late?" he said.

Zenon shoved open the window to Grace's apartment. "It's not."

He wasn't so sure—someone or something was blocking her from him, the same thing that had been gunning for them for months. He knew firsthand how powerful a force it was.

He climbed in after Zenon and was instantly assaulted by her familiar scent. He groaned as pain hit him, like someone had torn his heart from his chest all over again. He sucked in a breath and attempted to focus. He'd been here already, but with no leads, he was willing to try anything.

Zenon started in the living room and Chaos moved to her

bedroom. Images of her lying in her bed naked and wrapped around him flooded his mind, tore at his soul.

If someone's touched her, hurt her...if they...

He forced the thought from his mind before he lost his sanity completely. He'd failed her on so many levels.

Chaos tried to shut his mind down and started moving methodically through the room, searching every damn inch, but came up empty. The sound of a door slamming shut came from the other room, followed by a cry of alarm.

Someone had just spotted Zenon.

Chaos walked out and Vince was pressed up against the wall, cowering like a fucking pussy. Zenon was on the other side of the room, head tilted to the side, scratching his crimson head with a razor-sharp claw.

"What the fuck's wrong with you?" Chaos asked.

"But...you're...you look..."

"You know what we are, you're embarrassing yourself," Zenon muttered.

"What're you doing here?" Vince said, finally getting his shit together.

"Grace. She's missing," Chaos growled, unable to do anything else at this point.

"No...she's not. And I'm not expecting her back for a few days, either." His eyes were wide and filled with sympathy. "She wanted to tell you herself, but...she knew you wouldn't take it well."

Chaos stepped closer. "Tell me what?"

Vince stood to his full height, which was five-foot-fuck-all, and straightened his jacket. "She's with Oden."

He was lying.

In two steps Chaos was in front of the smaller male, fingers wrapped around his throat. He lifted him off the floor and his head connected with the wall a second later. "Why don't you try that again, Vince."

He pried at the fingers around his throat. "Look, let's just calm down here," he choked. "No disrespect, but Grace is f-family. I know you think she's your mate, but she chose him, Chaos, not you."

Vince blinked up at him, visibly paling.

"Grace *is* my mate, and she's not your anything, not anymore. So start fucking talking. The truth this time." The *or die* was left unsaid, but loud and clear all the same.

"She doesn't want you," the fucker said, stupidly sticking to his bullshit story.

He knew where she was. "Where is she?"

The male turned green. "I can't tell you..."

Chaos tightened his hold around the guy's neck and shook the shit out of him, then slammed him back against the wall. "It's taking every bit of control I possess not to snap your skinny neck."

Vince clawed at Chaos's wrist. "S-she said she wanted to go. I-I don't know how to f-find the place. I'm blindfolded and a driver picks me up. I-I couldn't take you even if I wanted to."

Was he telling the truth? Chaos was too far gone to read the male. "Zenon, call Kryos and have him take Vince to the compound." He let the sadistic darkness curling inside him show on his face. "You can't hide the truth from us, Vince. We can get in your head and extract it, all of it."

His eyes went wide and he broke out in a sweat. The male was a coward, if he knew how to find her, it wouldn't take much to get him to talk even without Eve's help. But Chaos didn't trust himself to get it out of Vince, he'd end up killing him before he got the information he needed.

Kryos strode in a few minutes later wearing an expression that was pure evil, despite the angelic blond curls— maybe that's what made it worse. The male looked like an Angel of Death.

Without a word, he strode to the smaller male, grabbed him by the back of the shirt, and shoved him out onto the fire escape. "I'll call when we know." His white wings snapped into place, and he glanced down at Vince. "If you piss yourself, I'm breaking your kneecaps."

There was a whimper, then they were in the air, Vince's body dangling below him.

"He knows where she is," Zenon said. "We'll get her back."

Chaos dipped his chin and climbed out onto the fire escape, taking flight.

He wouldn't rest until Grace was home.

CHAPTER 35

THE SECOND KICK to her ribs was brutal. The demon wasn't holding anything back, but Grace refused to cry out in pain. She could barely see at this point, her eyes too swollen to open properly. *Fuckers.*

"I thought I was a gift to some whacked-out demon cult leader? Won't he be pissed if you kill me?" She was pleased at how strong her voice sounded, even if it was kinda slurred, especially when her whole body felt, and more than likely looked, like raw roast beef.

Feeling helpless was not something she enjoyed, but with her hands and feet tied, lying on the cold, concrete floor, she couldn't do a damn thing to help herself. Vince knew what she could do, she'd stupidly told him, and the demons had made sure she couldn't touch them—add in the chains forged in Hell wrapped around her again, and she was utterly defenseless.

The demon fisted her hair, yanked her head back, and got in her face. His rancid breath washed over her. "Oh, I'm not going to kill you, demon butcher. Where would the fun be in that?"

She was in deep shit, and if she didn't find a way to get out of these chains, she was toast, no matter what this asshole said. "I can see you enjoy your work," she said to him. "I can respect that. You know, I don't think we've been formally introduced." She turned away and spat the blood welling in her mouth on the floor and smiled. "I'm Grace, and you're…?"

He stayed silent, but was still close, his blurry outline right in front of her, his rank odor singeing her nostrils.

"No name? No worries." Being as thick as a post, she doubted the male could multitask. Maybe if she kept him talking, he'd stop beating the crap out of her for a few minutes. "So how long have you been part of the commune? Sounds like a good deal. So when Diemos is freed from Hell, you what? Get some virgins to despoil and a pot of gold?"

His fingers were suddenly wrapped around her throat. "You have a smart mouth for someone tied up and lying at my feet. You're at my mercy, don't forget that. Vince isn't due back until tomorrow night. We could have a lot of fun in that time, couldn't we, demon butcher?"

"If you untie me, we could really party." She spat out some more blood. "Why don't you take off the chains and I'll show you just how fun it could be?" Yeah, then all she had to do was grab the asshole and suck the life right out of him, because getting to her feet so she could kick his ass, no matter how much she wanted to, might be out of the realms of her capabilities at that moment.

She was pretty sure a couple ribs were broken, possibly some internal injuries as well. Blood kept filling her mouth, and with how weak she was feeling, she was starting to think it wasn't just from her cut lips and gums.

"Do you think I'm stupid, female?"

Well, duh. "Course not—"

The slap was a shock since she couldn't see it coming, the

kick even more so. If she wasn't worried about what he'd do to her, she'd be hoping for blessed unconsciousness about now.

"I'll teach you, bitch, I'll show you—"

The sound of something heavy landing on the ground cut him off, followed by a whole lot of female cursing.

Grace recognized the low, husky voice instantly. "Goth girl?"

The chains fell away from her wrists and ankles. "You look like shit. Can you stand?"

If they were on their way out of this hellhole, she could dance a goddamned jig. "Yeah." With some help and a lot of hissing and cursing, Grace got to her feet.

"We have to be quick, the guards will be switching in about fifteen minutes."

Pain sliced through Grace's body as she worked at staying upright. Thankfully, goth girl clung to her, all but dragging her out of the room. Grace's sight was still for shit, but she could make out shapes and colors. "We have to get Hannah."

"Spencer, the male you met in the kitchen the night of the party already got her out. I thought it best if we split you up."

"The others?"

"Trust me."

"Why are you doing this? Why are you helping us?"

"Stairs," she said before Grace could trip.

Just when she didn't think the other female would answer, goth girl finally said, "I wouldn't wish this life on anyone."

"Come to the knights' compound, they'll keep you safe." Grace felt rather than saw her shake her head.

"I can do more good where I am. I'm his favorite, he trusts me." Her voice held an edge.

"The demon I met, the powerful one?"

Goth girl didn't answer, which was answer enough.

They went through a door that led to a garage and headed toward a black SUV.

"I'm going to have to ask you to cover your eyes, Grace."

She didn't bother to argue; this girl was risking her skin to help her out. They climbed in and she secured the scarf over her eyes. "At least there's no chance of me peeking," she said.

"I'm sorry you had to suffer through that. I would've come sooner, but I had to pick my moment."

Grace didn't get a chance to reply because the sound of feet pounding on concrete echoed in the distance. The car started and they gunned it out of the garage and onto the street. Goth girl could drive. Grace could feel the car weaving in and out of traffic, turning a dozen corners until she was sure they'd lost anyone following.

Grace turned to her, even though she couldn't see her. "They know what you've done. You can't go back."

"The windows are blacked out. They don't know it's me driving."

"Cameras?"

"None, it's too risky."

"Are you sure no one saw you?"

"Yeah, I'll be fine."

This female was a warrior in her own right, but they could break her other ways. How had she ended up where she was? Grace had so many questions, but she knew they wouldn't be welcome.

"Look, I know you can't tell me your name. But please, if you ever want to get out, if you ever need help...shit, just someone to talk to...call me. Will you do that?"

"Honestly...I hope I never see you again, Grace." There was so much weight behind those words, and she knew what they meant. If they ever saw each other again, Grace was screwed.

The car slowed, then stopped.

"You can take off the scarf."

Grace removed the strip of fabric covering her eyes, and could see a little better than before. "You're trying to stop him from releasing Diemos, aren't you?"

The female beside her held Grace's gaze, her violet eyes, so pale, so unusual. "I'm going to kill him before he gets the chance. No one gets to do that but me."

She'd been hurt badly by this sick, twisted demon, and she wanted revenge. Grace understood that.

She gave the other female a long, hard look. Something was different than the last time Grace had seen her. She was thinner, pale. "You're sick."

She shook her head.

"We can help you," Grace said, feeling even weaker, her chest painfully tight, her pulse racing. "P-please don't go back to that twisted fuck... You don't need to sacrifice your-self for this cause."

"I'm not sick." Her violet eyes moved over Grace's chin, down her throat, and lingered, her entire body freezing for a long moment. "I'll be okay...soon."

"Your eyes, they look...lighter?"

She quickly looked away from Grace. "You're mated to one of them, aren't you?" she asked, ignoring Grace's question.

"Yes." Her eyes felt heavy. She was so damn tired.

"Would you let your mate stop you from fighting? Even knowing the risks, could you stop?"

Grace didn't even have to think about it. "No. I'll n-never stop fighting."

"I can't stop, either. I need to be where I am. I can get closer to him than anyone else." Her lashes fluttered, and she looked away for a moment. Grace's stomach churned, thinking about what that meant. "I'm the only one who can kill him."

There was no use trying to talk her out of it, Grace could see it in her eyes.

"What about the other demi being held?"

"I promise, as soon as I get back, I'll get a message to your people, let them know where you can find them," she said.

Grace believed her.

The low-level hum that had filled the car since they left wherever the hell she'd been stopped, and a new silence settled over them.

Goth girl had dropped her block.

Silence filled the car, there was nothing else to say. There was no convincing this female to leave with her, she wasn't going to falter from her course, and Grace respected the hell out of her. It didn't stop her from being terrified for her, though.

"So now what?" Grace coughed, wincing in pain. More blood filled her mouth.

"We wait," goth girl said.

For Chaos. He'd be able to sense her now.

Grace glanced out the window. They were just outside of the city, parked in an empty parking lot outside of Chambers furniture store, one of the larger chains. The lighting was dim and they were surrounded by shadows. With a groan, she leaned forward and opened the glove compartment in front of her. She felt around and found a pen but no paper. "Give me your hand. My number."

The other female paused, then held out her hand, which told Grace that despite her words, she needed the connection, the possible out Grace had offered. The pen slipped through Grace's bloody fingers several times, but she managed to write her number just above the other female's wrist, so the sleeve of her top covered it. "I m-meant what I said."

Goth girl didn't answer, just offered a small nod.

Several more minutes ticked by—

The thump and screech of buckling metal above them was so loud Grace winced. He got there faster than she thought. She didn't have time to react because a fist smashed through the driver's window a second later. A massive hand came through and pinned goth girl to her seat and at the same time Grace's door was literally torn from its hinges on the other side and flung across the parking lot.

Chaos was suddenly there, cursing and growling as he slid his arms around her and lifted her gently from the car.

Gunner was on the other side, snarling down at the female who had risked her life to save her. She was blinking up at him, eyes wide, terrified.

"Gunner, *no*. L-let her go. She helped me." His pale-gold gaze lifted and landed on the male holding her tenderly in his arms. Chaos nodded, and Gunner released the female and stepped back.

"Bring her to the compound," Chaos said.

"No." Grace shook her head, her breathing becoming more labored. "W-we made a deal. Let her go."

Chaos scowled, but in the end gave Gunner another sharp nod. The curvy female turned to Grace and held her gaze for several seconds before glancing back at Gunner. She swallowed hard, then spun and ran into the night. Grace felt the second she lifted her block, the other female seemingly disappearing into the shadows.

Grace wanted to lift her head, but all her strength had drained away with her adrenaline, and the aches and pains roared back to the surface. She cried out in agony.

"Grace, Jesus, I thought I'd lost you." Chaos's distress was obvious in his voice, on his face.

The urge to reassure him was overpowering. "I'm o-okay." She forced a grin. "Killed Oden. Pussy screamed like a l-little bitch...t-took out a fuck of a lot more before they got m-me again." Blood filled her mouth, this time spilling past her lips. Breathing was serious work and hurt like hell. She opened her mouth to tell Chaos, but the words came out a bloody gurgle.

"Grace...*Grace!*"

Black spots moved across her vision as each breath became shallower. She looked up at the male holding her in his arms, wanting him to be the last thing she saw before she died. She'd never loved anyone else after the death of her parents, not like this, not until Chaos. He looked fierce, beautiful. Perfect.

Her lids grew heavy, and she struggled to keep her eyes open, just a little longer...

CHAPTER 36

CHAOS LANDED on the roof of the hospital. Jack was waiting for him.

"This way," Jack called.

They ran for the elevator. Chaos couldn't take his eyes off her, off the blood coming from her mouth, how so very still she was. How all color had drained from her. God, she looked blue, her breathing erratic. Her face was swollen, bruises already darkening. Grace was almost unrecognizable.

The skin around her wrists and ankles was raw and bleeding. Someone had tied her up, had beaten her while she was unable to defend herself.

He would kill whoever had done that to her. He would make them scream in pain.

Grace coughed and cried out. More blood leaked from her mouth, soaking into his shirt, into her pale blond hair. He couldn't think. The fear had all but paralyzed him.

He was losing her before he'd truly had her.

He was losing Grace.

She would die never knowing how much he truly loved

her. He'd told her, but words meant shit. He'd wanted a lifetime to show her.

The elevator opened and Jack raced into the emergency room, Chaos hot on his heels. There was another female there waiting. "Put her on the gurney."

Chaos didn't want to release her, but forced himself, knowing this was something he couldn't do for her. He couldn't save her.

"Stand back, give us room," Jack barked out.

Chaos had never felt more helpless in his life. He couldn't leave the room, couldn't leave her, so he stood in the corner as they worked on her, shoving tubes down her throat and needles in her arms. He knew it had to be done, but he couldn't stop the growl every time they poked and prodded her, when they cut off her clothes.

Jack cursed viciously, and when Chaos moved closer, he could see why. Her body was covered in bruises—her back, stomach, and ribs had taken the worst of it.

"Is she going to live?" Chaos choked out.

"She has several broken ribs and a punctured lung. There's more going on in there, but I'll need to open her up to figure it out."

"Fucking tell me, is she going to live?"

Jack met his gaze, full of sympathy. "I don't know."

They forced Chaos to wait outside while they opened her up.

Hours passed and still nothing. He paced the halls, going out of his mind, barely holding on to his demon. It wanted to find her, was fighting to get to her, to break free and take her home. Chaos shouldn't be here like this, around all the humans in this place, but there was no fucking way he was leaving. Here he could feel her, he could feel that she was still alive.

Kryos had called. As they'd suspected, Vince had been full

of shit. He'd known exactly where Grace was being held. He'd been handing over demi to the enemy, betraying his own kind for the promise of power. Chaos was going to put the fucker down for what he did. He knew Grace cared for Vince, or at least she had before he'd tried to deliver her to a soul-sucking demon. But he couldn't let him live, not after what he'd done.

He glanced up at the clock. The hands were still moving, but right then, it seemed like time was standing still.

Gunner strode down the hall toward him. "Thought you could use some company." He held up a bag. "And Eve packed some things she thought Grace might need while she's here."

"Thanks." He hadn't talked for the last few hours and his voice sounded like shit.

Gunner leaned against the wall and crossed his arms. "How you doing?"

Chaos met his brother's gaze. "Don't care about me. Just her. Only her."

"She's going to be okay. Any minute they'll wheel her through that door."

Gunner was right.

A short time later, the door opened, and she was there on the gurney being wheeled out, Jack following behind. Fuck, Grace was pale, and still, her eyes closed, but she was breathing. She was alive.

Moving hurt.

Hell, blinking didn't feel that great, either.

The sound of a door opening, then closing, broke past the brain fog and she braced. In her current condition, all she could do was lie there and take whatever punishment those sadistic bastards dished out.

The footsteps neared. She refused to show weakness and braced, forcing a growl past her lips, unable to form actual words. Pain shot through her side, and she struggled to breathe, her lungs working to inflate, like a truck was parked on her chest.

Someone cursed, then hands were on her. But not causing pain, no, these hands, despite the roughness of their skin, were soothing, warm. On her next indrawn breath, she got a hit of a familiar scent, one that succeeded in washing away any remaining fear from her body. She relaxed as one of those hands held hers, the other stroking her face, gliding over her forehead, brushing back her hair.

"Sleep, angel. You're safe now."

Chaos's deep, rumbling voice moved over her, through her, and she did as he said. She let all her fears wash away and let sleep claim her once more. He was here. That's all that mattered.

When Grace woke again, the first thing she felt was someone holding her hand. She didn't need to open her eyes to know who it was. She lifted her heavy lids and there he was. Massive, beautiful, fierce. The stark terror in his eyes made her chest ache.

God, how she loved him.

"You're here," she said, or more rasped past her dry throat.

Another emotion washed over his face, one that made her heart ache.

"I can't be anywhere else." He tightened his hold on her fingers. "I don't want to be anywhere else. I can't breathe when I'm apart from you, Grace."

She cupped his face. "I'm okay."

His expression was open and exposed, raw. "I'm the fucking walking dead without you, angel. Knowing you were out there...not knowing where you were, what they were doing to you—" He made a tortured sound. "I thought I was losing my mind. I can't lose you, Grace, I can't. Don't ever leave me, okay? You can't ever leave me."

"I won't. I promise," she whispered.

A tear slid down his cheek, his body held rigid, his dark gaze boring into her like he didn't believe her but was willing her words to be true. He practically vibrated with emotion. "Without you, I am lost, broken. Without you, angel, I am nothing."

She lifted a shaky hand and cupped his face, tears welling in her own eyes. "After I lost my family, I was so alone. I've been alone for so long. But with you, with my strong, beautiful, proud male at my side, I'm not alone anymore. I'm whole. I would never, could never, leave you, my love, because without you, I am lost, broken, *nothing*," she said, repeating his words.

"Grace," he choked, his big body shaking harder.

With the remaining strength she had left, she leaned in, pressed her lips to his, then tugged on his hand, asking without words for him to lie down beside her.

He gently wrapped her in his arms.

She sighed and kissed him again with all the emotion she felt swirling inside her, then rested her forehead against his. "Whatever the future holds, whatever this war brings, I will be at your side. And if anyone tries to tear us apart, I will always fight with everything I have to get back to you," she whispered.

His eyes drifted closed and he pulled her back in close, burying his face against her throat. He heaved in several large breaths, and she knew he was trying to keep it together. "I'll do the same, angel. Always."

She knew he was scared for her, terrified, because she felt the same way, but Chaos also knew she was a fighter, and no matter how scared he was for her, he would never ask her to stop fighting—just like she would never ask that of him.

Finally, he lifted his head and cupped her face with his strong, calloused hands, hands that could wield a weapon with ease, could kill an enemy with fast, brutal efficiency, and could touch her with a gentleness that should be impossible.

"I'll be by your side until the end of time." Then he kissed her again.

And with tears rolling down her face, Grace kissed him back.

EPILOGUE

GUNNER STOOD on the balcony off the control room and closed his eyes as laughter floated out to him from inside.

A moment of peace and happiness for his brothers and their mates among all the pain. Rocco was still refusing to return to the compound and the place didn't feel right without him. But seeing his brothers so happy with their females, while Kyler was still in Hell—Gunner thought maybe that was for the best.

The female who helped Grace escape had kept to her word and called with a location. And Roc had been by their side when they'd raided the warehouse, freeing the captured demi who had been held. He was there when they'd needed him.

Unfortunately, the powerful demon behind it all had gone to ground, leaving no trail. But they would find him. Fucking hopefully before Kyler came into her powers and Diemos was freed.

The compound was now filled to capacity with the demi who needed a safe place to stay while they recovered. And with Willow strengthening the wards, no one was getting near them.

Someone walked out onto the balcony.

Silas.

The angel had moved into the compound as well, his wings clipped by his own brethren for helping them, for stopping Zenon from walking into that warehouse, for saving him. He was putting on a brave face, but Gunner could feel his pain.

"Settled in?" Gunner asked as the angel moved to stand beside him.

"Yeah." Silas glanced back into the control room and made a rough sound. "Not sure everyone's happy I'm here, though."

Gunner followed his gaze. "Laz will calm down." Gunner wasn't sure he actually believed that, though. Silas had kept information from Lazarus when he'd first found Eve, and his mate had been used as bait to draw out Tobias when their brother had been lost to the darkness of his demon. That wasn't something Lazarus would just get over.

"No, he won't," Silas said. "I deserve it." The angel turned to him. "And I'm not the only one in pain. You gonna tell your brothers?"

Gunner stilled. "Tell them what?"

"I may have had my wings taken from me, but I'm not totally blind, and this weight you're carrying is not exactly subtle...or new."

No, it wasn't.

"I'm sorry, Gunner. I know that word means jack-shit to you right now. But fuck...I wish I could go back and change the way things went down."

Knowing that Silas *knew*, shit, made it all the more real. He hadn't imagined it, during that time when Lazarus brought Eve here. Her power had affected them all, but

Gunner the most. He'd spiraled into darkness, while he fought his inner demon for control. Still, deep down, he knew he'd felt it...felt *her*, his female, he'd just hoped he was wrong.

"Why are you sorry?" he finally said, voice rough as fuck.

The pain in Silas's eyes was stark. "If I'd told Laz what Eve was straight away, you wouldn't have been locked up, you would have been able to—"

Go to her.

Silas flinched like he'd heard the words that echoed through Gunner's mind.

Pain slammed into Gunner's chest. "She's gone, then, truly gone?" he choked out.

He'd never met her, had only felt her existence for a short time, but her loss was more than he knew how to live with.

"I don't know. The heavens, they're blocking you and your brothers from me. I think I knew...before they—" Silas stilled, the muscles in his inked arms flexing as he fought through the memory, the pain. The wounds where they'd mutilated him, where they'd sawn off his wings weren't healing as they should. "Now I see nothing, just...darkness ahead, only darkness."

Silas muttered another apology, looking lost.

Gunner had no idea how to help the male. Nothing he could say would make this okay for him.

"I'm just gonna..." Silas motioned inside, then the angel walked back in, striding past everyone and out to the hall, no doubt heading back to his apartment.

Gunner turned and looked out to the night sky as he listened to Meredith telling a joke, to the sounds of Mia, Eve, and Grace laughing. He didn't need to look back to know his brothers were watching their mates, unable to look away from the females who had them, heart and soul.

The ache behind his ribs increased.

He didn't have a right to play the grieving widower, not when Rocco was out there suffering even worse. Roc had actually met his mate, had held her, kissed her. He knew what his female looked like, had breathed in her scent, had heard the sound of her voice, her laughter.

No, Gunner deserved to suffer.

He'd failed his mate, had been so weak, so fucking pathetic that he hadn't been able to control his own fucking demon when everything went to shit and his brothers had needed him most. Had been forced to lock himself up or risk his inner demon running loose on the city.

They'd been out fighting, while he'd sat rocking in a fucking corner, or tearing his cell apart.

No one had been there to free him when he felt her for the first and only time, when breaking down the door with his body hadn't worked and he'd clawed at the fucking walls to get free until his fingers were torn and bleeding.

No one had been there to hear his roar of pain when he felt her being snatched from existence a short time later, like she'd never existed, like his fevered brain had imagined her.

Pulling off his shirt, he tucked it into the back of his jeans and extended his bronze wings, the gold flecks shimmering in the moonlight.

Yeah, he was a lost cause, but Rocco wasn't, not yet, and Gunner wouldn't rest until his brother was home with them and his mate was back and by his side.

ABOUT THE AUTHOR

Sherilee Gray is a kiwi girl and lives in beautiful New Zealand with her husband and their two children. When she isn't writing sexy, edgy contemporary and paranormal romance, searching for her next alpha hero on Pinterest, or fueling her voracious book addiction, she can be found dreaming of far off places with a mug of tea in one hand and a bar of Cadburys Rocky Road chocolate in the other.

To find out about new releases, giveaways, events and other cool stuff, sign up for my newsletter!

ALSO BY SHERILEE GRAY

Spin

Slide

Spark